BADLANDS

MORGAN BRICE

DARKWIND

CONTENTS

BADLANDS

By Morgan Brice

eBook ISBN: 978-1-939704-72-6
Print ISBN: 978-1-939704-73-3
Badlands: Copyright © 2018 by Gail Z. Martin.

Cover art by Natania Barron

Darkwind Press is an imprint of DreamSpinner Communications, LLC

SIMON

A t this hour of the morning, the boardwalk ghosts were silent. Simon Kincaide stared down the nearly empty, broad beachside walkway and breathed in the ocean air. Flags flapped in the breeze, waves pounded the shore on the other side of the dunes, and seagulls swooped. The tourists hadn't yet woken.

Simon looked, out of habit, to the places the spirits favored. The old man with his bicycle and his dog wouldn't appear until late afternoon, cycling down the boardwalk. Kevin, a dreadlocked man in his twenties, liked the stairs that led to the beach, perhaps near the spot where he drowned. Two children in Victorian clothing, spirits so faded that they could not even remember their names, would skip past near sunset. Other ghosts came and went, but Simon could set his watch by those appearances. Not everyone could see the ghosts—most of the people milling along the boardwalk could not and never would—but Simon did.

Sebastian Simon Kincaide had known he wasn't like other kids when he realized nobody else could see and hear the spirits he considered regular playmates. Discovering he got glimpses into the future from time to time made him even less like his friends at school. Figuring out that he was gay was just the icing on the cake.

That all happened long ago, but the sense of being an outsider never really went away, Simon thought, not even now at age thirty-five, with a prosperous business and a few bestselling books to his credit.

He worked the key in the front door. Grand Strand Ghost Tours, a small shop on the Myrtle Beach boardwalk, shared a building with a beachwear shop but had a coveted location between the legendary Gay Dolphin Gift Cove and the popular Myrtle Beach SkyWheel mega-Ferris wheel. Simon paused in the doorway, letting himself enjoy a moment of pride and satisfaction in the business it had taken three damn years to build.

Simon collected the mail, pocketed his keys, and locked the door behind him since the shop wouldn't open for another two hours. He switched on the lights and music, then went to the back to start a pot of coffee.

His phone buzzed, and he answered. "Hey, Seth. What's up?"

Seth Tanner chuckled. "You haven't had your coffee yet, have you?"

"I'm working on it." Simon held the phone between his shoulder and ear as he readied the coffee maker. "What do you need?"

Seth sighed. "I'm looking into a vengeful ghost problem near Breezewood, up in Pennsylvania. Salt and iron aren't doing the trick, but I'm sure it's ghosts, not demons, so exorcism won't work, either. Got any ideas?"

"Find the anchor object the spirit is tethered to," Simon recommended, measuring out the coffee. "Might not be near where the appearances are happening. Have an officiant from the deceased's faith tradition say a blessing and urge the ghost to move on. If nothing else works, there's a banishment ritual, but it's brutal on the spirits. And no matter what you've seen on TV, don't get yourself arrested trying to dig up the grave to salt and burn the bones."

Seth chuckled. "I knew you'd have the answers. You're a rare medium, Simon. Well done."

"Ha, ha. As if I haven't heard that one before," Simon groaned, rolling his eyes. He pressed the button, and the coffee maker chugged to life.

"Seriously, thanks," Seth replied. "Send me the bill."

"When I have to do some research, I'll charge for the time. This, I can give you off the top of my head. Next time you're in the area, stop in and we'll do dinner. Your treat."

"You're on," Seth replied and ended the call.

Simon headed out to the main room and started to get the shop ready for business. Shelves in the front held books about ghost stories from all over South Carolina and the Lowcountry, but especially those with tales of spirits, pirates, or old scandals of the Grand Strand. Prominently displayed were the three books on local folklore and ghosts that bore his name as author. The glass case by the register held gemstones and silver jewelry for healing and protection, colored candles, and sealed bags of the most common dried plants and flours used in rituals and aromatherapy. Shelves behind the cabinet held an assortment of candles in tall glass holders with pictures of saints on the front. In the back, a table and two comfortable chairs supplied a homey place to do appointment-only psychic readings, and the table could expand to hold six people for a full séance.

A rack on top of the counter held brochures about the Grand Strand Ghost Tours that Simon led four nights a week, as well as the "Pirates and Scoundrels" special tours and the "Lowcountry Legends and Lore" talk he gave twice a month at Brookgreen Gardens. The large sign on the wall behind the counter advertised ticket prices for the tours and special events, with a prominent reminder to "ask about rates for private spirit readings and séances."

Display racks offered t-shirts with the Grand Strand Ghost Tours logo, while others bore catchy phrases like "Ghosts Gone Wild," "Grand Strand Spook-a-palooza," and his favorite, a cartoon of a ghost holding a beach drink that read "Chillin' Out." The nearby shelves that held cups, stickers, and shot glasses with the same designs were a concession to tourist tastes.

Simon straightened some of the merchandise when his phone rang again. "Mark! You're up early."

Mark Wojcik grumbled something in response, and Simon grinned. Mark hated mornings even more than he did. "No, I'm up late and still haven't gone to bed," Mark muttered. "And I'm bruised from head to toe after I got my ass kicked by a were-cougar before we brought it down, so forgive me if I'm not Mr. Sunshine."

Like Seth, Mark was a real-life hunter of things that went bump in the night; part of a loosely allied group of people who by talent or personal tragedy found themselves initiated into a shadow world most people could live happily never suspecting. Simon's gifts as a medium and clairvoyant—and his training as a folklorist—made him a part of that hidden network, and his research skills provided a second stream of income.

"I finished the research on the kelpies you asked for," Simon replied. "Sent the files to the secure share drive."

"Okay," Mark said. "That's what I was calling about. I'll shoot the payment back atcha. Thanks."

Simon ended the call and ran a hand back through his shoulder-length brown hair. Four years ago, if someone had told him that he'd be making a living taking beachgoers on ghost tours, giving readings, and selling tchotchkes, he'd have laughed. But how he'd ended up on the Grand Strand was not funny at all.

Three and a half years ago, Dr. Sebastian Kincaide held a professorship at the University of South Carolina in the Humanities Department, teaching folklore and mythology classes and writing scholarly articles on legends and lore. He kept his abilities as a medium and clairvoyant hidden, although his long-time relationship with another professor on staff had been openly acknowledged, especially after he and Jacen had announced their engagement.

Even now, the memory brought a sour twist to Simon's stomach. Emerson Baucom Tallmudge, the father of one of his students, turned out to be not only a donor and a board member for the university, but a hard-core fundamentalist as well, of the "thou shalt not suffer a witch to live" variety. Apparently, after he'd gotten a glimpse of his son's textbooks for the class, Tallmudge got his dander up and lobbied the board to be rid of such an "evil influence." Simon thought he had successfully placated the board, citing the importance of classical mythology in a well-rounded education, but then Tallmudge found evidence online that Simon admitted to being able to talk with spirits, and everything came crashing down.

The board dismissed Simon with a severance package that told him they also thought Tallmudge's complaints were bullshit, but in the end, the prospect of an endowment beat out standing up for one of their faculty. Then Jacen broke off their engagement, too afraid that Simon's dismissal would compromise his bid for tenure, and Simon's world went up in flames.

Alone, unemployed, and unable to find another teaching job, Simon drifted down to Myrtle Beach, intending to stay for a week or so to regroup and lick his wounds. When his aunt offered to sell him the cottage in Myrtle Beach where he was staying, Simon took it as a sign to rebuild his life from the ground up. He put his folklore background to use writing a book on local ghosts and used the self-published book to leverage himself into jobs as a tour guide, haunted attractions actor, museum docent, and speaker while he put his plan together. Grand Strand Ghost Tours wasn't just a shop; it was Simon's howl of defiance at a universe that had fucked him over.

And which was still doing so, since the coffee maker had not only failed to produce a cup of java-rich goodness, but had sent a gush of murky water and wet grounds all over the floor.

"Shit." Simon grabbed a handful of paper towels and began mopping. The smell of burned electronics told him without needing to use his psychic gifts that the coffee maker was dead. He dropped the machine into the trash on top of the sodden towels, ordered a new one on Amazon with expedited shipping, and then contemplated the prospect of a morning without coffee.

"Screw that," he said, glancing at the clock. He locked up, turned out lights, and headed for Mizzenmast Coffee.

Before he'd made it half a block, his phone buzzed once more. This time he smiled at the number that came up. "Hi, Cassidy. Everything okay?" His cousin, Cassidy Kincaide, ran an antique store in Charleston, just two hours south of Myrtle Beach. They hadn't been close growing up, but now that Cassidy had discovered her own ability to read the history of objects by touching them, they had bonded.

"Fine. Just busy. Mostly regular stuff, but some of the other too, if you know what I mean." Cassidy's shop proved to be the perfect opportunity to get cursed and haunted objects out of the wrong hands. Simon and Cassidy often talked over whatever weird or supernatural situation they were currently navigating. Not to mention Cassidy had a gorgeous gay Weaver witch best friend as a partner in her supernatural escapades. It was another sign of the universe's contempt for Simon that Teag was already taken. "Is the store open yet? Can you talk?"

"I'm heading for coffee," Simon replied. "What's up?"

"I've got a carved mahogany trinket box with the name '*Jeremiah Holzer*' engraved on the bottom," Cassidy said. "There's a pretty nasty curse on it. I think Jeremiah was from the Myrtle Beach area, but Teag and I can't find anything about him online, and I thought maybe you could check some local archive stuff for me."

"Sure," Simon agreed. "How urgent?"

"We've got the box quarantined, so it's not doing any new damage, but two people were injured from the curse, and I have a feeling there's missing information that we need to break the bad juju. So, the sooner, the better."

"I'll work on it tonight, after the tour," Simon promised. "Say 'hi' to everyone for me."

"When are you going to come to Charleston? You know we've got the best restaurants on the Southeast coast," Cassidy replied. "Plus, Teag and Anthony have a couple of cute guys in mind they think you might hit it off with."

Simon cringed, glad Cassidy couldn't see his expression. Even after three years, he wasn't sure he was ready for a new romance. Perhaps he never would be. "It's the busy season," he begged off. "But maybe this winter. Or come visit me. Roads go both ways, you know."

"It's tourist season here, too," she reminded him. "But we'll get together soon, one way or another. And thanks for the research."

"You got that haunted painting off my hands," Simon replied.

"I owe you." He hung up, but couldn't shake the melancholy that had settled in. A couple walked past, hands clasped, talking quietly, and an ache he didn't want to acknowledge flared in his chest. As much as he feared being hurt again, Simon couldn't deny the fact that he missed being in a relationship, having someone to wake up with every day and fall asleep with at night. For a while, he'd buried himself in his work, and that had dulled the loneliness. Now that he was no longer in survival mode, the evenings were not completely filled with busyness, and the nights stretched long.

Simon chuckled at his fears. *Here I am, backing up people who hunt real monsters, and I'm too chickenshit to go on a date. I need to man up and...man up.*

2

VIC

"What a total bust." Homicide detective Lieutenant Vic D'Amato slammed the door of the police cruiser in disgust.

"Hey! Watch the door!" his partner, Lieutenant Ross Hamilton, protested.

"We've been up all night on a stake-out that yielded absolutely nothing," Vic growled. "We've got no new leads, no new evidence, and the killer is still out there. Zip. Nada. Zilch."

They walked into the Myrtle Beach precinct house, which was as quiet as it ever got this early in the morning. "I want to take a piss, because we've been in that car too damn long, drink some coffee, and take a walk before I have to be back here to do it all over again in a few hours," Vic added.

"Don't take it so hard. You know stake-outs define boredom, and it's the exception, not the rule when one pays off. We play the odds," Ross reasoned with him.

Both of them were hungry, tired, and frustrated. A serial killer was on the loose, preying on seasonal foreign workers, and it felt like they were getting nowhere. "Our tip didn't pan out. And tonight, or tomorrow night, somebody else could turn up dead, and we've got no way to stop it," Vic ranted, feeling all of the pent-up energy of the long night's vigil find release in his anger.

Vic stalked off to the men's room, ignoring the glances he received from the day shift in the bullpen. Draining the lizard was a blissful relief, and as he washed up at the sink, he couldn't ignore that his reflection in the mirror looked like shit.

He splashed cold water on his face, but that did nothing for the stink of sweat from being cooped up in a hot car. Vic thought about punching the wall, remembered how much breaking his finger hurt the last time, and kicked a stall door instead. When it bounced back and nearly clipped him in the head, he decided he was cursed.

Still, Ross was his partner, his best friend, and someone who didn't care if he was gay—even if his sex life was largely hypothetical considering how long he'd sworn off company. So Vic knew he needed to get his ass back out there and apologize, or at least offer to buy breakfast.

He wiped off his face with a scratchy paper towel, avoided his gaze in the mirror, and headed out. Ross was already at his desk, writing up the report.

"Shouldn't be much to tell the Captain, since nothing happened," Vic commented, perching on one corner of their shared desk. "How 'bout breakfast? My turn to spring for the bill."

Ross shook his head. "Tempting, and I'll take a raincheck, but I'm going to go home and crash for a few hours. Why don't you get out of here while the getting's good? I'll see you in a few."

On the surface, Vic and Ross were opposites. Ross had the tall, blond boy-next-door hometown football player good looks, rounded out with a wife and two kids, a dog, a cat, and more small furry rodent pets than Vic could keep track of. Ross had grown up in Myrtle Beach, thrived in sand and sun, and had a file full of commendations and awards.

Vic, on the other hand, had the dark hair and olive skin of his Italian heritage. His black hair was shaved, almost military, and he made no effort to hide either his tattoos or his orientation. He was single and gay, and even after two years, new in town. As for his file...the commendations he'd earned at his previous assignment in

Pittsburgh were buried under the reprimands from the incident that almost torpedoed Vic and his career.

"Something's eating you, aside from the stake-out." Ross didn't look up.

Vic shrugged uncomfortably. "You know how I feel about the way a lot of places bring in people from hard-luck countries and then work them like indentured servants," he said. "And I know that some of the hotels and restaurants wouldn't make it without the cheap labor and that what's 'cheap' here can be a good living back where they're from. I get that."

"I hear a *but*…"

Vic gave a bitter chuckle. "*But* some creeps don't treat their workers much better than slaves, and we've busted trafficking rings that take advantage of the workers not having anyone here who gives a damn."

"I seem to remember that, since I was there," Ross replied in a dry voice. "And your point?"

"I just hate to see a serial killer go after them, too. And the killer, something about him reminds me—" he realized what he had said and shut up, looking away.

"Of what happened back in Pittsburgh," Ross finished for him.

Vic didn't look at him. "Yeah."

Ross ran his hand over his mouth and chin; a clear tell that he was weighing his words. Officially, the only ones who knew the whole story about why Vic transferred down were their Captain and Ross. Vic wasn't stupid enough to believe that the other cops hadn't gotten the whole scoop from friends of friends. The "thin blue line" was an information superhighway.

"You've got a good thing goin' here, Vic," Ross said finally. "The captain likes you. The other guys think you're mostly okay. I tolerate you…" he added with a grin to lighten his words. "Don't fuck it up. People are monsters without needing any supernatural help. Just work the case. We'll figure it out."

Vic tamped down his anger, knowing that none of it was really aimed at Ross, reminding himself that his partner had his back and had been a champ about agreeing to team up with a damaged cop. "Yeah. I know that."

"Go on," Ross urged. "Take a break. If you don't want to go home, go for a walk. Clear your head. We'll figure out Plan B when we're back on duty."

Vic clapped him on the shoulder and left. A few of the other cops at their desks nodded in acknowledgment as he passed. He walked down the steps and onto the sidewalk, where the warm wind hit his face. From the precinct house, Vic knew he could be on the boardwalk by the beach in under ten minutes, and decided that a good cup of coffee and some time staring at the surf was just what he needed.

Myrtle Beach was a long way from Pittsburgh, but some days, the distance in miles and time wasn't enough. Back in the Burgh, Vic had his own house, a great work partner, a hot boyfriend and by all accounts was on track for another promotion, even though at thirty-one he was a little young to make Captain. Then it all went wrong.

The wind fluttered his jacket, and out of reflex, Vic shifted his arm to keep the flapping fabric from revealing his holstered gun. As a plainclothes detective, he didn't wear a uniform, and while he always had his badge, it didn't pay to freak the tourists. He tried to focus on the smell of the ocean, the distant cry of seagulls, the pounding of the waves that were the silent, throbbing beat beneath the hum of Myrtle Beach's activity.

Vic had dropped the subject with Ross because he didn't want to fight, but he couldn't change how he felt. Back in Pittsburgh, he and his former partner had tracked a serial killer through the city's neighborhoods, a real sick bastard who got off on pain and blood. Vic had been a cop long enough to have lost most of his illusions about human nature, but this guy, the one the cops called "Pop-eye" because he took eyeballs as souvenirs of his kills, seemed creepy even by serial killer standards.

He and his old partner had finally gotten a break in the case and tracked the killer down to his hiding place, where one of his would-be victims was still alive. But when they moved on the killer, everything fell apart.

The killer was ninja fast, dodging bullets like a superhero, and threw Vic's former linebacker partner across the room like a wadded up piece of paper. Vic opened fire, four bullets center mass, and the perp went down. What happened next doomed his promotion and almost finished his career. His partner was stunned. The perp had a big hole where his chest used to be. Then Vic saw a green glowing fog leave the dead perp and swirl around the screaming victim. And in the next instant, the victim had grabbed the perp's gun and moved into an expert firing stance, dead-eyed and ready to kill.

Vic shot first.

The victim, a petite young school teacher with no priors and no weapons experience, went down in a pool of blood, dead at the scene. Vic's partner woke, with no idea what had happened and unable to corroborate the story. The inquest had been brutal, worse because Vic had told the whole truth. He'd been placed on leave while Internal Affairs investigated, then sent for drug screenings and a psych evaluation. When he turned up clean, and the shrink cleared him, IA grudgingly allowed reinstatement. But at that point, Vic and everyone else knew it was over.

Nate, his boyfriend, had grown distant during the inquest. His tone and comments made it clear that he didn't believe Vic about the glowing fog and the whole Exorcist thing. When Vic brought up the possibility of moving, because nowhere close-by would hire him, Nate refused to even consider the idea. He didn't break things off between them in so many words. He didn't have to.

Vic took the carefully worded sort-of recommendation he got from his boss, packed his bags, and drove south, vaguely remembering spring breaks spent on the Carolina coast. With no one but himself to please, he headed for Myrtle Beach, working his old college network and family connections to put in a good word for him with the precinct there. Short on both prospects and money, Vic wasn't too proud to accept a favor.

Two years had gone by, but sometimes it felt like no time at all.

Captain Hargrove had been fair with him, better than his record deserved. The other cops gradually warmed up to him, and if Vic still wasn't exactly in the inner circle, they didn't shun him. Ross might have had something to do with that, going out on a limb to make his support glaringly clear. Vic had a nice apartment, some poker buddies, and a little money in the bank. And if he'd blamed the stress and demands of his job for why there was no significant other in his life, no one called him on the lie.

He stared down the beach at the 14th Avenue pier. Tonight, the huge Ferris wheel with its strobing, multi-colored lights would be the centerpiece, along with the two brightly-lit pylons from which screaming tourists gleefully paid to be dropped in a bungee harness for a thrill. All along the boardwalk were restaurants, bars, hotels, shops, arcades, and attractions eager to part newcomers from their money. Wednesday night fireworks lit up the sky, and weekend bands filled the park.

Vic hadn't grown up around the ocean. Pittsburgh had its famed three rivers, and friends had taken him boating or camping on lakes, but the ocean had always remained a special memory of his favorite childhood vacations. Just listening to the rush of the waves made Vic feel better, no matter how shitty the day might have been. And while he wasn't much for lying still in the sun, walking at the edge of the water and feeling the wet sand under his toes went a long way toward cleansing his mood.

The wind had picked up, and Vic glanced at the dark clouds coming in. Too late he remembered the predicted rain and grimaced at the thought of riding home and getting soaking wet. He thought about heading for his motorcycle, but the lure of some fresh air and a good cup of coffee kept him where he was. He could survive getting wet.

He rested his forearms on the boardwalk railing and looked out toward the ocean, in part to ignore the couples laughing and joking as they walked along with their ice cream. Maybe it was time to think about getting out there again, dating, finding a boyfriend and not just a hook-up. Vic snorted. Even his hook-ups had been few and far between because he didn't like being vulnerable with someone he didn't know. That nixed dating apps since the cop in him wanted to get a read on a prospective partner in person, not just swipe right. Then again, he hated going clubbing—no telling when one of those places would get busted for something—and cruising for a date in a bar just felt desperate.

Yep, he thought. That explained why he was still single and spending most nights watching TV, tuning up his cycle, or going for a long ride along the Coastal Highway. Maybe he should get a dog, and resign himself to spending the rest of his life wanking off in the shower. God, he needed to get laid.

Vic pushed off from the railing and ambled down the boardwalk toward Mizzenmast Coffee. He didn't usually pay much attention to the shops, couldn't remember the last time he had even noticed the signs. But today, the "Grand Strand Ghost Tours" window caught his eye. But what made him pause was the smaller lettering beneath *"Tours, Maps, Books, Candles, and Supplies."* In particular, the line that read *"Private Readings and Séances, by Appointment Only."*

What could it hurt, to come back and see if the psychic can contact any of the spirits of the dead workers? He thought. *Not like we've gotten any other breaks in the case. And if I get a tip that pans out, no one ever needs to know where it came from.*

3

SIMON

Simon had hoped to grab a quick latte at Mizzenmast Coffee—
or as the locals called it, Le Miz—but his heart sank when he
saw the line. He almost went back to the shop, but he remembered
that the coffee maker was dead, and desperation coaxed him to take
his place at the end of the long queue.

Le Miz had taken over the space that once housed a pirate-
themed exhibit. As Tracey, the shop owner and Simon's best friend
had once confided, she didn't have the money to renovate, so she
incorporated the pirate decor into the coffee house, which proved to
be a hit with both tourists and locals. Tracey was creative with the
specialty coffees, and they all boasted names of famous pirates, both
real and fictional. Simon had long ago gotten over the embarrassment of asking for a "Dread Pirate Roberts," which was a triple shot
of espresso in steamed milk with a shot of caramel syrup.

Simon glanced at the register, expecting to see Tracey holding
court, as usual. Instead, a woman he recognized but didn't know as
well, Lana, was ringing up purchases and calling out orders to the
baristas behind the counter. Le Miz had killer muffins and breakfast
breads, and Simon felt his stomach rumble as he remembered
leaving home with only a protein bar.

"Can you believe the line?" a voice said behind him. "Where did everyone come from, and why the hell are they between me and the coffee?"

Simon turned, thinking of a funny quip in response, and the words died in his throat. The man behind him was gorgeous. Short dark hair, caramel colored skin, and eyes the color of milk chocolate. Powerful arms crossed over a muscular chest hidden beneath a t-shirt, and a quick sweep of Simon's gaze suggested the thighs beneath those fitted jeans were mouthwatering. He had a bit of swagger and a cocky grin, but something about him came off worn and frayed, piquing Simon's interest beyond the man's good looks.

"That's the price of the Strand's best coffee," Simon replied with a smile. *Oh God, that's really lame. Shit, I've still got my glasses on. And my hair's a mess.* "Worth the wait though."

The dark haired man returned the smile, although it didn't reach his eyes. His gaze seemed to miss nothing, appraising and watchful. *Cop?* Simon wondered. *That would fit. Sweet Jesus, look at that body! Those arms—*

"I don't get over here often, and not usually this early," the man replied.

"It's my guilty pleasure," Simon confessed. "I'm kinda a coffeeholic. And the coffee maker at work died, so...here I am."

This time, the stranger chuckled. "Yeah, well. Work coffee sucks. Always tastes like it's been boiling all night, and I swear they never clean the pot."

Outside, thunder rumbled, and rain began to darken the boardwalk. Instinctively, the line moved closer together, away from the windows. "Hope you don't have far to go," Simon commented. "Because it looks like we're in for a downpour."

The man met Simon's gaze and kept eye contact for just a second too long, making Simon's heart pound. He felt a flush come to his face under that appraising gaze, unsure whether the stranger was really checking him out, or just giving him a cop's once-over. "I don't mind getting wet," the man replied, still not looking away, as if daring Simon to respond.

"Neither do I," Simon managed to reply, hoping his voice didn't betray his nervousness. A smile shared made Simon's pulse spike again. "Did you walk?" he asked, desperate to keep the conversation going as they inched closer to the counter. Simon wished Tracey was working because she remembered all her regulars and she'd be able to fill him in on the mystery man. Only three more people in front of them before he gave his order. Simon knew he'd need to get creative, somehow, if he wanted to share more than a few minutes of idle chatter.

"Nah. Rode my motorcycle." The cop—Simon felt sure the man was a cop—shifted, and he caught a glimpse of ink beneath the rolled up jacket sleeves. That observation went straight to Simon's cock. He didn't have any tattoos of his own, but the thought of an inked lover was a favorite midnight fantasy. Motorcycle cop came in a close second.

Get a grip, Kincaide. Horny is one thing. Desperate is totally not cool. "What kind of bike? Harley?" he asked, saying the first thing that came to mind.

"Nah. Hayabusa. Deep blue."

"I've got a friend who rides a Hayabusa," Simon replied. "I think it's black."

"You don't know what color it is?" Cop Dude asked with a smirk.

Simon shrugged. "He told me he bought it when he got out of the Army, but I haven't seen him in a long time."

Oddly enough, the cop seemed to relax a little, and Simon hid a smile. *He is checking me out. And he liked that Seth isn't around. Okay, let's see if I can figure out some way to get his phone number before we walk away with our coffees.*

"Bikes are a big deal here," Simon said to fill the pause. "I'm always amazed at how many come through for Bike Week." Several major motorcycle events each summer turned the Grand Strand into a cavalcade of the hottest cycles on the coast.

Cop Dude shrugged. "I always liked *Born to Run*. Springsteen fan. What can I say?"

"Sir?" the voice called from the counter, making Simon turn

away. "You're next." Simon had never been less happy to get to the front of the line.

"I'll have a Dread Pirate Roberts," he mumbled, not wanting to look like an idiot to the guy he was trying to impress. He handed over the money, took his change as she rang him up, dropped a one dollar bill in the tip jar, and moved down the counter to wait for his drink.

"I'll try that, too," the cop said, flashing him a grin. "What the hell? Live life on the edge."

Le Miz baristas were fast. Simon knew he needed to come up with a way to extend the conversation without looking like a creeper or lose the connection, maybe forever. Just as the barista handed both of them their drinks, a deafening thunderclap sounded, rattling the windows, and the rain came pouring down.

"Want to grab a table?" Simon asked, nervous enough that his throat felt tight. "We'll drown if we go out there now."

"Sure. Why not."

Simon led the way through the crowded outer room where the tables were all taken to the back room where there was once a display of pirate doubloons and recovered sunken treasures. The room kept its murals of sailing ships and scruffy pirates, along with the odds and ends left behind by the previous owners—a beat-up old chest, a pirate mannequin everyone called "Mo" and a bedraggled stuffed parrot on a perch, dubbed "Percy" by Le Miz regulars.

"You must come here a lot to know there's a second room."

"Told you, I take my coffee very seriously," Simon teased as he sat down. "I'm Simon, by the way."

"Vic," the man replied. "So what's in this mystery drink?"

"Do you like the smell?" Simon asked.

Vic leaned over his cup, took a deep breath, and his eyes fluttered almost closed. Simon's heart did a little samba, instantly imagining what Vic would look like blissed out and debauched after sweaty sex. Simon's erection strained at the fly of his jeans, and he was insanely glad they were seated at a table where Vic couldn't see how aroused he was.

"Good?" Simon asked, hating that he sounded a little breathless.

"Yeah," Vic replied, with a little moan that made Simon painfully hard.

"Glad I could turn you on to a good thing," Simon replied, hoping he hadn't read the signals wrong since he was blatantly flirting.

"Much obliged," Vic replied, and maybe it was Simon's imagination that the man's voice dropped a little lower, a bit huskier, than before.

"You've been here before, you said?" Simon asked, finding that his pick-up skills were as woefully rusty as his ability to make polite chit-chat.

"A few times," Vic replied. "I haven't gotten to the boardwalk as much as I'd like."

"I try not to overdo the special coffees," Simon said with a self-conscious smile. "I know the sugar adds up. But you've got to do something to make yourself feel good now and then, right?" *Oh lord, that sounded really bad. I can't believe I said that.*

A wicked twinkle came into Vic's eyes. "I'm all for feeling good," he replied, and his foot bumped into Simon's beneath the table.

It's just his foot. Doesn't mean anything. Could have been an accident, Simon told himself, but Vic didn't move away, and Simon hoped his smile looked encouraging instead of merely nervous.

"So are you in town for business or pleasure?" Simon asked, and cringed internally. *What's wrong with me? I'm never smooth, but I didn't used to be this awful at picking up a date.* "I mean, are you a local or just visiting?"

Vic's full, sensuous lips quirked in a smile. "Neither," he replied.

Simon tried and failed at not staring at his lips and imagining them around his cock. *Get a grip!* Shit, that only changed the mental image to a hand job. *So not working! Don't fuck this up.* That didn't help at all.

"Moved here not too long ago, so I don't feel quite like a local, but definitely not a tourist," Vic added.

"You can still take in the sights, even if you live here. Most people don't take time to enjoy what's in their backyards. I'd love to show you some of my favorite spots." *Oh, just shoot me now. That sounded like the worst line from a cheap porno. I totally suck at this. No, don't think about sucking...*

"Sounds fun," Vic said, and Simon was so lost in his embarrassment that he almost missed it.

"You would?" he asked, then cleared his throat. "I mean, that's great," he failed miserably to cover his awkward reply. Simon was just about to ask for Vic's number when Vic's phone went off.

The ringtone sounded odd, and Vic's manner shifted in the blink of an eye, going from casual and relaxed to tense and alert. "I've got to take this," he said, without even glancing at the number. "I'm sorry. It's work. Confidential—need to step away." With that, he got up and headed toward the service corridor that went toward the men's room, taking his coffee with him.

"Shit," Simon mumbled, running a hand over his eyes in utter frustration and disgust with his fumbling. Every phrase that came to mind about making a mess of things had a sexual connotation. Simon sipped at his now-cool coffee and glanced at his phone to check the time. *Crap! I need to open in five minutes.*

He got up and walked to the doorway to the main shop. The rain had stopped, and most of the tables were empty, awaiting the main tourist rush about an hour from now.

It won't kill me to wait a few minutes, Simon told himself. *With the rain, it's not like customers will be waiting at the door.* Then again, as two minutes stretched into five, Simon began to feel awkward sitting alone in an otherwise empty room when the other patrons left. He tried to remember if there was a back exit by the bathrooms. Maybe Vic had ditched him. Going to check on Vic was out of the question, but hanging around for no good reason looked pathetic.

This is why I'm single, Simon thought with a sigh. He finished his coffee, chucked the cup in the trash, and went out.

4

VIC

"There's been another one," Ross said when Vic answered the call. Vic gave Simon an apologetic smile, grabbed his coffee and headed to the back for privacy.

"Murder or missing person?" Anger and fatigue made Vic's voice raspy.

"Missing person," Ross replied. "Name's Iryena Kovaleva. She works an Italian ice stand on the lower end of the boardwalk. Came on a seasonal visa, been in the States for three months. We aren't releasing the name to the media just yet."

"Any priors?"

"Nothing in our system. I've asked for records from Belarus, where she's from, but I suspect if there was anything really bad, her employer would have known about it."

"Maybe it's not a local problem," Vic said, fiddling with his keychain as he thought. "Russian mob? Family debt from back in the Old Country?"

"Possible. We need more information," Ross replied. "Iryena's roommate reported her missing when she didn't come home last night. Says she always called to say where she was and when she would be back. Iryena returned the pushcart and the cash drawer, and that's the last time anyone saw her."

Vic listened as Ross filled him in on the rest of the details. "I'm heading back to the precinct," Vic said when Ross finally finished.

"Don't bother. Captain told us both to take the rest of the day off and pick up again tomorrow."

"But—"

"He's right, Vic," Ross reasoned. "We're waiting on reports to come in. Two officers already interviewed the roommate and spoke to her supervisor. There's nothing to do except stare at our screens and wait. Might as well sleep and hit it hard tomorrow, when we're fresh, and there's actual data to do something with."

"All right," Vic conceded reluctantly. "You're heading home, too?"

"Yeah," Ross replied. "I'm beat after being up all night. The kids have been sick, so I haven't slept a full night this week, and I'm feeling it."

"You're getting old," Vic teased. Ross was thirty-four, only three years older than Vic, but Vic had long argued that each child aged a parent at least five extra years, and Ross didn't contradict him.

"I feel old," Ross replied, sounding ragged. "Maybe we'll see something when we're fresher in the morning."

"Okay," Vic agreed, realizing that he had been gone from the table for a long time. Would Simon wait? Or would he figure Vic just slipped out the back? Damn, why hadn't he been faster to get a phone number? "Call me if anything changes." He ended the call, took a deep breath to clear his head, and walked back to where he had left Simon.

The table was empty.

"Damn." Vic strode across the back room to the main section of the coffee shop. Now that the rain had ended, the tables there had emptied out too. Simon was nowhere in sight.

"Hey, I have a question," he said to the woman behind the counter. "I was talking with a guy in line—couple inches shorter than me, glasses, brown hair that's almost down to his shoulders. He said he's a regular. First name's Simon. Do you know his last name? Or where he works?"

She gave him a skeptical look, and he dug out his badge. "Look. Not a creeper. I'm a cop."

"You're a cop. Doesn't prove you're not a creeper," she replied, giving him a look. "He seemed familiar, but I just fill in from time to time. Tracey—she's the owner—could probably tell you, but she's off today. If he's local, he probably works in one of the places along the boardwalk," she added with a shrug.

"Thanks."

The rain had done nothing to cool down the air; instead, it felt like a sauna, and it wasn't even officially summer yet. Vic stood outside Le Miz with his hands on his hips, debating what to do. *I've got the afternoon off,* he reasoned. *Been a long time since I've gone through the stores here. I might spot Simon. And if not, I should go check out that ghost tour person.*

He figured the tour guide/psychic was probably a middle-aged woman in flowing robes with a hokey Eastern European accent as fake as her so-called talent. Still, as long as a sign somewhere proclaimed *"for entertainment purposes only,"* she could avoid being charged with fraud. He didn't really expect a boardwalk medium to be able to provide a tip to break open the case, but Vic felt so frustrated with the lack of leads he was willing to take a chance.

Vic wandered in and out of the shops, inundated with the ticky-tacky-tourist fare of t-shirts, flip-flops, and shot glasses with the South Carolina palmetto tree, crescent moon, and star. He glanced into the restaurants, wondering if he would spot Simon, to no avail. When he got to the iconic Gay Dolphin Gift Cove—it had been a fixture on the Grand Strand for more than sixty years, long before "gay" took on a new meaning—he couldn't resist taking half an hour to wander the seemingly endless aisles of the three-story shop.

If I ever need seashells, wind chimes, an Elvis clock, or Christmas ornaments of Santa in a Speedo, I know where to find it, Vic thought, idly perusing the mind-boggling array of delightfully tacky collectibles. Still, the shop had a good-natured vibe to it, and he had to admit—

at least to himself—that his ten-year-old self would have been tremendously impressed.

By the time he left the Gay Dolphin, Vic realized he was stalling. Looking for Simon had been part of his quest for today, and he wasn't quite ready to give up yet, but if there was any chance that the Grand Strand psychic could shed some light on the case, Vic knew he needed to schedule a reading.

No one back at the precinct has to know, he told himself, realizing his palms were sweating, and not from the heat. *If I get a lead, I'll claim an anonymous tip from an informant. It's not like what happened in Pittsburgh. And even if someone sees me, or finds out, I'll get ribbed, but it won't cost me my badge.*

Vic mustered his courage and walked down the row to the Grand Strand Ghost Tours storefront. He opened the door, and the blast of air conditioning felt arctic and welcome. To his surprise, no one was behind the counter, so he had a moment to get his bearings.

The shop was nothing like he expected. Vic had figured there would be incense, flickering candles, and fabric draped like a fortune-teller's tent. Maybe even a haunted house vibe and plenty of creepy, cheesy souvenirs. Instead, he saw the neatly displayed, surprisingly high-end jewelry and merchandise inside the glass cases, the professionally printed tour brochures, and shelves of books, card decks, and items that looked more New Age than Nostradamus.

"Sorry, had to run to the back—" A man emerged from the bead curtain doorway and stopped in his tracks when he saw Vic.

"Simon?"

"Vic. Um, what are you doing here?" Simon replied, then winced. "That didn't come out right. Hi! Nice to see you again," he said with a self-conscious smile.

Simon was even better looking on second glance. He wasn't wearing his glasses, and while that gave Vic a better look at Simon's hazel eyes, he had kinda liked the sexy-nerd look the lenses gave him. The beautiful wavy brown hair Vic couldn't stop thinking about touching had been pulled up in a man bun, and from a certain angle, made it look as if Simon's hair was very short. He'd swapped out his plain blue t-shirt for one that had the store logo, and it showed off strong arms and hinted at a toned chest. Simon still wore the form-fitting jeans that let Vic admire his firm ass and nice thighs when they were in line at Le Miz.

"I take it you work here?" Vic said, looking around.

Simon chuckled. "You could say that. I own the place."

Vic looked at him in surprise, waiting for the punchline, but Simon appeared absolutely serious. "*You're* the Grand Strand psychic?"

Simon hesitated, then nodded. "Yeah. Tour guide, author, seminar-giver, medium, and psychic. Dr. Sebastian Kincaide, at your service."

"Sebastian?"

Simon shrugged. "My mother had a flair for the dramatic. I go by Simon. And let me guess. You're a cop."

Vic started at that, and his eyes narrowed, just a bit. Simon laughed. "No, I didn't use my *powers*," he said, waggling his fingers to underscore the last word. "You have cop eyes. And the call you took, back at the coffee house? Soon as it rang, you went on alert. Not too many jobs do that to a person."

Shit, Vic thought. Now that he'd found Simon, he sort of wished he hadn't. What were the odds that the first guy in forever that had really caught his eye would be a whack-job?

"I don't get the feeling you're a big believer in the Unseen World," Simon said, with an ironic tone, framing the last two words in air quotes. "So what brings you in? I promise I paid for my coffee this morning."

Vic cleared his throat. "Yeah, about that. I'm really sorry I walked off and left you. I've just been working a case—was up all night—and when my partner called, I knew it couldn't be anything good. Kinda goes with the badge. But I came back, and you were gone." Vic wasn't sure why it mattered so much what Simon thought of him, but it did. There'd been a spark of chemistry between them, more than Vic had felt in a long while, and he didn't want to come off like a jerk.

Simon gave him a half-smile in return. "I figured it was important. And I did hang around for a while, but I needed to open the shop." He gestured to the empty store. "As you can see, there were eager crowds waiting."

"You make a living from this?" Vic asked, and then could have kicked himself at how that sounded. "I mean—"

"We don't usually get busy until later in the day, but people do drift in earlier, and every sale matters."

"We?"

"I have a part-timer who watches the register while I do the tours, and if I've booked events," Simon replied. An awkward silence followed. "So," he said finally, looking a little flustered. "Can I show you around? Looking for anything in particular?"

Vic could hardly say *just you.* "I, uh, I've never been in a ghost shop before." He wanted to facepalm. *With moves like that, it's amazing I've ever gotten laid in my life.*

"We sell a lot of stuff, but not ghosts," Simon replied with a grin, and the awkwardness faded. He gestured for Vic to walk farther into the shop. "The tours and the t-shirts are for tourists. But a lot of locals come by for candles, hard-to-find botanicals—*legal* botanicals," he emphasized at Vic's side-eye. "And for the books, cards, and charms."

"Charms?" Vic asked, intrigued and suspicious at the same time.

Simon motioned toward the glass cases. "Legends all over the world credit certain metals, symbols, and semi-precious stones with protective abilities. It's a matter of belief, like with a religious symbol, but for those who do believe, having certain items makes them feel safer."

Vic reminded himself he had come for answers, and that going into skeptical cop mode would make Simon not only less willing to help with a reading but kill any chance of ever going on a date. "Interesting," he replied, trying to keep his tone as neutral as possible.

Simon had finished his mini-tour, and that left an awkward silence. "So…what brought you in today?"

Vic decided to tell the truth and see what happened. "I was hoping that if I wandered in and out of the places on the boardwalk near the coffee shop, I might run into you. I enjoyed talking, and wanted to get your phone number." Then he realized he knew nothing about Simon beyond the fact that he flirted back and wasn't wearing a ring. Maybe he was already with someone. The thought sent a stab of jealousy through him, hard to fight even though he knew it was absurd. "If, you know, you'd want to. Exchange numbers."

"You were looking for me?" Simon asked with a hesitant smile. "That's nice. And, yeah. Phone numbers. That'd be good." When Vic pulled out his phone, Simon told him his number. A buzz indicated that Vic had messaged him, returning the favor. "I enjoyed talking with you, too." That made Vic's heart speed up, just a little.

"And, I came into the ghost shop for another reason," Vic admitted. "But I've gotta know—are you for real? I mean, the talking to ghosts stuff? Or is it just a performance?"

Simon's smile faded. "It's real. Why?"

Vic swallowed down his fear and the bad memories of what happened in Pittsburgh. "This case I'm working on, I could use a break. And I thought that, if you really can speak with the spirits, well…"

"You want me to do a reading?" Simon asked, sounding surprised and unsure. "Is this 'Vic' asking or 'Officer…"

"Lieutenant. D'Amato," Vic replied. "Homicide. And right now, it's just me asking, unofficially. Because bad things are happening and at this point, I need something to go on." He glanced at the board above the counter and saw that a half hour reading was thirty dollars. "I'll pay you."

"I appreciate that," Simon replied, with a quirk of a smile, as if Vic had said something that was amusing but not really funny. "And you know that there's no guarantee the particular ghost you want to contact is going to show up. It's not like on TV. Ghosts don't participate unless they want to. And then they may not know the answers you want to hear, or sometimes, they can't or won't communicate."

Convenient, Vic thought and tried to shove down his skepticism. "All right." He pulled two bills from his wallet and put them on the counter. "How about now, before the wild crowds show up?" he added with a smile that he hoped smoothed over his skepticism.

"Sure," Simon replied, putting the cash in the register and flipping the sign on the door to read *"Back in 30 Minutes"* before motioning for Vic to follow him through the aisles to an alcove in the back with a table and two chairs.

"Isn't it kind of bright here?" Vic asked, looking around. The table had no cloth to obscure what was on or under it. The simple wooden chairs provided no place to hide wires or buttons.

"Expecting the Fox sisters?" Simon asked with an edge in his voice. "I keep my shoes on the whole time, and I don't make thumping noises with my toes," he added, referencing two famous mediums later revealed to be frauds.

"That isn't what I meant," Vic said, afraid that coming here was a mistake. He didn't seem to be getting off to a good start with Simon. The cop in him automatically began to look for reasons to discredit the reading before it began. But the other part of him, that had trouble not staring at Simon's lips or his long-fingered hands, hoped Simon could be trusted. Not just about the ghosts, but maybe, if Vic were lucky, with his heart.

"You know what they say," Simon said with a shrug. "Seeing is believing." He stood on the other side of the table from Vic. "If you want to look underneath the table, or check out the chairs and walls first, do it. Being unsure is fine, but the ghosts can sense hostility."

Vic got on his knees and ran his hands all over his chair, then examined the underside of the table, and finally, Simon's chair. That brought him dangerously close to Simon himself, and being on his knees when Simon's crotch was only a few inches away brought heat to Vic's face and sent a jolt to his cock. "Everything looks good," he said, and silently groaned at the way that sounded.

Simon chuckled. "Glad you think so." He sat, as Vic retreated to his chair and hoped he wasn't red-faced with embarrassment.

"Now what?" Vic asked, trying to regain a little control.

"Don't tell me anything," Simon said. "Just think about your

case, what kinds of things you want to know, the people involved."
He paused. "Um, it works best with physical contact. May I touch
your fingers?"

"Sure," Vic replied, leaving off that he'd be fine with it if Simon
wanted to hold hands. Despite his skepticism about psychics, Vic
found Simon even more appealing here on his own turf than he had
been in the coffee shop. Simon was rocking the slightly bashful nerd
vibe, and it looked good on him. Up close, the t-shirt pulled enough
to suggest lean muscles every bit as nice as the ass and thighs
revealed by his blue jeans. It hadn't escaped Vic that Simon was a
few inches shorter than his own six-foot, one. That meant they'd fit
together well, standing...or lying down.

"What now?" Vic asked, trying to shift a bit in his chair to
relieve his hard-on without being obvious. The hint of a smirk on
Simon's face told him he hadn't succeeded.

"Now I touch you, and we see what happens," Simon said.

So much for sitting comfortably, Vic thought, since his prick was back
at attention.

Simon's fingers were slim and strong as they brushed over Vic's
knuckles. Vic stifled a gasp at the spark that seemed to pass between
them and wondered if Simon felt it, too. From the way the psychic's
eyes widened and darkened, he suspected it was mutual.

"Keep your eyes open," Simon instructed, as his own fluttered
shut. "I don't want you to have any doubts. Both of my hands are
where you can see them. You can put your feet on my toes if you're
really afraid I'm pressing hidden buttons or something. Go ahead.
Do it."

Vic felt as if he'd been caught out in a secret, but he complied,
resting the tips of his shoes on top of Simon's. If the other man so
much as wiggled his toes, Vic would feel it.

"Think about what you want," Simon said. His voice had gone
low and quiet, a bit husky, and Vic couldn't help wondering what it
would be like in the heat of passion, to let that gorgeous hair down
and strip away the t-shirt and feel those legs around his waist.

*Shit. What if he can read minds? I'm so screwed. More like I'll never get
screwed, at this rate. Damn, damn, damn! Get your mind out of the gutter.*

Think about the case. Just the case. Vic took a deep breath, tried to ignore Simon's fingers against his, and found that picturing the bloodied remains of a serial killer's victims solved the problem of his erection. He felt his shoulders and arms tighten as he thought about the elusive murderer, the dead women, the scant evidence...

"Irene," Simon murmured. "No. Iryena. Thick accent. She's frightened. I don't think she realizes yet that she's dead. Oh," he groaned, but it was more in sympathy than theatrical. "Oh, my god. Her throat...Palm trees. Not...real ones. With lights. And a word, it sounds like 'ghost-in-eetza'. And a blue fish. Keeps repeating the word and the blue fish. Then what sounds like 'Bolshy-noss.'"

Vic held absolutely still, watching Simon with a gut-clenching combination of fear and fascination. Nothing about the psychic suggested that Simon was putting on a show. He sat with his head back, eyes shut, but his body did not move, and his tone did not vary dramatically. At the name "Iryena," Vic went cold. *Ross said we hadn't released her name to the media. How can he know? Shit, what if he's involved somehow? This was a mistake—*

Part of being a detective meant having a very good memory. Vic noted the details Simon revealed, making sure to remember the strange words. He could Google them later, or ask someone, although without admitting where he heard them.

Simon shifted in his chair, and his head turned as if looking at another speaker. "She says you did the right thing," Simon said quietly, his voice somber. "Mary? No. Maria. Last name...something like Colorado? She says you didn't have a choice, and neither did she. She would have killed you because of the fog—"

"That's enough!" Vic's voice was cold and almost shaking with fury. "I don't know what kind of game you think you're playing—"

Simon's hand jerked back, breaking the contact, and his eyes flew open as he stared at Vic with shock and hurt. "There's no game—"

"You're good," Vic said, pushing his chair back. "Did you snap a photo of me at Le Miz, then run it through some kind of facial recognition software? There's no way you should have known—"

"*I* didn't know," Simon replied, as the hurt in his expression hardened into anger. "*They* did. Almost none of that made any sense to me. It usually doesn't. Did it mean something to you? And if I got something right, why do you look like you want to take a swing at me?"

Vic tried to calm himself, but his heart was thudding so hard he felt light-headed. What if Simon was telling the truth about being able to speak to ghosts? Vic had gotten less coherent statements from real, live witnesses in the aftermath of a traumatic incident. Maybe dying shook up ghosts as much as almost dying rattled survivors. He was nearly willing to believe the information about the serial killer's victims. But as for the rest, Vic didn't know how Simon would have known enough about him to find out what happened in Pittsburgh, but that was the only explanation, right?

Because no way would the woman, who had tried to kill him when the green glowy fog possessed her, ever forgive Vic for shooting her dead.

"Look, I think you'd better go." Simon's voice had grown cool, not rude but distant and formal. "What I told you is either right, or it isn't—judge the truth about me by that. And no, I didn't take your photo, hell, I didn't even know your last name until you told me, here in the shop. You don't have to believe in me. But you don't get to accuse me of being a fraud."

By now, Vic's temper had cooled enough for him to realize how much he'd fucked everything up. "Sorry," he muttered, sure it was too little too late. He had been an ass when Simon had done exactly what Vic had paid him to do. It wouldn't take much to determine whether the "ghostly information" about the victims was real. But his reaction had certainly made a mess of any shot he might have had with Simon. "I was out of line."

"Yeah, you were. Don't worry; you're not the first person to figure it's a lark and then get their shorts in a wad when it's more than they bargained for." Simon frowned, and when he spoke, his voice was quieter. "Just don't write it all off, please. What she— Iryena—told me, it's true. And what happened to her, God, no one deserves that. Please don't ignore what she said because you can't explain it."

"I need to go," Vic said, torn between wanting to bolt and wanting to throw up. His chest felt tight, his gut was in a knot, and his mouth had gone dry. "You've got my number if any of your dead buddies start talking again." With that, he headed for the door with as much haste as his pride would allow.

5

SIMON

"**W**ell, that went to shit fast enough," Simon muttered as the door closed behind Vic. He sighed, and sat back down in his chair, resting his head in his hands. He knew he should go flip the sign, but he needed just a few minutes to compose himself.

Fuck. Or more to the point, no fuck. Simon didn't want to admit to himself how happy he'd been when Vic walked in the door. And when the cop had admitted looking for Simon to get his number, because they had *connected,* Simon had a roller coaster vertigo moment like an addled teenager.

As soon as Vic asked about doing a reading, Simon's self-preservation instincts started blinking a warning. He didn't have a problem doing readings for friends. Hell, he'd done plenty of readings for Jacen, when they were first dating, up in Columbia. Back then, when it didn't cost him anything, Jacen had believed in Simon's talent. But Simon got the feeling that Vic's skepticism wasn't as simple as not believing in psychics. He almost thought the opposite —that Vic did believe, or had, and got burned because of it.

Vic hadn't seemed freaked out until the second ghost showed up. He'd startled at the name "Iryena," so that must have been a hit. The other words were too vague for Simon to figure out the meaning, but ghosts didn't chit-chat, so if Iryena passed along those particular phrases, she thought they would help identify her killer. But the woman who would have killed Vic in the fog? What the hell was that about, and why did it make Vic take off like his tail was on fire?

Simon figured it didn't matter because he didn't expect to ever see Vic again. Unless the cop showed up to arrest him if something he said turned out to be details only the killer would know. Fuck. Why had he agreed to do the reading in the first place?

But he knew the answer to that. Vic had asked for help to solve a crime, and if Simon could lend a hand with his gift, he was willing, just like he would have assisted if he came upon an accident at the side of the road. *Next time, I'll tell my inner Good Samaritan to fuck off.*

He forced himself to get up, flip the sign, and sit behind the counter. Maybe his new coffee maker would come in the mail. That way, he wouldn't risk running into Vic again, since he felt certain the detective didn't plan on coming to his shop.

Dammit. Simon couldn't ignore the bitter disappointment churning in his gut. He'd felt a spark the first time he'd set eyes on Vic, and they'd hit it off so well talking over coffee. Not to mention that the cop was hella sexy. He was just enough taller Simon would have had to stretch to kiss him, and those inked arms would have felt solid and strong slipping around Simon's waist. And the way his jeans clung to his toned ass and muscular thighs? Lord have mercy, it made Simon stiff just thinking about it.

Except he wasn't going to get the chance to find out what that ink looked like, or get a piece of that tight ass. Because Vic either thought Simon was a fraud or had too many of his own issues to stick around for a one night stand, let alone a relationship. And how the hell had he gone from "call me, maybe" to fantasizing about Vic being a boyfriend anyhow? Simon chastised himself.

Maybe it had just been too long, he thought. Myrtle Beach had a vibrant gay community, with plenty of bars and nightclubs where he could certainly find some company. Then again, he'd never been much for casual sex. He liked being in a relationship, sticking around long enough to get out of the awkward "making a good impression" phase and into just being comfortable with each other.

Of course, if he didn't go out, he wasn't likely to find a new boyfriend. Especially since he'd already checked out the UPS driver, who was too old and married. *I wonder if the FedEx drivers are cute.*

Why not just order a pizza or call a plumber, he mocked himself. Shit. He needed to get his mind off Vic "the jerk" D'Amato and back in the game. But after he'd spent the next fifteen minutes staring at the door while absolutely no one even paused to look in the window, he realized that no distraction was likely to save him from his thoughts.

Vic hadn't said what case he was working on, but the image of the dead woman's bloody corpse and the Eastern European name—along with her accent and the foreign words—told Simon it had to be the "Strand Slitter." So far, the accounts in the media were short and to the point, no doubt thanks to the considerable pressure of the city fathers and the hospitality industry, which wouldn't want to scare off the tourists. The local news channels weren't even calling it a "serial killer." Just "the latest in a string of murders…"

But the locals talked. Simon knew all of the other store managers or owners in his block by name, and most of their regular employees, too. Cheap seasonal help brought in from less well-off countries kept hotel and restaurant prices low and translated into happy tourists. But he'd also heard stories about the darker side to the practice, and how the cops sometimes turned as blind an eye to abuses as did the employers. And all of them had heard of the Strand Slitter, warning their friends to take extra precautions.

Myrtle Beach—like any vacation spot—was a criminal's wet dream. So many transients—tourists, seasonal workers, drifters—that the pickings were easy and the odds of getting caught were worth the gamble. Unwillingness to make a fuss over problems, whether it was pickpockets, bed bugs, sharks, or thefts, kept the visitors blissfully ignorant and gave the perpetrators the advantage. And all too often the foreign workers were targeted because they didn't speak English fluently, were desperate to keep their jobs, and had no one to turn to. Simon had heard too many stories about those who were victimized getting brushed off by cops who didn't take their complaints seriously. People like Iryena.

So if Vic is looking into the Strand Slitter, at least he's willing to care about someone preying on transient help, Simon thought. It didn't fix his disastrous encounter with the detective, but it at least meant he might be an honorable man and a good cop. Not that those admirable traits were going to do Simon any good. Still, it mattered that someone was trying to stop the killer. And now that Simon had an inkling of what was going on, he knew he needed to check in with the network of special acquaintances that were going to be doubly at risk.

Right after work, Simon decided it was time to connect with his "skeleton crew."

His phone buzzed, and for a second, part of him hoped Vic had decided to call with an apology. Then he saw the number and sighed. "Hello, Mrs. Conrad. How can I help you?"

"Simon? I just wanted to remind you about the time for the library talk tomorrow. You can get someone to watch the shop while you're out, can't you?"

Fuck. He'd forgotten. "I'll make sure it all works smoothly," he lied, crossing his fingers. "It's at noon, right?"

"Noon to one, and you can bring some of your books to sell if you like," Mrs. Conrad, director of the Horry County Public Library, Myrtle Beach Branch assured him. She looked less like anyone's idea of a librarian, and more like a forty-something woman who came to the beach for a girlfriends' get-together and never went home. She seemed to own an unlimited variety of bright matching lipstick and nail polish to coordinate with the hair color that changed on a whim. Mrs. Conrad had been one of Simon's first friends when he had first moved to Myrtle Beach, and she remained a staunch supporter of his books and the tours. Despite himself, Simon smiled at her enthusiasm.

"Think we'll have a crowd?" he asked.

"I imagine you'll at least have warm bodies in the room since I advertised there would be refreshments," she confided. "That never hurts."

The library hosted all kinds of "lunch and learn" programs

throughout the year and tapped local experts, authors, and business people to do the free presentations. Mrs. Conrad had suggested six months ago that Simon do one on "unlocking your psychic potential," and he had agreed, but the time slipped by and what had been in the far future was now tomorrow.

"I'll put up a sign in the shop window," he promised. "And I'm looking forward to it," he fibbed. "It'll be fun."

"It's always fun when you're doing what you love," Mrs. Conrad chirped. He envied her seemingly endless supply of optimism. Maybe some of it would rub off on him and his non-existent love life.

Simon promised to be there early and ended the call just as two women in their thirties wandered in, looking for Tarot cards. After that, a constant stream of people made their way into the shop. Answering questions, ringing up purchases, and signing people up for tours kept Simon's mind occupied. By the time he was ready to close up for the night, he'd sold several books, a good selection of other merchandise, and booked his Thursday, Friday, and Saturday night tours nearly solid. Any other day that would have made him pretty happy, but after the clusterfuck with Vic, nothing seemed to raise his mood.

He locked up the shop and decided to grab a hot dog for dinner so he could check in with his "crew." As he paid the pushcart vendor, he realized that the dark-haired woman who usually sold frozen treats from a cart a little farther down the boardwalk was nowhere to be seen.

"What happened to the ice cream lady?" he asked the vendor.

"Who?" The man replied in heavily-accented English. Simon figured he was from the Philippines, maybe, or Malaysia.

Simon tilted his head toward the empty place on the boardwalk. "You know. The woman who sold ice cream, over there. She's always here."

The hot dog vendor shrugged. "Didn't show up today. That's all I know. Not my business. I stay out of it," he said.

"Yeah, I get it," Simon replied, thanking him and walking away. The boardwalk was lighting up as dusk fell. Upbeat music throbbed from the open-air bars and restaurants, tourists reeking of coconut sunscreen joked and laughed as they walked past, and in the distance, the huge Ferris wheel glowed rainbow colors that blurred when it started spinning fast.

The first bite of hot dog felt like a lump in the bottom of Simon's stomach as he tried to remember what the ice cream woman looked like. He'd never studied her features, but what little he recalled—dark hair, thin, heart-shaped face—was an unsettling match for Iryena's ghost. He had thought the spirit looked familiar, although at the time, he couldn't place her. Now, staring at the empty spot that usually held the brightly colored frozen treat stand, Simon feared that he already had his answer about why she wasn't at her post.

Simon didn't taste the rest of his hot dog as he hurried to finish. He washed the food down with a soda and headed for the first of several stops he intended to make before going home.

He walked down to the end of the boardwalk, then cut up a block to Ocean Boulevard. Cars formed a ribbon of red taillights driving along the iconic strip past surf shops, towering hotels, and neon-drenched attractions. The crowd in the cars and along the sidewalks would grow rowdier as the evening progressed, as the families with children gave way to drunken college students and twenty-somethings out for a good time. The Grand Strand wasn't Vegas, but that didn't stop it from having dirty dreams all of its own.

Simon lifted his head to the constant sea breeze, catching the tang of the waves above the car exhaust and cigarette smoke. He had liked living in the capitol, mostly, but he hadn't realized how much the ocean spoke to his soul until he ran away to the beach and decided it had been home all along.

He remembered what Vic had said about being from elsewhere, and his panicked reaction to the words from the second ghost. Maybe he ran away from something, too, only it followed him. Simon figured Vic's past would remain a mystery. He resolutely pushed down the hurt and disappointment and picked up his pace.

The Conch diner never closed. Its neon seashell was a beacon in the night to the hungry, the insomniacs, the stoned, and the inebriated, or those who had been tossed out at last call and had nowhere to go. The venerable eatery served greasy spoon comfort food, breakfast all day, and burgers from noon until sunrise. It anchored Ocean Boulevard just south of the 14th Street Pier, welcoming bar hoppers, fishermen, families, and travelers with its bottomless cups of coffee, Calabash-style seafood, and homemade banana pudding.

Simon walked into the Conch and found a booth near the back where he could see the door and the diner's patrons. He knew he wasn't the only one with psychic abilities in Myrtle Beach, but his gifts were among the strongest and the best trained of any he had discovered. Simon kept track of the others he had met who had traces of magic or supernatural talent, building a loose network of allies.

He thought of them as his "skeleton crew" because most worked the night shift. That kept dreams and premonitions at bay, and assured they were rarely alone in the wee hours, that time of night poets called the "hour of the wolf." Most of the crew struggled with their abilities, turning to whatever distractions could give them peace, dial down the psychic shitshow, mute the very real voices in their heads. Simon did what he could to help, but most of his crew had survived this long by being wary, and they valued their privacy and independence with fierce, if sometimes self-destructive, pride. Now, he feared that if his crew's gifts gave them glimpses of the Slitter and his victims, it could endanger them, all the more so since many of them were also seasonal help.

"Haven't seen you for a while." The server's blond hair had blue and green streaks, and her earrings shimmered with iridescent spangles. Tasha Ilicseu was a long way from her home in Bucharest, and her hit-or-miss telepathic abilities put her on Simon's radar.

"Been busy," Simon replied. "How are things?"

Tasha shrugged. "Things are what they are," she answered in heavily accented English. "Romanians, we understand this and have made our peace with it," she added with a nonchalant fatalism that never ceased to surprise him.

"Pick up any interesting news?" This time, he met her gaze and made certain that his foremost thoughts projected the Grand Strand Slitter and the missing seasonal workers.

"No," she replied, and Simon felt the barest touch of her power against his mind, something he would not notice or recognize for what it was without his psychic gift. "But I watch. And I listen. You know something?"

"Not yet," Simon replied. "If you 'hear' anything, let me know." He paid her two dollars for the coffee she brought and left a twenty for the tip.

"Of course," Tasha answered. "People like us, we have to stick together." She pocketed the tip and left Simon to drink his coffee, watching the crowds pass by the windows.

Of all his crew, Tasha was one of the most level-headed. Her telepathy was unreliable and her training minimal, but she'd learned the basics of shielding to keep out unwanted intrusions, and that meant she might live long enough to get her gift under control.

Simon sipped his coffee, killing time to make sure the next person he wanted to see would be on shift. The diner smelled of burger grease and vegetable soup, along with the aroma of pot roast laden with onions. Outside, the weather had changed from the morning's rain with the seaside's characteristic fickleness, and the nice night meant that being on foot was the best way to navigate Myrtle Beach's crowds and traffic. By the time he made the rounds, he'd have gotten in a few miles and hopefully tired himself enough to sleep without thinking about a certain troublesome detective.

A few more blocks brought Simon face to face with a life-size, roaring Tyrannosaurus Rex. The Lost Paradise mini-golf course was lit up brightly enough that it could probably be seen from space, and the velociraptors, pterodactyls, wooly mammoth, and stegosaurus howled and snorted and flapped in all their robotic glory. Dramatic music heightened the stakes for the laughing families and teenagers who played the multi-level course, and the lush palms, hibiscus, and oleander gave the attraction a jungle feel.

Simon tried to remember how long it had been since he had played a round or two of mini-golf and decided it must have been a year ago when friends from his old job in Columbia had come to visit. Myrtle Beach's mini-golf courses achieved a whole new level of epically themed entertainment, offering pirate adventures, shipwrecks, ancient sunken cities, and ferocious wild animals.

He stood in line behind a group of five college students who were almost too caught up goading each other about the upcoming game to pay for their balls and clubs. When they moved on, Simon glanced around to see whether anyone else was behind him, and then grinned at the harried young man behind the counter.

"Just another day in paradise?"

Quinn Radnor glared at him. "Come over to this side of the counter and say that," he grumbled, though his tone lacked heat. Quinn was tall and lanky, with skin the color of molasses and hair cut short and dyed bright red. A gold chain with a hamsa charm stood out against his dark skin. Unlike many of the workers in the beach town, Quinn was a true local. He huffed in exasperation and then offered a tired smile. "What's a guy like you doing in a place like this?"

"Fishing for information," Simon replied. "I know what my gift is picking up, and there's a storm brewing. Wondering what everyone else's 'radar' is saying."

Quinn read auras, which meant he had an inborn ability to size up people far beyond surface impressions and body language.

Quinn leaned toward him and dropped his voice. "Tourists are fat and happy. Locals, man, locals are scared. Leastwise the ones working the Strand are."

"The Slitter?"

Quinn nodded. "Yeah. People talk. Sayin' crazy stuff. Some I believe, some I don't, ya know? But couple of girls I know had themselves some near-misses, with this Slitter. Almost got grabbed, that kinda thing."

"And let me guess, no one wanted to call the cops?"

The man favored Simon with a withering look. "What do you think?"

"Got anything useful? Anything that could help people protect themselves?"

"How is this your problem?" Quinn asked warily. "Are you investigating this?"

Was he? Simon decided the answer could wait for another time. "I'm getting some disturbing visits from ghosts. And if there's anything *people like us* have picked up on that might keep the J-ones from getting killed, I figure we're all better off." He used the slang for the visa type that most of the foreign student workers carried, a term many employers on the Strand substituted for "seasonal worker."

"Maybe, maybe not," Quinn said. "I think you're crazy to get involved. But…if I pick up anything really strange, I'll let you know. Hard enough being a wage slave around here, without having a sicko running around."

"Thanks." Simon moved aside as another group crowded toward the counter, and he slipped past them into the night.

He dodged the throngs of vacationers who crowded the sidewalks. Simon decided to check in with one more of the crew on the way home, and leave the rest for another night. Quinn's ambivalence made him re-think his sudden involvement, but then he remembered Iyrena's ghost, and his resolve hardened. *What's the point in having talents if we don't use them to help?*

A few blocks away from the shop, Simon turned down an alley, walking away from the bright lights of Ocean Boulevard. The bars on the side streets catered to a different crowd than the neon-lit pubs and restaurants along the main thoroughfares. Bars like Crawdad Jim's pulled in a rough crowd. Some were local, others just passing through on the cheap. These watering holes weren't the kind that showed up on the Chamber of Commerce maps.

Out in the parking lot, Rennie puffed a cigarette. Her blue-black hair was as unnatural as her cherry red lips and the kohl that lined her flinty gray eyes. Rennie's outfit might have passed for club gear if the attitude didn't ask for a down payment before a trick ever got down to discussing business. Simon had no idea what her last name was, or whether "Rennie" was even her real name, but they had crossed paths when she had dropped by the shop for protective charms, and Simon had realized he'd just met the Grand Strand's only other true medium.

"Slumming isn't like you," Rennie said when she saw him approach. She took a long drag of the cigarette, then tipped her face toward the sky and blew out a plume of smoke.

"Maybe I just took a walk," Simon replied.

"Then you've got lousy common sense, wandering dark alleys. Ain't your mama ever told you to stay clear?"

"She said a lot of things. I only listened to some of them," Simon replied with a wry grin.

"So what you brings you out here? I know I don't have what you're looking for."

"Just wondering what you've been hearing...from the *others*."

Rennie dropped her cigarette and ground it out on the asphalt with her heel. "As little as possible. That's what the pills are for." Tattoos covered the scars from cutting and needles, but no matter what she used to numb her gift, nothing could hide the weary look in her eyes. He'd offered more than once to get her into rehab, and she'd turned him down.

"Has Iryena come to you?"

"Fuck," Rennie spat, giving him a baleful look. "What do you know?"

"Not much," Simon admitted. "Except that someone's killing J-ones, maybe others. Iyrena showed up in my reading today."

"Then there's nothing you can do for her," Rennie said. She lit up again, but Simon could see her hands shake. "Tell her to move the fuck on."

"There've been others. Have they told you anything?"

"I'm not like you," Rennie countered. "They don't show up and have proper conversations. I get flashes," she said and took a deep puff. "Godawful pictures. Drank myself shit-faced, and it still didn't stop them."

"Tell me," Simon said.

"What will it change?" Rennie argued. "If the cops cared, they'd have done something besides sit around with their thumbs up their asses."

"Then maybe if those of us who have a little *talent* work together, we can take care of the matter ourselves," Simon replied, his thoughts starting to come together.

"You're fucking serious," Rennie said, eyeing him. "Really?"

"At worst, maybe we come up with the anonymous tip that makes a difference. Because we *notice* things other people don't."

"I saw a blue fish, and some gibberish words, and a lot of blood," Rennie said, looking away. "Then another one—blond, sounded Russian or something—was all cut up, and all she showed me was fake palm trees all covered with lights." Another puff. "Seen other ghosts, but none you'd care about. Now get outta here. Gotta make my rent."

Simon left Rennie and headed toward the Ocean Boulevard, doing his best to tune into the party vibe of the tourists around him to lighten his mood. He hesitated outside Night People's Place, one of the better gay bars on the strip, then walked on. Cruising for a hookup wasn't something he felt comfortable doing even in the best of moods, and tonight he couldn't imagine anyone thinking he would be good company.

He headed home, a small blue cottage several streets removed from the beach. The 1950s bungalow had a tidy, retro look, with a tiny patch of grass and a carport for the silver Camry he rarely drove. His Aunt Karen and Uncle Jay used to winter in Myrtle Beach, until age and health made the trip less fun than it used to be. When he'd left Columbia, Aunt Karen had heard via the family grapevine and offered him the cottage with a sweetheart deal to buy them out. He'd taken it as a sign and snapped it up.

Usually, coming home after a day's work gave him a sense of peace. Simon had blended the house's vintage furnishings with what he'd kept from his apartment in Columbia, and the eclectic mix made him happy, from the kitschy cat clock with the wagging tail to the brightly colored Fiestaware dishes. But tonight, not even his favorite lime green pod chair raised his spirits.

Simon turned on the TV, but nothing held his attention. He poured himself a Jack and Coke and tried to read, then gave up, switched on music, and stared at nothing as he sipped his drink.

If Vic's phone hadn't rung when they were in the coffee shop, Simon felt sure they would have exchanged numbers, and maybe Vic would have asked him out right then. He hadn't imagined the chemistry between them, then or later at his shop. And if the second ghost had just minded her own business and stayed away, Vic might have been wary, but things still might have worked out between them.

Whatever the second ghost said did more than rattle Vic, and Simon had the sense the cop didn't scare easily. The ghost might have offered absolution, but whatever had happened, it seemed clear that Vic still bore the scars and the guilt.

"Cockblocked by a ghost," he muttered. "Just my luck."

To Simon's surprise, the library seminar room was nearly full. Apparently "Unlocking Your Psychic Potential" was a popular topic, or maybe Mrs. Conrad's spread of cookies and coffee had done the trick, but the twenty-five people who filled the space hung on Simon's every word. The presentation wasn't the difficult part; navigating the Q&A afterward required remaining polite even when faced with some of the most bizarre questions and assumptions.

"When you write your books, do you ever get the feeling that you're accessing the memories of past lives?" one woman asked. Her bottle-blond hair remained piled atop her head with what appeared to be real chopsticks.

Simon kept a smile plastered on his face. "Uh, no. Pretty sure that's all me. Current me."

"You write books about ghosts. Do any of the ghosts ever charge you to tell their stories?" a portly man in the second row piped up.

"I'm not sure how that would work since they're dead," Simon replied, feeling his face freeze with the effort to keep smiling.

"My astrologer told me that I'm the reincarnation of Judy Garland. Shouldn't I be getting royalties from all her songs?" another woman called out from the back of the room.

Simon fought the urge to smack himself in the head. "I really think that's something you should take up with a lawyer."

"And we're almost out of time," Mrs. Conrad chirped from the doorway, rescuing Simon. "Simon will have his books here at the front of the room if you'd like to purchase them, as well as information about his ghost tours and his fabulous shop down on the boardwalk."

Simon seized the verbal lifeline and left the podium to stand behind a table with his books and materials. The attendees filed past, most taking a brochure about the tours or a card with the shop's address. Two people bought books, and a few others snagged the last of the cookies on their way out.

One young woman lagged behind, obviously waiting for the others to go. Simon had noticed her in the back row, sitting quietly but paying close attention to everything he said.

"Dr. Kincaide—" she began.

"Simon, please."

"Simon," she repeated with a blush. "I'm Katya. Do you think it is possible to learn to, how you say, turn your...abilities...on and off?" The accent sounded Eastern European to Simon, and he wondered if she was a J-one.

"I *know* it is, Katya," he said with a smile, hoping she wouldn't rabbit. "I've had to learn how to set mental boundaries to keep from being overwhelmed."

"I can't help overhearing other people thinking," Katya confessed, avoiding his gaze. "It's not meant to be rude." She struggled for the words. "I'm afraid if my bosses knew, they would be angry or think I do not tell the truth."

"They don't have to know," Simon replied.

"But sometimes I know things, and I shouldn't," Katya went on. "I dream things, and then I find out they actually happened, only I dream them first."

"What kind of things?" Simon asked, his voice gentle. Fortunately, Mrs. Conrad busied herself cleaning up, so he and Katya could speak privately.

"Bad things," Katya said in a voice barely above a whisper. "I see strangers get hurt, killed. Sometimes, later, I see it on the news. Nobody I ever met, so how did I dream of them? I don't want to dream anymore."

"Take this," Simon said, grabbing one of his books. "It's my gift. Chapter twenty talks about ways you can teach yourself to shut the door in your mind. You can't leave it shut forever—that would cause other problems—but it can help you get some sleep, and keep from being overwhelmed."

"Thank you, thank you so much," Katya said, clutching the book against her chest.

"If you want to talk, come by the shop anytime," he offered. He grabbed one of the cards from the table, and then tore a strip from a piece of paper and wrote his cell phone number on it. "That's my personal phone. If it's an emergency."

"Thank you," she repeated, then glanced at Mrs. Conrad and scurried from the room.

"You're never going to get rich giving your books away," she mock-tutted as Simon gathered his things to leave.

"Nah," he teased back. "I give ghost tours for that. It's where the real money is." *Not.*

"I hear you," she laughed. "I'm making out like a bandit as a librarian!"

They chatted a few minutes longer, and Simon thanked her for the invitation to speak, then he hefted his backpack and started for the shop. The ten-minute walk offered a chance to clear his head. A pleasant breeze ruffled the stray hairs that had pulled loose from where he'd put it up in a knot, and for once, the humidity hadn't risen to stifling.

Simon admitted that he had hoped maybe Vic would show up to the library presentation. He knew it was a long shot, but part of him had remained optimistic, all the way to the end. Now, he felt down. He knew Vic's rejection had to do with the ghosts of his past, pun intended, but it felt personal.

Come on, snap out of it. Stop at Night People's Place, have a drink, get a little somethin' on the side, blow off steam, he thought. And just as quickly, he remembered how much he hated anonymous encounters. *Maybe see if there's someone new on the dating app—*

"Jump!"

Simon reacted before he could think, hurling himself into the bushes along the sidewalk as a black SUV hopped the curb and ran over the sidewalk where he had stood seconds before. It corrected course and roared off.

Simon stood, shaking, and looked around. There was no one in sight, and he wondered who had yelled the warning. As he brushed bits of twig and leaf out of his hair and off his clothing, he realized that someone was watching him. When he looked up, an old man with a shopping cart full of bundles stared at him.

"You warned me?" Simon asked in a whisper, in case anyone living might be near.

The ghost nodded. The spirit had mustered enough energy to shout a warning, but now either lacked the energy or the desire to say more.

"Thank you," Simon said. "Can I help you pass over?"

The old man shrugged and pointed to the park on the other side of the hedgerow. Simon took his meaning. The park had been the man's home in the last years of his life, and he wasn't ready to leave just yet. Fortunately, Simon thought, he hadn't wanted company.

"Thank you," he repeated, as the ghost's image faded. Simon grabbed his backpack from where it fell, brushed at the grass stains, and hurried his pace, although he only had a few blocks to go.

That car meant to hit me, he thought and felt chilled. *Someone steered toward me. That was too controlled to be an accident.*

But why? He wondered. Simon didn't have any enemies, at least, not in the murderous sense. The circumstances of his departure at USC had left bruised feelings and damaged egos, but in the end, the only person who sustained permanent injury was Simon, with the loss of his teaching career. After three years, he doubted anyone cared enough to try to kill him.

He didn't owe anyone money; at least, nobody but the bank for the loan on his shop. No gambling, no drugs, no blackmail, no crazy exes. *Unless someone thinks I told Vic something dangerous, or that I will tell him*—

Simon reached the shop, unlocked the door and turned off the alarm. He was breathing hard, and his heart still thudded against his ribs. Should he call Vic? He almost reached for his phone, then reconsidered.

And tell him what? A car jumped the curb? Everyone knows tourists can't drive. He'll say they were just on their phone or looking at their GPS.

Simon went to the break room, warmed up a cup of coffee, and flipped over the sign. He reached under the counter and pulled out a string of onyx and silver beads that usually helped to ground him and ease tension. They helped, but only a little.

The rest of the afternoon crawled. Simon jumped every time the door opened, then did his best to manage a greeting that didn't sound fake. By closing time, he was ready to go and grateful that this wasn't one of his tour nights.

Simon knew he should check in with the rest of his Skeleton Crew, but he felt too jumpy after the near-accident to walk around tonight. He did put up a sign in the window about starting a neighborhood watch program and picked a date for a meeting in his shop the following week.

He kept to the main streets on his way home, walking fast and staying as far off the road as possible. No one tried to run him down, and he couldn't see that anyone was following him. Simon threw together a grilled ham and cheese sandwich, curled up on the couch, and put in an action movie, promising himself that come the weekend, he would find himself a date. Maybe.

The ringtone on his phone woke Simon out of a deep sleep. He squinted, trying to figure out where he was and realized he had fallen asleep on the couch, with the movie long over and his contacts dried out. He pawed for the phone and saw the text message.

"Shit," he growled, jerking to alertness. "That's the shop alarm."

The LED display on his phone read 3:00. He debated taking the car, then decided he didn't want to chance walking after the SUV incident. Simon grabbed his keys and phone, locked up, and drove back to Grand Strand Ghost Tours, scared of what he was going to find.

He silenced the alarm from his phone when he reached the shop, then advanced warily, wondering why out of all the stores on the boardwalk, anyone would pick his to break into. He never left cash in the register and did a fraction of the sales the big gift shops made. None of his merchandise was particularly valuable, or even easy to fence. *'Cos I'm sure there's a big demand for stolen New Age crystals and books about ghosts.*

From a distance, the first thing he noticed was that the big plate glass window was still intact. The smell of blood stopped him cold.

"Fuck, fuck, fuck." No way could what he was seeing be real. But as he stepped closer, his heart sank and his breath came short and fast as fear slithered down his spine.

A plastic Bojack horsehead mask hung off one of the decorative boardwalk posts, with the face pointing at the shop. The mask and post were soaked with blood. To anyone else, it might look like a malicious prank.

To someone with a doctorate in folklore and mythology, Simon recognized it as a deadly threat.

"Niding horse," he murmured, unable to believe his eyes. Norse mythology, from the Viking days, a thousand fucking years ago. The custom was too obscure for him to have even brought it up in his classes, but he knew the lore. Vikings were hardcore on their gender roles. Weaving and magic were for women; men did the fighting and plowing. Men who did magic were killed, and so were gay men. The niding horse was a curse and a hate crime rolled into one.

Simon moved carefully, stretching out his senses for any indication of dark magic. The area around the bloody horsehead itself made him recoil with the taint of malicious power. The cops weren't going to show up; he had enough false alarms from drunks rattling doorknobs to only have patrols respond when he was out of town. That gave him a chance to handle the threat in his own way, since the police definitely weren't prepared for the paranormal.

Simon went around to the back door and let himself in, flicking on the lights so that they blazed brightly. Cutting down on shoplifting meant having good lines of sight in the store, and he always kept the door to the upstairs locked when he wasn't in the shop. That meant he could see everything, and no one lurked waiting to get the drop on him.

He grabbed some sage and an abalone shell, along with blessed salt, charcoal, and holy water. Then he filled a bucket with salted water to wash away the blood and dispel the bad magic. Simon went back around, avoiding the cursed area directly in front of the door, and took pictures of the bloody mask with his phone. He lit the sage bundle and placed it on the shell, and threw several handfuls of salt over the plastic horsehead and onto the area contaminated by blood, followed by holy water. Simon chanted a blessing and followed it up with a litany to dispel evil. When he finished, all that was left was a soggy pillar and a wet novelty mask.

Simon used a broomstick to lift the mask off the post. Then he locked the shop again and carried the mask down to one of the metal garbage bins on the beach, where he dropped it in and set it on fire. Starting a blaze on the beach was illegal, and it occurred to him that it would really suck to get arrested for burning a cursed object, but fortunately, the blaze died down before anyone noticed.

He went back to the shop and stretched out his senses again, but all traces of the dangerous magic were gone. Simon reset the alarm and turned off the brightest lights. He unlocked the stairs to his office, stretched out on the sofa he kept for emergencies, and tried, unsuccessfully, to go back to sleep until the sun came up.

Would have been nice to be dating a cop right about now, he thought as sleep eluded him. *One who believed in the supernatural. Too bad I'm not.*

6

VIC

"Another fucking murder, and we're no closer to catching the son of a bitch." Vic wanted to kick something, but that wasn't practical at a crime scene surrounded by other cops.

"You go talk to the roommate," Ross offered. "I'll babysit the forensics team."

Vic knew Ross was letting him off easy, and he almost argued, then changed his mind. He'd take the hard part next time. Changing off made it marginally easier to keep the awful details at bay.

He went back to the apartment's living room, where a woman in her early twenties sat on one end of a blue sofa that sagged in the middle, probably purchased at a consignment store or grabbed off the curb on trash day if the stained and threadbare fabric was any clue.

Like the dead woman, the roommate, Agata Marsalak was a J-one, here on a seasonal visa from the Czech Republic. Agata's dark hair was pulled back into a ponytail, a severe, unflattering look that made her tear-stained cheeks and red eyes all the more noticeable. She twisted a dish towel between her hands, looking desolate and frightened.

"Hey," Vic said, sitting down on the other end of the couch. He spoke softly, trying not to spook her. "I need to ask you a few questions. You speak English, right?" Technically, proficiency was a requirement to get the visa, but less scrupulous employment firms were known to fudge the facts in a hot market.

She nodded, and swallowed hard. "Well enough," she replied, her voice husky with tears.

"I'm Lieutenant D'Amato. I'm a homicide detective. And I'm very sorry about your roommate."

"She was a good girl," Agata said, with a look that dared Vic to say otherwise. "We work hard. Too hard sometimes, for not enough pay."

Vic didn't doubt that was true. He'd heard the stories of employers who abused their summer help but fixing it didn't fall to his unit. Murder did. "Tell me about her?"

"Her name is…was…Katya Buzek," Agata said. "We came over together. It was going to be, how you say? A lark. Fun. An adventure." She shook her head. "I don't know what I will say to her parents."

"Did Katya have any enemies?" Vic probed.

Agata shook her head. "No enemies. Like I said, she was a good girl. Didn't mess around with bad boys. No drugs. Didn't owe money. We both save everything we can, to take home."

"Was she afraid?"

Agata looked away, and Vic knew she was hiding something. "Please, tell me what you know. Keeping her secrets now might get someone else killed."

Agata looked like she was arguing with herself for a moment. "She had nightmares. Strange dreams. Not normal dreams."

Vic felt a shiver at Agata's words. "What do you mean, not 'normal'?"

"Do you believe in magic, detective?" she asked. "The, what's the word? Supernatural?"

"I'm more of a 'see it to believe it' kind of guy," he replied. "Did Katya think her dreams were omens?" At Agata's blank look, he searched for a synonym. "A bad sign?"

Agata nodded. "Many people believe such things, here, and back home. She told me that she saw things in her dreams she had not seen for real. People she didn't know, dead. Cut, like she is. It scared her."

"Did she tell anyone?"

"I don't know. She went to a class yesterday, to find out about how to control such things. When she came back, she seemed better."

"What kind of class?" Vic pressed.

Agata motioned toward a book and some pamphlets on the end table. "At the library."

Vic glanced at the materials, and his heart stopped for a second as he recognized the name of the author. Dr. Sebastian Kincaide. "Did she say anything about the class? Anyone she met there?" Vic slipped on a pair of latex gloves and picked up the book. A brochure for Grand Strand Ghost Tours slipped out, along with a card for the shop and a strip of paper, which fluttered to the floor. The torn paper landed upside down, revealing a handwritten phone number on the back.

"She said the class was very good. The instructor, he made her feel better, I think. Gave her the book. She didn't say much else."

"What did she do today?"

"We worked third shift. I was late coming back. About an hour. When I got here, I opened the door, and I saw her." She looked down but did not cry, although Vic could see the tension in her jaw as she tried to contain her grief.

"Did you see anyone else in the apartment?"

"No. Just Katya. The door was shut when I came home. I didn't think anything was wrong."

"All right," Vic said in his most reassuring voice. "That's it for now. We might have more questions for you later. And...I'm sorry."

Agata nodded, swallowing hard, looking like she had reached her breaking point. Vic picked up the torn paper and then pulled out his phone. When he entered the number, "Simon" popped up from his contacts. A glance confirmed that this number wasn't the same as the one for the shop on the business card.

Why the hell did a dead woman—a dead maybe-psychic woman —have Simon's personal cell phone number?

It took another couple of hours to clear the scene, as Vic and Ross coordinated with the beat cops, the forensics team, and the coroner's office, then filed their reports. By the time they were finished, Vic had a pounding headache, due in part to not having eaten for hours.

"You've been quiet," Ross said as they left the dead woman's apartment.

Vic shrugged, unwilling to put a name to the tangle of feelings churning in his gut. "It's the Slitter again, and we've still got nothing."

"Jumping the gun on forensics, aren't you?"

Vic glared at him. "Looks the same as the others—same pattern of knife wounds, same choice of victim. All that ever changes is the where and when."

"He'll slip up," Ross said with more conviction than Vic felt. "They always do. Maybe not as fast as we'd like, but sooner or later."

"The 'or later' part means more dead women," Vic growled. "We're missing something."

"Then we'll get a fresh start on it in the morning." Ross pulled up to the curb by Vic's apartment building. "Try not to spin your wheels all night. Let's see what the lab tests come back with."

Vic got out and wished him a good evening, wondering how the fuck his partner managed to compartmentalize so well. Ross cared about the job, Vic knew he did. But somehow, when it was time to go home, Ross seemed to flip a switch in his brain and let the crud they'd dealt with all day rest until tomorrow. Maybe it helped to have someone to go home to, Vic thought, which didn't help his mood as he pressed the passcode on the door to get into the building.

Vic needed a shower after the crime scene. No matter how long he'd been a cop, he'd never gotten over the smell of blood and shit that went with dead bodies. A hot shower with the strongest smelling soap he could find took the stench of death out of his nose, and he felt a little better just having a fresh t-shirt and jeans.

He headed down to the boardwalk, intending to catch Simon before the shop closed. When he got to Grand Strand Ghost Tours, Simon was in the back, straightening stock. He turned, and for an instant, he smiled when he saw Vic in the doorway.

"Vic—" His smile faded as if he recognized from Vic's expression and stance that this was not a social call. Simon's head lifted and his shoulders squared. "Lieutenant D'Amato. To what do I owe the pleasure?" His voice held a bitter edge.

"Where were you yesterday?" Vic asked, ignoring the way the hurt in Simon's eyes made his stomach twist. Damn, seeing him again stirred up feelings Vic wasn't ready to confront. Not that it looked like he'd ever get to act on any of the things Simon's smile made him want, or any of the dirty dreams that starred a certain long-haired ghost hunter up close and very personal.

"In the shop all morning," Simon replied. "Then I taught a class at the library and almost got killed walking back. Spent the afternoon—"

"You what?"

"A car tried to run me over. I went through a hedgerow to keep from getting hit. It sped off." Simon recounted the incident matter-of-factly, but the words hit Vic like a douse of cold water.

"Did you call the police?"

Simon gave him a look. "Black SUV. I didn't get the plates. No identifying marks. So, no. Nothing they could do about it. Nothing I could prove."

"Then how do you know they were trying to hit you?"

"Because the driver aimed," Simon replied. "Didn't try to correct until they realized I wasn't under the wheels.

Vic felt a surge of anger and protectiveness that surprised him. "And then what?" he ground out.

"Came back to the store, finished out the afternoon. Went home, fell asleep on the couch. The store alarm tripped at 3 a.m., so I came down to check and found a bloody horse head on a pole."

"Tell me that you called the police."

"Last summer, a bunch of teenagers thought it was fun to bang on the glass and rattle the doors along the boardwalk to make the alarms go off," Simon replied. "After the third or fourth false alarm, the cops got snippy. So I changed the monitoring protocol to just notify me, unless I'm out of town."

Vic pinched the bridge of his nose, trying to stop a migraine. "Did you have a weapon?"

"I don't own a gun." Not a real one, anyhow. A paintball pistol didn't count, from a disastrous "fun" outing Tracey had talked him into years ago.

"Did you say…bloody horse head? Like in *The Godfather?*"

"More Viking than Sicilian, in this case," Simon replied. "And the police couldn't have handled the situation. It was dark magic, a curse…and a death threat."

"Who the hell would leave a Viking curse for a shop owner in Myrtle Beach?"

Simon met his gaze. "Someone who knows I have a Ph.D. in folklore and mythology and would understand the message."

Vic wondered if apoplexy felt like this, the certainty that his head might explode. "But you didn't call in this new threat, either?"

Simon shrugged. "Cops don't believe in the supernatural. Why bother?" That last phrase was said without heat, but Vic knew it was aimed right at him.

"You have any proof?" Vic asked, refusing to rise to the bait.

Simon pulled out his phone and called up photos. He held it out for Vic to see but didn't hand it over as he flipped through the pictures he had taken of the niding horse.

"You know this isn't really proof," Vic said, frowning. "You could have staged that yourself."

"I didn't."

"Are you afraid?" Vic asked, watching his reaction.

"I'm a gay man in the South. I'm always afraid."

Vic chuffed out a breath and ran a hand up the back of his neck. So many instincts and feelings warred with each other, and the intensity of those emotions caught him by surprise. He'd been called to hit-and-run murders, and when his mind supplied Simon's lifeless body bloodied and broken in the roadway, a surge of rage bubbled up. *How the hell can he be so casual about his own life* turned to *who the fuck would want to kill Simon?*

"Tell me about the library program yesterday," Vic said, taking a deep breath to steady himself. "What happened there?"

Simon frowned as if the change of topic surprised him. "More people came for the cookies than for the information, but that's kind of the norm for a library talk. Sold a couple of books, chatted a little, and then I headed out."

"Why was your personal cell phone number in a dead girl's book?"

Simon looked confused, then as the meaning became clear, he gasped and went pale, reaching to steady himself against the counter. "Katya? Oh, god. What happened?"

"What did she tell you at the program?" Vic asked. He saw Simon's distress, and part of him wanted to pull the other man into his arms and soothe his pain. But the cop in him needed answers.

Simon hesitated, and Vic guessed he didn't want to break a confidence. "She's past the point of caring if you tell her secret."

Simon glared at him. "Do you have to be such a dick?" He squeezed his eyes shut and breathed deeply. "She said that she could overhear people's thoughts, and couldn't tune it out. That she had bad dreams, about strangers turning up dead. I gave her one of my books that has some techniques for shielding, and my phone number if she needed help."

"You just give your number out to total strangers?"

"Sometimes the risk pays off," Simon replied, refusing to look away. "Sometimes it doesn't."

Ouch, Vic thought. *Guess I deserved that.*

"Did she call you?"

"No. What happened to her?"

Vic saw the pain in his eyes and had to break off the stare-down. "Forensics is still figuring the fine points, but she was stabbed to death."

"She was a J-one," Simon said. "Like the others the Slitter killed."

"We didn't release any details—"

"Oh, come on!" Simon interrupted. "Do you think people can't figure it out for themselves? You think we don't talk to each other? The summer workers are terrified. They know who's been killed, they can connect the dots. You've got a serial killer targeting people who won't be missed, who can't fight back. Iryena. Now Katya. And all the others. So why are you here talking to me? You've already decided I'm useless."

Vic heard the pain beneath the anger in Simon's voice and winced internally. "I never said you were useless."

"You didn't have to. Walking out made that pretty clear."

Was it possible that Simon felt the same kind of connection between the two of them that Vic did? That might explain why the argument had a weird subtext that didn't seem to be about the case at all.

"Shit," Vic said. "Look, I'm sorry about that. You just…hit a nerve. I shouldn't have walked away like that. I'm sorry."

Simon regarded him in silence. "Did you follow up on what the ghost told you?"

"We've been a little busy—"

"No, huh? So you didn't believe it was real."

Vic opened his mouth to argue and shut it again. Simon was right. If a living witness had passed along a tip, even one that seemed incoherent, he'd have run it down. "Fair enough," Vic replied. Simon looked surprised.

"How about a truce?" Vic suggested, although his heart and his cock wanted far more. *Gotta make peace if you're ever gonna make out.* "I'll chase down Iryena's lead. And you—need to take the threats seriously. No more running around unarmed and alone in the wee hours if you've got someone who wants you dead."

"All right," Simon replied after a moment. The tension between them felt like it should be crackling with electricity. Vic had heard comments about "fighting and fucking," but he'd never really taken them seriously before. As much as he and Simon had just been at each other's throats, damned if Vic's cock hadn't gotten hard. Simon stood braced for an argument, and Vic's mind conjured up much better ways to work off all that tension, all of which involved getting naked and bending Simon over that counter—

"—protect the J-ones," Simon said.

Vic pulled himself out of his thoughts. "We *are* trying," he said, taking a careful tone so as not to destroy the fragile peace. "Hard to do when they won't talk to us."

"I'll let you know if I hear anything," Simon offered, looking as if he were waiting for Vic to mock the offer.

"You'd better," Vic replied. "And the same goes for near-misses and horse heads." He fully intended to keep an eye on Simon, and while he told himself it was just good procedure, Vic knew it was more.

7

SIMON

The next day dawned gray and rainy, like Simon's mood. Seeing Vic again had bothered him more than he wanted to admit, on more levels than he liked to think about. The way Vic had come barging down to the store to grill him rankled. At the same time, he'd caught glimpses of something else in Vic's eyes that resonated with desires of his own he'd almost given up on.

"Shit," he muttered, angry in equal measure with himself and with Vic. He couldn't deny the physical attraction; even if his brain tried to lie, his cock had a mind of its own. The dark hair and dark eyes, those tats, the muscular arms—

"Nope. Not going there," Simon grumbled, rearranging the displays and refreshing the stock to keep busy between customers. When his phone rang, he hated himself for the momentary hope it might be Vic and sighed when he recognized Tracey's number from the coffee shop.

"Hey, babe. Talk to me," he said, realizing that they hadn't connected in a couple of days, which was unusual. "What's up?"

"Had to make a trip back to Fort Mill," Tracey said. "My aunt's in the hospital. Turned out okay, but she gave us all a scare."

"Wondered where you'd been. The Mizzenmast isn't the same without you."

"Aren't you the sweetest thing," she said, in a thick Lowcountry accent she could turn off and on as the situation required. "You'll have to stop in. Got my braids re-done while I was home. Dyed the tips crimson."

Simon smiled. His best friend's love affair with hairstyles and colors knew no bounds. Tracey cycled through an endless variety of braids, cornrows, corkscrews, and other dos he could only think of as "sculptured." His admiration had grown when she let on just how long it took to get the complex styles done. "Bet you look absolutely fabulous," he replied.

"Nah, babe. You're fabulous. I'm marvelous." She paused. "So...dish. I hear there was a hot guy asking about you."

Vic? Then Simon remembered Vic's admission that he had gone looking for him after the ill-timed phone call that first day. "Um, yeah. It's complicated."

"Of course it is," Tracey chuckled. "If it were simple, you'd have just had it hard and fast back behind the bar."

Simon nearly choked on his coffee, and Tracey laughed. "Oh, I bet your face is as red as my tips right now," she teased.

"Look, I'll tell you the whole sad story," Simon promised. "But not over the phone. Come over on your dinner break, and I'll fill you in. Bring food. I'll pay you back."

"How could I resist an offer like that? I'll be by around four-thirty," she said and ended the call. Simon found himself looking forward to the visit. Maybe Tracey could make sense of his tangled feelings.

He went to the break room and poured another cup of coffee. At least the new machine seemed to be working right, a bright spot in an otherwise upsetting week. Back up front, he watched the rain sweep through and checked the forecast on his phone to assure himself that the storm would blow over and the afternoon would turn nice. He had two nearly full tours booked tonight, and no desire to have to refund for a weather cancellation.

Simon sipped the hot coffee and hoped it would wake him up.

He'd stayed awake late last night trying to communicate with the ghosts of the Slitter's victims, and Katya in particular, but no one answered his summons. That wasn't unusual; being a medium didn't guarantee the spirits were in the mood to talk. Katya might be too newly dead to manifest, and trauma victims were notoriously fickle about their interactions. He left the invitation and had to trust that when the spirits were ready, they would come to him.

At least he felt confident in his gift. As for Vic? Simon couldn't get the obstinate cop out of his head, but he had no idea what to make of Vic's reactions. Then again, maybe being a cop made it more difficult for Vic to figure out his own feelings. Last night, when Vic confronted him in the shop, he'd ranged from anger to concern, exasperation to possessiveness, all bound up in a simmering attraction that had Simon hard even when they were fighting.

"Fuck," he muttered, then rolled his eyes at his Freudian slip. So what if he'd been jerking off to thoughts about Vic since they'd met? That might be as close to the real thing as he'd ever get with the difficult cop, if things kept up the way they'd been going.

Maybe it's me, Simon thought. Jacen's betrayal had broken his heart, dented his pride, and shredded his ability to trust. His own parents had taken Jacen's side, and their comments about how they knew Simon's interest in "that occult stuff" would cause trouble still hurt. When he'd moved to Myrtle Beach, he had decided to steer clear of all entanglements until he got his head on straight again. Three years later, he was stuck in a safe but lonely rut.

Then again, maybe it's him. The truth was, if Vic didn't believe in Simon's talent, they'd never have more than a roll in the sheets. Jacen gave lip service to Simon's abilities as a medium and clairvoyant, but Simon had always suspected that his ex- thought the whole thing was an elaborate parlor trick. For Simon, his psychic abilities were as much a part of his core self as being gay or liking history. He'd learned the hard way that none of those things could be shoved aside or hidden without a cost Simon was no longer willing to pay.

Was Vic even out? Simon couldn't help wondering. Maybe Vic never was interested in more than being fuck buddies. The thought hurt Simon more than it should. Not that it mattered, since Vic seemed to consider Simon suspect just for trying to help. With a sigh, Simon went back over his script for the ghost tours, even though he could give the talk in his sleep. Anything to keep his mind off what he couldn't have.

Several minutes later Simon's cell buzzed, and he did a double-take at the number. "Hello, Miss Eppie. What can I do for you?" Ephigenia Walker, the most accomplished root worker and Hoodoo practitioner in Myrtle Beach, did not have time for idle chatter.

"Sebastian." Miss Eppie was the only one of Simon's new circle who called him by his given name, insisting it held truer to his energy. "What have you gotten yourself into?"

Simon choked, trying to figure out where to begin. "Quite a bit, actually. How do you mean?"

Miss Eppie might be in her seventies, but she did not suffer fools gladly. "I'm not talking about the new man who's put you twitter-pated. That will sort itself out in its own time. But I felt a surge of dark magic, and my spirit guides sent me word I should speak to you. Don't make me come down there and pound it out of you."

"Yes, ma'am," Simon replied. Since no one was in the shop, he told her about the black SUV and the niding horse, and about Katya and the ghosts.

"You have that jack ball I made for you?" Miss Eppie asked.

Simon reached into his pocket and found the protective ball of yarn and wax that was a powerful, personal Hoodoo talisman. "It's with me."

"Good. Keep it on you at all times," she said. "How 'bout that High John the Conqueror Root I gave you some while back? Wrap it in one of those little bags you put the crystals in and put it with the jack ball. It will strengthen your gift, and might could also solve that man problem of yours."

"My 'man problem' isn't a performance issue," Simon replied, feeling his cheeks color. "It's more of a showing up issue."

Miss Eppie's laugh was like honeyed bourbon. "Child, showing up is the first part of any performance. But you and that man who's caught your eye gotta live long enough to worry about such things.

So you keep those charms on you, and you say the protection spells I taught you. You remember those, don't you?" she asked, her voice suddenly sharp.

"Yes, of course." Simon felt as if he'd just been called to the principal's office.

"Now you listen to me, Sebastian. I'm not talking to hear myself speak. I know you've laid down salt along your windows and doors in that shop. Best you do so at home as well. And not just salt; get yourself some good Four Thieves vinegar and sprinkle it at every place something could come in and out. That means fireplaces, too," she ordered.

"Then you take that red brick dust I know you bought from me, and you fill up a wash bucket, and you scrub the entrance to your house and the shop. Mind you do it before dawn. Sprinkle the red brick dust onto the wet steps, and write the name of a policeman on a piece of paper. Burn the paper, and sprinkle the ashes with the brick dust. That will keep all but the strongest evil at bay."

"And how do I fight the strongest evil?" Simon asked. Miss Eppie's abilities were well-known throughout the Lowcountry, and he felt privileged to be her friend, even more so for his safety to be of concern.

"The only way anyone ever does," Miss Eppie replied. "With what you have inside you. It will have to be enough. But remember that two stand stronger against an enemy than any man alone."

"Thank you," Simon replied. "I'll do it. I promise." He paused. "What are you going to do?"

Miss Eppie sighed. "I'm gonna keep setting protection spells and selling amulets and charms and lifting curses. But I'm staying home to do it because I can't run as fast as I used to. I have helping magic, but it's not fighting magic, since I don't hold with cursing folks, unless they really, really deserve it."

"I understand."

"You're a good boy," Miss Eppie said, making Simon feel as if he were five instead of thirty-five. "Don't let yourself be addled, and you might just do all right."

Tracey showed up at four-thirty on the dot, and Simon put up the *"Back in 30 Minutes"* sign and led her to the back room. "I brought subs. That okay?" she asked. Tracey Cullen was only an inch shorter than Simon's five foot eleven, with a toned body like a competitive runner. She had a brilliant grin and a razor-sharp sense of humor. Her red-tipped braids contrasted with cocoa-brown skin and eyes so dark they might have been black.

Simon inhaled and groaned in happiness. "That's awesome. And...did you get them toasted?"

"Yep. I don't forget these things. I'd be the perfect boo for you, if I just had a dick," she joked.

"Speaking of boo, where's Sheyla?" Simon asked. Tracey's long-time girlfriend had an office job downtown with a real estate company and often worked late.

"She'll be along in a bit, but I was hungry now," Tracey replied. "I'll just nibble on a salad if she wants to go out."

"Thanks," Simon said, unwrapping the still-warm sub filled with ham, turkey, sliced veggies, and some honey mustard. "Believe it when I say this might be the best part of my week."

"Better than the hot guy you just met?" Tracey joked.

"A lot less complicated," Simon replied, taking a bite and making an exaggerated, orgasmic moan as he swallowed. "At least I know where I stand with the sandwich."

"I just spent three days dealing with enough family drama for a Netflix series," Tracey said as she chewed. "Fill me in."

Simon talked and ate, catching her up on meeting Vic, the unfortunate psychic reading, and the hot/cold attraction that was driving him crazy.

"You two just need to have a hot night together and get it out of your system," she said. "It's pent-up frustration. Probably been too long for both of you. Once you do, then you can walk away—or not —without twisting each other up."

Could it be that simple? Simon doubted it, but he didn't feel like arguing with Tracey. "Yeah, well. Not sure that's going to happen. Oh, and then I almost got hit by a car," he added, ready to change the subject.

"Seriously? Did your hot cop rescue you?"

Simon rolled his eyes. "No. Actually, a ghost told me to jump, or I'd have been road pizza."

"You have a strange life, Simon."

He told Tracey about finding the niding horse, but didn't go into detail about Katya or the other deaths, more to protect her than to keep from having to think about the grisly particulars. Tracey wasn't a J-one, but the killer could always change his pattern, and right now, it felt like no one was safe.

"So someone's tried to kill you—or at least warn you to go away —and you're just here at the shop, like usual?" Tracey finished her sub and balled up the paper.

"What am I supposed to do? Go into Witness Protection? I can't prove anything, and if the cop who maybe wants to get into my pants doesn't believe me, why would anyone else?"

"Uh huh. I think you need to work on the cop angle." Tracey sat back in her chair and took a long drink of soda through her straw. "Maybe if you're sleeping together, he'll be a little more protective. You know, like a live-in bodyguard."

Simon snorted. "Maybe I'll get a dog. Simpler."

"I'm talkin' friends with benefits, not man's best friend," Tracey said. "Seriously, did you buy a gun? Are you going to?"

"I'd probably hit everything except what I was aiming for," Simon answered, as he finished his sub. "That's not my thing."

"How about pepper spray? Or a knife? You need to have a way to protect yourself."

He knew Tracey was right, but buying a weapon made the threat all too real. "I'll get something," he promised.

She gave him a look. "Fine," she said, with an emphasis that made clear it wasn't. "Don't come running to me when you get killed." She checked her phone. "Shit. I have to get back." She lurched forward and folded Simon into a spine-snapping hug. "Seriously, fuck the cop—I mean that literally—and see if it makes him less grumpy. Trust me, I know about these things," she added with a wink. "Then come by and tell me how it went. I expect details." Tracey pocketed the cash he handed her for the food and tossed the garbage in a bin outside the shop.

Simon exhaled. Tracey was a whirl-wind of energy, and when she swept on to the next target, it seemed to suck the air out of the room. Still, he thought, maybe she was right on both counts. He ought to take the threats seriously enough to find some kind of weapon. And getting laid—especially if it involved Vic—would surely help both their moods.

He tidied up the back room, then took his soda up front to flip the sign back to "*Open.*" The rain eased up, as forecasted, and by the time the six o'clock group showed up, the sun had come out, and the sea wind dried off the boardwalk. But by the end of the early tour, the air had gotten cool as night fell. He wondered whether that would affect the turn-out for the late group. There were still a couple of spots left, and on a nice night, there were usually enough drop-ins to fill the tour to capacity.

At ten until eight, almost everyone scheduled had shown up, milling around the shop, picking up books, charms, and t-shirts. Simon was so busy ringing up customers, he didn't pay attention when the door opened.

"I'd like a ticket for the next tour."

Simon's head snapped up to find Vic standing on the other side of the counter, with a smile that was part bravado, part nerves. His stance signaled confidence, but his eyes suggested uncertainty. "Sure," Simon replied, taking Vic's cash and handing him the tour voucher. Their fingers brushed, and Vic didn't jerk away. "Didn't expect to see you here. I mean, I'm glad, but—"

"Thought I ought to try something new. Broaden my horizons," Vic replied. He looked good, with a black jacket over a concert t-shirt and worn jeans that clung to his muscular thighs. Simon caught sight of a dark bulge beneath one side of Vic's jacket and realized he was carrying. Somehow, that just made him hotter.

"Maybe I can teach you a few things," Simon answered, never looking away from Vic's dark eyes.

"I bet you could." Vic's slight smirk sent a bolt of lust right to Simon's cock.

The alarm on Simon's phone went off, reminding him it was time to start. "All right everyone, gather up front. Time to go!"

Myrtle Beach didn't have haunted old Victorian homes like Nantucket or Cape May, or ante-bellum mansions filled with ghosts and secrets like Savannah or Charleston. It hadn't been a city at all until around 1900 when a timber company decided to capitalize on the beachfront land it owned and started to develop an affordable seaside destination. But the coast had long been home to pirates, smugglers, and wreckers, and legendary shipwrecks lay beneath the waves not too far out from shore.

Simon's ghost tours weren't the dramatic presentations he'd enjoyed in New Orleans or the old cities in Europe. He told stories as the group walked along the shadowed side of the promenade, building drama and tension with his voice. He started with the tale of poor, doomed Alice Flagg whose parents kept her from her true love, throwing her engagement ring into the ocean and thereby trapping her spirit to wander forever.

Every ghost guide in town told Alice's story, but from there, Simon's penchant for research regaled the tourists with the ship-wreck *SS Georgiana*, a steamship full of guns and supplies whose iron hull proved no match to a Union blockade boat during the Civil War, sinking the craft and its cargo. That wreck led to two more, as the side-wheeler *Mary Bowers* and another blockade runner, the *Norseman*, were scuttled by the remains of the *Georgiana*.

He wove in the story of Captain Kidd and the rumors of buried pirate treasure, then came back to the shipwrecks, telling more tragic tales of unlucky sailors back to the Revolution, and the ghosts that still wandered the coast, looking for the sails that would carry them home.

That last, Simon could vouch for personally, and before their hour ended, he spun a few more stories he learned from the spirits themselves, dating back to the turn of the last century. They never left the boardwalk, but Simon led them down to a section where the bright lights from the bars and Skywheel were partly hidden by a curve in the walkway, and the jut of a hotel closed for renovation. The darkened, empty building added a sense of desolation and creepiness that had some in the group huddling together for his last, dramatic story.

Throughout it all, Vic had hung back in the second row, listening carefully, his eyes always on Simon. Simon felt self-conscious at first, but then as he warmed to the familiar tales and felt the audience buy into his storytelling, he almost forgot the weight of Vic's gaze. Almost, but not quite.

"And that wraps up our tour for tonight," Simon said as his final tale came to an end. "Don't forget to take your ticket stub with you —it's worth ten percent off at participating bars, restaurants, and shops."

He turned to lead the group out of the shadows, and felt the hair on the back of his neck rise an instant before a loud *bang* sounded, searing pain tore through his arm, and Simon fell.

"Gun!" someone in the tour group yelled. "Everybody down!"

Another tourist screamed and ran. A few followed her.

"Stay with him! Call 911!" Vic yelled, as two in the group knelt beside Simon.

Simon heard the pounding of running feet. He was dimly aware of the frightened voice of a man calling for an ambulance; then everything went black.

8

VIC

"Police! Halt!" Vic yelled, running in the direction the shot had come. As he ran, he pulled his cell phone and called the police. All he could see was a figure in a dark hoodie. The shooter headed into the crowd on the boardwalk, which parted sluggishly for Vic even as he shouted at them to move. A few steps farther, and he found the discarded hoodie, but with no idea of the clothing or hair color of the attacker, nothing called attention to any of the pedestrians.

"Shit," Vic muttered. He gingerly lifted the hoodie using a latex glove from the pocket of his jacket. Nothing on the hoodie was likely to ID the gunman at first pass, but if they arrested someone later and got a match, it would place the perp at the crime scene. He glanced at the buildings, looking for video surveillance that he could retrieve, without luck.

Vic had chased the shooter like a hound with a fox, training and instinct canceling out emotion. But as he jogged back to stretch of boardwalk near Grand Strand Ghost Tours, his heart was in his throat. *Please don't let this fall in my department,* he thought. Vic and Ross didn't chase regular perps. They only got involved with murder. *Simon was hit. He went down. Oh, god. What if...*

Vice saw the flashing lights of an ambulance and two squad cars which had driven onto the boardwalk. A cop tried to stop him as he approached. Vic pulled his badge. "Lieutenant D'Amato. Homicide." He lifted the hoodie between his gloved fingers. "I gave pursuit. The gunman was wearing this, and ditched it."

The cop jerked his head toward a knot of uniforms kneeling on the boardwalk. Vic handed off the hoodie to one of the patrol officers and then moved toward the others.

"Lieutenant—"

"My friend got shot," Vic snapped. "I'm damn well going to see how he is." He strode over, badge visible, barely breathing until he glimpsed Simon.

Simon's shirt was bloodied, and an EMT knelt next to him, bandaging his left bicep. Simon looked pale and shaken, but he answered the cop's questions.

"I don't want to go to the hospital," Simon insisted.

The EMT glanced at the cop. "It winged him, but the slug isn't in his arm." He nodded toward the dark boardwalk. "It's out there, somewhere."

"You patched me," Simon argued. "I want to go home."

"I've got this," Vic said, shouldering in as the EMT drew back. He flashed his badge at the patrol officer. "I'll make sure he gets home safely."

"I'm not sure—" the cop objected.

Vic gave a thin, unfriendly smile. "Protective custody. You've got your statement. I'll handle the escort."

The cop glared at Vic, then shrugged, and muttered something to his partner. By this point, the other two patrol officers had taken statements from the few ghost tour participants who had remained after the shot was fired.

"Come on," Vic said, steering Simon by the elbow until they were out of the crowd. Simon stumbled, and Vic slipped an arm around his waist. "I've got you," he said quietly. "You're safe."

"Thanks," Simon murmured.

"You really should go to the hospital."

Simon shook his head. "You heard the EMT—the bullet grazed

me. No evidence to recover, and that means it's just a deep cut. He fixed me up and said I didn't need stitches. I'm fine."

Vic didn't agree, but he also didn't want to argue. They were halfway to Simon's house before he turned to Vic. "How do you know where I live?"

Vic had the courtesy to look embarrassed. "I ran you through the system after you did the reading."

"Invasion of privacy, much?" Simon's voice lacked any heat behind it.

"Is it bad?" Vic said, taking in the blood on Simon's shirt.

"Still hurts like hell. But I'll be okay. Couple of butterfly bandages, an antibiotic script, and I'm back in business."

They arrived at Simon's bungalow. "Cute place," Vic observed. It wasn't at all what he had imagined Simon's house would look like. Too retro. Too…blue.

Simon fumbled the key. Vic took it from him and worked the lock, then stepped in front of Simon, gun drawn, as he flicked on the light. "Stay behind me," he growled, sweeping one room and then the next until he felt sure they were alone in the house.

"Vic, I don't think—"

"Someone just tried to shoot you," Vic snapped. "Let me do my job."

Simon walked into the living room and sank down on the couch. Vic guessed that his arm throbbed, and knew from experience that after the adrenaline rush of fear, the crash would bring him down, hard.

Vic returned from checking out the back rooms and stood in the kitchen doorway. "Cute place you've got here."

"Used to belong to my aunt and uncle. They can't come down anymore. He's got heart trouble," Simon replied.

"What did they give you for the pain?"

Simon frowned, trying to figure out the purpose for the question. "Just local anesthetic. They wanted to give me something stronger, but I didn't want to be… out."

"You got any beer?" Vic asked, and then headed into the kitchen to look for himself. He came back with two open bottles and handed one to Simon. In his other hand was a knotted plastic grocery bag filled with ice.

"Put this on it," he said, handing the bag to Simon. "Keeps the swelling down. It's gonna bruise like a mofo."

Simon nodded his thanks, took a swig of the beer, and then put the ice bag over the wound. He grimaced at the pressure against the injury.

"Yeah, it'll be that way for a while," Vic sympathized.

Simon looked at him. "You've been shot?"

Vic shrugged. "Coupla times. No big deal. I'm still here. Goes with the territory."

He had chosen a seat on the couch next to Simon, close enough that their legs touched. He reached up and pushed a strand of hair out of Simon's eyes. "Any idea—?"

"No. None at all."

Simon shuddered, and Vic slipped an arm around his shoulders. Vic wasn't sure whether Simon would pull away, but when he didn't, he drew him in close. "I'm sorry you got hurt," he said quietly. "And I'm sorry I didn't catch the perp. I saw you go down, and I was scared," Vic admitted. "I know we got off to a bad start. I suck at this kind of thing. But...I'd like to do better."

The brush of lips against his own surprised Vic. Simon stared up at him, so close, hazel eyes blown wide with desire and uncertainty. Waiting for Vic to make the next move. Vic cupped Simon's face in his hand, turning slightly to better press his mouth against Simon's full lips. He touched the tip of his tongue to Simon's mouth, and Simon opened to him. Simon tasted of coffee and cola and mint, and Vic's heart sped.

"This okay?" Vic murmured, reeling from the way they usually rebounded from desire to anger and back again.

Simon shifted, straddling Vic with a knee on either side of his thighs. The hard bulge in Simon's jeans rubbed against Vic's equally stiff erection, and Vic could not stifle a moan. "More than okay," Simon whispered. "Vic, help me forget."

Vic looked at Simon, brown hair loose around his shoulders, eyes dark and lips parted. "I don't want to take advantage."

"They didn't give me anything for the pain besides a local anesthetic," Simon breathed. "No drugs. I'm not high. Just...scared. Please, I need to feel you. Make me feel something good."

In response, Vic slipped his arms behind Simon, mindful of his wounded shoulder. He let his hands explore Simon's back, and discovered that while Simon might be a bit shorter and slender, he was all toned muscle beneath his shirt. Vic claimed his mouth again, deepening the kiss, and Simon ground their erections together, rubbing with enough friction that Vic thought he might come in his jeans like a teenager.

"Please, Vic," Simon whispered, and this time, it was his tongue slipping between Vic's lips, tasting, claiming, exploring. Vic reached down between them, moving slowly to give Simon a chance to pull away if he changed his mind, but Simon rolled his hips, making his intention clear. Vic worked Simon's belt buckle loose, then the button, and finally the zipper.

"I'm clean, just so you know," Simon spoke the words softly into Vic's ear.

"So am I," Vic replied. The department mandated regular bloodwork. Not that there'd been any partners recently. "Just so you know."

He pushed down Simon's boxer briefs and moved to wrap his hand around Simon's shaft.

"Together," Simon whispered. "I want to feel you."

Simon's breathy words and the vulnerability and need behind them made Vic painfully hard. He made quick work of his belt and jeans, lifting them both off the couch just enough to shove his pants down so he could pull his cock out from his briefs. Both he and Simon leaked pre-come, enough to slick his hand as he wrapped his fingers around both their shafts and began a slow, delicious slide that made them gasp.

Vic had jerked off to thoughts about Simon like this, in his arms, groaning with desire, but the reality was far hotter than the fantasy. Simon trusted his weight to Vic's supporting arm, letting his head fall back and his hair hang loose, eyes closed, face taut with hunger.

"I've wanted this since the first time I saw you," Vic confessed, working them slowly although he knew neither would last long. "Fuck, you're beautiful. Feel so good. You're so hard for me." He glanced down at his hand, holding both their swollen cocks together, and had to bite his lip not to shoot at the sight. "Gonna make you feel good. Real good. Let go. I've got you."

Simon cried out, sounding as if the intensity of his orgasm wrested the moan from his soul. Hot come spilled over Vic's hand, spurting between them, marking up Simon's shirt. A moment later, as Simon shivered and jolted through the aftershocks, Vic shot his load, climaxing hard enough that everything went white for a second. Simon fell forward, resting his forehead against Vic's, as both of them gasped for breath.

"Thank you," Simon murmured, brushing a kiss against Vic's jawline, barely a touch, but Vic felt it like a jolt of electricity.

"I'd say the feeling was mutual."

Simon glanced down at the sticky residue streaking their t-shirts, grimaced, and reached for a handful of tissues from the box beside the couch to daub them both dry.

Now that the passion had ebbed, an awkward silence stretched between them. Simon gently tucked Vic back into his briefs, meeting his eyes with a look that was both bold and challenging, before putting himself away. "Stay," Simon asked suddenly, looking as if the word surprised him as much to say it as it did for Vic to hear it. "I don't want to be alone."

Vic pressed a kiss against Simon's temple. "Are you sure?"

Simon nodded, blushing with the admission. "Is that weak? I mean, you get shot all the time."

"Not quite that often, thank God," Vic said. "It's not something that gets better with practice. And no, it's not weak. Sometimes mortality's a little too close for comfort." He didn't usually talk like this, didn't admit fear or discuss feelings. Cops didn't unpack the dark shadows in their minds unless the department shrink made them, and even then lies were easy to manufacture. So why did it feel right to console Simon, to reassure him that his reaction was normal, just human? Vic didn't know, and he didn't want to examine those questions right now, so he pulled Simon close.

Simon's head fell forward, resting against Vic's shoulder, and Vic brought both arms up around him, careful of his injury, holding him tight.

He toed off his sneakers, and Simon did the same. Vic took off his holster and laid his rig and gun on the coffee table. He pivoted, making sure Simon rested on his uninjured side, so that they lay back to front on the long couch, with Vic stretched out behind, one arm pillowing Simon's head, the other hand splayed over his abdomen, protective and claiming.

"Get some sleep," Vic murmured against his ear. "I won't let anything bad happen to you." Simon relaxed against him, and moments later, Vic could tell from his deep, regular breaths that Simon was asleep. Vic lay awake for a long while, trying to make sense of the tangled emotions warring in his heart, unprepared for how protective and possessive he felt of the other man pressed up against him.

Tomorrow, this will all probably seem like a really bad idea, Vic thought. *Hell, it* is *a bad idea. He'll probably throw me out in the morning when he decides I should have known better for both of us. But, dammit, we both wanted this. Now the question is, where the fuck do we go from here?*

Vic woke with a start long after midnight, alarmed and disoriented as he tried to recognize his surroundings. Then he felt a lean, strong body pressed against him and caught the scent of Simon's shampoo. Simon jerked and moaned, but fear, not passion, laced his cries.

"No…please, no. Blood and souls. Feed the beast. Please, stop!" Simon came awake with a shout, thrashing to free himself from Vic's protective embrace, only to cry out in pain as he moved his injured arm too roughly.

"You're safe," Vic reassured him, helping Simon sit up and wrapping around him from behind, one leg thrown on either side of Simon's hips so that Vic could stretch their bodies together. Simon's back was against Vic's chest. Vic's arms held Simon loosely, so as not to be a restraint, but supporting, secure.

"Vic?" Simon asked in the darkness, and Vic felt his heart plummet. Had he misjudged Simon's awareness last night? Simon closed his hands around Vic's forearms as if confirming that he was real.

"I'm here," Vic said, his mouth close to Simon's ear. "It's just a bad dream."

Simon tensed, then shook his head. "No. Not a nightmare. A vision. I'm sure of it."

Vic swallowed. Fuck, this was a bad time for psychic shit to pop up. He still wasn't entirely sure how much he believed—how much he dared believe—but Simon needed his support, so doubts and arguments would have to wait. "Tell me."

Simon hesitated, rightfully so, Vic thought. *I've done shit to earn his trust, at least when it comes to his abilities.* "I'm here for you," Vic said. "Tell me what you saw."

"It was a woman—I didn't recognize her, but she had been cut like the others. She stared at me, and then her mouth moved. I know she shouldn't have been able to talk, not with her throat slit, but she said 'blood and souls' and 'feed the beast.' Her voice was terrible," he admitted, and the words tumbled out fast as if he were afraid to slow down for fear he might not get them all out. "Wet, like she was drowning," he added in a whisper and shuddered.

"Does that mean something to you?" Vic asked because the image was terrifying, but the message eluded him.

"No," Simon admitted. "But the visions aren't always for my benefit. I'm just the messenger." He paused, and Vic wondered if Simon waited for him to make a cutting remark, or demonstrate his disbelief. "Did you ever follow up on the strange words from that first vision?"

Vic rested his forehead against Simon's head. "Hotel," he replied. "And 'big nose.' I asked one of our interpreters. She said it was Russian, but the woman in your vision, Iryena, was from Belarus. Russian is their second language."

Simon went still in his arms, and Vic wondered if he was surprised that Vic had asked for a translation. "I'm sorry to ask," Vic said gently, "but can you give me a description of the woman you saw just now?"

"Young, early twenties," Simon said, his voice raspy with sleep.

"Blond hair, cut chin-length, not symmetrical. She had piercings, her eyebrow and her nose—at least, those were the ones I could see. Short. Petite. And I think she was wearing a uniform of some kind, but there was so much blood—" He stopped, almost choking on the words.

Vic tightened his grip and rocked them back and forth. "Shh," he coaxed, kissing the shell of Simon's ear from behind. He'd never been this demonstrative with a lover before. Nate was another cop, and they'd kept to the script at home just like down at the precinct. The only emotions that they had ever both been truly comfortable with were anger and desire. *Maybe that's some of what went wrong,* Vic thought. *Maybe it was never more than fucking and fighting, and it never would have been.*

The feelings Simon woke in him were new, and frightening. Vic had never worried overmuch about Nate's safety. He was ex-military, and a street cop. He could take care of himself. But Simon didn't hide behind a macho facade, and he didn't even own a gun. As for his psychic gifts—if Vic believed in that sort of thing—they seemed to make him more vulnerable, instead of protecting him.

"You're quiet," Simon said, and Vic feared he had misinterpreted his silence.

"There's a lot to think about." Vic tightened his grip on Simon. Simon let his head fall back onto Vic's shoulder, and Vic pressed a kiss to his cheek.

"Do you believe me?" Simon asked, and the question hung heavy between them.

"I'm trying to," Vic replied honestly. "This is different for me. But, the reading you did before was dead on," he added, then cringed. "Pardon the pun. Even with the interpretation, I still don't know what her words have to do with all this, but they must have been important, right? So…I'm working on it."

The clock on the stereo said it was 3:50 a.m. "Let's try to get some sleep," Vic suggested, moving so that he and Simon could lie down again. "Everything is better in the light of day."

Vic's phone alarm woke him, and he sat up, groggy and alone. He pawed at his phone to shut off the alarm, and it took him a minute to realize where he was. Just after six in the morning, so if he got moving, he had time to go home, shower and change clothing, so he didn't go into work smelling of sweat and sex.

"Simon?" he called, his voice rough with sleep. The smell of coffee wafted out, enticing and welcome.

"I made coffee," Simon said, coming to the door of the small kitchen. He was barefoot and bare-chested, still wearing last night's jeans, and Vic's cock thickened at the sight, heedless of the fact that he needed to go to work.

"That sounds wonderful." Shit, this was the morning after the night before, and awkward as hell. He pocketed his phone and slipped into his holster. "I gotta piss," he said, and Simon pointed toward a door down the hall.

Vic closed the door, admitting to himself that he was hiding as well as heeding nature's call. Everything about Simon's bungalow was homey, ironically retro, and as genuine as the man himself. Compared to this, Vic's apartment had all the personality of a hotel room, revealing next to nothing of the man who lived in it.

He splashed water on his face and cupped a handful to rinse his mouth. It had been so long, years, since he'd stayed over after having sex, or allowed anyone to spend the night. Was there a graceful way to leave that didn't seem like a kiss-off? Vic didn't know exactly how he felt about Simon's so-called gifts, but he was more attracted to the psychic than he had been to anyone in a long time, enough to want more than a single night. He didn't trust himself not to fuck this up.

"You'd better get going, if you need to change before work," Simon said when Vic came back to the kitchen. He had his back turned, and Vic couldn't see his face. Was Simon having second thoughts about what happened between them last night? Did he regret asking Vic to stay, or was he still afraid of Vic's reaction to his vision?

"I'm sorry to rush off," Vic said and meant it. "Thanks. And, be careful. Someone took that shot at you. I don't want to handle your case."

Simon turned to look at him, his expression difficult to read, and nodded. "You, too. I don't want you to show up in one of my readings."

"I'll see you around," Vic said and decided he was terrible at flirting. He wanted to see Simon again but didn't want to pressure him. Did that sound like a promise? Or a brush-off? He couldn't tell what Simon was thinking.

"See you when I see you," Simon replied. Was that a promise or a challenge? Vic drained his coffee cup, murmured another thanks, and dodged out the door before the conversation could get any more awkward.

Vic tried to put Simon out of his mind as he rushed back to his apartment, showered, and changed. He carried his dirty clothes to the basket and caught a whiff of Simon's woodsy aftershave. Getting involved this much, this quickly, was dangerous, especially when Simon was connected—however tangentially—to the Slitter case. His cop instincts told him to put distance between them. But his heart—and he felt sure it wasn't just his dick talking—told him to hang in there. Now if he could only ditch the nagging fear that the woo-woo elements that were so much a part of Simon's life weren't going to cause the same havoc that they did in Pittsburgh.

Ross was waiting for him when he got to the precinct. He looked up from his desk as Vic brought in the two coffees he had bought at the donut shop next door. "Want to explain why you were involved in a shooting down on the boardwalk last night—and tried to chase the perp on foot?"

Vic set the coffee down, went to his side of the desk, and booted his computer. "I happened to be there when it went down. Made sure the victim had help and went after the shooter. Lost him in the crowd. Don't tell me you wouldn't have done the same." He figured a good offense was the way to go.

Ross didn't look convinced. "I'd believe that, except that Kenny Connolly, one of the officers who responded to the call, asked me if the guy who got shot was your boyfriend. Your *ghost tour-psychic* boyfriend." He didn't even try to hide the disdain in his voice.

Shit. Vic had been so worried about Simon being shot, the other cops at the scene had just been background noise. He remembered how he'd flashed his badge, bulled his way through, and taken possession of the victim. *In every sense of the term,* an unhelpful voice supplied. *Above and beyond the call of duty. Or is that booty?*

Ross lowered his voice. "Are you out of your mind, Vic? A guy who thinks he can talk to ghosts? After what happened the last time? Do you want to lose your badge?"

Vic's temper flared. "This is nothing like Pittsburgh."

"Isn't it?" Ross countered. "I heard one of the cops saying that it was too bad they couldn't just arrest him for fraud, for being one of those fake table rappers."

"He's not a fake, and he hasn't defrauded anyone," Vic retorted. "Geez, while they were at it, did they throw in any gay jokes?"

"This isn't about you being gay," Ross argued, struggling to keep his voice down. "No one cares who you sleep with—as long as they're not a laughingstock."

Vic's voice was a low growl. "I can't explain what I saw in Pittsburgh. And I can't prove Simon's abilities. I'm figuring that out as I go. But he's not breaking the law, and he's not a fraud, and the rest is none of anyone else's goddamn business."

Ross started at him. "Jesus. You slept with him."

"I'm not having this conversation." Vic pointedly looked away from Ross, intent on his computer screen.

"Watch your step, Vic. That's all I'm saying. As your partner— and your friend. This guy sounds like trouble. You don't want to have this conversation with the Captain."

9

SIMON

Simon heard the click of the door as Vic let himself out, and sighed, allowing his head to drop as he leaned against the kitchen counter. He didn't know what he had expected from this morning, but he felt oddly unsettled.

I didn't think he'd declare his undying love. Maybe a kiss before he left? Or something a little more definite than "see you around."

Simon took his cup of coffee out onto the small patio. If he angled his deck chair just right, he could see a sliver of the ocean between buildings. Usually, that sight helped to calm him, but now he felt more jangled than ever.

Someone had tried to kill him last night or at least had sent a dire warning. Vic had claimed him in front of the other cops and the EMTs, taking charge, getting him home, and making him feel safe. He had been more attentive and tender than Simon had dared to imagine. Just the thought of how Jacen would have reacted in similar circumstances coaxed out a bitter laugh.

Jacen would have run for the hills, every man for himself, Simon thought, and knew it to be true. *He wouldn't have noticed I was down until he was a mile away, and he would never have risked the "negative publicity" of being seen with me at the site of the incident.*

Which led him back to the million dollar question—what did Vic feel for him?

Simon sipped his coffee, black with sweetener, and let it burn down his throat as the breeze ruffled his hair. His arm ached, and it had been the pain that roused him from sleep, surprised to find himself tangled in Vic's arms. Simon hadn't wanted the moment to end, but he knew they both had to go to work, and he worried about how Vic would react in the light of day. He could barely believe that he'd worked up the nerve to ask Vic to stay and that the cop had agreed, let alone sleeping spooned together like lovers.

They weren't really lovers, were they?

Despite his injury, Simon remembered the kisses and the hot-as-hell hand job clearly. Vic had been caring and careful, so unlike the few one-night-stands Simon winced to remember. They hadn't fucked—at thirty-five he refused to think of it as "going all the way"—but the intimacy had been undeniable. Simon wanted more. Vic had seemed onboard, but then this morning it was hard to see his quick departure as anything other than extricating himself from an awkward situation.

It shouldn't hurt, but it did. Simon realized he knew nothing about Vic's past, except that something bad had happened in Pittsburgh that likely led to him coming south. Did he leave a lover behind? An ex-husband? Or just a string of nameless partners who had been fleeting encounters? Maybe Vic wasn't a relationship kind of guy.

And that right there was a problem because Simon knew himself, and he most certainly was a one-man man. The attraction he felt to Vic was dangerous, and last night in the wake of the attack, Simon had given in and let on how much he wanted the cop.

Probably scared the shit out of him, Simon conceded. But he couldn't deny the feelings that were growing beyond something sheerly physical. He'd been jacking off to fantasies about Vic since he'd met the cop, but the reality had been far better, even if it hadn't gone quite as far as Simon's imagination—

And it probably never will, he thought, draining the coffee that had gone cool. If only he hadn't had a vision right then, maybe this morning would have gone differently. Maybe Vic wouldn't have been put off by his panicked awakening in the middle of the night. But for anything beyond a fast fuck to happen between them, Vic would need to truly believe in and support Simon's gift, and that didn't seem likely.

I hid part of who I was before, and look where it got me. Never again. The best part of what I've built here is that for the first time, I'm completely honest about who I am—a gay clairvoyant medium history nerd with a passion for ghost stories. And I'm not giving up that truth for anyone —even Vic.

Simon forced himself to leave the patio. He filled a travel mug with the rest of the hot coffee, then went to get a shower and dress for work. A glance in the mirror told him that the wound on his arm had already bruised colorfully, but he knew it could have been far worse. Simon debated canceling the ghost tours scheduled for that night but decided against it. *This is my life, the way I make my living, and I'll be damned if some coward in the shadows is going to make me stop doing what I love.*

Maybe he could make a few adjustments, for safety's sake, he thought. He wouldn't take the group as far down the boardwalk, sticking closer to where there were more people. That would make him harder to hear above the noise, and detract from the spooky feel, but he and his customers might be safer remaining in a better lit, busier area. Perhaps the cops would catch the shooter, and find it was all a dreadful mistake, or some kind of random incident that had nothing to do with him, his visions, or the Slitter. Much as Simon wanted to believe that, he didn't really think so.

Vic didn't take his visions seriously, and the police weren't likely to find the person who shot at him, so it was time for Simon to make the next move. Simon had always regarded the ability to hear spirits as a solemn responsibility. Iryena, Katya, and the unnamed woman last night appeared to him because there was no one else who could hear their plea. If the cops couldn't, or wouldn't, do something with that information, then Simon intended to provide the police with evidence they'd accept, a solid lead that would keep other J-ones from dying.

And tonight, after the last ghost tour, Simon would check in with the rest of his Skeleton Crew and get some answers.

———————

His phone rang around ten o'clock, and he knew from the ringtone it was Tracey. The early morning rush would be over at the coffee shop, and more of her staff would be on hand to serve customers, giving her the chance to sneak off to drink a cup of her own java.

"Did you hear about the shooting on the boardwalk last night?" Tracey greeted him. "Shit, if it happened while you had a tour, did you see something?"

Simon groaned. "I did better than see it. I'm the one who got shot."

Silence answered him. "That's not funny, Simon."

"No kidding. It hurt like fuck."

"You're serious?"

"Unfortunately, yes."

"If you got shot, why are you at work?" Tracey's voice sounded like she was straining not to yell into the phone. "Shouldn't you be in the hospital?"

"The bullet grazed my arm. It didn't even need stitches," Simon replied, sorry he had been so honest. "I'm bruised, but fine."

"Oh, my god," Tracey breathed. "You're serious. Does your cop know? What did he say?"

"Vic was on the tour when it happened. He made sure I got home okay."

"Did he take *real good* care of you?" Tracey asked.

"I'm not going to answer that."

"Shit! You slept with him, didn't you?"

"It's…complicated," Simon replied with a groan.

"Honey, it really isn't. You do know how sex works, right? Either you had it, or you didn't. Unless you hit your head and don't remember, in which case he's a total creep for taking advantage of you."

"Oh, for fuck's sake! It didn't get quite that far."

"Define 'quite.'"

"No."

Tracey chuffed into the phone. "You take all the fun out of things. You're my best friend. We're supposed to share things."

Simon couldn't help smiling, despite everything. "Maybe so, but I'm also not going to come over to get our nails done together, or braid each other's hair."

"Spoilsport," Tracey teased. "That just means I need to have you over to binge-watch Netflix and drink wine until you tell me everything."

"Not going to happen," Simon countered, although more than once, he and Tracey had done exactly that.

"But you like him, right? Really like him?"

"You make this sound like I'm worried he won't ask me to prom. Yes, I like him. No, I'm not sure it's mutual. I don't actually know anything about him. Maybe he's not boyfriend material."

"Well, that would be his loss, because you'll make some man a fine husband," Tracey declared loyally. "And he's a shithead if he doesn't appreciate that."

"Thanks, I think," Simon said with a chuckle, finding that Tracey's steadfast support eased his disappointment, just a little. "Look, I'm all for doing a Netflix night, but I need to get back to work. Just—be careful," he added. "There's bad stuff happening, and so watch yourself, okay?"

"I'm not the one who just got shot," she replied. "So, back atcha. Double."

During the slow times, Simon searched online to make sense of the hints from that first vision. The Russian words meant "hotel" and "big nose," which were rather vague, and the images of blue fish and twinkle-lit palm trees hardly helped narrow things down in a town like Myrtle Beach, where hundreds of hotels lined the shore and decorating with fish and white Christmas lights was an obsession.

The Slitter had so far chosen his victims along the main stretch of Myrtle Beach, not in the more upscale reaches of North Myrtle, and not as far south as Surfside. That made sense, Simon thought, because the main drag of the Grand Strand didn't have the gated resorts of the north or the family-run campgrounds and motels of the south. Central Myrtle Beach was a middle-class Vegas on the beach, minus the casinos: loud, neon-lit, a little out of control and not a bit subtle. The unspoken promise that kept families coming back year after year was that you could go a tad wild here, and nothing bad would ever happen.

Which wasn't exactly true. While the city's PR machine tried to keep things quiet, Myrtle Beach had a larger number of missing persons than normal for a town its size. Then again, people came here, drank too much, partied too hard, and made bad choices. Some of those tourists and spring break revelers didn't get a do-over. Others came here to disappear. Simon had done just that three years ago, and while he hadn't vanished into a "long weekend" gone bad, he hadn't hit rock bottom, either. Those who had often rose again only when they floated to the top.

By the end of the day, Simon had a short list of hotels that might match the glimpses from his vision. He had contacts among his Skeleton Crew at some of those hotels and elsewhere who should be working nights, available after he wrapped up the last ghost tour.

Simon felt nervous about walking the Strand alone at night for the first time in years. He had lived in Columbia, a much bigger city, without incident, and he knew enough to stay clear of the less savory parts of town. But if he could narrowly escape being shot just a few yards from his shop on the Boardwalk, anything could happen, anywhere. The new canister of pepper spray that hung from a carabiner on his belt and the small knife in an ankle sheath —a gift from Tracey—reminded him that things were different now.

To his relief, both ghost tours were uneventful, and only two people either canceled or failed to show. Simon found himself much more tense than usual, but the audience seemed just as happy with the experience, and his tips were a bit more than usual. He said goodbye to the last of the tour-goers, watched them disperse down the boardwalk, and then headed for Ocean Boulevard, on a mission.

The Blue Conch Hotel was the first on his list, and Simon

wandered into the lobby, hoping he blended in with the guests who belonged there. It was a mid-price, family-oriented property geared to families with children, and as he wandered around the restaurant, bar, and pool areas, nothing in the decor resonated as matching what he had glimpsed in his original vision.

Discouraged, Simon headed back out onto the street, and when he ducked into the Golden Strand Hotel, he had a different agenda. The Strand was one of the grande dames of Myrtle Beach, a hundred-year-old luxury resort that had weathered history and hurricanes and emerged with the faded dignity of an aging movie star. Celebrities for ten decades had graced the Strand's stage or stayed in her rooms, and their photographs lined the main hallway. Newer, glitzier resorts shouldered into the beachfront on either side, boasting waterslides and swim-up bars, but the Strand harkened back to elegant days and celluloid glamor with a siren call that kept patrons coming year after year.

Despite the grim business that prompted his visit, Simon couldn't help smiling as he walked into the Strand's opulent lobby, past the uniformed doorman. The high ceiling with its stained glass dome, the expanse of marble flooring and white columns, and the formal mahogany check-in counter with its crisp-suited staff made him feel like he had walked into another era. His inner history geek and movie buff did a little happy dance until he reminded himself why he was there.

Knowing he intended to stop at the Strand, Simon had dressed up for his ghost tours, favoring a collared shirt and khakis instead of his usual t-shirt and cargo shorts. While the Strand's staff, not the guests, adhered to an elegant dress code, Simon still felt under-dressed as he strode into the intimate bar. One wall opened to a panoramic ocean view. High-backed chairs flocked in faux-velvet clustered around small tables. The huge wooden bar and mirror-lined backbar gave the room the Great Gatsby extravagance of a vanished era.

Simon spotted Michelle from across the room. Her dark hair was swept up in a neat chignon, and paired with striking make-up and her high-collared, retro bellman's uniform jacket; she exuded cinematic chic. Simon had known her since she came to Myrtle Beach within a few months of his own arrival, but she'd been Michael then, fleeing the Midwest for a chance at anonymity and total reinvention. Desperate questions about her own untrained and sporadic telepathy had brought her into Simon's shop, and they'd been allies, if not quite friends, ever since.

Simon picked a spot at a distance from other patrons and waited for Michelle to notice him.

"Simon. This isn't your usual haunt," she said when she made her way over. He couldn't tell from her voice whether she was pleased or wary.

"Unusual things are going on," he replied with a shrug. She got him a rum and Coke without him having to order, and he laid down cash for the drink and a twenty for the tip. "See anything interesting lately?" Anyone else would have mistaken their small talk to be about movies or television, but Michelle looked daggers at him, taking his meaning.

"Fear," Michelle said quietly, glancing around to make sure no one was listening. "Lies and lust and greed and jealousy—the usual," she added bitterly. Simon wasn't always happy that the fates gifted him with the ability to speak with the dead and glimpse the future, but he couldn't imagine trying to live with unwanted peeks into the cesspools of the human mind. "But there was one person— didn't get a look at the face. Might have been a guy—not sure. With him, the lust and rage was all tangled up. And something else—he was looking forward to killing again."

Simon's stomach churned. He'd bet a week's pay that was the Slitter. "Think hard. Can you give me anything about him?"

Michelle looked at him as if he were crazy. "Why do you want to know? You should be running away, not looking for him."

"Long story," Simon replied, knowing their time to talk was limited. "Anything?"

"I saw glowing seashells," Michelle replied.

"Like the Conch Diner?"

She shook her head. "No. Smaller, all different shapes, like a light-up border. The feeling that went with it was awful," she added, shivering. "Hunger and…anticipation."

"Thanks," he said, downing the rest of his drink and pushing away from the bar.

"Stay clear, Simon," she warned. "Let the right people handle this."

"You know they won't," he replied. "But somebody has to."

Simon checked out the lobbies of three more hotels along the beach, looking for blue fish and bedecked palmetto trees. There were plenty that had a variation of one or the other, but not a match to what Simon saw in his vision. He had tried to figure out whether the symbols were what Iryena saw at her work, which might indicate the larger hotels, or something from the location where she died, in which case the shabbier, older motels a block or so from the waterfront would be a better bet.

As he walked Ocean Boulevard, Simon tried to keep a lookout on both sides of the street, frustrated that something seemingly so simple could prove elusive. As the crowds moved around him, jostling his shoulders and occasionally requiring a sidestep to avoid collision, Simon couldn't help wondering whether the Slitter was among them. Twice now he'd been targeted, but not in the killer's usual method of attack. Was it a warning to back off? Or a message that his time would come?

Gym-tastic's yellow illuminated sign outshone the streetlights. The 24-hour gym offered locals and tourists the chance to tone up with free weights, cycles, treadmills, weight machines, and more by the month or for a cheap day pass. On other visits, Simon had paused to enjoy the view of toned bodies in sweat-slicked, clinging Lycra flexing and stretching. The gym catered to men and women, but the late-night crowd was usually exclusively male. Those in the know regarded Gym-tastic as a prime spot to work out and hook up, but neither were on Simon's mind as he walked in, obviously overdressed.

"I need to see your card," the harried man in the Gym-tastic t-shirt behind the check-in counter said without looking up. When Simon didn't reply, he glanced at the newcomer. "Oh, it's you."

"Nice to see you, too, Marcus."

"Looking to shape up for the beach?" he asked with an expression that told Simon the man knew exactly what need had brought the tour guide to his door.

"Not exactly."

Marcus rolled his eyes. "Aw, man. Gimme a break. I'm workin' here, you mind?"

"Just take a second of your time," Simon said, glancing at the glass case of accessories for something he might actually use. "I'll take one of those green t-shirts. Size Large."

"Buy the black. It's more your color," Marcus countered, reaching down and pulling out a black shirt as Simon moved to pay.

"Talk to me," Simon said, holding out cash, more than the shirt cost.

"You know I don't control this shit, it just comes to me or not. Mostly not," Marcus replied, not looking at Simon. His pre-cognition worked differently from Simon's visions. Where Simon's gift usually served up a mix of reality and symbolism, Marcus saw snapshots from the future. Simon considered Marcus's talent to be the crueler of the two since he was burdened with foreknowledge but rarely had enough context to affect the outcome.

"Take your time and count the change, maybe a dollar back in pennies?"

"Screw you."

Simon gave a wry smile. "Anything for an excuse to keep chatting. What did you see?"

"I saw a blond white girl get real dead," Marcus said under his breath. "Chin-length hair, pierced nostril, eyebrow and snake-bite piercings. Wore a uniform like some of the hotel maids. Too much blood to be sure."

"Could you tell how soon?"

Marcus's dark eyes were haunted. "You want me to dredge up that kind of shit; you need to pay enough for a bottle, not a shot."

Simon slipped him another ten. "I can't say for sure—you know how this stuff is—but I'd say soon, real soon, if it hasn't happened already."

"Anything in the background?" Simon pressed. "Something to help me find her?"

"How is this your problem?"

"It just is," Simon said.

"Okay, I had the weirdest sense she knew she was broadcasting," Marcus answered. "Like she had a little bit of a gift, and was scared enough to use it. She blasted a signal, I felt like my head would explode, and it all went dark."

"So this wasn't the usual, where your gift only serves up snapshots. You think she contacted you?"

Marcus shrugged. "I didn't come with an instruction manual. I'm making this shit up as I go, same as you. That's all I've got." He nodded toward the door as a few more late-nighters headed their way. "Gotta work, man. See ya 'round," he added in a tone that told Simon not to come back too soon.

Simon checked his watch as he left Gym-tastic. It was after eleven, but the weekend night meant the sidewalks were crowded and the late-night partygoers hadn't yet gotten started. He meandered through half a dozen more hotels, finding plenty of lighted palmetto trees and fanciful fish, but none that matched his vision, not even those decorating the pools. And certainly no light-up sea shells other than the giant Conch Diner sign that was a beacon to the whole middle Strand.

He had one more stop before he could go home, a place that definitely wasn't part of his normal routine. Fox and Hound strip club featured only female dancers, and while Simon had an artist's appreciation for the form, even the best endowed did nothing to rouse his dick. He'd only stopped in a few times over the years, always to touch base with Cindy, a lithe redhead whose hair color was as fake as her name, but both seemed to suit her.

The club smelled of alcohol, sweat, and sex, but somehow so different from the all-male dance club over on King's Highway. He wasn't a regular at Aloha Cowboy either, although he'd admit to having dropped in once and again when the long nights tried his resolve. Both clubs tried for an upscale look and failed, managing instead to match the decorating taste of a pretentious drug dealer.

It hit Simon that the club had redecorated. A new decorative border ran around the main room, different types of seashell cutouts on a metal strip with a backlight. *Glowing seashells.*

Simon ignored the hint of weed in the air and didn't have to guess what the rowdy young prep school men in the corner were snorting when they leaned toward the table. He'd never dared try to blunt his gifts with drugs, although a glass or two of whiskey had taken the edge off more than one awful reading or vision.

Simon didn't have to stretch his imagination to figure that most of his Skeleton Crew had habits, or records, or both, trying to keep their unwanted powers at bay. They were young, haunted by their untrained gifts, wary of asking for help, and even more afraid of coming to the attention of authorities. From the little they confided in Simon, most of them had fled homes that condemned the very existence of their talents, on top of abuse, neglect, or intolerance for any way they didn't measure up to someone's bullshit standards. Outcasts and misfits found their final destination at the ocean's edge just as surely as the rivers that flowed down to the sea.

He settled into a seat in a silver vinyl-covered booth that allowed him to see the stage and audience while keeping his back to the wall. The two dancers borrowed their flexibility from Cirque and their moves from PornHub, which seemed to be a big hit with the rowdy men waving sweaty dollar bills in the front row.

"What'll you drink?" the server asked, wearing nearly as little as the dancer, but looking far more bored.

"Rum and Coke," Simon replied, figuring the bar couldn't screw it up too badly. "When is Cindy dancing?"

The server's lips pursed like he'd offered a lemon. "She's not. Didn't show up yesterday or today, didn't call off. So if you want to see her dance, it probably won't be here after Billy fires her ass."

Simon leaned back, watching the crowd and ignoring the dancers. *I guess that proves, again, that I only play for one team.*

"I'm an old friend," Simon said. "Is she all right?"

The server eyed him like she'd heard the story before, then something in her gaze faltered. "I don't know. She didn't answer her phone, and Billy went over to her place, but she wasn't there. I thought she would have called me or Billy if she needed something, but she didn't." Her voice held a combination of worry and abandonment.

"Did anyone report her missing?"

"To the cops?" The server looked at him like he was crazy. "Yeah, that would go over real well. Look, you better finish up and move on. Billy doesn't like friends and family showing up, you know what I mean?" She flounced away, and Simon knew she wouldn't be back. A glance toward the bar where she was talking with a brawny guy that might be Billy suggested Simon shouldn't linger, especially when Billy fixed him with a glare.

Simon knew Cindy a little better than some of the crew. Enough to know that she always worked not just her own shift, but as many extras as she could manage. Cindy might have been in her late twenties or early thirties, but already she worried that she couldn't compete with the never-ending flow of younger women that got off every one-way bus. She had gotten her GED and was working on an Associate's Degree at the community college, but in the meantime, she needed cash for the constant nips and tucks that kept her face and body looking youthful.

Cindy's story was just one of the dirty little secrets of every beach community. Tourists rewarded servers, bartenders, lifeguards, and every other kind of performer for their looks and figures as much as for the quality of their work, and tips were the lifeblood of J-ones and locals alike. News stations occasionally trotted out sad stories about eating disorders, plastic surgery gone wrong, or shooting up to slim down, but budget money never showed up to help those the power brokers considered to be disposable.

Simon walked out. There was no point pressing the server for details which he knew she wouldn't share. But after a moment's hesitation, he pulled out his phone. His finger hovered above Vic's name, then he sighed and hit the button.

"Simon?" Vic didn't sound like Simon had woken him. Was he working? Relaxing? Or maybe moving on to better company?

"I got a line on another missing person," Simon said. Even on the sidewalk, the booming base of the dance music made the glass windows vibrate.

"God, Simon—where are you? Did you go clubbing?" Vic sounded irritated, but Simon figured it had more to do with reducing his homicide workload than jealousy.

"For a good cause," Simon replied. "Look, I think the Slitter has a new victim. Goes by 'Cindy,' strips for Fox and Hound. Didn't show up tonight or call off. That's not like her."

Vic was silent for so long Simon thought the call had dropped. "I didn't think you swung like that."

"I don't," Simon snapped. "She's an empath—she's come by the store now and again. The point is, she wouldn't just disappear."

"People do it every day, for all kinds of reasons, and they aren't all dead," Vic replied. "You got a phone number for her? Address? Hell, last name?"

"No."

"Then until someone reports her missing, the cops can't do anything," Vic said, sounding worn. "And I'm homicide, so I don't get involved until someone turns up dead, remember?"

"I'm worried."

"I'd say, 'file a report' but you can't without that information. I'm sorry, but there's nothing to do but wait." Vic hesitated. "Look, I really am sorry. I hope she's okay. Can we meet up and talk in person? I'm even worse on the phone than I am one-on-one."

"What did you have in mind?"

"Lucca Trattoria, seven p.m. tomorrow," Vic answered. "Nice and quiet, good food, and we can talk without getting interrupted."

Simon couldn't tell from Vic's tone whether this counted as a date or meeting an informant. Deep down, he didn't care. He hadn't been able to get the stubborn detective out of his mind, and while he cautioned himself not to read too much into the invitation, he figured Vic didn't usually meet his snitches in nice restaurants. "I'll be there."

"Simon," Vic said, his voice low and urgent. "It's after midnight. Don't walk home alone."

"I'm a big boy."

"I remember," Vic replied, and Simon could picture his knowing smile. "But someone's tried to kill you twice. You know what they say about the third time."

"Yeah, okay. I'll get a rideshare—"

"No. A real cab. Someone with a license and a photo and a dispatcher," Vic cut him off. "Please."

At least it meant Vic cared a little, right? "Okay, although it isn't very far."

"Humor me. I don't want to get stood up for dinner tomorrow."

"Don't worry—I'd haunt your ass."

"Not funny."

Simon sobered. "All right. I'll see you tomorrow. And…thanks."

Vic ended the call, having likely expended his conversational reserves. Simon hailed one of the cabs idling outside the club, checked the driver's face against his license, and rode home in silence. His dreams that night were quiet.

VIC

I *t's not a date.* But he wished it were. Vic had changed outfits twice, trying to decide what looked nice but not too nice, flattering yet effortlessly casual. In the end, he went with a burgundy shirt, black tie, and dark jeans over nice boots—fitting for Lucca's dress code but not too fussy.

He wondered what Simon would wear, whether he'd dress up, maybe try to impress him a little. Vic had been fantasizing about Simon ever since he had slipped out of Simon's house two mornings ago, and his libido warred with his lack of self-confidence. If he had it to do over again, he wouldn't have left without a kiss, without something to indicate his interest. Had Simon already written him off? After all, he'd been at a club last night. Vic assumed Simon had left alone, hence the cautions about travel. But maybe Simon had moved on to someone more fun, and less difficult. The thought of Simon with someone else hurt.

Would he show up? Or call off at the last moment? Simon was too well-mannered to just not show, but "emergencies" could be invented as needed. Vic popped a mint into his mouth, checked to assure no lint from the bath towel clung to his short hair, and let out a long sigh. He hadn't cared this much about a date—or a not-date

—since high school. Even with Nate, back in Pittsburgh, things just seemed to happen without any real planning.

And maybe that was part of the problem. Vic knew he had to stop comparing Simon, comparing everyone, to Nate. Ross's warnings rang in his mind, and he did his best to squelch them. *The ghost tour stuff is just for entertainment,* Vic thought. *Just like all the other performances on the Strand.* As for the readings and witchy merchandise…Simon said it was a matter of belief.

He believes he can talk to ghosts, and that ghosts talk back. Compared to most of the stuff from my catechism class, that's not even half-way weird. So what's the difference? But there had been a difference, back in Pittsburgh, between what people considered to be blessed and miraculous, and suspiciously supernatural. And if Simon's involvement—tangential as it was—with the Slitter case blew up, Vic had the feeling those old prejudices would resurface fast. If that happened, it could go badly for Simon—and burn down everything Vic had painstakingly rebuilt for himself.

Vic adjusted his tie and refused to let anything spoil the evening. Even if they talked shop—and he felt certain Simon would—Vic intended to use the chance to get to know Simon better, less as a cop and more in a potential boyfriend. He wheeled his motorcycle out of its parking space and wondered whether Simon had remembered about the bike. The thought of having Simon pressed up against him from behind, arms tight around Vic's waist, made him half-hard, and he adjusted his snug jeans that left little to the imagination.

He grabbed his jacket, pushed his badge into a pocket, and holstered his gun. After what had happened on the ghost tour, Vic wasn't taking any chances. Then he headed out, wondering if Simon felt as nervous about the evening as he did.

"You want me to ride on that?" Simon asked skeptically, as Vic idled the motorcycle in front of his house.

Vic grinned. "Gotta live a little. Come on; I can hardly open up the throttle on the streets around here."

Simon tucked his hair under the black helmet and looked at the Hayabusa as if it might bite. He had chosen a dark blue collared shirt that brought out the flecks of gold and green in his hazel eyes, over black casual pants and dress shoes. No tie. Vic felt a bit overdone, but he couldn't stop staring at the hollow of Simon's throat where his shirt opened.

Simon gingerly swung one leg over the bike, and wrapped his arms around Vic's waist, sliding forward as he did so until his chest pressed against Vic's back and his knees hugged the other man's hips. Vic shifted since the contact went straight to his dick.

Vic eased the motorcycle into traffic, and when they started to move faster than a walking pace, Simon tightened his grip. Vic had been riding long enough that he forgot how much faster and closer traffic seemed to someone who wasn't used to being on a bike. The short trip to Lucca's barely let him reach twenty miles an hour, given the congestion and out-of-town drivers who didn't know where they were going. But when they parked at the restaurant and Simon removed his visored helmet, his face was flushed and his eyes bright.

"That's…nice," Simon said, managing a self-conscious smile.

"We'll have to take it out somewhere I can open it up and let her fly," Vic promised.

"I might have to work up to that."

Vic locked the bike and secured the helmets, then walked beside Simon to the door. He didn't reach for Simon's hand, just a subtle, claiming touch to his lower back, enough to let anyone watching know that they were together. *Are we together? Shit, I hope so. If I don't screw it up.*

They followed a server to their table, a quiet spot where they had some privacy, for which Vic had tipped generously. He hesitated, unsure whether to pull out Simon's chair, and then felt awkward when Simon seated himself.

"Come sit down," Simon said, smoothing over the misstep. "I've never been here. If the food is as good as it smells, this might become a new favorite."

"It's not my grandma's cooking, but nothing is," Vic said with a grin. "Short of dinner at nonna's, this is pretty good."

Vic ordered a bottle of wine and kept the conversation light as the server brought bread. They chatted about the menu options, Vic pointed out what he'd had or what he liked from his family's recipes, and by the time they ordered, the awkwardness had faded.

"So tell me about Dr. Sebastian Kincaide," Vic prompted, letting his right hand brush Simon's fingers on the table. He did his best to keep his voice light, not to sound like a cop, and since Simon didn't flinch or pull away, Vic figured he might have done all right.

"It's a pretty boring story," Simon said with a shrug, but for the first time that evening, he refused to meet Vic's gaze, suggesting the tale was anything but. "I spent far too much time in college studying the myths and folktales people have been telling around the campfire since campfires were invented. I taught classes, wrote tedious scholarly articles to impress my colleagues, and researched regional ghost stories for some books I wanted to write that the department thought were too 'trivial' for a 'serious academic.'" His voice gained an edge, but mostly Vic thought Simon just sounded resigned and a little sad.

"Did you like it? The teaching part."

"Mostly," he replied. "It was safe. Steady paycheck. My parents could brag that I had a Ph.D. But always neglected to mention in what," he added with a dry chuckle. He took a sip of his wine. "The university had its perks. I was comfortable."

"Kind of a big shift, moving down here and opening the shop."

Simon's mouth tightened, and for a moment Vic feared he'd ruined things again. Then Simon shook himself out of his thoughts and managed a self-conscious half-smile. "The father of one of my students was afraid I was luring young minds to the dark side and had enough money and influence to get me fired."

"You should have known that the Defense Against Dark Arts position never works out."

Simon burst out laughing, a sound as musical as it was unexpected. "That…that's perfect!" He said, and all the tension drained away. Vic grinned back and held his gaze. This time, Simon edged his fingers close enough to touch Vic's hand, and neither man pulled away.

Simon caught his breath. "I'll have to remember that. Wow— didn't expect you to be a Potterhead."

Vic smiled. "Kinda hard to overlook the books and movies, unless you spent your formative years under a rock."

Simon leaned back, removing his hand just long enough to tear off a piece of warm bread and dip it in olive oil while Vic did the same. "Anyhow, I wanted a change, and I came down here to get my head together, then my aunt offered me a good deal on the house, and I realized I could do just what I wanted, and be me. All of me."

"And what is, 'all of you'?" Vic asked, his eyes serious even if he tried for a light tone.

"A gay psychic medium with a nerd-on for ghost stories and a flair for storytelling," Simon said, without a hint of challenge. Vic envied that utter conviction and the balls to claim what mattered to him. Simon watched Vic as if wondering what he might say.

"I'm glad you're here," Vic replied, covering Simon's hand with his own. "And I'd like to get to know you better. All of you." He knew from the slight blush that came to Simon's cheeks that the double meaning registered.

"That might be arranged," Simon replied. "How about you? You're not local."

Turnabout was fair play, Vic thought, although his heart rate spiked and he wondered whether he would be able to tell his story nearly as gracefully.

"I'm a cop, from a family of cops. Lived in Pittsburgh all my life, and liked it—snow and all," he added with a rueful smile. "Then I saw something I couldn't explain when a bust went wrong, and a civilian got killed. My story was a little too woo-woo for the brass to believe, but I got cleared, only I knew it wouldn't ever be the same." He looked down.

Unlike Simon, who had told his story without seeming to be

embarrassed or ashamed, Vic couldn't escape the sense that he had, somehow, fucked the whole thing up.

"What happened?" Simon asked quietly, and when Vic met his gaze, he saw only concern and sincere interest.

Vic glanced around them, but no other diners were seated nearby. He wet his dry mouth with a swallow of wine. "I'd been chasing a guy who had shot up a convenience store and took a hostage into a basement. I went in after them, and shot the guy dead, but then…" His voice trailed off, and he closed his eyes. *Here's the part where Simon decides I'm too damaged to be worth the trouble.*

Simon waited, attentive but not pushing, fingers light against Vic's knuckles. "Then I saw a green, glowing fog come out of the shooter's mouth and it zoomed over and into the hostage—a civilian—and she grabbed his gun and aimed it at me. I shot her," he said, looking down again. "And the fog came out of her and disappeared." He waited for Simon's outrage, for the condemnation he heard every night in his own mind.

"I believe you," Simon said simply. "There are other kinds of spirits out there besides ghosts like I mentioned before. Some nice, and some very, very bad. You're lucky that the entity didn't try to possess you."

Vic unbuttoned the second button of his shirt and withdrew a religious medallion. "Saint George. Patron saint of cops. My nonna gave it to me when I made the force. Maybe it helped."

"I don't doubt it," Simon replied, without a trace of sarcasm or irony. "Belief is a powerful thing."

"Um, talking about belief…I sent some uniforms looking for your pal, Cindy," he said. "Got her address from her boss. Real name is Callie Franklin, from Conway, SC. No priors. Didn't have cause for a warrant, but the uniforms went to her apartment. From the way the mail's stacked up, she hadn't been around in a few days. Neighbors didn't know anything, of course. So there you have it."

"Thank you." Simon was watching Vic with a curious expression as if the few minutes he had taken to follow up on the tip mattered.

"I hope she's okay," Vic said. "Gotta say I'm curious—can't quite imagine you being buddies with a stripper."

"She's one of my Skeleton Crew," Simon admitted.

"Your what?"

"It's just a name I came up with because most of them work night shift. People with minor psychic gifts. Not that the abilities aren't important, but they don't have a lot of strength, and most have them have no training," Simon explained. "They like night shift, so they don't have to sleep when it's dark."

Vic gave him a look as if he were remembering Simon jolting awake with his own nightmares. "Oh yeah?"

"It's a bad combination, talent and no training. People write them off as crazy—hell, sometimes they think that themselves," Simon said with a harsh, bitter laugh. "There's a tendency to 'self-medicate' to make the voices and the dreams shut up."

"You know from experience?"

Simon shrugged. "Some. But I was lucky. I've found people along the way who helped me piece together enough to gain control, create boundaries—at least, most of the time." Vic's dubious expression didn't need words.

"So…you're running a halfway house for damaged psychics?"

"Not really. But at one time or another, they've drifted into the shop with questions. I try to stay in touch, be helpful if I can. A lot of them are runaways, or come from families where having some kind of supernatural gift is even more suspect than being gay."

"Gotcha," Vic replied. "So what made you go looking for Cindy?"

"There's a theory that incidents of severe emotional trauma can cause 'psychic bursts,'" Simon replied, lapsing into lecture mode. "So if there's a disaster or big tragedy, it sets off some kind of energy beacon, and everyone with a bit of psychic ability in range picks up on the transmission. Only it's not a clear signal, or some people have broken radios. So they only get bits and pieces."

"And you wanted to see what some of your Skeleton Crew picked up from the 'airwaves'?"

"They won't talk to cops," Simon said as if he guessed Vic was about to jump on him for detecting without a license. "For good reason. They're on the fringe. So far, I haven't gotten much. But one of them, a telepath, picked up on really malicious, predatory thoughts from someone in her bar, and an image of glowing sea shells—like the decor at Fox and Hound."

"That's kinda thin, don't you think?" Vic asked. He knew he should shut down Simon's Hardy Boys game, but he was intrigued. And while he'd never be able to sell the woo-woo leads to Ross, his partner would be the first to remind Vic that he had chased tips just as flimsy.

"Got something better?"

Vic shook his head. "No. And you know I couldn't tell you if we did. But at this point, a lead is a lead. I hope you're wrong about Cindy, and that she just hared off for a better job or to skip out on the bills."

"I hope so, too," Simon said, although his tone suggested that he didn't believe his words.

"How's your arm?" Vic asked, noting when Simon bumped against the table and winced.

"Sore," Simon admitted. "I took some ibuprofen, and that helped. It's manageable."

Just then, the server returned with their entrees, steaming hot and piled high. Vic's chicken Marsala smelled divine, while Simon's eggplant Parmesan came on a bed of spaghetti with Lucca's signature house-made sauce.

"No more shop talk," Vic said, meeting Simon's eyes. "Let's enjoy the evening."

Simon returned a smile that looked almost bashful. "I like the sound of that."

For the rest of the meal, they chatted about TV shows, recent movies, video games, and sharks. Simon didn't share Vic's passion for the Pittsburgh Steelers, Penguins, or Pirates, or any sports team, so Vic segued to favorite road trips or places each of them someday wanted to visit. Despite their different career paths, they found plenty to talk about, and Vic found himself relaxing for the first time in forever.

They finished the bottle of wine with the last of the meal and ordered a tiramisu to share. Since Vic was driving, he let Simon have the extra glass, and could have sworn it added a flush to the other man's complexion and brightened his hazel eyes.

"I already arranged for the check," Vic said when they pushed the empty dessert plate aside. "So we can wander on whenever you're ready." He chuckled as Simon started to protest. "I didn't want to argue about it. You can get it next time if you want." He found himself hoping very much there would be a next time.

"All right," Simon conceded. "Do you want to come back to my place? Doesn't have to be late…I know we've both got work tomorrow."

There it was; the invitation and the graceful out to avoid another awkward leave-taking. Vic slid his hand over and tangled his fingers with Simon's. "I'd like that."

When Simon slid up behind Vic on the bike, he pressed them together so tightly Vic could feel the other man's hard-on against his ass. The promise of the night yet to come gave a whole new meaning to the term "crotch rocket," and Vic struggled to keep his motorcycle's speed down since the last thing he needed was a ticket.

They arrived at Simon's house, and it struck Vic again how settled Simon seemed. How rooted. He felt the transience of his own apartment, despite its newness. This blue bungalow had a calm vibe as if it were as content with itself as its owner.

Simon checked the lock before entering, but to Vic's relief, the mechanism hadn't been tampered with. With a few taps on his phone, Simon started up quiet background music and brought the lights up to a warm glow. He grinned when he caught Vic staring at the app.

"What? Just because I study old stuff doesn't mean I don't live in the modern era," Simon teased.

Vic took a step toward him, backing Simon up against the door. Simon reached behind and turned the deadbolt. Vic set the chain lock and left his hand on one side of Simon's shoulder. They fit together just right, and Simon brushed up to kiss Vic's lips.

"Tell me what you want," Vic said, his voice husky with need. Simon's eyes were already dark with the answer.

"I want to taste you," Simon replied, pressing his hips forward to rub against Vic's crotch and his already stiff dick. "And I want you to suck me."

"That can be arranged," Vic growled, dipping in for another kiss, and this time, his tongue slipped between Simon's lips, exploring and claiming, picking up traces of marinara and coffee and something totally Simon. He pulled back, just enough to see Simon's flushed face. "Do you want to take turns or—"

"Together," Simon replied, and while his cheeks colored, he did not drop his gaze.

I like a man who knows what he wants, Vic thought.

"Show me," Vic dared.

Simon took his hand and led him to the oversized couch. It was long enough for both of them—they had proven this the last time— and by tossing the pillows off the back, was as wide as a twin bed, more than enough for what they intended. Vic didn't miss the nuance that keeping their liaison in the living room avoided the issue of staying over. He wondered if, in time, they would make it into the bedroom, and what his imagination pictured made his cock achingly hard.

"Come here," Simon said, pulling Vic close. They were both still standing, and Simon kept eye contact as he let his hand slide down Vic's shirt, pausing to flick his tight nibs. Vic brought his hands up Simon's sides, slipping one beneath his shirt and working the buttons impatiently with the other, careful to avoid his sore shoulder. Simon tugged at Vic's tie, loosening it and casting it to the side, then opened enough buttons to where he could slide the shirt over Vic's head.

They fumbled with each other's pants until the last of their clothing pooled around their ankles, and they toed off socks and shoes. Vic pressed up against Simon, buzzed on the high of being completely skin to skin. He wrapped his fingers around Simon's rigid cock, jacking him a few times to feel the warm, slippery pre-come bead from his slit. Simon met his gaze like a challenge and did the same, pausing first to roll Vic's balls in his palm.

"Not going to last long if you do that," Vic said, his voice far breathier than he intended. Damn, Simon made him hungry and reckless, and the feeling was exhilarating and terrifying at the same time.

Simon walked them backward until Vic's knees bumped the couch. They let go of each other long enough for Simon to settle onto the couch, one leg bent, looking wanton and debauched before they had even gotten started. Vic took a moment to admire the long, lean muscle, defined but not bulky, and the smooth skin that was lighter than Vic's olive complexion. Simon didn't have a lot of body hair—Vic was fine with that—and what he did have had been groomed, neat and trimmed. He had a whipcord strength that intrigued Vic, and once again, he couldn't wait to feel those powerful legs wrapped around his waist.

He'd wondered whether Simon would prefer top or bottom, and maybe this answered his question. Then again, if they ever got to that point, Vic would be fine discovering that Simon liked to switch. Vic himself preferred to top, but for the right guy, a permanent guy, he'd always figured he could learn some new tricks.

Vic leaned down to kiss him, a brush of lips and a swipe of tongue, teasing and promising. Then he climbed on top, offering up his swollen cock to Simon's hungry mouth, and licking Simon's dick like it was the best course at dinner.

Simon grabbed his ass, fingers digging into his cheeks, and pulled him close, licking and exploring, laving Vic's balls and his sensitive taint. When Simon's grip pulled him open, and his tongue slipped back to rim Vic's tight pucker, Vic groaned, and swallowed Simon down to the root.

Vic savored the tang of Simon's pre-come, burying his nose in his wiry, light brown pubes. He smiled to himself when he caught a whiff of soap along with sweat and musk, telling him that for all Simon's reservations, he had been ready for them to go further. *Maybe not tonight, but soon. God, I won't be able to hold out forever.*

Simon sucked and licked, moving from Vic's hole to his balls, then up his sensitive, throbbing member, loosening his hold to pull Vic into his mouth and then he closed his plush lips around Vic's skin.

Vic fought the urge to fuck Simon's mouth, and Simon's grip held him just so, letting his lover set the speed and how deep he took his cock. Simon ran the pointed tip of his tongue up Vic's shaft, swiped the broad, flat surface across his knob, and then closed his lips and took him deep, sucking and humming until Vic thought he would explode.

Hard to tell if this was a race to win or lose, he thought as he doubled his attention to Simon's dusky, hard cock. They were both clean, so Vic wasn't worried about swallowing Simon's shoot, but maybe some other time, he'd get to spill his seed all over Simon's gorgeous chest. His mind conjured the image, and then another with him balls-deep in Simon's ass, and Vic lost what little control he had. He came hard, and Simon took it all, as Vic tightened his mouth around Simon's dick and the other man came a few seconds later.

When Vic could breathe again, and his vision cleared, he cleaned up the last drops of Simon's spend and had the presence of mind to fall to one side so as not to crush his lover. *Lover. I like the sound of that.*

Simon released him with a kiss on Vic's spent cock that seemed almost more intimate than everything else they had done. Determined to do better this time on his "boyfriend etiquette," Vic maneuvered to lie beside Simon face to face, fitting Simon against his shoulder.

"You look amazing," Vic murmured, pushing a lock of chestnut hair out of Simon's eyes. "That was...really good."

Simon smiled, sated and vulnerable. "You're pretty awesome yourself," he replied, tracing Vic's jawline with a finger. Vic turned to slowly pull the digit into his mouth, sucking and tonguing it to leave no doubt he wanted more.

"I want to see you again," Vic said, propping himself up on one elbow. "I don't know where...this...will go, but I want to find out."

Simon's gaze grew melancholy. "Can you afford to? I mean,

you're a cop…"

"I'm out at work," Vic replied. "I mean, I don't wear rainbow t-shirts, but the people who need to know, know. Just, don't become a suspect. That would get sticky."

Simon put his fingers to his mouth with a sinful grin. "We're already sticky."

Shit, the mouth on that man. Vic hoped he didn't look hopelessly sappy. "You know what I mean."

"And the psychic stuff?" Simon asked.

"We'll figure it out," Vic promised. "Wouldn't be the first cop to work with a psychic. Happens all the time on TV."

Simon's smile wavered, and Vic planted a kiss he hoped was claiming and reassuring. "We'll find a way." He saw the doubt and reservation in Simon's gaze and wanted to punch the son of a bitch who had taught him to be so afraid.

They stayed like that, naked and entwined until the old mantle clock chimed midnight. "It's late," Simon said. "And we've both got work tomorrow."

Vic kissed him again. "All right. But for the record, I liked sleeping here. So…maybe another time?"

Simon smiled, and this time it reached his eyes. "That would be very nice. I liked it, too."

After that, it didn't feel awkward as they got up and dressed. They remained standing close, little touches that made all the difference between a fledgling relationship and a hurried one-night stand.

"Be careful in traffic," Simon warned. "I have to admit I'm partial to having tons of steel wrapped around me, especially the way tourists drive."

Vic chuckled. "It's bad luck to hit a cop. And I've been riding since I was sixteen, so I'm experienced."

Simon stretched up to kiss him. "You certainly are," he breathed, holding on to Vic's hips with both hands. "Don't stay away too long."

"And you, watch your back," Vic cautioned. "We still don't know what we're dealing with, but someone's out for you." He raised a hand to cup Simon's face. "Don't get dead."

SIMON

"So...tell me what happened?" Tracey whispered as Simon treated himself to a latte at Mizzenmast.

"Not here," Simon murmured, feeling his cheeks color.

"You go, boy!" Tracey replied, as if he were a chick leaving the nest.

"I really like him," Simon said as she swiped his card.

"I can tell. It's about time! You're overdue." She handed back his card. "I'll be by for the neighborhood watch meeting tonight. See you then."

Shit, that was tonight. When Simon posted the sign in the shop window, he had hoped to attract not just nearby store owners, but perhaps some others with untrained talent whom he hadn't met. His goal had been to band together and share information, keep eyes out for anyone who seemed suspicious. Now he hoped that no one with abilities would show up. *I might as well just put a big target on their backs,* he thought, angry at himself for not foreseeing the danger.

He walked to the shop with his coffee, considering possibilities. It was already too late to cancel the meeting. People would still show up and possibly out themselves to a killer. Better to have the gathering and provide a warning, both to those who had no psychic gifts and to the others whose help might provide the information neces-sary to stop a killer.

Simon turned on the music and readied the shop for another day. He plugged in the scented oil warmers that gave the store a vibe that he hoped was more New Age than head shop and swept the sand off the stoop, being careful not to disturb the red powder. Simon had used the brick dust, as Miss Eppie had advised, and figured every layer of protection helped. Even with the wide board-walk and a stretch of seagrass between the shops and the beach, sand was everywhere.

He caught himself humming a Springsteen song that reminded him of Vic, and smiled. Last night, after Vic left, Simon had gone to sleep feeling happier and more content than he had in a long time. Longer than he could remember. *Maybe since the first days with Jacen?* He thought. The last months with his ex- certainly hadn't been warm or sweet. As Simon's problems with the university escalated, Jacen withdrew, protecting his career instead of defending Simon. When Simon finally decided to resign rather than to have his repu-tation further tarnished, Jacen hadn't even tried to dissuade him. *Hell, he practically packed my bags for me.*

Looking back, Simon couldn't remember why he'd fallen for the uptight academic. Jacen was nothing like Vic, not in looks, or in bed. Jacen had been fussy, fastidious to the point of prissiness as if he barely tolerated the mess of sex or the complications of trying to fuse two lives into a relationship. Simon found he much preferred Vic's unconcealed hunger and unbridled pleasure.

So much for going slowly, Simon thought. *I'm in way too deep, too soon.* He liked the new side of Vic he had seen at their dinner together, and whether it had started off as a date, it had certainly become one by the time dessert was served. Vic had taken him seriously, tried hard to be accepting of the psychic gifts Simon knew the cop still thought of as "woo-woo," and had done his best to make up for the abrupt ending to their first night together. The sex last night had been intimate and urgent, but with an underlying tenderness that gave Simon a warm feeling in his chest.

Maybe when the Slitter case is over, we can move from lovers to partners,

Simon thought and found himself hoping very much that would be the case.

A bright day without too much humidity made for good strolling weather, and the shop stayed busy all day. Advance sales for the next ghost tours were going strong, and Simon felt a surge of pride when several customers bought copies of his ghost books. It didn't escape his notice that he did a better than usual business in protective medallions, candles, crystals, and jewelry. He didn't know whether any of the buyers harbored psychic gifts themselves, or if word that a killer was on the loose had spooked enough people that they were covering all bases.

Simon watched the customers as they wandered through the store, wishing his gift included the ability to sense talent in others. Today his clientele ranged from plump grandmothers, goth teens, and patrons who wanted to get into serious conversations about the books and supplies for their own practice, to joking twenty-some-things teasing about love potions and potency charms. At one point, when the shop was so full Simon couldn't see past all the people in the aisles, he felt a chill go down his back. He looked up sharply, abruptly turning from the customer he was waiting on, but only caught the back of a man's head as he left the shop, a baseball hat covering his hair.

"Can I have my card back?" the woman at the register said with enough impatience that Simon suspected she had asked more than once.

"Oh, um. I'm sorry," Simon faltered and handed back the woman's credit card and her purchase. "Thank you for stopping in." He looked past her, out the store's large glass window, but saw only the top of the baseball cap disappearing into the crowd.

What the hell was that? Simon wondered. He knew his abilities didn't include empathy or telepathy. But intuition was psychic-independent, at least the common garden-variety "gut feeling." Simon had learned a long time ago to trust his hunches, and if he'd run into the baseball-capped stranger on the street, he would have crossed to the other side, driven by a vague sense of uneasiness and danger.

Could that have been the Slitter?

The next time the store had a brief lull, Simon backed up the single security camera and surveyed the crowd. He spotted the cap first, as the man entered with a group of other customers. The man —Simon thought it was a man—kept his head down, and between the aviator sunglasses and the beach towel slung around his neck, his face was obscured. With the stranger's slouched posture, he couldn't even be sure of height, and the man always remained in the middle of a group, so clothing and body build were impossible to see clearly.

"Dammit," Simon muttered, then looked up and plastered on a smile as the door chimes jangled and more customers entered. He glanced at the display case, noting that he would need to reorder amulets and protective crystals soon. He'd gone through more in the past week than he had in all the previous month, and while no one who bought the charms had volunteered the cause of their worry, Simon guessed from their ages and accents they feared the serial killer.

He wondered again about the blond woman from his vision; the one Marcus had also glimpsed. Unlike with Cindy, Simon had nothing to go on to guess her identity. He could only hope that she decided to leave town before she became the Slitter's next victim.

By the time Simon rang up the last purchases and shepherded the customers out the door, he was more than ready to go home and collapse. But he had the Neighborhood Watch meeting to deal with first. He hadn't been able to escape a feeling that something was going to happen, although there had been no repeat visit by the man in the cap, and his patrons had all been generally pleasant. The receipts for the day were better than average, which should have lifted his mood, but somehow did not change the worry in the pit of his stomach.

He hand-wrote *"Private Event: Neighborhood Watch"* on a piece of paper and taped it to the front door, to discourage after-hours shoppers. The store didn't have room for seating, but he figured that for the short meeting, people wouldn't mind standing. Simon ducked into the back for the tray of cookies he had picked up at the grocery store, which he hoped helped with the "neighborly" feeling.

Right on time, Tracey showed up, and shortly afterward, ten others Simon recognized as managing nearby stores. Everyone chatted and helped themselves to cookies, and the fresh pot of coffee Simon set out, and when he figured no others were likely to show up, he cleared his throat for their attention.

"Thanks for coming," he said, oddly nervous although addressing a lecture hall of students had never bothered him. The door chime jangled, but Simon couldn't see the newcomer over the heads of those clustered around him.

"I think we've all seen the recent headlines, and I'm guessing that by now you've heard that the woman who sold ice cream from a cart on the boardwalk near here was one of the victims of the criminal they're calling the Strand Slitter," he said. "So far, it looks like all of the victims have been seasonal help, but there's no guarantee it'll stay that way—and our livelihoods depend on tourists feeling safe here. So my thought was simple. Just to ask that we all keep an extra-sharp eye out for anything that seems unusual, and report it on the tip line the police have set up."

"Since when have the cops cared about J-ones?" a man asked from the back. Simon recognized him as the owner of a t-shirt store a few doors down, a recent immigrant himself.

"They're trying to find the killer," Simon replied. "But we come in contact with a lot more people every day than they do, and we're here in the heart of the Strand. Maybe if we all keep our eyes open, someone will spot something that is the tip they need. So, it's kind of 'if you see something, say something.'"

"Yeah, we can do that," a heavyset man said from near the tray of cookies through a full mouth. "But I gotta say, if the cops can't catch shoplifters, I don't know how they're gonna find a serial killer." He reached for an oatmeal raisin cookie.

The small crowd grew still at the words. "That's why we can help by staying alert," Simon replied. "Plenty of cases have been solved from someone calling in something that looked strange."

"That's it? That's the whole reason for the meeting?" The

speaker was a tall, thin man named Jay who ran the tattoo parlor a little farther down the boardwalk. Jay was usually quiet, and Simon couldn't remember having spoken more than a few sentences to him in passing. He had a good reputation not only for the quality of his art but also for having a level head, and many of the other shop owners thought well of him. His Grand Strand Ink had been a fixture on the boardwalk for more than a decade, nearly forever in a transient town like Myrtle Beach.

"Is there something else you want to mention?" Simon hadn't intended to expand the scope, but Jay seemed intent on saying his piece.

"Just that whoever this Slitter is, he must spend a lot of time in and around the hotels and kiosks, finding his next victims." Jay shrugged at the looks the others gave him. "So sue me. I watch Dexter and Criminal Minds. The point is, Simon's right. This nutcase is probably right under our noses, and sooner or later he'll slip up. The more people who are watching, the more likely someone will notice."

Jay looked at Simon and nodded. "Count me in. And I'll talk to the other shop owners down my way who didn't make it tonight." He leveled a look at the others in the store. "I think we can all bring some more people to the party."

"Be careful," Simon warned. "Someone took a shot at me a few nights ago, and it wasn't even ten o'clock." The group murmured in surprise and shock. "Be on the lookout for a guy wearing sunglasses and a baseball cap who goes out of his way to hide his face. He might be involved. And don't forget to check your video feed if someone makes you uncomfortable. That's why we all bought the cameras."

"I heard about the shooting," Jay said. "Didn't realize it was you. Glad you're okay."

"Thank you," Simon said and handed out slips of paper he had printed with the police tip line as the small crowd filed for the door once the last of the cookies disappeared. When all the others had gone, he turned to the tiny woman who hung back.

"Hello, Gabriella. I didn't think I'd see you here."

"I respect what you're trying to do, Simon, but this is a matter you should leave to the police." Gabriella Hernandez was a *bruja*, a witch of some power, and someone who had been a mentor of sorts in both magic and the inner workings of the Myrtle Beach community when Simon moved down.

"You don't usually have a lot of faith in the cops," Simon replied. "What changed?"

She gave an eloquent shrug. With her short, fashionably trimmed dark hair and a coral twinset that brought out the warm undertones in her cocoa-brown skin, Gabriella didn't look like anyone's stereotype of the witch next door. "I still don't have much faith in them," she said. "That's not the point. It's too dangerous for *our kind* to get involved in this, Simon."

Since he'd seen pictures of Gabriella's numerous children and grandchildren and her husband of fifty years, he knew she didn't mean "gay." "You think the Slitter is targeting people with abilities?"

Gabriella nodded. "I do indeed. The killer is starting with easy pickings, the ones who don't have families to notice right away if they go missing. Ones with just a little bit of power, so there's not much risk. But I don't think he—or she—is just interested in killing. There's something else the killer wants, and it's tied into the magic. It's not safe here, Simon. We're all in danger."

"This is my home now," Simon said. "I won't be chased out."

Gabriella snorted in disagreement. "Young people. So eager to stand and fight. You get old; you learn that sometimes, running is better. You live longer that way."

"So you're running?"

"Tomorrow I'm going up to Virginia to stay with my oldest daughter and her husband for a few weeks, maybe longer. Until things here settle down. Spend some time with the grandchildren. Lie low."

Simon wanted to argue, but Gabriella had a point. Stepping up to hunt down the Slitter, especially if the killer was singling out victims with psychic gifts, was sure to draw unwanted attention. Perhaps there had been other battles Gabriella had been willing to fight, in her younger days. Who was he to ask her to endanger her life now when she had so many loved ones who relied on her?

"I'll miss you," he said simply, bending over to kiss her on the cheek. "Drop me an email now and then. I won't know what to do without new pictures of your grandchildren."

She chuckled. "You're a good boy, Simon. Be brave, but not foolish."

"Did your gift have any wisdom for me?" He walked her to the door.

She shook her head. "Only that there will be more blood before all of this is over. Just remember, magic can be a powerful weapon. You don't see it like that, but others might. Be careful, and stay safe." With that, she let herself out and vanished into the boardwalk crowd.

Simon watched Gabriella go, fighting the sadness he felt. While rationally he understood her reasons, Simon couldn't help feeling deserted by one of the only other practitioners he knew in Myrtle Beach who had more than middling power. Gabriella had mentored him, teaching him techniques from her tradition, and helping him strengthen his ability to shield his thoughts, as well as showing him helpful blessing and cleansing rituals.

He locked the door, then picked up the empty cookie tray and the coffee pot and walked to the back room. As psychic abilities went, clairvoyance and being a medium were defensive, not offensive. A true witch like Gabriella could use her spell craft as a weapon, or at least, to contain an enemy. Simon had learned how to defend himself from predatory spirits and how to shut out the never-ending voices of the dead, but nothing in his psychic "tool box" would provide a physical defense. He felt more aware than ever of the pepper spray that hung from his belt and the knife near his ankle.

His phone rang as he rinsed out the coffee pot and dumped the grinds into the garbage. He frowned, not recognizing the number.

"Simon?"

"Tasha?"

"I'm scared," Tasha said in a breathy whisper. "There was a man in the diner earlier. I couldn't get a good look at him—"

"Let me guess. Big sunglasses and a baseball cap."

"Yes," she replied. "He wouldn't look up from his newspaper when he ordered. But I touched his mind. It was foul, like garbage. Full of hate. And…violence. I think he might have been the Slitter."

"Where are you?" Simon dried his hands and headed for the light switches to lock up.

"At work. Please, Simon. Come get me. I don't want to walk home alone. I'm sorry—there's no one else I can call."

"I'll be there in about fifteen minutes," Simon said, flipping on the security system as he exited and locking the door behind him. "Stay put."

"Put where?"

Simon sighed at the language barrier. "Stay inside, in the light, where people can see you. I'll get there as quickly as I can."

He unhooked the pepper spray from his belt and turned the safety off, keeping it in one hand as he jogged toward the street. After the stranger he'd glimpsed in the shop, Simon felt insecure enough about his own safety; he didn't want to imagine how fearful Tasha would be after making any contact with the Slitter. Had the killer been aware of her abilities? It seemed like too much of a coincidence for the man to show up at the workplace of one of Simon's Skeleton Crew. Did the Slitter know she touched his mind? If so, Tasha was in more danger than ever.

Simon debated whether to go home and get his car, then looked at the solid red glow of tail lights on Ocean Boulevard, and reconsidered. Not only would it take him twice as long in traffic, but finding parking would mean more time lost. He'd pick up Tasha, and figure out the next steps later.

He considered calling Vic, then discarded the idea. Too much "woo-woo," not enough evidence. Someone who didn't believe in Tasha's talent could easily dismiss her reaction as nerves, or an overreaction to backroom gossip. The cops could hardly be expected to escort every seasonal worker home after dark. But Simon didn't doubt that Tasha had not only glimpsed the Slitter, but that he was the same man who had been in Grand Strand Ghost Tours earlier that day. How he could keep Tasha—and himself—safe, he wasn't sure.

Running had never appealed to Simon, although his workouts at the gym kept him in decent shape. Jogging outside, in the ever-present humidity, dodging clueless tourists, left him soaked with sweat and panting. He reached the Conch and searched for Tasha through the big picture windows, feeling his heart clench when he didn't see her. He paused outside to catch his breath, then pushed open the outer door, ignoring the condensation that ran down the glass. A quick glance assured him that the man with the baseball cap was gone.

Just as he was about to find a seat, he spotted Tasha peeking out from an *"Employees Only"* door. Simon strode toward the back as if he belonged there, and Tasha opened the door for him.

"Simon. Thank you. I just couldn't—"

"That's okay. Where do you want to go?"

"To my apartment," she said. "It's not far. Most of the time I don't mind the walk, but today—"

"I've got you," Simon said reassuringly. "Come on. I'll get you home."

They walked shoulder to shoulder, keeping to the well-lit, busy sidewalks along Ocean Boulevard for several blocks. Once they were out of sight of the diner, Simon stepped off into a parking lot. "How far away is your place?"

"About four blocks," she said, with a nod that indicated the side streets.

He knew the area, right at the end of the boardwalk. That meant less foot traffic, but plenty of cars. Simon kept a grip on the pepper spray as he and Tasha left Ocean Boulevard and headed up a darker, less traveled side street. The garden apartments in this area were small and old, but relatively cheap, especially when split among more residents than officially permitted. Street lights illuminated small areas but shadows stretched between the lamp posts, and without the garish lights of hotels and restaurants, the residential area seemed ominously dark.

"We're close," Tasha said. Simon tensed as they passed every fence and driveway.

"Are any of your roommates home?" he asked.

"I don't know. They work nights, mostly. My shift changed because Amy was sick. Usually, I have friends to walk with."

"You were right to call me," Simon said, wishing he had thought to bring a stronger flashlight than the light on his phone, although that might have seemed strange when they were on the brightly lit main drag. Many of the windows of the homes and apartments around them were dark, a clue that their residents also worked nights, or were already in bed for an early morning shift. Few bothered with porch lights, an unnecessary expense.

"Get your key ready," Simon said, standing at the edge of the nearest pool of light to Tasha's doorway. He felt exposed as if they were in a spotlight, but he wanted to minimize the time either of them had to spend in the dark.

"Got it." He could see the key clutched in her right hand. What he hadn't noticed before was the steak knife she must have concealed in her sleeve, gripped tight in her left.

Something made the hair on the back of Simon's neck stand up, but as he turned to take in their surroundings, he saw no movement, no one loitering, no idling cars. "Come on," he said, as they made a dash for the door.

Just before they reached the stoop, Simon sensed that they were being watched, but before he could shout a warning, a disembodied force lifted him off his feet and hurled him back toward the sidewalk.

"Tasha!" he yelled in warning. A dark shape rushed toward Tasha, where she hurried to get the key into the lock. Simon climbed to his feet and ran toward the attacker. "Cover your eyes!" He yelled, gambling that whatever mojo the stranger had used on him couldn't be summoned up again quickly.

The man turned, and Simon saw only sunglasses and a hat before he set off the spray. He danced backward, trying to avoid being blinded by the same chemicals, and heard Tasha choke out an angry shout. The attacker cried out, and then a rush of cold energy sent Simon staggering. By the time Simon caught his breath and got his balance, the stranger was gone.

"In!" he ordered as he scooped up his phone from where he dropped it, still choking and gasping, and he pushed Tasha ahead of him. Simon slammed the door behind them and locked it, although the flimsy knob and chain wouldn't hold off a determined attacker.

"Oh, god. My eyes!" Tasha wailed.

"Get us to the kitchen," Simon said, with his own eyes nearly swollen shut. She took his wrist and led him into the small galley. "We need to wash our hands with dish soap," he directed, his voice a raspy growl as they made room for each other at the sink. "Then rinse your eyes with cold water. Do you have milk?"

"Some. In the refrigerator."

"Once we can see, we'll pour some milk in a bowl and soak a cloth to put over our faces. Takes the sting out."

"How do you know this?" Her voice sounded raw, but she no longer gasped for breath. Simon felt some of the burn in his lungs subside, though his throat felt scorched.

"I accidentally sprayed myself when I first got it," he admitted. She recovered first and readied the milk-soaked cloths. Simon let the almost-too-wet dish towel ease his stinging skin.

"It's good you know this. Handy," Tasha said.

"We weren't supposed to get messed up as much as the bad guy," Simon lamented. *And let's hope he doesn't recover faster than we do, and that's he's long gone.*

"I think, he got it worse," Tasha replied. "You sprayed right at him. We just got the—how you say—overflow."

"Close enough," Simon agreed. Tasha handed him a cold glass of water, and he drank it down, soothing his irritated throat.

"When do your housemates get home?" he asked.

She looked at the clock. "Very soon. Then, there will be five of us. I don't think the man will come back with so many, do you?"

"I hope not," Simon replied. "But you need a better lock."

"Tell my landlord."

The door was only part of the problem, he realized, looking around the old, hard-used apartment. The windows didn't look any more secure than the door, and even if the landlord could be persuaded to pay for good locks, it could take a week or more to get them installed. *This is why the Slitter goes after J-ones. Easy pickings,* his mind supplied.

"Can you leave town for a little bit?"

Tasha shook her head. "My visa, remember? If I don't work, they send me home. If I leave, I break the law. They would deport me."

They heard the door rattle, and the click of the chain. "Tasha? Open up! Why the chain?" an exasperated voice yelled through the gap.

"Sorry! Sorry!" Tasha rushed to open the door, but Simon made her look through the peephole first.

A flurry of questions and answers were traded in what Simon guessed was Romanian, and now and again one of the three girls looked his way, sizing him up as if to determine whether he was a problem. Finally, Tasha turned to him.

"I told them what happened, how you walked me home from the diner after a man got too pushy, and how he followed us here and you fought him off." Tasha made it clear with her recap that the others did not know about her abilities. "If I see him again, I will let you know." She grabbed his arm. "Please, don't call the police," she begged in a whisper. "They will tell my landlord too many people live here. My friends will get in trouble."

"There isn't much I can say that they'd believe," Simon replied. Much as he wanted to tip off the cops, he could hardly report having a "bad feeling" about a man whose description matched half of the tourists in town. He didn't want to think about telling the police that an attacker threw him into the street without even touching him. *Yeah, right. That would go over real well.*

"Don't go out alone," Simon cautioned, blinking a few times to assure himself that his vision had cleared. "Don't be home alone. Please. This guy is dangerous." He paused. "In fact, I'm going to call a cab. Just in case."

"Thank you," Tasha said, laying a hand on his arm. "I appreciate what you did."

"I just want you and your friends to be safe," Simon emphasized. "So don't take any chances."

She managed a wan smile. "Same for you."

Simon climbed into the cab, feeling self-conscious about calling a
ride to go such a relatively short distance since it wasn't even past
ten. But he had no doubt that the attacker had been the Slitter, and
no desire to meet up with a frustrated serial killer who blamed him
for spoiling the night's "fun." The pain of the pepper spray had
mostly faded, and Simon hoped that the stranger had gotten a much
more potent dose that would keep him from trying again, at least for
tonight.

Knowing that the man with the cap had been in Grand Strand
Ghost Tours made Simon's throat tighten. The cab pulled up to his
house, and Simon hesitated before he paid the driver, trying to see
whether anyone lurked in the shadows. He palmed the small knife
from his ankle holster as he got out and sprinted to the door, not
caring what the cabbie thought.

Once inside, Simon locked the door and then collapsed against
it, feeling reality sink in. He and Tasha had eluded the Slitter, a man
who had a string of murders to his name. Simon knew he was shaking, and barely had enough time to make it to the bathroom before
he fell to his knees and threw up into the toilet.

Fuck. We faced off with a serial killer.

Simon felt the sudden need to get clean, to be rid of any taint
left behind from the pepper spray and especially from the dark
energy he'd sensed from their attacker. He stripped off his clothes,
deciding he'd need to figure out how to remove the residue later,
and stepped into a cool shower, letting the water sluice over him,
cleaning away the sweat and fear. His hand trembled when he
reached for the soap, and he steadied himself against the wall.

I'm not cut out for this hero stuff.

By the time he had toweled off and changed into sweats, Simon
had regained most of his composure, though he still felt off-kilter.

He walked to the kitchen, lit a bundle of sage for cleansing, and poured himself some whiskey. When his phone rang, he saw Vic's name, and relaxed, just a little.

"Hey. You home?" Vic asked, his voice low and sultry.

"Yeah," Simon replied. "It's been…quite a night."

"You don't sound good. Did something happen?" Vic's tone shifted immediately to concern.

"I'm pretty sure Tasha and I fought off the Slitter."

The phone was silent for long enough that Simon thought Vic had lost the call. "I'm coming over," Vic said. "Don't go anywhere."

"Don't worry. I'm definitely in for the night. And yeah, I was going to call you, as soon as I caught my breath."

Simon wasn't surprised when his phone rang again fifteen minutes later. "I'm outside," Vic said tersely. Simon still checked, then unlocked the door and stood aside for Vic to enter. He had barely gotten the door shut when Vic pushed him against it and held him pinned with a hand against his chest, checking him over from head to toe.

"What happened? Are you hurt?" Vic's voice sounded angry, but the look in his eyes was pure worry.

"I'll have a nice bruise on my back from hitting the pavement, and I've been reminded why pepper spray is no fun, but I'll live." Simon locked the door, then let Vic take his hand and lead him to the couch. Vic sat on the coffee table and leaned forward, elbows on his thighs, to look right at Simon.

"Tell me."

Simon recounted the whole adventure, from Tasha's call to the cab ride home. He left nothing out, hoping he was doing the right thing by trusting Vic to believe the paranormal elements of the story. When he finished, Vic was watching him with the analytic stare Simon thought of as "cop face." "Say something, please," he muttered, not sure how to take Vic's scrutiny.

"You said that the attacker picked you up off your feet and threw you onto the road, which was at least a yard away?"

Simon nodded.

"But your impression was that the man was shorter than you,

and not some kind of crazy weightlifting hulk. How is that possible?"

"He didn't touch me. He just threw me," Simon replied. "I've suspected for a while that the Slitter has some kind of abilities. Apparently I was right—and I think he's choosing victims who also have gifts."

Vic bowed his head and laced his hands behind his neck. "Shit," he muttered. "I don't even know what to do with this."

"Believe me?" Simon asked, hating that his voice sounded vulnerable.

Vic looked up and took both of Simon's hands in his. "I *do* believe you. That's what's eating me. You could have been killed tonight. I don't know how to protect you."

"Apparently, pepper spray is a good start," Simon replied, trying for shaky humor. "And I think Tasha might have cut him with the steak knife she was carrying. It proves the Slitter is human."

"Human? Was there another option?" Vic's eyes went wide.

Simon managed a wry smile. "You're talking to a folklorist. You don't want to know how many creatures fit the Slitter's description."

"Okay," Vic replied, drawing out the syllables. "I'm not gonna go there. You both saw a man in a baseball cap and sunglasses. Could you give a description to one of our sketch artists, down at the precinct?"

Simon shook his head. "Whoever this guy is, he's good. Had a beach towel around his neck in the store, so I never got a look at his face, and Tasha said he kept a newspaper up when he ordered at the diner. When he attacked, it was too dark to see much of anything."

"Shit," Vic muttered. "So this guy knows who you are and where you work, same with Tasha, and where she lives." He threaded his fingers with Simon's. "Probably knows where you live, too. I want you to leave town, Simon. Far enough away this guy won't follow you."

"I can't do that," Simon replied. "I've got a store to run. It's my livelihood."

"That won't matter if you're dead!" Vic's heated gaze stirred something deep inside Simon, as he realized that what sounded like anger in Vic's voice was protectiveness and fear. It felt nice to be on the receiving end of that, comforting in a way Simon had never known.

"Tasha and the others, they can't run away," Simon reminded him. "And with Gabriella gone, I'm one of the people with the strongest gifts left."

"That makes you even more at risk."

Simon closed his hands around Vic's and forced the other man to meet his eyes. "That means I'm responsible. With great power, and all that stuff."

"You aren't a superhero. You're a civilian," Vic ranted. "And talking to ghosts or getting visions—that doesn't protect you in a fight. You're not safe here."

"No, I'm not," Simon said quietly. "But I have a job to do. I might be the puzzle piece you need to catch this guy. Your job isn't exactly safe, either."

"That's different," Vic argued, looking away. "I'm a cop."

"Doesn't mean I like it any better knowing you're in danger whenever you're working," Simon confessed, and realized what he had just admitted.

A smile touched Vic's lips. "You worry about me?" He looked surprised and inordinately pleased.

"Maybe," Simon replied, feeling a blush color his cheeks.

Vic reached out to trace Simon's jaw with his fingertips. "I like that," he said, meeting Simon's gaze.

Simon shifted in his seat and winced.

"What's wrong?" Vic asked sharply, coming to sit beside him on the couch, so close that their legs touched from hip to knee.

"Nothing," Simon said, wincing. "Just, my shoulder's sore where I landed. It's the same arm that got shot."

Vic reached for him, running his hand through Simon's loose hair, still damp from his shower. "You scare me," he said quietly, and Simon wasn't sure whether that meant tonight, with the attack, or something deeper. "I worry about you, too. Especially now. I try to understand the psychic stuff, but it's hard because I can't imagine what it would be like, to be able to do that. And this thing...us..."

scares me too." Vic's voice had grown low and husky, and Simon couldn't decipher the mix of emotions he saw in the other man's eyes.

"Why does it scare you?" Simon asked, just above a whisper.

"Because it's more than I bargained for," Vic replied, letting the pad of his thumb skim over Simon's cheekbone, and gently trail down the scruff to his jaw. "You're more than I expected."

"Is that a bad thing?" Simon found himself holding his breath.

"No," Vic replied, quickly enough to ease Simon's concern. "Just, different. More. It's been a long time since someone mattered like this."

Simon slipped his hand up to cup Vic's face. "You matter to me, too."

Vic pulled him in for a kiss. It began slow, but deepened quickly, as Simon drew Vic closer, and Vic's tongue slid between his lips, tasting, claiming, teasing. Vic crawled into his lap, running his hands all over Simon's arms and chest as if assuring himself once again that there was no blood, no new wounds. Simon returned the kiss, wrapping his arms around Vic's back, holding onto him like an anchor to ground himself to reality.

"What do you want?" Vic breathed, lips brushing lightly over Simon's cheeks.

"I want you to fuck me." The words seemed to surprise Simon as much as they did Vic, but once he said them, Simon knew it was true.

"You sure?" Vic asked, pulling back far enough to meet Simon's gaze. "You've had a rough night—"

"Remind me that I'm alive," Simon replied, refusing to look away. "Make me feel something that isn't fear."

Vic kissed him, and the passion and hunger sent a surge of heat through Simon's body. "I can do that," he growled. "He can't have you. Do you understand?"

"Yes. God, yes. I just want to feel you. Please, Vic. I need this." Simon knew he should have felt embarrassed at the plea, but being with Vic made him feel like he had found a safe harbor, something he had never sensed with any other lover. Simon had always been proud of being able to take care of himself, and he knew he could—he had fought back a killer just tonight. But now he craved connection, a reminder that he wasn't alone.

"Come on, then," Vic said, as he stood and reached out for Simon's hand. "Show me what you want."

Simon led the way to his bedroom, his stomach tight with anticipation and nerves. Vic's hand was warm in his, the grip reassuring. He felt oddly glad he had bothered to make his bed that morning and tried to remember if he'd left clothing on the floor. There was lube and condoms in the bedside table, though it had been so long since he'd needed the condoms that perhaps they should check the expiration date.

He flicked the switch, and a corner lamp provided soft light. *Whew. No dirty laundry.*

Vic tugged Simon toward him, until they were standing close, face to face. He put his hands on Simon's hips, slipping his fingers through the belt loops. "Are you sure?"

Simon nodded. "Very. Please. I need this. I need you." *Tonight. Maybe forever.*

"I'm right here. Not going anywhere." Vic tilted his head down and brushed his lips across Simon's forehead, his nose, and finally his mouth. His hands came up under Simon's t-shirt, gentling it up and off, careful with his sore shoulder and arm. Warm fingers slid down Simon's back, then teased around the waistband of his sweats, as Simon gasped and pressed his hips against Vic.

Simon slipped his arms around Vic, deepening the kiss, as Vic tangled his fingers in Simon's hair.

"I like your hair long," Vic murmured, edging away from Simon's mouth to kiss his chin. They moved together, ending up with Simon on the bed, bare-chested, his erection obvious beneath his sweatpants, as Vic stood at the bedside.

"Take them off," Vic growled, never breaking eye contact. "I want to see you."

Simon blushed as he shucked off the soft fleece, and saw the heat in Vic's gaze when he planted his foot on the comforter and drew one knee up, letting the other leg fall open, offering himself up for inspection. "Like what you see?"

"Very much." Vic took off his holster, and set it and his gun and phone on the nightstand. Then he wriggled out of his shirt, finally giving Simon the view he had been waiting for of Vic's chest and those mysterious tats.

Black ink against Vic's naturally bronzed skin stood out in a full sleeve of symbols on his right arm, blocky curls and geometric designs than ran from his bicep down to his wrist. On Vic's left shoulder the same symbols formed a whorl that wrapped around his upper arm like a snake. On his left forearm, a tribal band of repeating angles and arrows complimented the other tats. Simon wanted to learn the story behind all of them.

Vic pushed his jeans down in one move, and his cock sprang free.

Commando. Nice touch, Simon thought, feeling his own dick beading with pre-come.

Vic crawled up the bed toward him, feral and hungry. Simon wasn't sure where to look. Vic's eyes were dark with lust, and he licked his lips as if Simon were the perfect meal. His powerful shoulders and arms rippled sinuously with every move, and Simon couldn't wait to trace those intricate tattoos with his fingers and his tongue. Then again, he'd gotten a good look at Vic's package, and his thick, cut cock was every bit what Simon had imagined in his fantasies.

"Come here," Simon managed, hoping his voice wouldn't fail him, that Vic wouldn't notice the slight tremor. He shouldn't be nervous. This wasn't his first time, not by a long shot. But it was the first after a long, voluntary dry spell, and it was Vic, dammit, and that mattered. Maybe more than it should, perhaps more than it did even to Vic, far more than was safe.

"I'm here," Vic said, hovering over Simon, then lowering his mouth to land light kisses on Simon's shoulders, his collarbones, and sensitive neck, and to lap at the hollow of his throat, drawing an involuntary groan in reply. "That what you like?"

Simon could only nod.

Vic grinned, continuing his downward trek, drawing first one of Simon's nipples into his mouth and then the other, taking turns at running his tongue over the sensitive nibs, rolling them between his lips, lightly plucking at them, and then giving a slight tug with his teeth until Simon bucked beneath him.

"Going to make you feel good," Vic promised in a voice like sin and whiskey. He settled onto his elbows, into the V of Simon's legs, his chest pressing against Simon's straining erection, a sweet friction that had Simon panting as Vic intentionally shifted to increase the connection. He chuckled and began to kiss his way down Simon's abdomen, following the happy trail of chestnut hair until he moved backward to give himself access to Simon's engorged cock.

"So beautiful," Vic murmured, licking up the pearl of clear liquid that beaded from the slit, looking up to make sure Simon was watching before he licked his lips and took him down to the root.

"God, Vic! Fuck! Oh, please. I'm not gonna last," Simon warned, afraid he would shoot too quickly.

Vic pulled off with a pop and grinned. "So, come. I'm the one fucking you, remember?"

Simon shook his head. "Not like this. Want to come with you inside me. Please, Vic."

"And you will. I promise." Vic lowered his head again, but this time, he only favored Simon's sensitive shaft with a long, slow lick and a twist of his tongue around the head before he nipped and kissed at the hollows of his thighs, then pushed his arms under Simon's legs, lifted him up, and buried his face in his balls and taint.

Simon tried for words, but only managed a groan that egged Vic on, exploring his sac and then his taint as if it were a feast and Vic was a starving man. Strong arms held Simon in place, giving Vic full access as he gently rolled first one of Simon's balls and then the other in his hot mouth, sucking lightly, just enough to make Simon's pulse skyrocket. Vic's tongue slipped lower, stroking along Simon's taint, and then even farther, to rim his tight hole.

"Fuck. Vic. Please." Simon's post-doctorate vocabulary failed him, and he was left with a primal language of panting and moaning as Vic ignored his pleas and laved his tongue over his pucker, broad strokes and then kitten flicks, then the tight point of it tracing the sensitive ring of muscle as Simon writhed in his grip.

"In the nightstand," Simon gasped. "Top drawer."

Vic lowered him gently, moving up between his thighs and spreading his legs wider as he reached over Simon for the nightstand and pulled the top drawer open, then settled back with a foil packet and a tube.

"This still what you want?" he asked in a husky voice that went right to Simon's bloodstream like good scotch.

"Yes. Fuck, yes. Now!"

"Bossy bottom," Vic chided, his voice warm. "I like that." He rose up on his knees, so Simon was sure to watch as he gloved up, then ran a lube-slicked hand over the latex and drizzled more of the slick substance onto his fingers.

"You're tight," Vic said, lowering himself again. "Need to get you open."

"I don't care," Simon panted, too far gone to worry about it.

"I do. Gonna make this good, remember?" Vic lowered his head and began to suck Simon's cock again as one finger found Simon's furl and gently worked its way inside. Simon bucked impatiently, but Vic kept licking and sucking, first with a single digit and then two, scissoring them and stretching him open, until three fingers could fit easily.

"Vic!" Simon begged, then gasped as Vic turned his fingers just so to stroke his spot, and Simon saw stars. Vic clamped a hand around the base of Simon's cock just when Simon was sure he was going to shoot.

"Not just yet," Vic coaxed. "You're so tight."

"Told you, it's been a long time."

"It's easier if you're on your stomach, but not with that shoulder and arm," he said, looking down at the bruise Simon had glimpsed in the mirror and the half-healed gash. "And I like this better where I can see you," he added with a wicked grin.

Vic slipped his arms beneath Simon's legs again, lifting him up, and positioned the head of his stiff, thick cock against Simon's furl. He pressed in slowly, giving Simon time to adjust, and Simon panted as he took in every inch of Vic's hard length until Vic was fully seated inside.

"So good," Simon managed, trying to keep his eyes open so he could watch Vic's face. For the first time, all of Vic's defenses were down, the "cop eyes" were gone, and the unguarded emotion on the other man's face made Simon's heart clench. Simon already knew he was too far gone over Vic to be safe. Maybe, just maybe, Vic felt the same about him.

Vic pulled out, then plunged back in again, and set a rhythm, slow at first and then faster, rocking them together and filling Simon over and over, so hard and thick and *right*. Vic curled his fingers around Simon's dripping cock and stroked him once, twice, and then Simon came hard, shouting Vic's name and painting his chest and chin with thick strands of come.

Simon clenched hard around Vic's cock, and that tipped the other man over the brink, finishing in just a few hard, fast thrusts until he spilled into the condom, filling Simon with warmth.

"My god," Vic gasped, as he shifted forward to look down at Simon's face. "That was—"

"Yeah," Simon agreed, not caring if the grin he wore looked like he was completely high. "It was."

Vic kissed Simon, slow and gentle; their bodies still joined, both hearts pounding. "It really was," he repeated in a throaty voice just above a whisper. He moved back reluctantly, reaching down to hold the condom in place as he pulled out, then tying it off and tossing it into the waste can beside the bed.

"Stay right there," he said as he got up and went to the bath-room to clean up, returning after a moment with a warm, wet towel to wipe off Simon's chest and then between his legs. It seemed so simple an act, so natural as if Vic hadn't even given it a second thought to tend to his lover, but Simon's throat tightened at the inti-macy, something no one had bothered to do for him before.

"Better?" Vic asked, tossing the towel on the floor as he lay beside Simon, pressing his front against Simon's side.

Simon turned onto his good shoulder to face Vic, and let his fingers ghost down over his brow, his cheekbones, lips, and chin.

"Much. That was—" *Perfect? Amazing? Heart-stopping?* "—Just what I needed."

Vic kissed his cheek. "Just what I needed, too. I care, Simon. More than I should. I'm going to do my best not to let the job get in the way."

"I care, too," Simon murmured. "We'll figure it out." Simon kissed Vic lightly on the lips. "We can do this our way." He glanced at the clock on the nightstand and saw that it was after midnight. "I know we both have to work tomorrow. Can you stay?"

Vic smiled. "I was planning on it, no matter what happened tonight. Brought a change of clothes. Figured you wouldn't want to be alone."

"You figured right." They moved off the bed just long enough to pull down the covers, then Simon slid inside and held out his hand for Vic to join him. Vic's smile made Simon's heart flutter, and a warm contentment coiled in his belly as Vic slipped beneath the sheet and pressed against his back.

Vic settled an arm over Simon's hip; his fingers splayed possessively over his abdomen. "Sleep tight," Vic murmured against Simon's ear. "I'm here. And I won't let anyone hurt you." Simon fell asleep to that sweet promise, listening to the sound of Vic's breathing and the beat of his heart, and prayed that this was something he could keep.

1 2

VIC

"You're whistling Springsteen. You never whistle," Ross said as Vic walked to their shared desk and hung up his jacket.

"It's a nice day out. Whistling isn't a crime."

"Springsteen isn't meant to be whistled, or hummed," Ross grumbled. He looked up, eyes narrowed, assessing Vic like a crime scene. "Dammit. You slept with him again, didn't you?"

"Since anything I say can and will be used against me, I'm not going to answer that," Vic replied. His leave-taking from Simon that morning had gone much more smoothly than before, with some kisses and a sleepy make-out session that left them both hard and breathless. He had promised to have Simon over to his apartment, although Vic knew it lacked the charm of the blue bungalow and he intended to text at least once during the day.

"Seriously, Vic? There are plenty of fish in the sea—surely some of them aren't crazy."

Vic rounded on him. "You want to back that up, or walk that back?"

Ross's eyes widened at the change in tone. "Whoa, partner! I guess this guy's really gotten under your skin."

"His name is Simon. And, yes, he has," Vic admitted. "And he's not crazy."

"I kinda get the ghost tour thing," Ross said. "It's entertainment, like the pirate show. But if he's claiming to give séances and readings that aren't just putting on a play, then that's either fraud or crazy."

"My nonna could put the Evil Eye on someone," Vic replied, logging into his computer. "Nobody in the neighborhood would cross her."

"That's hardly the same thing."

Vic struggled with himself over the need to defend Simon. He hadn't told Ross about his visit that first day he and Simon met, or his tip about Iryena's ghost. And while the hotel with the blue fish and the light-up palm tree hadn't materialized into a solid lead yet, Vic wasn't ready to give up on it. But if he told Ross, his partner would fault him for revealing police business—or worse, think Simon was somehow involved. So he kept that to himself, at least for now.

"It's a matter of belief," Vic muttered, as he waited for his email to load. "Cause from what I remember out of catechism, the saints had all kinds of visions and heard plenty of voices."

Ross gave him a look. "That's different. At least back off until we catch the Slitter. You don't want rumors to start. Like last time."

Vic glared at him. "I'm well aware. Drop it."

Ross raised his hands in a gesture of surrender. "This is me, dropping it. But don't say I didn't warn you."

Vic knew he shouldn't be more than mildly pissed at Ross; after all, it was a good partner's job to butt in and push back when their counterpart was about to do something stupid. Then again, Vic kept his mouth shut whenever Ross vented about marriage or parenting, aside from a few snarky comebacks. Or maybe Ross's warnings sounded too much like that fatalistic voice in the back of Vic's head that always told him everything was about to go to shit.

He focused his attention on email, opening a file he had requested a couple of days ago. Simon didn't know Vic had spent an evening following him as he ducked in an out of beachfront hotels and touched base with his Skeleton Crew. Vic felt guilty not telling Simon about the recon, but if Simon was determined to play detective, Vic was equally determined to keep an eye on him. He told himself it was to keep Simon safe, but the cop inside wanted proof that Simon was who he claimed to be. Especially now, when Vic knew he cared far more than was prudent and caught himself hoping the relationship might deepen further still.

The file revealed the police record for Marcus Walker, who worked at Gym-tastic. Grew up in foster care, busts for underage drinking, an arrest for weed, cops called to his apartment once for a noise complaint. Nothing damning, but not a sterling resume. The list of arrests for the sex worker who called herself Rennie was much longer. Prostitution, soliciting, disturbing the peace...the busts weren't violent, but she wasn't going to win a citizenship award.

Vic sat back in his chair, staring at the information. He had no way to confirm whether Marcus or Rennie had low-level psychic abilities, as Simon claimed. If they did, and they'd grown up without anyone to train them or help them make sense of the weird things happening to them, he could see how that could get a kid into trouble. But that involved a very big "if," and that key element was something neither Vic nor anyone else could substantiate.

They might just have untreated mental health issues arising from childhood trauma. Vic had seen enough in his time as a cop to know just how much a crappy family life could screw over a person and point them in the wrong direction. Not that it gave someone a free pass for crime, but a bad start certainly made it harder to stay on the proverbial straight and narrow.

What if Simon was wrong—mistaken or misled? What if the misfits he was getting information from, and risking his life to protect, were delusional? Or what if one of them was the Slitter?

Vic felt his chest tighten. *Simon's gift is real. There's no way he could have known about Iryena and Katya. I might not have been around for that bloody horse head or the car that tried to run him over, but I know for sure someone took a shot at him. Why would they, if all this is fake?*

Ross mumbled something about getting more coffee. Vic was glad to have a moment to himself as he tried to sort through the information. His heart wanted to believe Simon. But his head, and his cop training, made him look at all the evidence objectively. Deep down, Vic desperately hoped that the evidence would come down on Simon's side.

He looked at the rest of his email, and saw another new message, from an old friend now working for the Columbia police.

Hi Vic.

Great to hear from you. Myrtle Beach sounds like it's treating you well I called a friend with the university. Off the record. That professor you asked about, Sebastian Kincaide? He taught there for several years, humanities stuff— history, mythology, that kind of thing. Seemed to get on well with the students, was engaged to one of the other professors. What happened to him depends on who you ask.

One group says he was the victim of a witch hunt, because some kid's father got bent out of shape over him telling ghost stories and teaching folklore. But talk to some other folks, and they'll say he was odd, secretive, always going on about strange things. Creepy, even. Big into occult stuff like witches and magic, not just stories, but like he believed it was real. Hard at this point to figure out the rumors three years later, but the wilder tales about sacrificing cats and dancing around bonfires are probably hearsay. Although, I don't know, man. It sounds like he was into some weird stuff. What'd he do, kill someone?

Keep in touch. Brad.

Vic's chest tightened. He knew how unreliable hearsay was, and how once someone was singled out, others would pile on, inventing wild stories to get attention. South Carolina was still part of the Bible Belt, and claims that someone teaching folktales might be subverting young minds wasn't as impossible to believe as Vic might wish. He didn't think it was likely that Simon was inducting students into a secret coven or trying to summon eldritch monsters. But did he have a clear grasp on what was real and what wasn't? Could his love for the subject matter have clouded his judgment?

Vic wanted to believe he was a better judge of character than that, but he knew he'd been fooled before. Yet Simon had answered all of his questions, shared his information, and provided tips that panned out. Vic saw how scared Simon had been after the attacks, and seen the damage inflicted with his own eyes. No, he refused to credit the naysayers. Simon's story about what happened at the university made sense, and Brad hadn't found anything to prove it wrong. He was going to put his money on Simon, unless or until something could prove he should do otherwise.

Vic pulled out his phone. *Day going well so far?*

Hard to beat the early morning.

Vic smiled, remembering the warmth of waking up with Simon in his arms, and the burn of Simon's stubble against his cheek. *Agree. Dinner at my place?*

I don't close up until 7. That okay?

I rarely get home earlier. See you at 7:30?

Sure. What can I bring?

Just yourself. For dessert, Vic added. Simon returned a few smileys, along with a couple of eggplant emojis.

"Geez, you're as bad as my kid sister," Ross growled, returning to his desk.

"Have you had your blood pressure checked lately?" Vic asked with contrived innocence. "Or maybe get checked for a blocked colon? What next? Tell me to get off your lawn?"

"You're pushing your luck, D'Amato," Ross muttered. "Just keep your wits about you with this psychic guy—"

"Simon."

"Simon," Ross repeated. "Maybe cool things down until the investigation is over?"

"And then what? Because there's always going to be another investigation." Vic leaned back. He didn't want to argue. Ross was a good partner, and while they weren't best friends, they worked well together and got along most of the time. "See, I'm thinking that's how people end up like Mosley and Dawson, forty years on the force, no partner, no kids, no friends," he replied, mentioning two of the department's longest-tenured officers.

"There's a reason cops don't tend to stay married," Ross said and shrugged. "We're not easy to live with, and neither is the job."

"You're managing."

Ross sighed. "And it's harder than it looks. We promised each other we'd get up every morning and fight to keep what we've got one day at a time."

Vic felt a pang of jealousy at the thought of sharing that level of commitment with a partner. Could he and Simon be like that? He'd moved in with Nate, largely because it was convenient. But they had never discussed the future, certainly never contemplated marriage. Vic hadn't spent much time thinking about a forever partner, at least not once he realized that he wouldn't ever have a big traditional Catholic wedding like his siblings had.

But having someone to go home to at night and wake up with in the morning, the same someone? Vic thought he could get used to that. And while it was far too early to have any thoughts like that about Simon, Vic surprised himself to find that the possibility didn't panic him.

"Earth to Vic!" Ross said, clapping his hands in front of Vic's face. "Geez, you really are a poor besotted fool, aren't you?"

"Fuck off." Vic's voice lacked heat, although his cheeks colored at being caught daydreaming.

"Yeah, I'm right," Ross replied with a grin. "Just do me a favor and keep your wits about you, so you don't get canned. You don't fart like my last partner. And Jonesy's new partner sweats like a stuck pig."

"See, I'm a diamond in the rough," Vic teased.

"You're rough, all right." Ross stretched and flexed his shoulders. "You got anything new on the case?"

Vic refused to glance at the two emails in his inbox. "Nothing that pans out. There's got to be something we're missing. Guys like the Slitter always slip up."

Ross gestured toward the piles of paper on his desk. "He's got his pick of J-ones, and we're trying to play catch-up."

"Are we sure all the deaths are foreign help?" Vic asked, thinking back to Simon's theory that the real common factor was untrained psychic talent. He had no idea how to come up with a reason Ross would accept, but maybe they could find a pattern aside from a fondness for easy kills.

"You know something?"

Vic shook his head. "Just found myself thinking they were all seasonals, and then thought I'd better fact-check."

"Good point. Let me look." Ross pulled up a file and checked down through it. "Seven kills over six months, but the last three have been closer together than the first several. Like maybe he's preparing for something? Nobody's figured out a pattern for where the bodies have been found, except that he likes parking garages. Ah...here's the list." He frowned as he read the names silently. "You're right. Two weren't J-ones."

"What about missing persons in the same period?" Vic asked. "The foreign workers can't leave without defaulting on their visas. So if they go missing, they might be victims we haven't found. Has anyone figured out what the two who weren't seasonals have in common?"

Ross scanned the report again, though Vic knew the two of them had read it many times. "Nope. So guess what we're gonna do for the rest of the afternoon?"

Seven thirty found Vic fidgeting, waiting for a knock at the door. He had texted Simon his address earlier in the day and decided at the last minute to pick up Pad Thai for dinner rather than fail at cooking for company. In the half hour after he got home from work, he tore through the apartment to clean up, make the bed, check to confirm that condoms and lube were in the nightstand drawer—just in case—got a shower and ran the vacuum. If Ross could see him, he'd be laughing his ass off.

He'd turned on music—a Springsteen list from one of the streaming services—and the familiar songs eased his nerves.

Vic looked around his apartment, wondering how Simon would see it. Compared to the blue bungalow, the sleek lines and modern furnishings looked stark, cold, and impersonal. Now that he thought about it, he'd put out very few personal photos or knick-knacks. He had his TV/stereo/gaming console set up in the living room, with a decent library of favorites. But he'd switched to downloading or streaming music, movies, and games when he moved from Pittsburgh, just like he'd moved very few of his paper books and given in and bought a Kindle. That left his shelves a little too bare.

And maybe that was the heart of the matter, Vic thought, punching one of the throw pillows on his leather couch to fluff it up. Maybe he'd never unpacked himself after Pittsburgh, just like he hadn't bothered unboxing his things. Was he waiting for the other shoe to drop? For something to go wrong here, like it did before? Or holding himself in reserve, keeping himself safe by not committing all the way?

He heard the knock at the door, and couldn't help smoothing a hand down his t-shirt and stealing a quick glance in the mirror. Simon waited in the doorway, looking completely edible in a dark green t-shirt and a pair of worn jeans that left little to the imagination. He held out a bottle of wine and a potted orchid.

"I didn't know if you had a vase," Simon said when he handed the plant to Vic. "So I got something that didn't need one." Then he took the initiative to stretch up and kiss Vic on the mouth as he stepped inside.

"Thanks," Vic said, taking the wine and orchid and setting them aside. He locked the door behind Simon, then drew him close for a proper kiss, long and lingering, letting his tongue explore Simon's mouth, attuning himself to the other man's quiet moans when their bodies brushed together just so.

Vic slid his hands down Simon's back, liking the firm muscles beneath the soft shirt. He cupped Simon's ass with both hands and smiled into the kiss as Simon slid his hands into Vic's back pockets.

Vic's stomach growled, and they pulled apart, flushed and breathless, then they both laughed. "I guess we ought to have dinner," he said with a grin.

"I'm holding you to dessert," Simon said with a wicked smile. "Been thinking about that all day."

Vic gave his ass a squeeze. "Oh, really?"

Simon pinched him lightly through the denim. "I've got all kinds of ideas," he said, and the look in his eyes made it clear how those options ended. Vic found himself hard and his mouth dry.

"Let's eat," he managed, and Simon looked triumphant at flustering him.

Vic took his lover's hand and led him into the living room. "Well, what do you think? This is it. Kitchen's over there," he said, pointing to the small galley area with a raised bar that was not fully separated from the loft-style living area. "Bathroom and two bedrooms are that way," he added, gesturing in the opposite direction, toward a partition wall that separated the public and private space.

"Modern, clean, very nice," Simon said, glancing around. "Streamlined."

Vic cleared his throat. "I have a bunch of personal stuff I just never got around to unpacking," he added, feeling as if he needed to explain. "I hit the ground running at work when I moved here, and the only company I have is when the guys come over to watch the game, or play poker and they don't care—"

"No explanation needed," Simon said, kissing him on the cheek. "Now, you said something about food?"

Vic removed two bowls of spicy noodles with chicken from the oven where he'd left them warming, then opened the bottle of wine Simon brought, and poured them each a glass. He felt strangely awkward, being on a date in his own home as if he were trying to be on his best behavior.

Simon, on the other hand, looked completely at ease. If he thought the place lacked any of the personality and charm of his bungalow, he didn't show it, and after an initial glance around, he kept his attention focused on Vic.

Supper conversation stayed light, remarking on the weather, complaining about traffic, and commenting on the status of the area's never-ending construction projects. Through it all, Simon joked and flirted, and Vic flirted back, finding excuses to brush their fingers together or touch the other man's hand, bumping knees or feet under the table, making eye contact. It felt strange and wonderful at the same time, and Vic never wanted it to end.

"So tell me about your family," Simon said as he helped Vic clear their plates from the table after they had demolished their servings. "Is that their picture in the living room?"

Vic nodded. One of the few items he had unpacked was a photo of the whole D'Amato clan, taken right before he left Pittsburgh. "We're a loud, rowdy bunch, three generations of cops, with a few other black sheep thrown in. Those black sheep are the teacher, the pastry chef, and a lawyer since they strayed from the family profession."

"Utterly shameful," Simon teased. "So you've got a big family?"

Vic shrugged. "Pittsburgh Italian Catholic. Five kids. That seems big nowadays, but both of my parents were one of ten, so they thought they settled for a small family. We could fill a park shelter just with the cousins!"

"Sounds like fun," Simon said, a wistful note in his voice. "It was just my brother and me. He's five years older. We weren't close. I think I met my cousins on either side of the family once or twice in my life. My parents weren't big on get-togethers."

"It was a good thing we had so many cops in the family because our Fourth of July picnic got kinda loud," Vic remembered with a smile.

"You must miss them. Do you go back often?" Simon asked.

Vic looked away. "I do miss them. But it's a long way from here, and the weather sucks for half of the year. I go back now and then, and I call my mom or she gets worried. Everyone else, I hear from on email."

"I hear from mine on birthdays and Christmas," Simon confessed. "We aren't close. And what happened at the university just seemed to make things worse."

"That wasn't your fault." Vic reached out to take his hand. But he remembered the tone of Brad's email from earlier in the day.

How many others had said the same thing, or worse, as the scandal unfolded, and how much had that betrayal scarred Simon?

"It was the wrong place to try to be open about a lot of things," Simon said. "So far, Myrtle Beach has been a lot more welcoming."

They went into the living room and settled on the black leather couch. Vic had always loved the couch because it was long enough for him to lie down, and the soft leather conformed to his body. Simon sat next to him, and Vic slipped an arm around his shoulders, letting Simon rest his head against him.

"Dinner was good," Simon said, in a warm, relaxed voice that made Vic half hard just listening to him. "Thanks."

"It's my favorite Thai place," Vic replied, absently toying with Simon's hair. He noticed that after his comment about liking Simon's hair down, the ghost guide had shown up tonight with it cascading around his shoulders. The realities of Vic's job demanded that he keep his own hair short, but he found himself utterly intrigued with Simon's thick, chestnut waves.

"I've got an Indian place I need to take you," Simon murmured from against his chest. "Kind of a nice change from all the burgers and seafood." Myrtle Beach catered to tourists on vacation, and while the shore was a great place for fresh crab, fish, and other delicacies, those who lived there year-round soon craved variety.

"Sounds like a plan," Vic replied, enjoying the feel of Simon, warm and solid against him. In just the short time he and Simon had been seeing each other, Vic already realized how much had been missing from his relationship with Nate. Nate hadn't liked being openly affectionate or looking like a couple in public, and he tended to touch Vic only when he wanted to have sex. Vic liked the casual contact that seemed to come naturally to Simon, the easy, unapologetic way they moved together, even though they were still so new in whatever this thing was between them.

Relationship, Vic told himself. *It's called a "relationship" and it's what happens when you start falling for someone.* He wasn't ready to use the "L" word yet, and he didn't think Simon was either, but it no longer seemed impossible to imagine that the attraction—hell, the magnetism—between them could grow into something deeper. Something more permanent.

"I seem to remember that you promised me dessert," Simon said, and let his hand slide down to cup Vic's crotch. "You know that false advertising is illegal."

"We wouldn't want to break the law," Vic replied with a sexy chuckle, drawing Simon toward him. Christ, he was perfect, with his hazel eyes already wide and dark with desire, his lips pink and swollen from kissing, and his fingers teasing up Vic's inseam and dipping down between his legs to stroke his balls. Vic was already painfully hard, and he knew from the bulge rubbing against his thigh that Simon was very ready for the next step as well.

"Come here," Vic growled, pulling Simon onto his lap. Simon was a couple of inches shorter and not as heavily built, but he was all lean muscle, and the memory of how good he had looked naked made Vic's pulse race. He pushed a thigh between Simon's legs, letting the other man rub off on him, getting his own satisfying friction against Simon's leg, rutting against each other as they kissed.

Simon's hands slid up Vic's chest, exploring the hard muscles, tweaking his nipples beneath his t-shirt. He bent and traced the swirls on the tattoo sleeve with his tongue. Vic's breath caught. No one had ever done that before. He'd gotten the tats after he left Pittsburgh, part of creating a new life, and he hadn't taken a real lover since then. Simon took his time, exploring the dark ink, sometimes with the very tip of his tongue, other times with the flat or even the side, all of it intimate and erotic. Vic wondered if he could come just from watching Simon follow every scroll and detail as if committing the pattern to memory.

Simon glanced at him. The sight of those hazel eyes giving a knowing look from beneath his lashes nearly undid Vic. "Do you like it when I do this?" Simon's voice was whiskey-rough, with the hint of a smile that said he knew exactly what his attention was doing to his lover.

"Fuck, yes. That's...real good."

Simon licked a few more of the geometric designs, tasting the salty skin beneath the pattern, following the outline with his tongue and lips. "I want to do this for all your ink," he promised. "Memorize you with my tongue."

Shit, Vic was in trouble, because he already felt closer to creaming his jeans than he had since he was a teenager. He brushed the knuckles of his right hand against Simon's cheek, fluttered the touch against his throat and collarbone, and then let his fingers glide down Simon's back, toying with the tender skin right above his waistband.

"I'd like that," Vic managed to stammer, too aroused to care if his voice wasn't entirely steady. Damn, he loved what Simon did to him, brought out in him, things he never thought he'd find comfortable and now discovered he did not want to live without.

Simon paused long enough to strip off his shirt, exposing that toned chest and a dusting of dark hairs. Vic pulled his shirt over his head, and Simon stared at his tats like they were their very own erogenous zone. Shit, Vic hadn't thought he might have a lover with a tattoo kink; the designs had been strictly for himself. But he wouldn't turn down that added bonus, not when Simon looked ready to devour him.

Vic's phone rang, in the shrill tone reserved for work.

"Sorry, I've got to take this," Vic said, as Simon shimmied off him, back to the couch where he watched, curled up with his knees in front of him, as Vic reached for his phone.

Ross's voice sounded harsh and fast. "Gotta go. Grab your coat. Parking attendant just called in a body. Sounds like the Slitter again."

Vic looked up, meeting Simon's eyes. He saw the same disappointment there that he felt, and a frustration he bet matched his own. "I'm sorry," he said when the call ended. "It goes with the job."

Simon leaned forward and kissed him. "I understand. Just be careful." He stood, all graceful, lean muscle, and reached for his shirt, pulling it on and then shaking his head to free his hair. "Call me, okay? I'll worry."

Vic had already gotten his shirt on, and he pulled Simon to him by his belt loops, kissing him again, a promise. "I'll call. You drove here?"

Simon nodded. "Yeah. Didn't think you'd want me walking back late."

"Next time, figure on staying," Vic said, as he collected his wallet from the side table, then went into the bedroom to retrieve his gun and holster, shouldering into the rig like a second skin.

"That's hot as hell," Simon said, eyeing Vic and then heading for the door. "Happy hunting." He shut the door behind him, and Vic closed his eyes, taking a minute to shift gears from being a few minutes away from a night of hot sex into the headspace to go look at a corpse.

Vic angled his motorcycle into the parking garage where Ross had said to meet him. The lower level was already swarming with police, and Vic flashed his badge, then parked his bike and followed a patrol officer's directions to the rear of the fourth floor.

The smell of blood had already drawn flies, a given with the South Carolina heat. Vic pushed through the crowd of police and the forensics crew to find Ross, who stood off to one side, letting the others do their jobs. Vic paused as he passed the dead woman.

Cindy, the stripper from Fox and Hound, lay in a pool of blood. He didn't need the lab team to tell him that the pattern of knife wounds matched the Slitter's signature.

"Want to tell me why dispatch says you ran her through the system, before anyone filed a missing persons report?" Ross asked, giving Vic a hard look.

"I got a tip from someone that she hadn't shown up for work, and they were afraid she was in danger."

Ross gave him the stare he usually reserved for perps in interrogation. "Try again. Because a homicide detective doesn't usually go out of his way to run down details on a stripper who isn't even dead yet, just because she didn't turn up for her shift. Especially when I know you aren't sleeping with her."

Vic pulled Ross over to one side, where they were less likely to be overheard. "Simon has a loose network...of acquaintances...who he says all have minor abilities—"

"Psychic abilities?" Ross pressed.

"Yeah," Vic replied. "Not enough to do much with, but enough to screw up their lives. Since he hasn't been able to come up with any solid leads with his own gifts, he figured he'd ask around, see if one of these acquaintances had seen something that might be important."

"You brought your ghost whisperer boyfriend in on a case?" Ross growled, face coloring with anger. That rankled with Vic, who felt his temper flare.

"Lots of cops have used psychics to get a break when they hit a dead end," Vic countered. "There are psychics who work with police departments all over the country. It's not like we've got this sewn up on our own."

"They get clearance, D'Amato. They don't just go to some fortune teller on the boardwalk and divulge confidential police information!"

"Back that right the hell up," Vic argued. "First of all, I didn't divulge anything confidential. The city PR people might be trying to keep a lid on the news, but everyone knows about the Slitter, and they've figured out we haven't caught him yet. And second, Simon isn't a fortune teller."

"He's a fraud, and he's going to take you down with him if you're not careful, Vic. Do you know what the Captain would say if he found out you consulted with a guy who gives ghost tours—let alone started sleeping with him?"

"Who I sleep with is no one's business."

"It is when it could compromise an ongoing investigation," Ross snapped.

"So I'm the first detective to go to questionable sources? Really? How many junkies and dealers and thugs are we paying as informants? And you're mad because I went to a business owner who might have connections we could use?"

"Connections with ghosts!" Ross retorted. "He talks to invisible people."

"He was right about Cindy." Vic knew he was walking a dangerous line. If he told Ross about Simon's visions, his foreknowledge of Iryena's death and his link, however circumstantial, to Katya, he could end up making Simon a suspect. But if he protected his source, and the information came out later, both Simon and Vic could be in for a rough time.

"It's like you want to blow up your career all over again!" Ross threw up his hands.

"We canvas people who might have seen something or know something all the time," Vic said, barely keeping his anger in check. "Sometimes, we give a little info to get a little new info. That's how it works. I saw a chance to get a break, and I took it. It's no different than what we do every day."

"I can only cover for you so far, Vic," Ross warned. "I want to give you the benefit of the doubt. And I will...for now. But I won't sacrifice my badge just because you're not thinking with your upstairs brain. You hear me?"

"Loud and clear." Vic turned away. He was furious with Ross for not trusting him, and underneath that, angry with himself for creating a situation that could get ugly fast. Part of him was pissed at Simon because his involvement complicated everything. *I didn't have to get involved. I'm the one who went looking for him. He's only tried to help—and nearly got killed for it.*

Vic walked a few steps down the outer side of the garage, trying to get his emotions under control while the photographers and forensics team finished. He looked out at the view of the taillights on King's Highway, the wall of lit-up high rise hotels along the beach, and the neon mayhem of signage that lined the road.

This particular garage sat next to an older hotel which could boast about low rates even if it couldn't offer a beachfront location, and a high rise closed for renovations. As Vic walked along the outer wall of the garage, he looked down, getting a unique aerial perspective of the hotel pool below.

The pool was in the shape of a huge blue fish, surrounded by palm trees spangled with white sparkling lights. Across the street, a garish sign enticed shoppers to Big Al's Beachwear, with a caricature of a man with a huge nose.

"Gos-teen-eetsa." "Bolshoy-noss." The Russian words Simon had

reported from Iryena's ghost rang in his ears as he looked down on a match too perfect to be coincidence. Vic intended to run with it, see if that meant the Slitter had his bolt hole somewhere close. But he knew what Ross would say. Ross would turn his attention to Simon, not as an informant, but a suspect. The cop in Vic knew Ross had a point, much as his heart fought that conclusion. Maybe he did need to keep a little distance, for Simon's sake—and his own.

13

SIMON

"Quinn Radnor doesn't work here anymore," the big man at the mini-golf clubhouse told Simon the following evening. "He just up and quit, said he needed to get out of town for a while." The man shrugged. "He didn't say where, and I didn't ask."

Simon nodded, feeling the worry ratchet up. "All right. Thanks, man."

"Do you know if he's in trouble?"

Simon hadn't expected concern from the mini-golf manager. Plenty of people came and went in Myrtle Beach, and jobs like this, handing out clubs and balls at a golf course, turned over quickly. "I don't think Quinn did anything wrong," Simon said carefully. "But I think he might have been afraid, with all the stuff that's been happening."

"You mean that Slitter guy," the large man said. "Hell, who ain't afraid of him? But I thought he just killed women?"

Simon sighed. "I don't know why Quinn ran. He isn't answering his phone."

The manager looked as if he were debating something, and then met Simon's gaze. "If you talk to him, tell him to come back, and

I'll find shifts for him. I liked that kid, and he always did a good job."

"Thank you," Simon replied, now more sure than ever Quinn had fled because of the killer. "If I find him, I'll let him know."

Simon had given Quinn a ride back to his apartment once and remembered where he lived. That was his next stop, and when he saw the light on inside, his heart rose. But an unfamiliar young man came to the door.

"Quinn? He grabbed his stuff and bugged out of here like his ass was on fire two days ago," the man said. "Paid us the rent for the rest of the month, and said he'd let us know if he decided to come back." He shook his head. "You looking for a place to stay? We've got an open bunk."

"No, thanks," Simon said. "I'm a friend of Quinn's, and I'm just worried about him. Did he say where he was going?"

The man's eyes narrowed. "Are you a cop?"

"No. Like I said, a friend."

"He didn't stay to talk," the roommate said. "He looked freaked out, but he wouldn't answer any questions except to say that he didn't know if he was going to come back."

"And he took everything?"

"Yeah, which makes me think we can rent out his half of the room," the man replied. "Tell your friends. It's a nice place."

The small apartment had at least four men living in a space meant for two. "I'll keep it in mind," Simon replied as he turned away.

"Hey, are you Simon?" a new voice called to him before he had gotten down the sidewalk.

"Yeah, why?"

"Quinn said to tell you 'black and red, like lava.' Does that make any sense to you?"

"Sort of," Simon replied. But the important thing was, to someone like Quinn who saw auras, it would have made perfect sense. Quinn had glimpsed the Slitter by his aura and run for his life. "Thanks."

Simon headed home, deciding against trying to touch base with his crew tonight. He had seen the news account about Cindy's death, and now With Quinn's disappearance, he feared that he might draw attention to the very people he was trying to protect. Simon had another purpose in mind. It had been a few days since he had attempted to contact the ghosts, and instinct told him he needed to do so soon.

He grumbled under his breath as he wove through Myrtle Beach traffic. Simon appreciated Vic's concern and knew that he was right to drive instead of walk, but he hated the stop and go crawl. Still, it gave him time to think, since he had nothing to do but stare at the tail lights ahead of him.

Vic had texted him today, but he had seemed distracted and deflected Simon's questions about the incident that had called him out the previous night, which Simon guessed had been finding Cindy's body. Simon tried not to let it raise his fears about whether Vic had second thoughts about getting more serious. Vic had been caring and protective, thoughtful and attentive, and while Simon knew Vic wasn't completely on board yet with the psychic stuff, he knew the other man was making a real effort to understand. And as much as Simon cursed the phone call that interrupted their love-making, he knew that he'd need to learn to accept that kind of thing if he intended to be a cop's partner.

He pulled into the carport and took a good look around to assure the way was clear before sprinting to the front door. Simon let out a long breath once he was inside and the door was locked. Even so, he switched on all the lights and made a quick inspection before he felt truly safe.

Simon appreciated being invited over to Vic's apartment, but he much preferred the vibe of the bungalow. Vic's place was upscale and modern, but impersonal. It made Simon wonder how much of himself Vic was used to sharing with someone else, and how accustomed the cop had become to keeping his personal life out of view in the course of his job. Simon had lived through hiding parts of who he was, and he remembered how dislocated it made him feel, as if he'd lopped off part of himself. Did Vic feel incomplete keeping so much of himself hidden, or was he so used to it by now that he no longer noticed?

Simon didn't question whether Vic cared. He'd seen that clearly in his lover's touch, in his eyes, in his kisses. He wasn't certain that Vic was as far gone on him as he was on Vic, but that would resolve itself in time. Simon had already admitted to himself that he was in love with Vic…whether or not the cop was ready to hear that, or accept it. And that made the whole Slitter mess even worse because Simon felt sure that at some point, his sleuthing was going to run afoul of Vic's by-the-book approach, and that was a recipe for trouble.

But not tonight. Tonight, Simon intended to eat dinner and then see if the spirits would heed his call.

You home? Vic's text made Simon's phone buzz.

Eating dinner. You?

Still at work. Door locked?

Yep. Even drove the car today. Parking's a bitch.

Yeah, well. You in for the evening?

Planning to be. You want to come over?

Wish I could. Gonna be here late. Just…be careful.

You too.

Simon waited for further conversation, and when none came, he set the phone aside, feeling an odd pang of loneliness. His relationship with Vic had already progressed farther and faster than he had dared hope at the beginning, but past experience warned him not to expect a smooth ride. Still, he'd caught himself daydreaming about being with Vic this summer, or at the holidays…the kind of future plans he'd rarely made, not even with Jacen. Thinking about the future with Vic came easy, and Simon fervently hoped that the possibility wasn't just in his imagination.

A quick meal of leftover pizza later, Simon put his dish in the sink and went into the living room. He didn't need much to open himself to the spirits, just a quiet space, a point of focus, and his willingness to open the door to the other side. Simon lit a candle and a bundle of sage and sweetgrass and set them in glass holders on the coffee table, then settled on the couch and got comfortable.

He took several long, deep breaths, centering himself and running what he thought of as a "self diagnostic" to make sure he was properly attuned for spirit work. That meant letting go of any anger, worry, negative thoughts, or doubts that would cloud his vision. Simon tried to clear his mind as he breathed, and gradually he felt his shoulders loosen, and then little by little, the rest of his body.

The smell of the sage and sweetgrass grounded Simon, making him feel safe. He reinforced his mental wardings, the psychic barriers that helped him remain in control of the conversation and protected him from spirits that might be angry or aggressive. Finally, when he was relaxed enough to go into a trance, he closed his eyes and sent out his energy, calling out to the ghosts, asking for their help.

His breath caught when Quinn Radnor appeared.

"Damn, Quinn. What happened?" Simon felt a stab of grief at the young man's death. It was unusual for such a fresh kill to manifest as a ghost, but Quinn had always been a stubborn man, determined to make his way. Simon had the distinct impression Quinn was fighting to make himself seen and get his message heard.

Red and black. Simon's gift didn't lie in seeing auras, the energy vibrations given off by all living things, but Quinn had a talent for it. The image Quinn's ghost conveyed showed a man with a baseball cap and sunglasses, face still in shadows, but limned with gray and crimson that pulsed like a lava flow. The picture vanished, replaced by a close-up of a man's hands. A lattice of pink scars covered the pale skin, branching like lightning. The scars flowed across the backs of both hands, veining over the fingers and twining up the wrists.

"Blood and souls," Simon heard himself say as Quinn's spirit wavered. "Beyond the limit." With that, Quinn's ghost vanished, and Simon found himself alone.

Before the vision could fade completely from Simon's mind, he grabbed a piece of paper, traced one hand and then the other, and recreated the pattern of the branching scars as best he could. Then he sat back and looked at the drawing. The Slitter could hide his face, but it would be very hard to hide his hands, here in a place where the weather never required gloves. Someone must have seen a man with hands like this and remembered such unusual markings.

Simon felt a surge of excitement at the lead, followed by a crashing wave of guilt. Quinn was dead. Simon closed his eyes and took several deep breaths, trying to deal with his grief. Quinn wasn't a close friend, hardly more than an acquaintance, but Simon had felt responsible for him, at least when it came to magic. He had tried to be a mentor to Quinn and the rest of his Skeleton Crew, insofar as they would let him, and instead of helping them be better able to use their magic, Simon wondered if he had somehow drawn a killer right to them.

The cops couldn't do anything with Quinn's tip about the Slitter's aura. The words "blood and souls" were the same as what Iryena's ghost had shared days ago, confirming to Simon that the Slitter had some occult purpose behind his killing. Did he hate people with "magic"—psychic gifts? Or was he trying to steal their power, to prepare for some bigger attack? Either way, the cops wouldn't be able to make sense of the verbal tip. But the scars, that might be a solid lead.

Simon debated calling Vic, and decided against it. Vic had said he was working late, and he might even be dealing with Quinn's murder. He didn't need to confront Simon's "woo-woo" on top of everything else. But Simon could still report the lead...just not to Vic.

He got in his car—Vic would be happy he drove, if he ever found out—and went to Jackalope's, a local dive bar about half a mile away. It wasn't one of Simon's favorite hang-outs, but he did recall seeing an old fashioned pay phone in the back by the men's room and hoped it was still in service. He looked up the number for the police anonymous tip line on his cell and then juggled enough change to use the old wall phone. To his relief, a recorded line answered, and asked him to leave his tip at the beep.

"Quinn Radnor has gone missing, after reporting a stranger creeping him out," Simon said, muffling his voice. "Look for a man with branching pink scars over both hands. He's the Slitter."

With that, he hung up, glanced around to make sure no one was watching, and just for good measure, wiped off the handle and mouthpiece of the pay phone before sauntering back out to his car. The whole adventure probably took fifteen minutes, but Simon's heart pounded the entire time, certain he would either be accosted by the police or ambushed by the Slitter.

When he was back inside his house, doors locked and lights on, Simon collapsed onto the couch. "I'll find him, Quinn," he said to the empty room, hoping Quinn could hear him. "And I passed along your message. You did good."

The next morning, before the shop opened, Simon had just made a fresh pot of coffee when his phone buzzed.

You at the shop? Vic asked.

Yeah, why?

I'm outside. Can I come in?

Simon headed to the front, knowing that it was at least an hour before he was due to open, which might mean Vic had already gone by the house. He had a feeling this wasn't just about Vic missing him.

"You're out early," Simon said as he let Vic in. He leaned in for a quick kiss, which Vic returned. Then he locked the door behind him and gestured for Vic to follow him to the kitchenette. "Coffee?"

"Sure," Vic replied, leaning against the counter. He accepted the cup from Simon with a tired smile. "Sorry I haven't been around."

"You've got a big job," Simon replied. "It goes with the deal."

Vic took a sip of his coffee, and the met Simon's eyes. "I might be able to keep you out of trouble if I were home more."

Simon's smile faltered. "What kind of trouble do you mean?"

Vic set the cup aside with a sigh. "You called in that tip last night, about Quinn Radnor and the scars, didn't you?"

Simon was certain Vic wasn't pleased, but he didn't want to lie and make it worse. "Yeah. I went by his work to ask him a question, and the boss said he'd quit without warning. His roommates told me he took everything and ran." He debated mentioning the aura and decided to tell the whole truth. Even if Vic didn't believe him, he wouldn't be able to say that Simon hid evidence.

"Quinn had left them a message for me. About the man's aura being 'black and red.' That means anger and violence," Simon explained. "He must have seen the Slitter, glimpsed his aura, and it freaked him, so he ran. When I came home, I tried to contact the spirits. I've been attempting to keep an open channel in case any of the victims have something they want to tell me. Instead, I got Quinn."

"Quinn's ghost?" Vic clarified, eyes narrowing and going into cop mode.

Simon nodded. "He must be newly dead, because his spirit was having a lot of trouble making the connection. But he told me 'blood and souls' like the other ghost said, and he gave me an image of a man's hands, criss-crossed with scars." He pulled a copy of the drawing from his pocket and handed it to Vic.

Vic studied the paper and scrubbed a hand over his eyes. "The tip got handed to me because Ross and I are on the Slitter case. I didn't have to recognize your voice to know it was you. Payphone?"

"I drove," Simon mumbled, not looking up.

"Thanks for that," Vic replied sarcastically. "At least you're listening to half of what I tell you."

Simon looked up, searching Vic's face to figure out just how angry he was. Vic's expression was worried, not furious, and Simon took cold comfort in that. "I do listen. I've been driving everywhere, even though it's a pain in the ass. I didn't expect anything bad to have happened to Quinn, and I certainly didn't know he was going to be murdered."

"I know," Vic said, closing his eyes and shaking his head. "Just… try to see how this looks from the other side. You know things that you shouldn't. You were right about Cindy—"

Simon looked up sharply. "When?" he asked, although he was certain he already knew the answer.

"That was the call I got when you were at my place," Vic replied tiredly. "I'm sorry."

Simon slammed his fist into the small table. "I wanted to protect her—"

"You had a connection to Katya—"

"I met her once, for ten minutes."

"You knew Cindy, and now Quinn."

Simon met Vic's eyes. "Am I a suspect?" He saw pain and uncertainty in Vic's gaze.

"No. But if you keep showing up in the wrong places with the right information, I'm going to have to report it. I'm pushing 'confidential informant' boundaries to the limit," Vic said.

Simon felt his chest tighten. All he'd wanted to do was help find a killer and protect the people around him, and now he'd jeopardized Vic's trust, and possibly destroyed their budding relationship. "Vic, I—"

"They found Quinn's body this morning, behind a bar called 'The Limit,'" Vic said and frowned as Simon flinched. "What?"

"Quinn told me 'blood and souls,'" Simon said quietly. "But he also said 'beyond the limit.'" I didn't know what that meant, I never thought about it being a place instead of a boundary."

"Fuck! Simon, you've got to stop playing detective!" Vic growled. "Don't you get it? If the Slitter wanted a perfect fall guy, he couldn't do better than you."

Simon shivered, cold with the realization that Vic was right, at least for how it could look to the cops. "I don't think he wants to set me up," Simon said quietly. "I think he wants me dead."

Anger and protectiveness sparked in Vic's eyes. "All the more reason to stay out of it," Vic argued. "Please, Simon. Listen to me. I...care about you. I want to see where this thing between us goes, I really do. But it doesn't do anyone any good if I get kicked off the force because I'm shielding you. And if it were any other cop, you'd probably be down at headquarters for questioning."

"You believe me?" Simon asked, fearing the answer.

"God help me, but yes, I do. Against all common sense," Vic admitted. "I just want you to stay safe, and stay out of trouble. Leave the job to the police."

"The cops don't usually pay attention to people like Quinn and

Cindy and Katya," Simon said quietly. "Not until they're dead. And they won't listen to anything that comes from their gifts."

Vic pinched the bridge of his nose as if fending off a headache. "I don't want to fight with you," he said quietly, and moved over into Simon's space, taking the cup from his hands and setting it aside, then settling his hands on Simon's hips. "I want to protect you, find the killer, and keep my job. Two of those you can help me with."

Simon managed a faint smile. "Best two out of three?"

"Not funny."

"What about the ghosts?" Simon asked. "They can't talk to the police. Who speaks for them, if I don't? And the workers down here on the boardwalk—they won't talk to the cops. If they're not J-ones and scared about being deported, they've got reasons they don't want the police looking at them too closely." Simon and Vic both might have come to Myrtle Beach to outrun their pasts, but for many people without the luck of an education or a profession, they merely drifted or ran until they hit the ocean, and waited for their old mistakes to catch up with them.

"What did you have in mind?" Vic asked, looking as if it pained him to speak the words.

"Let me take the drawing around to the shops and bars on the boardwalk, where people know me," Simon suggested. "I've already started a neighborhood watch with the other shopkeepers, trying to look out for the hat guy. If anyone recognizes the scars, they're more likely to tell me than to tell a uniform."

Vic was silent for so long Simon feared he might explode, and then Vic closed his eyes and sighed. "All right," he said quietly. "Just on the boardwalk, not all over town," he cautioned. "Because I can't stop you from doing that. And I think you're right about the trust issue."

"Thank you." Simon slipped his arms around Vic's waist and pressed himself against his lover's chest, nestling his head beneath the taller man's chin. He was afraid for a moment that Vic would step away, and then Vic tightened his hold, moving his hands to grip Simon's back and draw him closer.

"Be careful," Vic murmured. "I don't want you to get hurt, and I don't want you to get arrested. Just...try to stay out of trouble? Please?"

"I'll try," Simon replied because that much was true. He had no desire to cause problems, for himself or Vic. "Can you come by tonight?"

Vic shook his head. "I barely got out of there long enough to come over here, and Ross will be on my ass about it when I get back. I'm going to be pretty tied up for a while. I'll text, but we'll have to play the rest by ear." He lifted a finger to trace Simon's jaw. "Not forever, I promise."

"I'll hold you to that," Simon said, and this time it was Vic who leaned in for the kiss. His lips were warm, and he tasted like coffee and mints, but he pulled back before their clinch could become more.

"Be careful," Vic warned one more time as he reluctantly let go and headed for the door. "I mean it."

"You, too," Simon echoed, watching as Vic let himself out and headed down the boardwalk.

He glanced at his phone. Still half an hour until the shop was due to open. Time enough to run down to Mizzenmast Coffee and see if Tracey could help him make sense of the jumble in his heart and his head.

When Simon got to Le Miz, the line was no worse than he expected, but Tracey was not behind the counter. He got in the queue but had barely moved forward when he looked up and saw her motioning to him from the back room. Curious, Simon left the line to follow her into the pirate room.

"I wondered when you'd show up," Tracey said, and then ducked into the kitchen and returned with two cups of coffee. "I came in early to do paperwork, and so Lana's covering the front. Come with me," she ordered, and Simon followed her into the tiny office that barely had room for a desk and two chairs. "Sit. And tell me what's going on with you."

Simon caught her up on everything that had happened since their last chat and gave her a copy of the scar sketch, which she promised to show her staff. Tracey's eyes widened as he finished his story. "Damn, boy! When you do something, you don't do it halfway!"

Simon sipped at the hot drink, knowing that the coffee should be making him jittery by now, but with how poorly he had been sleeping, it barely kept him coherent. "I don't seem to be able to do the right thing no matter what I do," he confided. "I thought I could help by seeing if my crew noticed anything funny going on, and I might have put them in worse danger. I've tried to help by talking to the ghosts, but the more on-target their information is, the more I seem to be putting a bull's eye on my own back. I don't want to end up dead or in jail. And I don't want to lose Vic."

Tracey watched him, her dark eyes stormy. "You never met my grandma, but she would have had a few words for you." She lifted her chin like a matriarch. "First off, you haven't done wrong trying to look out for people who aren't as blessed as you are. That's no sin. Money, education, even gifts like yours—when you've got more than some do, you've got a responsibility. Nothing wrong with taking that seriously."

"But—"

"Did I look like I was done talking?" Tracey challenged him, winding one red-tipped braid around her finger as she spoke. "Secondly, the ghosts don't have any voice but yours, Simon. If they were alive, the police would be all over them as witnesses, but the police can't reach them. You can. They want to testify," she said, dark eyes boring into him until he felt like squirming in his seat. "They have a powerful testimony, and you're the only one who can hear it. That's important."

"All right," Simon agreed. "But—"

Tracey held up a hand, palm out, and Simon went silent. "Now about that man of yours," she said, and her eyes narrowed. "He's either with you, or he isn't. It's as simple as that. Because if you go forward with him, there are things both of you are gonna have to adjust to, like his crazy schedule and working all hours of the night, and your talent. Those aren't negotiable," she warned. "Don't be thinking either of you is going to change. That's what got you where you were *before*," she added, with a look that made Simon cringe as he thought of Jacen.

"So he's going to have to figure out whether he's in or out," Tracey went on. "Whether he's in love, whether he's out of the closet, and whether he's in your corner when it comes to believing in your talent. It's not enough that you've made up your mind about him," she said with a knowing grin. "He's got to *decide* about you."

"I know he cares," Simon defended Vic, remembering the kiss from earlier, and the conflict in Vic's eyes. "And I think he believes in the supernatural deep down, but he got hurt for it before, and now it's harder for him to trust."

"That's what he's got to *decide*, sweetie," Tracey said, laying her hand over Simon's. "Because real love isn't easy, and there's always a price to pay."

14

VIC

"Do I want to know who you got the tip from about the scars?" Ross asked. "Or the blue fish hotel and big nose?"

"Don't ask, and I won't tell," Vic replied. The tension between him and Ross had grown over Vic's admission that he had brought Simon in on the case. While he hated being at odds with his partner, he still believed he had done the right thing. The big question was, how could he make use of Simon's insights without making Simon a prime suspect?

"So you think that maybe the Slitter had a bolt hole around here?" Ross waited while Vic parked the car, and they both got out and headed for the street. Vic had parked in the bottom of the garage where they had found Cindy's body. He climbed to the top level to get its view of the Grand Strand, and that's when pieces started to click.

"Yeah, I do. From the top level of the garage, you can see the locations where all the other victims have been found," Vic replied.

Ross snorted. "From that high, you can see half of Myrtle Beach. That's not a real revelation."

Vic gave him a look. "It's probably what, a mile radius? Two miles? And all the bodies have been left within that area."

"Why leave bodies near his own hiding place?" Ross argued. "You don't shit where you sleep."

Vic sighed. "I can always count on you to be a class act." He couldn't help teasing Ross, even if they were a bit on the outs with each other.

"So? It's a good point. Why leave bodies near where he's holed up?"

Vic frowned, thinking. "Maybe we're missing the point. What if it's not about where he lives, but where something important happened to him? Where he worked, or where he had a run-in that set him off?"

"It's possible," Ross admitted grudgingly. "So you just want to hit the streets asking people if they've seen a guy with scarred hands?"

"A guy who usually wears a baseball cap and aviators, and who has weird pink scars on his hands," Vic corrected. "That's pretty specific."

"This is a beach town. Most of the men here wear a baseball cap and sunglasses," Ross protested.

"But they don't give off the vibe that they're hiding something," Vic replied. "If he's been around here, either someone's seen him or one of the video cameras has picked up images we can use. Now we've just got to find out about it."

They each took a copy of the drawing Simon had made and split up to cover both sides of the street. After a block, they regrouped.

"So why do you think the Slitter killed that guy?" Ross asked. "Kinda late in the game to switch targets, don't you think?"

Vic remembered Simon's theory but knew he couldn't back it up with any evidence Ross would accept. "There's probably a link we don't know about between the victims."

"The victims didn't work together. As far as we can tell, they didn't know each other. No schools in common, no club memberships. The first several kills were J-ones, but now these last two aren't," Ross grumbled. "You know how rare it is for a serial killer to change his habits."

"So we need to assume he didn't, and that there is a link we just aren't seeing," Vic replied. And while he knew that Simon was acquainted with Quinn, Cindy, and Katya, he'd found no connection between him and the other victims. He hated checking up on Simon, but the cop in him had to know.

"I can't shake the feeling that he's building up to something," Ross said. "And that worries me. The killings have gotten closer together. What's next? A bomb?"

Vic shook his head. "That doesn't feel right. But I agree there's a build-up going on, or maybe he's losing control, and he can't stop himself."

"He's too meticulous for that," Ross disagreed. "He hasn't left us a bit of evidence yet. I think he's all about control, and he's got a master plan we aren't going to like."

Three more blocks passed the same way, with shrugs or shakes of the head from all the merchants, restaurant servers, and ice cream stand workers they questioned. Finally, Vic scored a win with the hot dog vendor across the street from the hotel he had glimpsed from the parking garage.

"Scars? Yeah, I remember a guy like that," the man said, pushing up his striped cap and stepping back from the steaming cart. "Used to come by every week and get hot dogs on Friday. Mustard, no ketchup or onions, pickle on the side like this was Chicago, if you can believe it."

"Do you remember what he looked like?" Vic pressed, trying to keep his excitement in check.

"Other than the scars?" The hot dog man shook his head. "I keep my eyes on the money. You'd be amazed how good some people are at shorting you if you aren't watching every move. Never him, though. He always paid."

"Does he still come around?"

"Nah. Haven't seen him in three, four months, give or take," the vendor said. "I figure he changed jobs. Most of my regulars work around here. They like my dogs because they can get a quick meal on their break." He grinned. "I'm cheap, fast, and good, but I ain't easy."

Vic chuckled at the bad joke. "If you see him around, try to get a look at his face, but don't do anything unusual to draw his attention. That's important," he said, meeting the man's eyes. "This guy is dangerous."

"Yeah? Didn't seem like an imposing guy to me. Wasn't real tall, or a weightlifter. Just a regular dude. But, hey, what do I know? I just sell hot dogs."

Vic gave the man his card and thanked him, as the wheels spun in his mind. The killings had started four months ago. If the Slitter had been laid off from one of the places in the radius of where he left the bodies or had a run-in with a co-worker or lover, maybe they could guess his end game. Vic glanced around and remembered the large area visible from the top of the parking garage. Trying to gather a list of everyone who had been laid off four months ago from all the businesses in that range would take forever.

Which meant they needed to get started right away before the killer struck again.

Vic's phone buzzed, and he pulled it out. A new text from Simon. Despite everything, it made him smile.

Having a nice day? Been busy here.

Boring legwork, the curse of all cops everywhere.

Don't forget to eat. Vic loved that Simon worried about him. Nate had shared the demands of being a cop, so he never had any sympathy when the weight of it bore down on Vic. Simon's quiet nurturing made Vic feel wanted, treasured, and valued without being smothering or controlling. He had never realized how much he liked being cared for until Simon.

I'll eat. Can't promise it'll be healthy. Donuts, you know.

Defy the stereotype, Simon texted back.

Vic was thinking of how to reply when Simon wrote again. *Can you come by the shop later? I've heard some things.*

Sure. I'll be there by seven, Vic promised. He had been thinking of asking Simon to see if he could pick up anything else from the ghosts, anything that might corroborate his theory about the Slitter having had an upsetting experience with either a business or an individual linked to the area of the kills. He'd have to be careful how he phrased the questions, but years as a cop had trained him how to ask for what he needed without giving anything away.

Looking forward to it. Be safe.

Vic stared at the message for a moment before pocketing his phone. Despite Ross's warnings and Vic's unfortunate past, he couldn't get Simon out of his mind. Yes, the dark-haired ex-professor was surprisingly hot and enthusiastic in bed, a compatibility Vic had feared he might never find in a partner. But what he felt was grounded in more than just mind-blowing sex. Simon set him at ease, made it possible for Vic to let down his guard, and that was something very few people managed to do. Being with Simon felt *right;* and thinking about being with him for the long-term was ridiculously—frighteningly—easy.

Now if Vic could just protect Simon from the Slitter, and from Simon's own misguided amateur detecting.

The rest of the afternoon passed in a tedious slog, going door to door, showing the drawing and being turned away without leads. A few people remembered seeing the man, but not recently, and no one knew where he worked or why he was in the neighborhood.

"I'm beat," Ross confessed when he and Vic met up as the sun was low in the sky. "We didn't get much, but at least we confirmed you were right about him having some tie to this area." He cleared the sweat from his face with his sleeve. "We gonna do this again tomorrow?"

"You got any better leads to track down?"

"Nah. This is more than we've had to go on in a while. Good thinking, by the way."

Vic shrugged. "You'd have come up with it, too. Eventually," he added with a grin.

"I need to get home," Ross said, checking the time. "My wife is very patient with the job, but she's starting to send me pictures of the kids to remind me of their names. I can take a hint."

"Go," Vic replied. "I'm planning to grab something to take back with me for dinner and crash in front of the TV."

Ross gave him a skeptical look. "No psychic action on the side?"

Vic was surprised how quickly his anger spiked. "I know you don't like Simon—"

"I don't trust him," Ross corrected.

"Fine. But I'm tired of you talking about him like he's just a piece of ass."

Ross's eyebrows rose. "Isn't he?" He gave Vic an assessing once-over. "Shit, Vic. You care about this guy."

Vic swallowed. "Yeah. I do. And the timing is lousy, and it should be all kinds of wrong after what happened in Pittsburgh, but…it's different than with anyone else."

Vic expected a lecture from Ross about his stupidity, about being conned by a man Ross considered to be a fraud, about putting his career and their partnership in jeopardy. Instead, Ross just shook his head like he was having a conversation with himself. "Huh," he replied.

"That's it?"

Ross huffed out a breath. "I still don't like it. I'm still on the fence about his motives, and I worry about you being played—"

"You're worried about *me* being played?" Vic echoed incredulously.

"It happens to the best of us."

"How is being involved in this to Simon's benefit in any way?" Vic demanded.

"He has a cop in his corner, defending him, for one thing."

"Ross, if you—"

Ross held up a hand to stop Vic mid-argument. "I'm not saying that he's the Slitter—"

"He isn't."

"Or that he's an accomplice. But Jesus, Vic, this is like basic police academy stuff. The guy that keeps showing up for no good reason usually has a bad reason."

Vic rubbed his neck, trying to keep his temper in check. He knew Ross was worried about him, and if he were in Ross's place, he'd probably have been even less tactful. But Ross didn't know Simon—had never even met him—and Vic had to trust that his ability to read witnesses was as good as it always had been. There'd been no gain for Simon in any of this, except for his relationship with Vic, and no way that Vic could see for Simon to benefit from the deaths. Until something proved him wrong, Vic was going to trust his gut—and his heart.

"I hear you, Ross. But we've played hunches before, and they've worked out. That's part of being a detective, isn't it? Intuition? So trust me a little bit longer on this, will ya? Because I think Simon's the key to this, not because he's guilty, but because he's got a perspective we don't."

"You mean, he talks to dead people."

"Look at it as debriefing hard-to-reach witnesses," Vic said with a wry grin, and Ross groaned. "Seriously, if we could talk to them, we would. But we can't. So if he can—"

"You sound crazy."

"Belief," Vic replied, raising his chin and meeting Ross's eyes. "Think of it as a matter of belief."

Ross dropped the subject as they drove back to the precinct, and they parted for the evening with a little less tension between them than before. Still, Ross's lack of faith in Simon nagged at Vic, and he didn't need to ask to know where their captain would come down on the matter.

Vic picked up his motorcycle and made his way through traffic until he got to the boardwalk. He found a parking spot and walked the rest of the way to Grand Strand Ghost Tours. He knocked on the window, and Simon looked up from behind the counter and went to unlock the door since the shop was closed.

Vic pulled him in for a kiss, inhaling his scent of incense and aftershave, liking the way Simon pressed against him, responding to the brush of his lips with gentle hunger. Simon reached behind them and locked the door.

"Hey," he said, looking a little uncertain.

"Hey, yourself," Vic countered. "You all right?"

Simon didn't look all right, but he nodded anyway. "Thanks for meeting me here. I had another vision—not sure what it means, but I wanted to tell you about it. And I thought you might want me to reach out to the ghosts again."

"You'd rather do that here than at your house?" Vic asked.

Simon sighed. "I've tried talking to the ghosts at home and remembered why I stopped doing that. Once I open the door, so to speak, they don't want to leave me alone. Ghosts aren't good at boundaries, especially when they find someone who can hear them." He gave a wry grin. "Lucky me. So I had to do a major cleansing just so I could get a full night's sleep without being interrupted. I'd rather not undo that and have to go through it all again if there's a choice."

"All that from the Slitter's ghosts?" Vic looked at Simon incredulously.

"What? No. A lot of people die in Myrtle Beach with unfinished business." Simon gave a shaky laugh. "Sometimes I get the feeling everyone here is outrunning something in their past. And it's not just people who die violently. Natural causes catch people who think they've got time to put things right and find out too late that they don't."

"And what do they want from you?" Vic asked, never having thought about this part of Simon's talent. "I mean, it's not like you're a priest. You can't give them absolution or Last Rites."

Simon shook his head. "Some of them aren't sure they're dead. Those are the easy ones. Once I convince them that they really are, they find their way."

"To the light?" Vic asked, his tone lightly sarcastic, although he found himself truly interested.

Simon shrugged. "Onward, wherever that leads. Most of them go pretty quietly. Then there are the people who are angry about old grudges, or upset about something they left undone. If I can get them to let go of the anger and the guilt, they move on. Otherwise, I have to throw them out, and they get pissy. And then there are the ones who want me to pass along a message. Sometimes I can; sometimes I can't. Usually, I try to show them how to make themselves seen to the person they want to talk to so they can do it themselves."

"Geez, you sound like Dr. Phil for ghosts."

Simon chuckled. "Feels like it sometimes. That's why the bound-aries are so important. I knew that, but I just wanted to find some-thing that could help." He headed toward the back room, and Vic followed.

"The coffee's gone, but I've got water and soda in the fridge," Simon offered. Vic chose water, and Simon put down two bottles in front of them.

"So…" Simon said. "I had a vision earlier. Practically knocked me on my ass right in the middle of ringing up a customer. It was Cindy. She's pissed, to say the least."

"I'd imagine so," Vic replied, doing his best to set his skepticism aside.

"It felt like she used all her energy to shove an image at me because new ghosts aren't very strong. But the problem is, it doesn't make sense."

"Try me."

Simon sighed. "Billy Bass."

Vic laughed. "You're kidding. The talking mechanical fish?"

Simon's cheeks flushed, and he nodded. "See, that's what I mean. If you've only got a little juice to send an important message, why would you send that?"

Vic leaned back in his chair and took a sip of the water, consid-ering possibilities. "There are plenty of bars that have one of those things on the wall for kicks," he said. "Maybe Cindy met the Slitter at one of those bars."

"That's a pretty big 'maybe,'" Simon said. "The image got shoved at me with so much force I know I didn't mistake what I saw. But I'm at a loss. I thought maybe it would mean something to you."

Vic shook his head. "No. At least, not yet. Have you heard from any of the other victims?"

"Not since when Quinn showed up," Simon said. "But after Cindy sent me the vision, I thought I'd try again, and I figured you might want to be here for it."

"I'm game," Vic replied. "How do you want to do this?" If he had his way, they'd go back to Simon's house and have a quiet dinner, then a rowdy night of sex. But Simon seemed preoccupied, and Vic figured it was best for both of them not to push.

"Like the last time. Concentrate on what you want to know, who you want to hear from. You don't have to say anything, just think hard," he said with a self-conscious smile. "I'll open the gate, and we'll see who shows up."

"Isn't that dangerous?" Vic asked, thinking about how vulnerable Simon would be opening himself up to other energies. "What's to stop something bad from sneaking in?"

Simon smiled. "Another benefit of doing the readings here. I've had the shop blessed, cleansed, and warded multiple times. It's not a guarantee, but it tends to keep out the riff-raff."

Vic didn't like things he couldn't prove or didn't fully understand, but at least Simon was including him, and he'd be here if anything went wrong. "Okay. Let's do it."

Simon closed his eyes and reached out both hands across the table. Vic took hold, twining their fingers together. He kept his eyes open, watching Simon as the medium took several deep breaths and then relaxed. His face went slack as if he was sleeping, but the twitch of his eyes beneath the lids suggested something far more active.

"He didn't just cut their throats," Simon said in a dazed tone. "Stabbed through the heart. Needed heart blood. For his power. Blood for power." He went quiet for a moment, canting his head as if listening to someone speaking off to one side.

"Didn't want the money. Didn't take anything except blood. Getting stronger. Needed to drug the first ones. Held the new ones by himself. Stronger from the blood. Not done yet. There'll be more."

Simon grew more agitated, but nothing about his actions suggested a performance. He looked genuinely distressed, and his grip on Vic's hands tightened. "No…" he murmured. "No."

"Simon!" Vic called, worried that this had gone too far. "Simon, wake up!"

Simon came back to himself with eyes open wide and a gasp as if he had been too long underwater. He was shaking and had visibly paled. Vic came around to kneel in front of him, pressing a bottle of water into his hands.

"Drink," Vic instructed. He helped hold the bottle since Simon's hands shook. Then he set the bottle aside and pulled Simon down with him onto the floor, holding him against his chest and stroking his long chestnut hair. "You're all right. You're safe. I'm here. You're okay. Just breathe."

Simon buried his face against Vic's chest and wrapped his arms tightly around him, and Vic held him close. After a while, Simon's breathing slowed and he shifted so that his head was tucked up under Vic's chin.

"Did you hear all that?" Simon asked.

"I heard plenty," Vic replied. Many of the details Simon reported from the spirits were already known to the police—that the victims hadn't been robbed or otherwise assaulted, that the cuts were on the throat and to the heart, that the first kills had traces of chemical sedative in their blood, but not the later ones. None of that had been released to the public. Those details were known only to the police and the killer—and the victims' ghosts.

"He's picking victims with psychic power and using it somehow to make himself stronger," Simon said, and while his voice was now steady, he still sounded pretty freaked out.

"Is that possible?"

"There are legends...folktales where witches can steal someone's power. But, hell, I never heard of someone actually doing it," Simon replied. "That day, at Tasha's, when he threw me out of the way—that wasn't physical strength. He never touched me, and I went flying. So maybe if he can throw someone, he can hold them still. Maybe that's why he didn't need to drug the latest victims."

"Whose ghosts did you see?" Vic asked, still holding Simon close against him, stroking his hair.

"A couple of women I didn't recognize. One had long, straight black hair. The other was a redhead with a ponytail."

Vic startled because the descriptions matched two of the first women killed by the Slitter. "No one else?"

"Katya," Simon said sadly. "She's the one who said he didn't drug her."

"And at the end, you kept saying 'no.' What did you see?" Vic kept his voice quiet and reassuring, the way he did with spooked witnesses, which he guessed described Simon more literally than most.

Simon leaned into him, burying his face against Vic's shirt once more. "He's not done yet. There'll be more deaths before he's ready for the 'big show.'"

"What is the big show?" Vic pressed.

Simon shook his head. "They didn't know, but he must have bragged about it, that he was going to do something really big, prove something, get back at someone. But they didn't know who or what."

"Did they know who he's going after next?"

Simon hesitated. "No. Just that there'll be more."

They sat in silence for several minutes, Simon clinging to Vic like he was drowning, and Vic doing his damnedest to think his way out of the problem. "You can't talk about what you've seen—to anyone," Vic warned. "They won't understand."

"You mean, they'll arrest me."

Vic pulled him tighter. "Maybe. Let's not find out."

"I'm causing a lot of trouble for you," Simon said quietly. "I don't want you to lose your job."

Vic bent to kiss the top of his head. "Let me worry about that. We get plenty of tips from people on the wrong side of the law every day—mobsters, dealers, guys who run chop shops and fence stolen goods. And we overlook that because they have intel we need. I don't see why an honest psychic shouldn't get the same treatment."

"Thanks," Simon said. "I wasn't sure I'd hear you say 'honest psychic' in this lifetime."

"Hey," Vic replied. "I'm learning. My nonna used to get dreams that turned out to be right a surprising amount of the time. Not to mention giving the evil eye. And my aunt reads tea leaves." He shrugged. "No one thought twice about it, back in my neighborhood in Pittsburgh."

"But the cops there did," Simon said quietly. "I don't want to make you have to choose between me and your job."

Vic didn't want to have to choose either, because losing Simon or his badge would tear him apart. Surely he could manage to keep both. "I'll figure it out," Vic assured him. "We'll find a way." He straightened out his leg, which had begun to cramp.

"But right now, I think we need to get off the floor, and I need to get you home. Did you drive?"

Simon nodded, giving him a final squeeze before letting go. Vic got to his feet first and pulled Simon up, folding him close again to steady him. "All right then, I'll follow you back to your house, make sure you get in okay. And then I'm going to go run some Billy Bass possibilities through the computer and see where it leads."

"Thank you," Simon said, brushing a kiss across Vic's cheek. "I'd ask you to stay, but I think I'm going to collapse as soon as I get inside."

"You look beat," Vic said, smoothing the hair back from Simon's eyes. "I'll call you tomorrow. Just take it easy."

Vic followed Simon all the way to the blue bungalow and watched until he was safely inside with the lights on.

Did you lock the door?

Yes.

Back door?

Yep. Windows, too. Thank you.

Get some rest. And please, be careful. I care.

I care about you, too.

Vic stared at his phone, surprised how hard that last text from Simon made his heart beat. How the hell did he fall in love with a ghost whisperer? And why was he afraid that the odds were fifty-fifty whether Simon would get arrested or killed before Vic could figure out how to stop the Slitter from striking again?

15

SIMON

S imon leaned against the door and heard Vic's motorcycle roar away. He slid down and sat on the floor, too shaken to stand. He hadn't told Vic the whole truth about the vision, because he feared that either Vic wouldn't believe him, or would take it so seriously he'd put Simon in custody for his own safety.

Simon had seen himself die.

He had been in a room that appeared to be under construction, like the gutted floor of a high rise, and another man was there, wearing a surgical mask so his face couldn't be seen except for his eyes. In the vision, Simon had been restrained, or perhaps too injured to fight back, because there had been so much blood. The man—the Slitter—had raised a dagger, eyes glinting in triumph, and brought it down with all his strength, driving the blade into Simon's heart.

Just thinking about what he had seen made Simon's heart pound and his mouth go dry. He tried to tell himself that premonitions showed what *could* be, not necessarily what *would* be. The future was always in flux, changed by every choice, every action. He told himself that while some of his visions showed what had already happened, he obviously wasn't dead yet, and so there was still time to change the future.

Or maybe, to shift the manner of his death. If he foresaw something fated to happen, then Simon vowed to go down swinging, not as the Slitter's hapless captive, but as the agent of the serial killer's downfall. If he ended up in that room with the murderer, Simon swore that should one of them survive, it would be him; otherwise, neither he nor the Slitter was going to leave alive.

Something about the room he'd glimpsed in the vision niggled at the back of his brain, a memory he couldn't place, familiar and yet not. The harder he tried to identify the location, the more the connection eluded him. With a sigh, he pushed off the floor and stumbled to the kitchen. Simon poured himself a few fingers' worth of whiskey and dropped into one of the kitchen chairs, head in his hands, carding his fingers through his hair as he thought.

Vic had been so good with him back at the shop. He'd been trying to believe and had managed to keep his skepticism at bay. From Vic's reaction to some of what Simon relayed, he felt sure that the information had been on point, details the police had not released.

That might prove Simon's gift. Or, more likely, it pointed suspicion right at him. Vic had begged him not to tell anyone about the messages, and Simon knew that while his lover was worried for Simon's safety, he was also afraid for his badge.

Could they make this attraction between them work? Would Simon always be a liability to Vic's career, a cause for ridicule among his peers even if Vic did come to believe whole-heartedly? Sometimes, Vic's hesitation reminded Simon too much of Jacen. Attraction alone couldn't overcome a lack of faith.

As much as Simon wanted to find a way for them to be together long term, he didn't know how much Vic was willing to risk. Simon already knew he loved Vic, and what he wanted wasn't a whirlwind secret affair. If they did this, Simon wanted a shot at forever. And although he knew Vic cared about him, Simon still wasn't convinced that Vic felt as deeply for him, certainly not to the point of risking his job.

Simon could see how much being a cop mattered to Vic, how much pride he felt in his work, the satisfaction of carrying out a family tradition. There were plenty of guys Vic could date who wouldn't cost him his badge, who wouldn't threaten his credibility or make him a laughingstock to his colleagues. Vic deserved someone he could be proud of, not someone he had to make excuses for and constantly defend to his friends. And while it warmed Simon's heart that Vic would stand up for him, he knew that would get old fast and be a constant strain that would eventually tear them apart.

Then again, if Simon died confronting the Slitter, he really didn't have a future to worry about.

Simon sipped the whiskey, restraining himself from knocking it back to ease the pain and fear that shuddered through him. He refused to accept the vision as a death omen, telling himself it was merely a warning, foreshadowing one of many possibilities. Regardless of what the future held, he had work to do.

His phone buzzed, and Simon glanced down, hoping it was Vic. Instead, the caller was Marcus. He'd given his number to Marcus months ago when he had first learned that the young man had some talent, but Marcus had never called him. This couldn't be good. "Hello?"

"Simon? Man, I'm freaked out. I need to know what to do."

"Talk to me. What happened?" Simon asked, sitting up and alert.

"This guy started coming into the gym. Gave me really bad vibes, you know? Never did anything or said anything out of line, but he made my skin crawl. I've been around a lot of people, but nothin' like him, and I've known some real scum."

"White guy, baseball cap, aviator sunglasses, maybe about five-ten or so, fit but not muscle-bound?" Simon asked.

"Yeah. You know him?"

"Listen to me carefully, Marcus. That's the Slitter. You need to get out of town right now. Are you home?"

"Yeah, I came straight here when my shift ended. I couldn't shake the feeling I was being watched."

Simon cringed. "Do you have any religions medallions—St. Jude, St. Christopher, crosses, crucifix, Star of David—anything?"

"I've got a bunch of cross necklaces. My grandma buys me one every year."

"Okay. Put them on. Put them all on, and say a prayer to bless them and awaken their protective power," Simon instructed. "Do you have any sage?"

"I've got weed. Will that do?"

Despite the danger, Simon smiled. "Um, no. How about salt?"

"I've got a salt shaker."

"That works. I want you to pack a bag—take what you can't do without, and some clothes to last a while. Fast. Do you have a car?"

Marcus snorted. "Are you kidding? I have a bike—the kind you peddle."

"Call a cab. Not a rideshare—a real cab. Get out of Myrtle Beach. If you can, hop a bus once you're out of town to somewhere that's as far from here as you can go. Stay there until the Slitter is caught or killed, because if he's hanging around the gym, then he's noticed you, and that's really bad."

Simon wished he dared go pick Marcus up, but doing so might call the Slitter's attention even more, and besides, between the visions and the whiskey, Simon was in no shape to drive.

"Okay. Okay," Marcus said, and Simon could hear him hyper-ventilating.

"Breathe," Simon warned. "You've got to hurry. If your gut is telling you that you're in danger, trust it. I think the Slitter has magic. Real magic. Don't let him get near you. Don't tell anyone here where you've gone."

"Gonna lose my job."

"Can't work if you're dead."

"Okay, I get you."

"There's a cop I know. I could call him and have him escort you—"

"No cops, man. If they don't bust me for the weed, they'll find something to get me on, and I don't want any 'three strikes' bullshit."

Simon wanted to argue that Marcus would be safer in jail, but he knew the other man wouldn't agree. "Call me and let me know that you're somewhere safe," Simon said. "But don't tell me where you are. If I don't know, I can't tell."

"Shit, you're serious about this, aren't you?"

"As a heart attack," Simon replied. "Hurry. Run, and don't look back."

He ended the call, and let out a long breath, then swallowed down more whiskey. He had traded phone numbers with very few of his Skeleton Crew, and now Simon debated calling the ones he could reach to warn them. But what if they weren't on the Slitter's list after all? The J-ones couldn't run, and the others needed their jobs too much to just leave. All the more reason to find the Slitter and stop him, once and for all.

Simon finished his whiskey, letting the burn fill him and drive out the cold. He debated having another and decided to wait a while. He reached into his pocket and wrapped a hand around the jack ball and High John the Conqueror root Miss Eppie had given him. He'd already taken her advice about using the red brick dust and the Four Thieves vinegar to protect the shop and his house, and he wondered if that had helped to keep the evil at bay. But now, he needed to step up his game.

In the three years he had lived in Myrtle Beach both Miss Eppie and Gabriella had taken him under their wings, nurtured his gift. Simon didn't have the kind of abilities they had, either as a root worker or as a *bruja*, but they had both assured him that with his native energy, some magic could be learned. They had taught him ways to protect himself, and some low-level spells that could be used for defense.

First, he rifled through his kitchen for basil, then went to find patchouli and St. John's Wort from another cupboard. He ground the protective herbs together, mixing them into powder, and filled several small cloth bags, which he tied shut. Then he went to his bedroom and rummaged through his bureau to find all his protective medallions, as well as silver rings and an onyx bracelet. He brought them all to the kitchen and lit a bundle of sage, smudging the four corners of the room, then the corners of the house, and finally marking the four points of the compass before he wafted the smoke over the jewelry, invoking a blessing and visualizing them glowing with energy.

Vic would probably tell him to get a gun. This was South Carolina; getting a handgun wouldn't be difficult. But Simon had never shot a real gun, and if his aim at darts or paintball was any indication, he couldn't hit the broad side of a barn. He had his pepper spray and his silver knife. Those were helpful, but if the Slitter could throw him bodily a distance of several feet and immobilize his victims with magic, then Simon needed weapons of an entirely different kind.

It had been a while since Simon had practiced what Gabriella had taught him, and the little he could do was paltry compared to the *bruja's* abilities. But if he was gathering his defenses, then he was determined to use every advantage he possessed.

Most of his lessons with Gabriella had been on shielding and warding, learning how to create boundaries with the spirits. She had helped him focus his energy, place protective wardings on his house and the shop, and cleanse himself from the stain of despair and malice that some ghosts brought with them.

But Gabriella had also taught him what she called "rote magic," spells that he could work drawing not on any special powers but on his own life energy. They were more than magician's tricks but far less than a true witch could do. Still, the Slitter might not expect any magical defense from Simon, and surprise could be a life-saving advantage.

Simon stilled his mind and took several calming breaths, centering himself. He held out one hand palm up and focused all his concentration on willing a small flicker of flame into being. It took several tries—he was rusty—but finally, after he had started to sweat and his head began to pound, he managed to bring a tongue of fire to life in his palm, no larger than the flame of a taper candle, but real and burning at his command.

Simon released the flame with a gasp at the effort required and leaned on the back of the nearest kitchen chair to catch his breath and still the ache in his head. He was heartened by his ability to work the minor spell despite how out of practice he was, and knew he needed to refresh his few other workings.

He gripped a paper towel in one hand, held it at arm's length, and focused once more on his inner energy, the core from which he drew his mediumship and the source of his visions. Simon pictured his hand growing warm and then hot, not burning his flesh but radiating enough heat to singe the paper. Once again his head pounded and his vision blurred, but Simon knew he would be working under much worse conditions if he ever faced off with the Slitter.

Gradually he felt heat rising from his fist, higher than a fever until he could smell paper scorching. He cried out and relaxed his grip, and the napkin fell to the floor, with the faint brown outline of his hand imprinted where he had burned it.

Simon stumbled and almost fell, but he caught himself on the kitchen chair. His head throbbed, and he felt far more light-headed than he could blame on the whiskey, but he had one more spell to try, and then he would head to bed if needed to crawl to get there.

Simon summoned his waning energy and stood in an open space in the kitchen where he had a few feet of empty floor around him. He closed his eyes and visualized himself inside a glowing circle that pulsed with silver fire. It took several tries, but finally Simon felt the power answer his call, and when he opened his eyes, he saw a thin shimmering curtain of energy surrounding him. He only held the protective ring for a few moments, just to assure himself he could sustain it, and then dismissed the magic with gratitude. He did not know how strong a barrier the energy curtain would provide, or what kind of attack—if any—it might stymie, but at least he didn't feel like he might face the Slitter entirely unarmed.

Simon's phone rang. He answered without looking at the ID. Unlike the phone for the shop, Simon gave his personal number to very few people, so he had a short list of who might be calling. "Hello?"

For a second, the line was silent, and Simon thought it had been a wrong number. Then a heavily filtered voice came on the line. "You can't stop me. Your time is coming." The line went dead.

Simon swallowed hard and realized he was shaking. He checked his phone history, but when he tried to return the call, he got a recorded message that the number was out of service. He thought about calling Vic and decided against it if he didn't even have a number to trace. Vic would worry without being able to do anything about it. He already knew Simon was in danger; the caller's vague threat provided no clues to stop the killer.

Simon had never been big on true crime books, but he had watched enough TV to know that serial killers liked to toy with their victims, enjoying the mind games as much as the actual murder. He shuddered and went to check that the locks were in place. Simon put on several of the blessed medallions, tucked one of the bags of protective herbs into the pocket of his sweatpants, and set both the pepper spray and his knife on the nightstand. He fell into bed, utterly exhausted, but too afraid to fall into a restful sleep.

Simon headed to work the next morning, still groggy from a night of waking at every noise. He wore several of the amulets and tucked the rest around his house and saved some to bring to the shop, adding the herb bags for good measure. But when he approached the store, he saw a dark stain just in front of the door.

The smell told him what the liquid was before he had time to think about it. Blood, quickly turning sour in the heat. Bile rose in Simon's throat. He had no idea whether the blood was human or animal, but he did note that it did not cross the protective line he had set down with Miss Eppie's Hoodoo vinegar.

Again, Simon debated calling Vic. He knew he should report the vandalism. But...Simon was afraid of drawing the attention of Vic's fellow cops, whom he felt certain wouldn't give him the same benefit of the doubt. If they found out the things he'd told Vic, things no one should know, he'd end up as a suspect. Maybe they'd think he dumped the blood himself, as a red herring. Simon shook his head, coming to a conclusion. He couldn't afford the scrutiny, not if he didn't want to end up as a convenient fall guy.

"Shit," Simon muttered. He went around to the back door, relieved to find there was no similar vandalism, let himself in, and turned off the security system. While the alarm had cameras on the inside of the shop, none of them faced outside. Simon thought maybe that was an oversight to correct, and he'd ordered another camera, but it hadn't come in yet. Right now, he needed to wash down the sidewalk before anybody noticed.

He went to the utility closet, grabbed a gallon of bleach, and mixed it up with water in a scrub bucket, then attached a hose to the faucet in the mop sink, and dragged the hose with him out the front door. He opened the door and found Jay from the tattoo shop eyeing the mess.

"Did you piss someone off real good?"

Simon shrugged. "Maybe one of the feral cats got a rat." He took a photo with his phone, although it showed little than a dark stain.

Jay raised an eyebrow. "If all that blood came from one rat, then we need to call in the National Guard instead of Animal Control."

Simon waved for Jay to step back, and sluiced the bleach-water down over the stinking puddle, washing it away. He sprayed it with the hose until long after the last of the blood was gone, and poured straight bleach on it for good measure before rinsing it again.

"You gonna call the cops?" Jay asked.

"What are they going to do?" Simon asked wearily. "They'll think it's just some dumb frat boy prank."

Jay gave him an appraising look. "Maybe starting the neighborhood watch made someone nervous."

"Could be," Simon said, winding up the hose. "I got a threatening phone call last night, but it must have been a burner phone, and the number says it's disconnected. Nothing to trace."

"Damn, boy. You better watch your step. I haven't seen that guy with the scarred hands you asked me about, but maybe he got wind that you were looking for him."

"Maybe," Simon replied, sure that was the case. Or else, as the late-night caller had warned, he was just being reminded that he was next in line to die. "Thanks for helping keep an eye out."

"Just part of being in the neighborhood." Jay shrugged and ambled off.

Simon took his bucket, bleach, and hose back inside and then went back out front to set down another line of Four Thieves vinegar at all the doors and windows. When he was finished, he lit one of his protective candles behind the counter and placed some of his blessed charms and herb bags near the register and in the break room.

Once he'd finished his second cup of coffee, he made a call. "Cassidy?"

"Hi Simon! That lore you called me with helped a lot with the cursed box. Thanks!"

"Glad to hear it. Hey, do you have a minute?"

"Always," she replied. "What can I do for you?"

Simon had spent the past hour trying to figure out how to get more information than he gave away, mostly because he didn't want to drag Cassidy and her friends into his mess, even if they did have some occult skills. Simon was still mostly certain the Slitter was more criminal than cryptid, and more a problem for the police than for monster hunters. Mostly.

"I know lore, but you've got a lot more hands-on experience," he said. "Is it possible for a person to steal magic from someone else?"

Cassidy paused. "Are you sure the thief is human?"

Simon found himself nodding, even though he knew Cassidy couldn't see him. "Yeah. At least, I think so. He might have some rote magic, but I don't think he's got much natural power. But he's causing problems, trying to leech off other people's magic."

"What kind of problems?" Cassidy pressed.

"People have gotten hurt."

"If it were a creature, there would be ways to kill it, but that's a lot harder when the monster is human," Cassidy replied. "This sounds like it might be more in line with your witch friend."

"Gabriella had to go out of town for a while," Simon replied. "I'm the last deputy left in Dodge City."

"And I don't have a good answer for you," Cassidy admitted. "The police won't consider it battery or theft, and you can't warn everyone with a bit of psychic gift. Encourage people to wear protective jewelry and strengthen their personal defenses. But even if you could throw a person like that in jail, he'd be able to draw off the energy of other inmates—gifted criminals can have magic, too."

"Okay," Simon agreed, knowing his reluctance was clear in his voice. "I thought the same thing, but I figured I'd bounce it off you."

"Are you sure you're okay?" Cassidy might not have clairvoyance, but sometimes Simon swore her psychometry managed to work through the phone.

"Yeah," he lied. "I'm fine. I just thought you might know how to get this guy to stop bothering people."

"If you need help, Teag and I can be there in an hour and a half," she offered, including her best friend in the offer. But since Simon had never heard tell that either Cassidy or Teag had powerful magic of their own, Simon would be putting them in mortal danger by bringing them to the Slitter's attention. This was a battle Simon knew he was going to have to fight himself.

"I appreciate that," Simon said. "And if I need help, I'll holler. But you gave me everything I needed for now. Stay out of trouble," he added affectionately.

"You, too," Cassidy replied. "And figure out when you can come visit. There are a couple of new restaurants I know you'd love."

Simon ended the call with a promise he wasn't sure he could keep and tried to shift his attention to the store since it was time to open for customers. He had ghost tours to lead that night, and once again sign-ups had been busy, so the tours were full.

Today he noticed that more locals than tourists came into the shop, heading right for the protective candles and amulets. Simon had already placed a reorder but wondered if he would run out before the replacements arrived. With the Slitter's death toll climbing, even the city's PR department couldn't keep word about the killings from spreading, and while the tourists didn't seem to be worried, Simon could sense a new tension in the air among the merchants and regulars on the boardwalk. Everyone was waiting for the next murder and wondering why the hell the cops didn't do something.

Several times throughout the day, Simon had the feeling of being watched, but when he looked around the shop, he saw no one staring in his direction. The wardings he had done at the doorways were supposed to keep evil out, and Simon hoped that included crazy serial killers. But he couldn't shake the apprehension that kept him tense, and when he glimpsed the top of a baseball cap through the store window above a crowd outside, Simon ran for the door, standing on tip-toe to spot the wearer.

If there had been someone outside his window, they were gone now, and Simon couldn't see any caps in the mass of sunscreened beachgoers. He went back inside, apologized to the customer he'd been waiting on, and tried to calm down. But his gaze repeatedly strayed to the window.

Get a grip. He's playing with your mind, Simon told himself. *It's a psych-out, and if he can get you flustered, he wins.* Intellectually, Simon knew that was the truth, but his senses spun every time he thought he saw someone linger outside the window.

He jumped when his phone buzzed. A glance confirmed it was Vic, and Simon felt both relief and guilt.

Having a good day? Vic asked.

Pretty quiet so far. You?

Another day in paradise. Are you okay?

Simon swallowed, hating to lie to Vic, but until he could turn up real, solid evidence the police would believe, he needed to keep his own counsel. *I miss you.* That was true.

Miss you, too. They've got us pulling double shifts, so I don't know when I can come by. Don't forget about me.

Who? Simon teased. *No danger about that happening. Just, be careful.*

You, too. Stay out of trouble.

If I don't, can we play with your handcuffs? Simon flirted.

Now my pants are tight. I'll see you as soon as I can. Be good.

Simon stared at the screen for a moment after Vic ended the call. He wished he could confide in Vic, and he promised himself that he would, just as soon as he had something he could prove.

Fortunately, the rest of the afternoon went well, and Simon's mood lifted. Tracey had called and insisted on coming over to the bungalow after his last ghost tour to watch Netflix and drink wine. Shayla was at a conference, and Tracey decided Simon needed to lighten up. As worried as he was, he didn't have the heart to turn her down, and he promised that he would give her some protective charms to wear, just in case. Then again, Tracey didn't have a bit of magic, so she was probably safe.

Simon had an hour between when the shop closed to customers and when he opened back up for the tours, time enough to tidy up and grab a quick dinner. But as he headed to the back room to finish off the coffee, a vision hit so hard he fell to his knees, bruising his sore arm against the doorframe.

He saw an abandoned hotel, one he recognized as being just a block or so farther south on the boardwalk. It used to be the Moonlight Bay before it closed several years ago. It was an older property, slated for renovation, but despite the chain-link fence around it, vandals had gotten into the pool area and covered the walls with graffiti, completely obliterating their original theme of shells, fish, and sand. Simon braced himself on his hands and knees, ready for a horrendous revelation, but as abruptly as it had appeared, the vision faded without any additional information.

"What the fuck?" Simon groaned, toppling over to sit with his back braced against the doorway. He had walked by the old hotel just this morning on the way from where he had parked, and nothing looked different from any other time he had passed the derelict structure. If it hadn't been for the defaced mural around the pool, Simon might have wondered if the vision showed the same place. At any given time there were plenty of motels and condos being built, torn down, or renovated. Even the locals couldn't keep track. Simon promised himself that tomorrow he'd pay the Moonlight Bay a visit.

Both ghost tours were packed, and the tourists had started drinking early, so they were a rowdy, fun crowd. Clouds occasionally swept over the moon, adding to the atmosphere for good ghost stories, and the people who had signed up were in the mood to have fun. Simon felt his spirits lift, enjoying spinning the yarns and sharing some of Myrtle Beach's more salacious history.

He didn't take the tours as far down the boardwalk as he used to, and even as he told his tales and answered questions, he remained alert. Customers filled the shop between tours, buying up merchandise and books. Once on each tour, Simon felt a prickle at the back of his neck like he was being watched, but he couldn't spot anyone suspicious at the outskirts of his tour group, let alone the baseball-capped Slitter. Still, it was enough to temper his good mood and make him happy when the second tour ended, and the last customer pressed a tip into his hand in parting.

Simon went back to check that the shop door was locked, and found a large brown envelope leaning against it. It only read *"Simon"* without a delivery or return address. He pulled a tissue from his pocket and used it to pick up the envelope, just in case the sender had left behind fingerprints. As much as he wanted to see what was inside, he had no desire to hang around a darkened shop this late in the evening.

"You ready?" Tracey asked as Simon slid the envelope under his arm.

"More than ready," Simon agreed.

Tracey had grabbed a ride in with a friend that morning, so they both walked briskly on the best lit path back to Simon's car and hurried to the blue bungalow. He glanced around to make sure no one lurked in the bushes, shoved the envelope under his arm, and went to let them both into the house.

"So where's your sexy cop?" Tracey asked as Simon led the way to the kitchen. He set the envelope on the table and took the two bottles of wine she handed him, as she shrugged out of her backpack.

"Working a late shift," Simon replied. "No surprise, given what's been going on."

"He's cute. I can see why you like him." She put her hands on her hips. "And you don't break any mirrors yourself. I mean, if I noticed that kind of thing about guys." It was an old joke between them when it came to compliments, and Simon felt himself unwind, just a little. He decided that the contents of the envelope could wait. He was long overdue for a little time off.

"I stocked up on cheese and crackers the last time I went to the store," Simon replied as he moved around the kitchen, getting out wine glasses and plates. "Some fancy salami, too, and a nice crusty loaf of bread if you want to do the picnic thing while we watch TV."

"Sounds like heaven. I've been looking forward to this all day."

To Simon's great relief, Tracey didn't bring up the Slitter or ask more questions about Vic. Simon resolutely refused to think about either one and threw himself into enjoying the good wine, tasty food, and great company. Tracey always knew just what to say to lighten his mood. They picked a few movies specifically for their awful ratings, then poked fun at the acting and mocked the special effects in their own private *MST3K* until after two in the morning.

"Damn. It's late—"

"Early. It's early," Tracey corrected, her voice just slightly slurred.

"Time to get to sleep," Simon replied, gathering up the debris of their living room picnic. "The guest room is made up. And you know where everything is in the bathroom."

Tracey eyed the couch. "I think I'm just going to crash out here if it's all the same to you. I like your couch."

"Whatever," Simon said, carrying the empties and leftovers to the kitchen. "Just don't bitch at me tomorrow when you've got a stiff neck."

"Me? Never. I do not bitch," Tracey corrected imperiously. "I merely uphold a higher level of standards."

"Uh-huh," Simon replied noncommittally. "Just make sure to set your alarm, so you and your 'high standards' can get through the shower in time for both of us to get to work on time."

"Spoilsport," Tracey grumbled, crawling up onto the couch and pulling a throw over her as she punched the pillows to get comfortable. Simon flipped her off with a grin and blew her a mocking kiss good night, feeling better than he had all day.

16

VIC

"That's all of them," Ross said, dropping a pile of folders onto their shared desk. "We've also asked for their credit card and phone histories going back three months. That'll help us retrace their steps, see if there are common touchpoints."

Vic looked at the folders and let out a long breath. He'd reached the point where the break room coffee ate at his gut more than it cleared his head. Myrtle Beach didn't have a huge homicide department—this wasn't Atlanta or Columbia. Ross and Vic had been put on the Slitter case exclusively since the pace of killings had sped up, but the two other detectives in the precinct were being run ragged just following up on the normal activity usually split among both teams.

Like New Orleans or Las Vegas, Myrtle Beach was a place people went to drink too much, party hard, and let their inhibitions run wild. Sometimes that included really bad life choices. The town's transient nature coupled with tourists who weren't always careful enough could be a recipe for tragedy— on top of domestic violence, hold-ups gone wrong, and bad tempers mixed with strong drinks. Being put on the Slitter case was a change of pace, but hardly a respite from the dark, troubling realities of being a homicide detective.

"Let's go over them again. I'm pretty sure I've got them memorized, but maybe something new will jump out at us," Vic said.

Ross pulled up a portable whiteboard. "I'll write—no one can read your chicken scratch," he said, moving over to the side. "Oh, and do you want to explain why you ran 'Billy Bass' through the system? Was that some kind of joke?"

Vic shook his head. "No joke. Just a tip. It's got to mean something, just not sure what."

"A tip. From Simon."

Vic shrugged, not wanting to fight. "Whatever happened to respecting a source's confidentiality?"

Ross leaned in so only Vic could hear him. "All bets are off when you're sleeping with the informant."

"Not relevant."

"It *so* is."

Vic glared at his partner. "You gonna write? Or do I need to take possession of the marker?"

Ross muttered something under his breath that Vic didn't quite catch. He drew lines down the board for several categories: address, work, hobbies, associates. They would likely add more before they were through. Vic and Ross had done this before, when there were fewer victims, and found no glaring connections. But now, with more data points—and some additional new interviews with the victims' families and friends—something they hadn't seen before might show up.

They reviewed the cases in order, from oldest to newest. Vic read the notes aloud, and Ross scribbled on the whiteboard. In his head, Vic kept his own scorecard, alert for any red flags that suggested more connections between the victims and Simon than he already knew about. He hated himself for doing it, but the cop in him didn't have a choice. Vic didn't believe Simon was involved; hell, the Slitter had come after Simon several times. But deep inside, Vic knew Ross was right to be skeptical, and that he owed it to himself to look for evidence that might cast doubt on

Simon, even as he owed it to Simon to look for ways to exonerate him.

After a few hours, Vic set the most recent file down with a thwack. "That's the first five," he said, stifling a yawn. "All J-ones, all worked within the two-mile radius around the parking garage, no obvious connections."

"Once we get through the main files, we'll go down the list of places that laid people off," Ross replied, taking a swig of coffee and grimacing at the bitter taste. "That's a hell of a long list."

It had taken plenty of legwork to hit all the businesses in the sightline of that parking garage and convince them to turn over names of people recently fired. A few of the places volunteered information about individuals who reacted with threats or outbursts, and those names went to the top of the list.

Ross stepped out to get them both more coffee. Vic took the opportunity to text Simon. He felt guilty as hell for not being able to see him, especially since their last "date" had deepened the growing connection between them. Still, maybe a little enforced distance was for the best, his cop brain warned, even if just for appearance's sake. Once the killing spree had ended and the culprit jailed, Vic could make up for lost time. He put his phone away just as Ross returned. Ross noticed as he put down his phone and frowned but wisely chose to say nothing.

They started back into the files. Ross had brought in a second whiteboard with a map, and they'd drawn a circle to show the radius around the parking garage. He marked the locations in which the bodies were found, but the pattern still looked random to Vic.

As far as Vic could tell, none of the first five deaths had any connection to Simon. Simon hadn't claimed them as part of his "skeleton crew," so if they did have any psychic abilities, they weren't known to him. Iryena had worked various locations on the boardwalk; she and Simon might have crossed paths, but for that matter, so had half of the beachgoers on any given weekend. The only connection as far as Vic could see was that he had asked for Simon's help, and Iryena's spirit had responded. He hadn't confided that to Ross and didn't see a reason to do so now.

Katya was the one who had shown up at the library event Simon gave. "So listen to this," Ross said. "According to her roommate, Katya belonged to a local group interested in the occult. A statement from her roommate said she was into reading Tarot cards and had 'spooky friends.'"

"What next?" Vic mocked. "Are you going to tell me she played D&D and that obviously made her a Satan-worshipper? Come on. That's so 1980."

"No idea whether she was into role-playing games, but according to her medical records, there was a history of drug use, and during one hospital-mandated psych evaluation, the interviewers suggested that she was prone to delusions."

Katya had told Simon she dreamed things that came true. That wasn't so far off from the claims Vic had heard growing up from his nonna and some of the older women in his neighborhood. Did she have ability? Or was her belief a symptom of fragile mental health?

"Half the women in my mother's book club also read Tarot cards or went for regular readings," Vic replied. "It's not really that far out. Doesn't make the readings true, but it's hardly fringe behavior."

"Maybe," Ross allowed.

"Then there's Cindy, the stripper you ran through the system because Simon thought she was in danger."

Vic rolled his eyes. "So now anyone who gives us a tip is suddenly a suspect?"

"There's a track record for civilians who get too involved in cases that don't concern them, and it isn't good," Ross reminded him.

"Maybe Cindy read tea leaves in between pole dances?" Vic asked as Ross put another dot on the map.

"You tell me. You're the one with the folder."

Vic glanced down through the interviews they had collected after Cindy's death. The dead woman liked to binge watch the Hallmark channel and Netflix, and she also baked good cookies. To Vic's relief, no one said a word about any psychic abilities, so whatever she thought she could do, she must have shared that secret only with Simon. He wasn't sure whether that was good or bad.

"And then there's Quinn, the most recent kill," Ross replied, making another dot on the map. Vic read out the rest of the details from the folder and watched as Ross marked on the whiteboard. Three of the victims had some personal connection to Simon; two of them were acquaintances if not friends. Tasha, the woman Simon had escorted home who barely evaded the Slitter, would have been another death that linked Simon to the killings.

Vic felt his stomach tighten. He'd seen how upset Simon had been over the readings, and how distressing the visions and nightmares had been, how panicked Simon was the night of the attack. Either Simon was one hell of an actor, or he was genuinely concerned—and at risk. But Vic also knew how anxious the Mayor and the Commissioner were to be able to announce an end to the Slitter's reign of terror.

With billions in tourism at stake, would they care if they got the wrong guy, or would any possible suspect do? Deep down, Vic believed that most officers wanted to do the right thing. But he'd also been around long enough to know that not every cop was honest, and sometimes people's rights got railroaded. The evidence linking Simon to the crimes was flimsy. But would the D.A. be in such a rush to score political points by putting away the Slitter that he might rush to judgment?

Until he had something more concrete, truly damning, Vic intended to keep his mouth shut.

He could cost you your badge, an unpleasant voice in his mind taunted. *Just like before. Honest to a fault. Just remember, no good deed goes unpunished.*

"Quinn's the last one," Vic said. He rubbed his eyes and blinked, feeling the effects of recirculated air and the faint second-hand smoke that clung to the clothing of the detectives who chain-smoked out behind the building and came back in reeking of Marlboros.

"And our outlier," Ross noted, marking a ninth dot. "The only guy."

Vic read the information out of the file once more and paused.

"Okay, one of his roommates said that Quinn belonged to a group that looked into paranormal phenomena."

"Like those ghost hunters on TV?"

"There's a webpage," Vic said and pulled the site up on his computer. "Shit. This group's been active for a couple of years. There are a couple of hundred people signed up."

"Does it show what their meetings have been about, and who attended?" Ross asked, coming to look over his shoulder.

"Yeah," Vic replied, clinking on links. Despite the large number of total members, it appeared that most meetings were attended by twenty or fewer people. "Looks like there was a core group that showed up most of the time, and other people came and went, or tried it and didn't come back," he mused.

"And look at who spoke to the group six months ago," Ross said, pointing. Vic felt his heart speed up when he saw Simon's picture in the "guest speaker" announcement. "Dr. Sebastian Kincaide, author of several books on ghosts and hauntings, will be on hand to talk about spirits, mediumship, and clairvoyance," Ross read aloud.

"The group has several hundred members," Vic countered. "And they've been meeting every month for years. They've had dozens of guest speakers."

"Do a search," Ross instructed. "Let's see how many of the victims either belonged to the group or signed up for a meeting."

With a leaden feeling in his stomach, Vic ran the names. Every one of the victims had, at sometime in the past year, attended at least one of the meetings. Quinn and Cindy were at the program where Simon spoke—not surprising if they were already acquainted, or perhaps that was where Simon met them.

"Contact the administrator. We want a membership list," Ross said. Vic sent an email. "Now let's go back through the past six months and see who the attendees were."

"There could be people who showed up but didn't sign-up through the site," Vic said, battling the nausea rising in his gut.

"We'll see if there were sign-in sheets."

"And if the Slitter went to these meetings looking for a hit list, you think he used his real name?" Vic's worry and uneasiness found a vent in anger.

"Maybe he's a cocky bastard. After all, six months ago the killings hadn't happened yet."

Vic printed off what he could from the group's site. "We should run the rest of the names against the 'recently fired' list," he said. He leaned back in his chair and looked at Ross's dots on the map, and his eyes narrowed as he saw a pattern.

"What?" Ross asked as Vic rose abruptly and walked over to the whiteboard, grabbing the marker. Vic connected the points in silence until he had a five-pointed star.

"It's a pentagram," Vic said quietly. "Simon has a theory that all of the victims were killed because they had some kind of psychic gift."

"Then if he's not a fraud, that either suggests he's the killer—or he's going to be a victim," Ross replied. Vic felt sick at the thought of Simon facing down the Slitter for a third time. He thought about calling to warn him, but what would he say that Simon hadn't already figured out for himself? No, he thought, better to wait until he had something tangible.

But what if Simon's involved? That dark voice in his mind murmured. *He wouldn't have to be the Slitter himself. An accomplice, perhaps? After all, he can't prove those attacks ever happened.*

Vic found himself clenching his jaw as he pushed back the poisonous thoughts. But it was impossible to silence the voice altogether. After all, he was a cop, raised by cops, and he'd been taught since the time he was a kid to be suspicious, look for hidden motives, not take things at face value. He'd seen more than one fellow officer turn mean and cynical, because the truth was, trust came hard for a cop. And, dammit, he'd trusted Simon. Trusted him in bed, and beyond that, with his heart. He'd started to think about being not just lovers, but partners, not just for fun, but maybe forever.

Now, that trust felt fragile. He wondered if Simon had told him everything. There had been times he thought the other man might have been holding back information and had figured Simon was gun-shy about sharing "woo-woo stuff" Vic might not believe. He didn't want to ascribe a darker motive to it, but his cop brain wouldn't shut up, tallying the evidence and whispering suspicions.

"You're going to break your pen," Ross said, and Vic realized how tight his grip was on the ballpoint in his fist. "Something you want to share with the class?"

"No. Just pissed that we still don't have a solid lead," Vic replied, avoiding Ross's gaze.

Vic and Ross ordered from the Lucky Pearl Chinese restaurant across the street from the precinct headquarters. The food was middling at best, but the price was right, and they delivered. They ate quickly, and then Vic and Ross traded roles, with Ross reading off names from first the paranormal group attendees, and then the list of fired employees. By the time they finished, they had a dozen people who had either been fired or laid off that appeared on both lists.

"Tomorrow, we'll run both lists through the system, and see what comes up," Ross said, pushing aside the remnants of his dinner. "You might have your Billy Bass results by then, too. And then maybe you and I go pay a visit to the people on the shortlist."

"Tomorrow," Vic echoed. "Because it's—fuck, it's ten o'clock. No wonder I'm beat."

"And I'm in the doghouse," Ross said with a sigh. "Maybe Jenny'll forgive me when I bring home the overtime pay." He gave Vic a worried look. "Are you going to see Simon tonight?"

Vic wanted to drive over to the blue bungalow, wrap Simon in his arms, and take them both on his bike to someplace far from Myrtle Beach. Or at least, he wanted to fall asleep with Simon, listen to his heartbeat reassuring Vic that they were safe. But even though he was still convinced of Simon's innocence, he knew keeping a little distance was best for both of them.

"I already told him I'd be working late," Vic replied. "And I'm too beat to be good company."

Ross snickered. "Gettin' old, D'Amato," he joked, then grew serious. "Look, I know you like this guy. And I hope he turns out to be legit. But for your sake, please think about how this could look to the Captain while the investigation is ongoing. If Kincaide is cleared, then you can tell everyone—including me—to fuck off."

Vic snorted. "Won't be the first time."

"Probably won't be the last, either," Ross replied as they closed down for the night and walked out together. "Just watch your back."

"Always," Vic assured him, but as he headed for the motorcycle, he had a gut feeling that the worst was yet to come.

By six in the morning, Vic was back at the precinct. The Captain had authorized overtime, and Vic couldn't sleep anyhow—not with real data to parse and Simon's life on the line. He figured he might as well be productive.

The Billy Bass search turned up nothing except jokes at Vic's expense. Vic went back over the whiteboard points, but couldn't find a connection between the talking mechanical fish and any of the bars where the victims had been employed, or their addresses.

At seven, Vic started calling down through the shortlist of paranormal meeting regulars, while he waited for the system to send something back on the longer lists of members and people who had been fired. Later in the day, he and Ross would personally follow up with the dozen names where the two lists intersected.

When his first call—from a phone line that didn't show up on Caller ID as the Myrtle Beach Police Department—got a groggy roommate who swore the person Vic asked for had run off, Vic chalked it up to coincidence. By the fourth call with a similar response, Vic knew they had a pattern. By the end of the list, a third of the people had fled town within the last month, suddenly and without apparent planning.

Vic sat back and stared at his notes. He didn't think the missing attendees had been killed; instead, he figured they had gotten spooked and run for their lives. The unusually high number of sudden departures gave credence to Simon's theory, or at least to the idea that people with low level abilities might have felt targeted and left while they could.

At eight, Vic's personal phone rang. He frowned when he saw Ross's number, but before he could say anything, Ross started talking. "D'Amato. There's been another killing."

"Where?" Vic asked, rising from his chair.

"I've got this," Ross said. "Stay where you are."

"What the fuck?" Vic protested. "Like hell."

"You will stay where you are, or I tell the Captain everything," Ross said in a low rumble. Vic felt a cold chill slither down his spine.

"Simon?" he asked, hating that his voice tightened, as his heart sped up. Another killing and Ross didn't want him there? Did that mean Simon—

"He's not dead," Ross snapped. "But he's the dumbass who found the body and called it in."

Vic sank into his chair, torn between relief that Simon wasn't dead, and panic that his lover had put himself squarely in the crosshairs. "What?"

"You know the old Moonlight Bay hotel? The one that's only a couple of blocks down from his shop?"

"The abandoned one that's been sitting for a while."

"Yeah. With the pool that the taggers have gone nuts with," Ross muttered. "Your boy apparently had a premonition and showed up to check it out—which is at least trespassing, breaking, and entering—and finds a body. Of someone he knows. Now at least he had the sense not to touch it or approach it, but he called it in."

Shit. Fuck. Damn. Vic swung from fear to anger and back again, as the implications hit him. "Why didn't I get the call?"

"Because you've apparently been on the phone for two straight hours," Ross growled. "But Vic, you can't touch this. For his sake, and for yours."

"The hell—"

"Listen to me." Ross shifted to the "command voice" he had learned in the military. "You come forward now, and you get tossed off the case, maybe the unit. Stay behind the scenes, and if there's anything that vindicates him and points to the real killer, we'll find it." He paused. "For what it's worth, I don't think he's the Slitter. He's entirely too freaked out."

Vic closed his eyes and pinched the bridge of his nose, visualizing Simon, panicked and alone, at the murder scene of a friend. "Who died?"

"A guy named Marcus Walker. Worked at Gym-tastic. Ring any bells?"

Vic recognized the name as someone Simon had mentioned, but he hedged. "Maybe."

"I'm going to bring Kincaide in for questioning," Ross said, keeping his voice level as if he were talking to a spooked horse. "You need to be out of sight."

"I want to watch the interrogation." Vic's tone didn't leave room for argument.

"From behind the mirror," Ross conceded.

"And how are you going to explain to the Captain that I'm not where your partner should be?"

Ross sighed. "I'm gonna tell him you're acquainted socially, and so you're staying behind the scenes."

That might work. But the thought of Simon being perp-walked through the precinct in handcuffs made Vic's stomach turn. At the same time, he realized that Ross was taking a huge risk on his behalf. If Simon was the Slitter—or an accomplice—both Ross and Vic would be fired when the Captain found out the truth about Vic's relationship with him and Ross's knowledge.

"Thanks," Vic replied. He felt jittery from the adrenaline flooding his system both from fear and anger, and his hand shook holding the phone.

"Just stay out of the way. I mean it. Fuck this up, and it all goes south." Ross hung up.

Vic passed a hand over his face, trying to get a grip. Simon had found a body and acknowledged he had seen it in a vision. At least he'd had the presence of mind not to contaminate the scene or get blood on himself. Thank God for crime shows. That would have made it worse, but even without fingerprints on the murder weapon, there was plenty of circumstantial connections that wouldn't work in Simon's favor.

Maybe he played you. The dark voice in the back of his mind whispered. *Used you. Lied to you. Conned you. That's what serial killers do. And you thought he cared. You fell in love with him. You've been owned.*

Vic shook his head, resisting the treacherous suspicions. The details that linked Simon to the case could be easily explained—if you believed his abilities were real. But this was South Carolina, and the God-fearing jurors likely to hear the case weren't prone to thinking kindly of anything that smacked of the occult or the supernatural. The D.A. would make Simon out to be crazy or a fraud. Even if he didn't go to jail, he'd be ruined.

Vic heard a ruckus near the doors and drew back to a spot where he could see without being seen. Ross came in first, then two uniforms with Simon between them, cuffed and quiet, head down. Vic's utter relief that Simon hadn't been the victim warred with anger over seeing Simon taken into custody, and fear of what could happen soured his stomach. Mostly, Vic wanted to go to him, comfort him, and take those fucking restraints off. Simon's joke about handcuffs from the day before now seemed like an omen.

Simon raised his head, looking around the room, looking for Vic. When he didn't see Vic, Simon's expression went blank, and his shoulders slumped. Vic hung back until after Ross led Simon into the interrogation room, then slipped into the viewing area behind the one-way mirror. Captain Hargrove was already there, along with a tech to handle recording the audio and video.

"Nice work," the Captain said. "You and Ross have been working it old school. Looks like it might have paid off."

Vic didn't trust himself to speak. He clasped his hands, afraid he would give himself away with their trembling. The uniforms escorted Simon to a chair at the table, leaving him cuffed. Both cops pulled back to stand on either side of the door opposite the mirrored wall, while Simon sat in silence. It was standard procedure to let the anxiety percolate, but Vic hated seeing Simon on the receiving end. Worst of all, he knew Ross would do his job without remorse, and he had seen his partner be a real son of a bitch when it came to questioning a suspect.

Simon turned and looked at the mirror. Vic met his gaze through the glass, although Simon couldn't see him. He had never seen such a bleak look in Simon's eyes, like he'd been gutted, abandoned. Vic knew that's probably exactly how his lover felt since Vic hadn't even shown up to show silent support. Simon looked away, apparently deciding he was entirely on his own, and Vic's heart ached.

"I heard this guy thinks he can talk to ghosts," Captain Hargrove said. "Must think we're stupid."

Vic didn't reply. Ross made a dramatic entrance, throwing the door open so that Simon startled, and then striding across to sit down on the other side of the table.

"State your name," Ross snapped.

"Sebastian Simon Kincaide. Ph.D."

"Employment?"

"I own Grand Strand Ghost Tours."

"You knew the victim?"

"We were acquainted. Not really friends."

"So if you weren't friends, why was a call to your phone one of the last the victim made?"

Simon cleared his throat. "He was afraid. I told him to get out of town."

"Afraid of what?"

"The Slitter."

"And why did he happen to call you, if you weren't friends?"

"He knew me from the shop. He thought the Slitter might be picking victims who had some psychic talent."

Ross let that ride. "Why did you go to an abandoned hotel this morning?"

"I had a dream about something bad happening there, at the pool."

"Most people would have called the cops."

Simon turned to look at the mirror. "The cops wouldn't believe that kind of thing. So I figured I'd see for myself." Vic felt Simon's accusing gaze, and the sadness and betrayal made Vic's throat tighten.

"Damn right," Captain Hargrove muttered behind Vic.

"And what happened when you got to the pool?"

"I saw a body," Simon said. "I recognized Marcus from a distance." A bitter smile touched his lips. "I've watched enough to TV to know not to touch anything. So I called it in."

"You could have used an anonymous tip line. Why use your own phone and wait for the police?"

Simon raised his head and looked Ross straight in the eyes. "I didn't know Marcus well, but he deserved some dignity. That's why I stayed."

Vic closed his eyes, fighting back emotion. The answer was so totally *Simon*. Vic was more sure than ever that he loved Simon and certain that he'd just lost his chance at earning Simon's love in return.

"Maybe you stayed because you wanted to show off your handiwork," Ross said, upping the ante.

Simon's expression grew cold, and as terrified as he must have been, none of that showed in his eyes. "I want my phone call. And I want a lawyer."

Ross tried several other lines of questioning, but Simon only repeated his requests. When the two uniforms led Simon out to use the phone, Ross put both hands on the table and let his head hang. The tech in the observation room turned off the equipment.

"He can lawyer up all he wants," Captain Hargrove said. "If he did it, you and Ross will nail him for it." He left the room, and Vic trailed behind, feeling like his entire world was coming unglued.

Ross was waiting when Vic returned to their desk. His partner looked worn thin, and Vic knew that interrogation was partly real, and partly a high-energy performance. "What now?" Vic asked tonelessly.

"Now, we put Kincaide on ice until his lawyer gets here."

Vic frowned. He had somehow expected Simon to ask for a public defender. "Who's his lawyer?"

"I don't know. He called someone in Charleston to arrange

counsel. I guess we'll find out soon enough." Ross looked away. "Look, I know this is hard—"

"You don't know shit," Vic snapped. He realized that Ross wasn't the right target for his anger, but after seeing his lover frightened, humiliated, and intimidated, Vic barely restrained the urge to punch something.

"I know that he didn't give you up to us," Ross said in a low voice. "He could have thrown your name around, tossed you under the bus with him. But he didn't. Not once."

Probably because there was no relationship left to rely on from Simon's perspective, Vic thought. It was more likely that Simon thought Vic had somehow betrayed his confidence, or at least no longer believed in his talent or his innocence. There wasn't any way to come back from this, Vic thought sickly. Too much damage, too many bridges burned even if Simon was ultimately vindicated.

That hurt even more than his long-ago break up with Nate, Vic realized. Nate's leaving had hurt Vic's pride and his ego, saddened him, but nothing like the way the thought of losing Simon ached so bad Vic could barely breathe. It killed him thinking that Simon was locked up in a cell, certain that he had been completely abandoned. Everything in Vic wanted to comfort and protect, and not being able to do so was an unbearable helplessness.

"It's not over yet," Ross said, jolting Vic out of his thoughts. His partner's eyes were sympathetic. "I don't think he did it. Any of it. I'm not ready to sign on to get my palm read, but I just don't think he's a killer."

"I don't, either," Vic said. He took several deep breaths and felt himself growing cold, the way he always coped with loss and grief. Bury it deep, and don't deal with it until it digs its way back up out of the grave. After a few moments, he could function, as long as he didn't think about Simon. "I found some information this morning that I think you'll want to see."

A little over two hours later, Vic and Ross looked up as two strangers walked in like they owned the place. One was a man in his early thirties, blond hair, broad shoulders, and a suit that easily cost a couple of grand. With him was an older man in a bespoke seersucker suit and bow tie, the hallmark of blue-blood Charleston aristocracy. The older man spoke to the desk sergeant, who called over a uniform to escort the two men to the cells. They walked back out with Simon between them, much faster than usual. Simon never even tried to look for Vic, just kept his eyes straight ahead.

"Holy mother of God," Ross muttered. He called up to the front. "What law firm were those guys from?" he asked, and paled a bit when he heard the answer. "Shit. Thanks." Vic raised an eyebrow.

"Your boy has connections—and money. Those lawyers were from Benton Connor Hawthorn in Charleston, and to get here this fast, they must have left almost as soon as he placed his call."

Vic recognized the name. BCH handled high-profile litigation, and their criminal defense attorneys were the best in the state. "Fuck. How—"

"Not only that, but the blond guy? He's Anthony Benton, son of the main partner, great-grandson of the founder," Ross went on like he'd just seen a celebrity. "And the old man? Drayton Conrad. Ring a bell?"

Vic felt gobsmacked. Drayton Conrad represented big-shot celebrities who got on the wrong side of the law, politicians whose improprieties caught up with them, and CEOs who ran afoul of the rules. "Yeah, I've heard of him."

"I'm guessing their hourly fee is more than my car payment. Hell, more than my mortgage," Ross said. "So how does a guy who runs a ghost tour store afford that kind of representation, let alone have two of the best lawyers in the state hotfoot it over here when he whistles?"

"I have no idea," Vic replied, mystified.

"Well, I don't think you've got to worry about your boyfriend taking the fall for this," Ross said quietly. "Because they'll shred the circumstantial evidence and burn our case to the ground if we even tried to take this to court."

That was good, Vic thought. With that kind of representation, Simon wouldn't get railroaded by an ambitious district attorney. But that didn't mean he was safe from the Slitter. And it didn't change a thing about the damage done by Vic's absence and perceived betrayal.

"I think I know what we need to do next," Vic said, in a voice he barely recognized as his own. "Come on. We've got work to do. We both think the Slitter is out there. Let's find him."

17

SIMON

The day had started off so well, only to go straight to hell. After their late-night movie binge, Simon had set his alarm for six, giving him just four hours of sleep but assuring he would wake up in time to get Tracey off to work. Although Tracey ran Mizzenmast Coffee, she wasn't a natural morning person, to say the least.

By six-thirty, the coffee was ready, Simon had laid out muffins and butter, and Tracey was up, showered and reasonably coherent. He pushed her out the door after a hug and a quick breakfast, promising to stop by Le Miz later that day, and not to let so much time go by between movie nights.

Now that he was fully awake, Simon took his second cup of coffee to the table and pulled out his laptop. His night had been restless, despite several glasses of wine, and the Billy Bass clue had churned in his mind. *What if it's a symbol, not a real thing? Billy is Bill is William. And Bass?*

He fired up his browser and pulled up a search engine, then looked for 'last names starting with "F." Scrolling down, Simon found plenty of sites and started taking notes. "Fish, Fishback, Fishbaugh, Fishbeck, Fishbein, Fishburn, Fisher, Fisherman, Fishman," he muttered, noting that all those could also be spelled with an "sch" as well. "Oh, and let's not forget Marlin, Pike, Cod, and Shad," he said.

Next, he put the first name "William" in front of each surname and searched for hits in South Carolina. That eliminated quite a few options, leaving him with ten names. Glancing down the search results, he eliminated three more people, since the information showed them to be over seventy years old.

Simon had thought about this all night as he tossed and turned. He remembered some of the other store owners talking about how they ran potential new hires through an online background check, looking for bad debts, criminal records, and other red flags. A search pulled up several options, and after a few minutes, Simon chose one with the features he needed, paid the fee for the first month's subscription, and entered the seven remaining names.

Since it would take a while to get results, Simon turned his attention to the envelope he had found by the shop door last night. It had been pushed aside in the rush to get breakfast. Simon grabbed a pair of latex gloves from a box under the kitchen sink, and handled the envelope gingerly, spreading clean paper towels on the table to try to keep from contaminating the contents.

He worked open the flap, and four large photos slid out, gruesome close-ups of the Slitter's victims. These weren't police pictures, Simon knew by looking at them. These were the killer's personal trophies. A sticky note attached to the top photo read *"You're next"* in block print marker.

Simon shoved the photos back into the envelope and ran to the sink to throw up. He braced himself on the edge of the basin, shaky and lightheaded. He had barely glanced at the pictures, but beneath the blood, he had recognized Quinn, Katya, Cindy, and a dark-haired woman he thought might be Iryena from the ice cream cart. It was no accident that out of all the Slitter's victims, he had chosen photos of people Simon knew for his vicious taunt.

It took a few minutes for Simon to collect his wits. He put on fresh gloves, wrapped the envelope in paper towels, and put it in a folder he got from his home office. He added the list of fish-related names, and printed out the pictures from his phone of the niding horse and the bloody puddle at the shop's front door, and added those to the folder as well.

Simon grabbed a tablet and started to jot down a timeline, from the first reading he had done for Vic, through the other dreams, visions, and ghostly appearances, noting the dates and times. He added the date and phone number of the threatening call, as well as the other attacks, and finally, the death omen dream and the call from Marcus. Then he set the tablet inside the folder as well and finished his coffee, debating his next move.

He looked at the folder and considered calling Vic. But Vic had seemed distant lately, wrapped up in the case, and Simon knew that what he had collected were mere odds and ends, nothing that might turn the tide of the investigation. Vic would worry about the envelope's threat, but there were no markings to identify the sender, and although he had been careful handling the paper, he doubted the Slitter would be careless enough to leave a fingerprint or DNA evidence.

Simon wasn't even sure where he stood with Vic right now. More than a one night stand, but less than a boyfriend. Simon would willingly give the relationship time to grow if Vic seemed inclined to deepen their connection. But Simon's psychic ability was the big ghostly elephant in the room, the thing they didn't want to talk about and couldn't evade. No, he thought with a sigh. He couldn't take the jumble of information he'd collected to Vic. Not yet. Not until he had something that would stand up to police scrutiny, something that could be proven.

He had one lead he hadn't followed up on. The vision of the graffiti-tagged pool at the old Moonlight Bay Hotel had been a strong one. He checked the time and saw that it wasn't yet eight a.m. If he hurried, he could stop by the abandoned site on his way to work. If he found something useful, he'd take photos, and maybe then Vic would believe him. Since the background check would take a little while to run, and Simon needed to get to the shop, it seemed like the best option to stay one step ahead of a killer.

The boardwalk was quiet when Simon arrived. Most tourists

didn't wake this early, the shops weren't open yet, and early-bird walkers tended to prefer the beach. A chain-link fence surrounded Moonlight Bay, but it had been bent and breached numerous times by thrill-seekers and urban explorers, so getting through a gap posed little problem.

In its day, Moonlight Bay might have been charming, with its white walls and blue balconies just a stone's throw from the beach. Now, rust streaked the white paint, and the balconies looked likely to collapse. Draperies sagged in the windows, and vandals had broken out some of the glass on the first floor.

Simon headed right for what had once been an indoor-outdoor pool. In bad weather, large Plexiglas panes could be slipped into place, keeping the pool warm while protecting against the chill. During temperate seasons, the pool was open air with the glass removed, and back in the day would have had a clear line of sight right to the ocean.

Graffiti artists had "decorated" the walls in overlapping colors with designs, gang signs, and funky murals that vied for attention. Very little of the original beach-themed painting showed through the layers of spray paint. As Simon reached the pool deck, he realized that the motel hadn't truly been abandoned, merely co-opted, given the amount of garbage, used condoms, and drug paraphernalia left in the corners. He walked carefully, sniffing the air. The hotel smelled of water damage and mildew, and another scent that grew stronger as he neared the long-empty pool.

Simon reached the edge of the pool at the same instant he recognized the smell of blood and decay. A body lay on the cracked tile at the bottom, surrounded by a large enough circle of dark liquid Simon had no doubt the person was dead. From this angle, he could recognize the face. Marcus.

He stumbled back, sickened and horrified. Simon's first impulse was to leave and call in the murder from a pay phone. Then again, that hadn't shielded his identity before, and someone was likely to see him fleeing the scene of a crime, which would only make things worse. Calling Vic would be a mistake because it would compromise him even more than he already was by his connection to Simon.

Still in shock, Simon pulled out his phone and dialed 911. "I'd like to report a murder."

Ten minutes later, when the police arrived, Simon hadn't moved from where he had backed away from the horrific view of Marcus's dead body, to stand against the wall. He knew enough not to touch anything, and so he waited, hands clasped in front of him, for the officers to swarm in, wondering if Vic and his partner would be among them.

A tall, blond man with a football player's build headed right for Simon. "Simon Kincaide?" The man gave him the once-over. Simon nodded in assent. "You called 911?" Again, Simon nodded, as the reality of the situation overwhelmed him. He'd gone from being the target of a serial killer to being a murder suspect.

At least if I'm in jail, maybe the Slitter can't get me.

"Have you touched anything? Handled the body in any way?"

That startled Simon out of his shock. "No. Of course not. I saw the body from the edge of the pool and backed away. Then I called you. I didn't touch anything."

"I'm Detective Hamilton, Myrtle Beach Homicide. I need you to wait right here, and then you'll need to come down to the station and give your statement."

Simon nodded, feeling like he had been suddenly transported into one of the crime dramas he occasionally watched on TV. He recognized the man's name. Ross Hamilton was Vic's partner. So why the hell was he teamed up with a different man now? Simon could see Hamilton was heatedly debating something with another cop on the other side of the pool.

Vic wasn't coming. Had Simon's involvement somehow gotten Vic in trouble, maybe even taken off the case? Simon's heart sank. A man he knew lay dead in a garbage-strewn hotel. The Slitter had his sights on Simon for his next victim. The cops were going to have a field day with this new twist, making Simon a suspect. And Vic? If he had any sense of self-preservation, for his reputation and his career, he had probably turned over everything Simon had confided and washed his hands of his troublesome lover. Just like Jacen had.

A uniformed officer walked over to Simon, his face grim. "We need you to come down to the station and give your statement," he said, pulling out a set of handcuffs.

"Am I under arrest?" Simon blurted, eyes wide.

"Just questions right now," the cop said. He held out the cuffs. "Standard procedure." Simon's heart sank as he felt the cold metal click around his wrists.

Across the pool deck, Simon could see Detective Hamilton on his phone, scowling. He ended the call, pocketed the device, and strode over to the two uniforms who had come to wait with Simon.

"Let's go," Hamilton said, not giving Simon a second look as he led the way out of Moonlight Bay.

Hours later, after he had survived Hamilton's interrogation, spent time in a jail cell, and finally been rescued by lawyers he had never met before, Simon was back home again. The lawyers had warned him to stay away from anyone involved in the case, to lie low, and to not yet hand the photos over to the police. His cousin, Cassidy, had come through big-time by sending the lawyers. Simon had called Jay and asked him to put a sign on the door to Grand Strand Ghost Tours saying that the shop was closed for a death in the family. That was near enough to the truth and the kind of excuse that might temper a customer's ire.

Throughout his ordeal, Simon wondered where Vic was. But he hadn't spotted him in the police department as he'd been walked in and out, and Vic didn't join Hamilton for the interrogation. Maybe he had been behind the mirrored glass window, but he hadn't been anywhere to offer even silent support.

What did you expect? Did you think he was going to sweep you up in his arms and protect you? A noxious voice in his mind taunted. No matter how Vic felt about him, Simon knew the man couldn't afford to show that kind of support, not in the middle of a murder investigation when his lover had just become a prime suspect. Unfortunately, that didn't soothe the ache of abandonment in Simon's heart or the bitter sense of déjà vu. Vic might well cut ties to save his badge, but it didn't change how Simon felt about him. Tracey said Vic needed to decide what he wanted. It was clear he had made his choice.

"Picked a helluva time to fall in love, Kincaide," he muttered to himself.

His phone rang, and Simon hated himself for wishing, just for an instant, that the caller would be Vic. Instead, he took a deep breath and answered. "Cassidy?"

"Simon! Are you all right? My god, what happened?"

Simon had used his one phone call to let Cassidy know he was sitting in jail on suspicion of murder after Hamilton had detained him following the interrogation. "I'm home," Simon said. "And it's a mess, but I didn't do anything, Cassidy."

"I know you didn't," his cousin replied.

"The cops don't like psychics or mediums," Simon said miserably. He gave her the key information, including his ill-fated affair with Vic, but left out some of the details. The last thing he wanted was for Cassidy and her friends to have their own abilities come to the Slitter's attention.

"I don't know how to thank you for sending the lawyers," Simon said. "And honestly, I'm not sure how long it'll take me to repay you. BHC is a big deal."

"Anthony Benton is Teag's Anthony," Cassidy said, reminding him about her best friend's long-time romantic relationship. "He's one of *those* Bentons. And Sorren said he'll pay the bill for your defense if it comes to that. Says we owe you far more for all the lore you've looked into for us over the years." Her business partner was a very wealthy man, from an old European family. If Simon weren't so completely freaked out, he would have been less comfortable about accepting help. As it was, all he could do was accept with an overwhelming sense of relief.

"Thank you," Simon said. "I don't know what I would have done."

"You're welcome. It's what family does," Cassidy assured him. "Do you need anything?"

"I've warded the house," Simon replied. "I'm safe for now."

"Stay that way," she ordered. "And when all of this is over, come down and take some time off."

"I promise," Simon said. "And, thanks." He ended the call and stared out the window.

His budding romance had gone down in flames. A serial killer was hunting him and had just killed another of Simon's acquaintances. Simon was too shaken to go down to the shop today, and god knows who from the stores along the boardwalk had seen him led out to a police car in handcuffs. On the bright side, there hadn't been any news crews to splash his face all over TV. It wasn't much of a win, but Simon would take what he could get.

Simon made a fresh pot of coffee and turned his attention to his computer. He logged into the background search site and pulled up the results of his query. Out of the seven names he had supplied, five of them had no prior arrests, no run-ins with the law worse than parking tickets or speeding violations, and no other red flag indicators like bad debts or old restraining orders.

Two of the names, however, caught Simon's attention. William Fishbein had a long record of theft, had done time in the South Carolina state penitentiary, and had recently been arrested for check fraud. One look at his picture told Simon this wasn't the man he'd glimpsed in the cap and sunglasses.

William Fischer, on the other hand, had been picked up a couple of times on drunk and disorderly charges and had a DUI on his record. Those were several years old, and not in Myrtle Beach. For the past two years, he'd been working construction with one of the companies Simon recognized as being a leading builder for the local hospitality industry. He'd also been laid off, six months ago.

Simon looked at the man in the photograph. Fischer was in his early thirties, with short blond hair and cold eyes. The face structure fit the man Simon had glimpsed on more than one occasion, the one he believed to be the Slitter. Interestingly enough, the site showed an address for Fischer only up through five months prior. Now, the report read "*address unknown*."

Simon printed the report and added it to his folder. He pulled up his browser and searched on the name of the builder that had employed Fischer. Simon frowned as he read the results. As it turned out, Bolton Construction had run into financial difficulty lately, according to several news sites. Recent storms, price hikes in building materials, and clients who went bankrupt or were bought out had forced the company into crisis. As a result, they had stopped work on some of their more ambitious projects and laid off much of their workforce.

The list of Bolton's construction projects was fairly long, but Simon's heart thudded as he focused on the shorter list of buildings whose progress was put on indefinite hold due to the company's hardship. As he skimmed the names, his breath caught at one in particular.

Three Triton Place was a twenty-story hotel with shops and restaurants on its lower floors, not far from the boardwalk. It wasn't a new building, but rather an ambitious remodeling and repurposing of an older tower. Simon had watched it be gutted and made over during the past year or two and then noticed when activity stopped short of completion. All the windows were in place, and at a glance, the structure looked ready for business, but none of the inside finish work had been done beyond basic wiring and plumbing. Simon remembered hearing gossip at Le Miz about local subcontractors complaining that they were stuck holding onto shipments of carpet, wallpaper, fixtures, and furnishings because the project had stalled.

The dream. When I died. Something about the setting in that dream had tugged at Simon's memories as if he had forgotten something important. Now that he saw the before and after pictures of Three Triton Place and is predecessor, Poseidon Plaza, Simon remembered a party he had attended during the first year he had lived in Myrtle Beach, at the Poseidon. It was a charity fundraising dinner held in one of the upper floor ballrooms, and an unusual view of the SkyWheel and the ocean beyond had mesmerized Simon at the time.

The same view he had seen and not quite recognized in the vision that foretold his death.

Simon scrambled to print out a map of Myrtle Beach, and then checked news sites about the Slitter murders to find the locations of the victims' bodies. He plotted them on the map, and then connected the dots into a five-pointed star. Five points, and five places the lines crossed. Ten bodies, including Marcus. And in the middle of the pentacle was Three Triton Place.

Simon's mouth went dry. He knew who the Slitter was, and where he would kill again—and who the victim would be. And the police would never believe him. Simon lost his inside contact with Vic and his credibility after today's debacle. But if the police did corner Fischer, and the man had been able to "steal" the magic or psychic energy of his victims, then they would be walking into a deadly trap without any way to counter their quarry's attack.

All at once, Simon figured out the missing piece that had eluded him, the Slitter's real end game. What was the point of bleeding off the psychic energy from other people unless you intended to do something with it, something big?

Fischer had a history of anger management problems and impulse control. He'd gotten laid off right before the killing started. Simon wasn't his last victim, just his final "battery charger." Fischer intended to go out with a bang. A big, magically powered explosion, to get back at the company that had let him go. Fischer meant to go postal, and he was going to do it with stolen magic.

Simon might be the only one who could stop him.

He thought about his contacts, the people who depended on him to help them hunt things that went bump in the night with ancient lore and obscure translations. Seth Tanner was somewhere up north at the moment, and so was Mark Wojcik. It would take them at least two days to reach Myrtle Beach, and neither of them had psychic abilities of their own.

Cassidy was closer—Charleston was less than two hours away. But Cassidy's ability was psychometry, reading the history and emotional resonance of objects by touching them. Teag had some kind of Weaver magic, something about weaving spells into cloth. Neither sounded to Simon like they involved defensive skills, nothing that would be good in a fight. He did not want to bring anyone else into a situation where they could get hurt. That left the task to Simon.

He let out a long sigh, drained his now-cold cup of coffee, and tore a sheet of paper out of the tablet. Mustering his courage, Simon wrote a letter to Vic, all the things he hadn't had the nerve to say in person, and everything he had uncovered about the Slitter. He paused after he signed his name, and felt the ache of losing Vic. But one way or the other, it was over. If Simon faced off with the Slitter and lost, the future was moot. But even if by some miracle Simon managed to stop the killer, it wouldn't make Vic suddenly believe in his psychic abilities. It would always be a choice between Simon and Vic's badge, and Simon felt certain that answer was already decided.

With my luck, I'll stop the Slitter and get charged with his murder.

Simon folded up the letter, put it in an envelope, sealed the flap, and wrote Vic's name on the outside, placing it inside the folder on top of everything else. He went to the windows, glancing out from all corners of the house, but he couldn't see any surveillance. Still, Simon figured the cops would have someone watching him. Whatever he did next, he'd need to make sure he wasn't followed.

He spent the next few hours gathering materials and making a plan. It wasn't necessarily a *good* plan, but it was better than nothing, and the best he could manage, given the circumstances. Simon drew on all the knowledge of lore he had gained in his years of study, but William Fischer wasn't a demon or a warlock, or a monstrous beast out of legend. He was a sick, sadistic bastard who had stolen power that didn't belong to him for the purpose of getting revenge, a supernatural terrorist.

Simon glanced at his phone. No calls or texts from Vic. He hadn't expected any. Well, he might have hoped, but he didn't really *expect* any. There were at least twenty missed calls from Tracey. He couldn't face talking to her right now. Simon imagined that she'd heard he'd been led away in handcuffs this morning, and seen the sign on the shop window. He listened to the increasingly shrill messages and knew her anger covered fear and concern.

Another glance at the time, late afternoon already, assured him that Tracey would be in the end of day rush and not answering. His call went to voice mail as he planned.

"Hey Tracey. It's Simon. Hasn't been my best day. I figured you heard. No matter what anyone says, I didn't hurt anyone. But I've got to take care of something, and no one else can do it. If you don't hear from me in twelve hours, I need you to call Homicide Lieutenant Vic D'Amato and let him into my apartment. There are papers on the table that he'll need. I hope I'll see you tomorrow for coffee. But if I don't, take care of yourself. And, thanks for everything. Gotta go."

He paused, then touched another contact in his list. After a few rings, Miss Eppie answered. "Sebastian? Is that you?"

"I need a favor," Simon said, hoping his voice sounded normal because his heart seemed to be in his throat. "Do you remember when you told me you didn't curse people unless they really, really deserved it? I found out who the Slitter is. He's after me next. Can you curse him?"

"How do you know he's after you?" Miss Eppie's voice was sharp and worried.

"He told me so."

"Son, you just can't help stepping in it, can you? What kind of curse did you have in mind?"

"What can you do? I think he's been stealing power from low-level psychics, and I'm afraid that's going to make him hard to fight. I don't want the police to get slaughtered, and they won't listen to me if I warn them." It was close enough to the truth, for now.

"You have anything that belonged to him? Hair, clothing, that sort of thing?"

Simon looked at the envelope. The only things there that had belonged briefly to the Slitter were important pieces of evidence. "No, not really."

"That's going to make it harder, but I will try," Miss Eppie said. "Tell me his name, his address, anything personal you know about him. I'll do a crossing spell. It's more potent if I have personal objects, but information will do in a pinch."

Simon gave her all the details he knew about William Fischer, while Miss Eppie listened attentively. When he finished, she was quiet for a moment.

"Sebastian Kincaide, I don't think you've told me everything. I'll do as you ask because he does deserve it. But you listen to me, son. Whatever you're gonna do, you be careful. You carry those charms I gave you, and don't think my curse is going to make a snake like that less dangerous all by itself. It'll help—I do good work—but he can still bite. You hear me? Best way to fight evil is with what you have inside you. That's the strongest magic you've got."

He thanked her, ended the call and turned it to silent. Simon gathered his small cache of weapons—three knives and an ice pick —as well as his protective charms. He added a paintball gun and some extra clips. Those all went into a small gym bag, along with a couple of flashlights, a length of rope, and a few other odds and ends that might be useful. His entire plan lay in surprising the Slitter in his lair, and facing off with him, pitting his scant magic and inborn psychic energy against what the killer had managed to steal from his victims.

No matter what it cost, Simon intended to make sure the killing ended tonight.

18

VIC

"Slow down," Ross urged, jogging to catch up with Vic.

"I've lost enough time already," Vic replied, not altering his pace. *I've lost Simon, but I'm not going to let him get charged with a murder I know he didn't commit.*

After Simon's lawyers had freed him—and simultaneously put the Myrtle Beach PD on notice that they'd better have a *damn* good reason to continue bothering Kincaide, Vic had thrown himself into the case for the rest of the afternoon. He wasn't ready to face the heartache of the fallout from Simon's arrest. Simon had clearly been looking for Vic, and Vic wouldn't fault him for considering his absence a betrayal. On top of Vic's unsteady belief in Simon's psychic gifts, it was probably the last blow to their budding relationship.

Vic and Simon had barely gotten started, so why did it feel like Vic's chest was being crushed? He kept his phone out, hoping against hope for a text. He'd picked up the phone to send his own a dozen times or more, and put it back down, at a loss for what to say. All he knew was that he wanted far more time with Simon than they had spent together, and he had hoped for a future that now looked highly unlikely.

Now was not the time to grieve, not when the Slitter remained on the loose and Simon had as much to risk from a killer as he did from the police. The best way Vic could show his love was by getting to the bottom of this mess and hoping there might be a chance to fix things between them later.

By five, Vic's eyes blurred, and he had reached a dead end with the files. That's when he had announced he was going down to interview boardwalk regulars, in case anyone had seen something out of the ordinary. So here they were, working door to door, while Vic tried to come up with what he planned to say when they got as far as Grand Strand Ghost Tours.

They had already been in and out of four shops, with no luck. The staff hadn't come in early enough that morning to notice anything at Moonlight Bay before Simon got there or hadn't worked late enough the night before to get a glimpse of the murderer.

"The timing is all wrong," Vic grumbled. MBPD already had an approximate time of death—between 6 p.m. and 11 p.m. the previous night. Vic bet on the later time since the boardwalk would be quieter then, making it easier to slip into the old hotel unnoticed.

"You know we have to look closely at whoever finds the body," Ross replied, sounding aggrieved. Vic knew he shouldn't be pissed at his partner for bringing in Simon, but watching Simon's interrogation had been one of the worst experiences of Vic's career.

"If he'd been the one to leave the body there at midnight, he'd have no reason to go back at eight the next morning," Vic responded. It was unfair to be angry with Ross, but right now the storm of feelings he struggled to repress had to come out somewhere.

"I'm on your side, remember?" Ross said. "And on his."

Vic sighed. "I know. Sorry. It's just—"

"Yeah. I get it. Come on," Ross said. "Next up is a tattoo parlor. You need to add anything to your collection?"

Fuck, that just made Vic remember how it had felt to have Simon's tongue trace the swirls on his shoulder, the pattern of his sleeve. He'd been ready to get new ink in the cleft of his hip just for Simon. Now, those memories just made the ache sharper.

"This is where I got the others done when I moved here," Vic replied. He walked in first, and Jay, the owner looked up.

"Vic! Great to see you. Looking to add to your collection?"

Before Vic could answer, Jay's expression darkened when Ross walked in. "What are you doing here?" Jay's voice was suddenly cold.

"This is my partner, Lieutenant Hamilton—"

"I know who he is," Jay said, crossing his inked arms over his chest. "I saw you take Simon away from the old Moonlight Bay hotel this morning like he was a goddamn criminal. But where the hell were you day before yesterday, when some asshole dumped blood all over his doorstep? What did you do about the threatening phone calls?"

Vic felt light headed. "What blood? What calls?"

The friendliness that had greeted Vic earlier had chilled to wary regard. "Day before yesterday, I was walking to my shop and I passed Simon's place. He wasn't in yet. Looked like someone had dumped a bucket of blood all over his doorstep. Stank like high heaven," Jay said.

"Simon got there a few minutes after I did. He went in through the back, washed it all down with bleach, and hosed it off. Said he'd had a threatening phone call, too, but there was nothing for the cops to do about it because the number was out of service." Jay looked at Vic and Ross like he'd just thrown down a gauntlet.

"He never told me," Vic said. "I swear, I didn't know."

Jay looked unconvinced. "I think there've been other threats. That's why he started the neighborhood watch. And you know what? I bet whoever's behind all this didn't much like having the rest of us on notice. So maybe you need to arrest the right guy, and give hardworking guys like Simon some protection."

Out on the boardwalk once more, Vic walked to the railing and braced his arms, looking at the ocean. Ross came to stand next to him.

"Talk to me, D'Amato. I know the wheels are turning."

Vic never took his eyes off the sea. "Simon didn't trust us— didn't trust me—enough to tell me about either the blood or the phone call," he said, his voice rough. "We probably couldn't have traced them. But if we'd been notified, it would be in the record—"

"And it would count in his defense if anyone seriously looked at him for the murders," Ross added. He turned to lean his back against the railing so he was facing Vic. "There's got to be some connection, some reason for the threats."

"Simon thought he knew what it was," Vic replied tonelessly. "And it wasn't one we'd believe."

"Hey! D'Amato!" Vic turned at the shout, and Ross stood, warily moving up beside him. A tall woman with dark brown skin and long braids tinged in crimson came striding toward them, glowering. She stopped in front of Vic, and he noticed she was about Simon's height, so she didn't have to look up much to meet his gaze. Something about her looked very familiar, although he couldn't place her.

"You're Vic? Simon's Vic?" she demanded.

"Yeah," Vic replied, hoping that was still true.

"Who are you?" Ross had shifted a half-step ahead, expecting trouble.

"Tracey Cullen. I own the Mizzenmast. And I'm Simon's best friend."

Now Vic knew why she looked familiar, and he had an inkling as to why she was also so angry. But before he could say anything, Tracey held up her phone.

"Do you know what's going on with him? Jay calls me to tell me he's been arrested, and that the cops found a dead man in that fleabag motel. I called Simon twenty times since this morning, to find out why he never showed up at the shop. And what's with that 'death in the family' notice on the door? He ignores my calls all day, and then he leaves me this," she said, cycling through screens on her phone until she played a voicemail on speaker.

"Hey Tracey. It's Simon. Hasn't been my best day. I figured you heard. No matter what anyone says, I didn't hurt anyone. But I've got to take care of something, and no one else can do it. If you don't hear from me in twelve hours, I need you to call Homicide Lieutenant Vic D'Amato and let him into my apartment. There are papers on the table that he'll need. I hope I'll see you tomorrow for

coffee. But if I don't, take care of yourself. And, thanks for everything. Gotta go."

She lowered the phone and stood, hands on hips, staring at Vic. "That was three hours ago. He called during the late rush when that boy knew I wouldn't be able to pick up. I heard that message, and I said, 'fuck no, I'm not waiting twelve hours,' but then I didn't know what to do. And now Jay calls me again and says you're down here asking questions, and I'm wondering why the hell you aren't out looking for him."

Vic's whole body had gone cold, numb. He heard sadness and resignation in Simon's recorded voice, as well as a grim determination that chilled Vic. Somehow, Simon had cracked the case, and he'd decided to make the next move on his own. That scared Vic down to his bones, but even worse was the assumption in Simon's wording that he wouldn't live through whatever he had planned.

"Can you get me into his house? So I don't have to break down his door? Do you know what he left there?" Vic had always been able to lock a mental steel firewall on his emotions when the going got rough, but the iron willpower that usually came easily from long practice eluded him tonight.

"Yeah, I can get you in. No, I don't have any idea about what he left." Tracey turned and walked away, then stopped a few paces later. "What are y'all waitin' for? Come on!"

They hiked the few blocks to the blue bungalow at a brisk pace. Sweat plastered shirts to skin and sent rivulets down their faces and arms. The air conditioning hit them like a sledgehammer of ice when Tracey unlocked the door.

"I figure you know your way around," Tracey said, and her tone carried a hint of censure, making Vic's face warm. Had Simon discussed their fledgling relationship with her? Obviously so, and from Tracey's protective attitude, Vic guessed that Simon might have also confided misgivings about Vic's depth of commitment.

"Yeah, I can find the kitchen," Vic replied, refusing to meet Ross's gaze. Ross followed as he led the way, with Tracey trailing behind.

"You know, I saw on TV that they took someone into custody

for maybe murdering that guy this morning, and then Jay said it was Simon, and I thought for sure his detective boyfriend would take better care of him than that." She sounded just like Vic's disapproving aunt. Even Ross flinched.

"'Cuz you see, there's no way Simon had any time at all to go kill someone yesterday," Tracey continued. "He opened that shop at nine, and the two of us, we text back and forth all day. He told me he was slammed so hard, he didn't even get to eat except up at the register, all the way through until it was time for the tours. He's got security cameras on the shop, so I bet there's footage showing exactly where he was. Then he had two sold-out ghost tours, and the people from the first tour stayed to buy things, so he barely got them out the door so he could take the next group. That's forty to fifty people who can vouch for where he was from six until nine."

She barely took a breath. "Then I met him at the shop door right at nine 'cuz we had plans. And I know for damn sure he didn't kill anyone after that, because I went home with him and spent the night."

Ross raised an eyebrow, and Vic felt a stab of confusion. Tracey rolled her eyes. "Hell, no. I don't swing that way, and neither does he. My girlfriend would kill me. But Simon and me, we watched stupid movies and drank wine and ate junk food until two in the morning. Then he woke me up at six to get to work. I slept on the couch, between his room and the door. And lord knows, that boy is as stealthy as an elephant in oversized combat boots. He sure didn't sneak out past me. I was tipsy, but I wasn't blacked-out drunk."

Vic and Ross exchanged a look. *He had an alibi. And airtight alibi for the whole time.* And although Vic had never seriously thought Simon was involved in Marcus's death, his cop brain sighed in relief.

They walked into the kitchen, and Vic saw a Manila folder on the table. On top of the folder was a sealed letter-sized envelope that just said "*Vic.*" The sight of that envelope sent a current of fear through his body.

"Read it," Ross urged quietly. "I'll start on the rest of the folder."

Ross sat at the table with Tracey hanging over his shoulder. Vic walked a few paces away and tore open the envelope.

Dear Vic,

I love you. No matter what happens, I needed to say that. I know it's too soon, and that you probably don't feel the same way, but I wanted to tell you.

I had nothing to do with Marcus's death. A premonition sent me to Moonlight Bay. At least we found him.

In the folder is everything I've worked out about the Slitter. His name is William Fischer, he got laid off from the construction project at Three Triton Place, and I'm positive he's stealing energy from low-level psychics to build up his power for some kind of attack to get revenge on the people who fired him. If I'm right, and the cops try to stop him with regular weapons, it'll be a bloodbath—theirs. I might be able to do something. It's a long shot. Unfortunately, I'm the best chance we have to bring him down.

There were several threats and attacks I didn't tell you about, because there was nothing you could have done about them. I wasn't keeping secrets, just trying not to strain your belief any farther than I'd already stretched it.

If I've gotten you in trouble or screwed up your career, I'm sorry. I never meant to hurt you. You need someone who isn't a liability, someone you don't have to defend to the other cops. Please don't stop looking for the right person.

I don't think I'm going to come back from this. At least, that's what the dream told me. But if I can stop the Slitter from killing more people, that's worth it. I wanted more time with you, maybe forever, but it's not going to work out that way. So please, Vic, take care of yourself, be careful, and think about me now and again.

Love, Simon

Vic squeezed his eyes shut tight against the tears that threatened to break loose, holding the letter crumpled in his fist. He had never cried on the job, and he wasn't going to start now. There would be time enough for that, later, in private. He had never hoped so much for Simon's clairvoyance to be wrong.

"Vic?" Ross called, in a tone that let him know it wasn't the first time he'd spoken. Ross was turned around at the table, looking at him with worry in his eyes, and Tracey watched him with a wary, appraising look.

"Simon knows who the Slitter is, and where to find him. And he's gone after him by himself."

Tracey's eyes widened. "Oh, no, no, no, no! That boy did not do something that stupid. Fuck!" She yelled, turning to slam her fist down on the kitchen counter. "I'm gonna kill him—" her voice broke off in a strangled choke when she realized what she said.

"You need to see this," Ross said, pushing back from the table so to give Vic a look at the contents of the folder.

"Shit," Vic murmured as he took in the pictures with the threatening note, the map with Simon's own pentagram and Three Triton Place in the center, and all the rest of the evidence.

"This is persuasive," Ross said. "Even without anything from his visions or the ghosts' testimony, he took that 'Billy Bass' clue and ran with it." He held up a sheaf of printouts from the background search site. "This fits with what you suspected, and the placement of the bodies."

"And Fischer wants to kill Simon because he was afraid Simon would find him?" Tracey asked.

"Maybe," Vic replied. "Or maybe he changed his mind when he realized Simon's abilities were real, and he'd be a big juicy psychic battery for whatever workplace murder spree he's planning."

"You better do right by him," Tracey said, meeting Vic's gaze. "He believes in you."

"I will. I promise." Vic tried to take deep breaths and slow his pounding heart. "We know where he was headed. I'm going after him." He couldn't say out loud that it might already be too late.

Ross rose and blocked his way. "No, we're going," Ross corrected him. "And we're taking a SWAT team with us."

19

SIMON

In the time it took to walk from the blue bungalow to Three Triton Place, Simon's nervous jitters and sweaty fear shifted to cold certainty. He wondered if this was what soldiers felt going into battle, a sense of purpose, and no assurance that they would come back alive.

Sweet Jesus, he didn't want to be a hero. He just didn't see any other way that the police could act on his information without walking into a trap. And he knew that if the cops thought they were closing in on the Slitter, Vic and his partner would be right there in the line of fire.

Vic might have made his choice, but so had Simon. There was no way in hell he would put Vic's life at risk, not if he could do something to prevent that scenario. Which meant it was all up to him.

The information he'd left in the folder would provide context, no matter how tonight went down. By the time Tracey called Vic, it would all be over, one way or the other. And if Simon was successful, and the Slitter was stopped, then even if Simon didn't survive, Vic would have real evidence that would help him close the case.

Simon suspected that if this was indeed the Slitter's falcon nest, he would have trophies and hard evidence the police couldn't overlook.

Simon stopped beside the parking garage where one of the bodies had been found and peered up at the abandoned hotel across the street. Iryena's clues had described the pool area of a different motel to Simon's left, from where there was a perfect view of Three Triton Place. The abandoned high rise wasn't the place the killer was going to hide a body; it was the Slitter's secret lair.

How many nights had Simon glanced up at the hotel as he passed and noticed a single light burning and a ceiling fan rotating in a high window in the otherwise dark building? He'd noticed it, but figured that it would just be someone working late or an oversight of the cleaning staff. He hadn't stopped to think that wouldn't be the case in a building that had been gutted but not remodeled, where even the construction crews hadn't set foot in six months. The Slitter had been taunting them all along in plain sight.

Simon tilted his head back for a better look and counted the floors. Twenty stories above Myrtle Beach. No way would Simon trust the elevators, even if the power to them had been turned back on. That meant a long hike in a building that probably didn't have air conditioning. He peered up again at the single lit window, trying to work out its location on the floor of the tall, round tower. Once Simon was inside, he couldn't afford wasting time searching for the right room.

He headed across the street toward the chain-link fence, as ready for the confrontation as he'd ever be. Simon had brought a pair of wire cutters, thinking he might have to make a hole, but the gate near the parking garage swung open at a touch, although it appeared locked at a distance. Moving cautiously, Simon headed into the black maw of the garage beneath the building that looked more like a darkened cave.

Once inside, he turned on his flashlight and wondered whether the Slitter had left the gate unlocked—another taunt—or if some of Myrtle Beach's homeless had found shelter inside the deck's deeper levels. The flashlight had been a last-minute purchase at a convenience store whose window display advertised *"stun gun flashlights"* to a populace frightened by a serial killer on the loose. He had no idea whether it would work as advertised, but he figured he needed all the help he could get.

Simon headed for the stairs, once again wondering whether he would find the door locked. He'd thrown a legal lock pick kit into his pack just in case, something he'd purchased after the fifth time he had to pay a locksmith to let him back into the shop when he'd locked himself out. He was hardly good enough with the tools to get a door open—no risk of becoming a cat burglar—but he figured they might come in handy. The stairs door was unlocked, and Simon didn't know whether to feel relieved or suspect he was being drawn into a trap.

He reached out to the spirits and felt their presence. The Slitter's victims were watching him, supporting their champion. None of the ghosts offered advice, and his visions did not provide insight, so Simon kept on going, hoping he had surprise on his side.

As he feared, the building's main air conditioning was turned off. But once he got above the second floor, the security lights burned in the concrete-enclosed stairwell. There had been none on in the garage or the first floor. Then again, if the Slitter had made the half-finished hotel his hideout, he had the skills to know his way around a construction site. A smaller company might have noticed electric bills for a shut-down building, but Simon guessed that in the midst of its financial chaos, the holding group owners never caught the questionable expense.

Simon made his way up the stairs, moving as silently as he could. Tracey often teased him about his lack of stealth and her humor was justified; Simon wasn't athletic or naturally graceful, and he had a tendency to trip even on bare pavement. *I'm so not a super-hero*, he thought, figuring that if fate had chosen him, then it was betting on a dark horse. But by moving slow and keeping his mind on what he was doing, he managed to keep climbing in relative silence.

His shirt plastered to his skin with the sweat that ran down his back and soaked his hair. His pepper spray hung from a carabiner on his belt, and a knife was in a sheath beside it. He had his phone in the pocket of his jeans, and before he burst in on the Slitter Simon intended to turn on its recorder so that if he didn't survive to testify, the police could replay what he hoped would be Fischer's confession, and if not, then proof that Fischer had killed him.

By the fifteenth floor, Simon was breathing hard, glad he'd thrown a bottle of water in his pack. He stopped to rest, knowing that if the Slitter somehow anticipated his arrival, Simon would be no use in a fight if he was too winded to catch his breath. The pause gave him a chance to go over his options once more. There wasn't much of a plan, except to go in strong and hit the Slitter with everything Simon had. If by some miracle he managed to get the killer down, he had zip ties in his pack. That had been an optimistic addition on his part, but he'd tried to cover everything.

As he let his breathing and heartbeat slow to normal, Simon couldn't help wondering what Vic was doing now. Was he still at the station, plowing through data? Had he made any of the same connections Simon had found? Nearly four hours had passed since he'd left the message on Tracey's phone, so if she followed his request, that left another eight before Vic would know where Simon had gone. By then, it would all be over.

He wished he'd had a chance to tell Vic good-bye, wished that he'd at least caught a glimpse of him in the squad room that morning. But it was probably better this way. A clean break—at least for Vic.

Mustering his courage, Simon started up the last five flights of stairs, with the same grim resolve he'd felt the day he defended his Ph.D. thesis to an unwelcoming committee. That hadn't been a life and death situation, but it felt like it at the time, and Simon told himself that he needed to put up a confident front, no matter that his insides quivered like jelly.

He paused again in the stairwell of the twentieth floor to finish the bottle of water, and get his breath before the confrontation. Simon had wracked his brain to recall the long-ago party at the former version of Triton Place, trying to remember the layout of the ballroom or at least where the walls and doors had been. Of course, with the renovations, that all might have changed, but since the light visible from the street appeared to be confined to a single area, Simon guessed that some of the room might be as he pictured it. If so, the stairwell and elevator lobby would open into a circular central reception area with doors to different pie-slice shaped ballrooms that had curved window views onto the city and the ocean.

He had his stun light and his knife handy. The pepper spray was a last resort since it had nearly incapacitated Simon as well as the Slitter the last time he used it. Simon had the spells Miss Eppie and Gabriella had taught him well-rehearsed, and he was hopeful that his scant magic could do something against the power the Slitter had amassed from his victims. And for good measure, he had the jack ball and conjure root charms in his pockets. Clutched in his right hand was his paintball pistol, with a fresh CO_2 cartridge and a full clip of orange paintballs. He had more clips in his bag, but he doubted he'd get the chance to reload. Simon had marshaled every resource available to him, and it would have to be enough.

When Simon stepped into the central rotunda, security lights cast a dim glow. He reached into his pocket and started the recorder on his phone. Under the door to one of the rooms, a much brighter light shone, and Simon felt his heart thud as he closed in on the killer.

In the movies, the hero always knew just what to do. Simon had never felt less heroic in his life. *Then again, wars are fought and won by scared farm boys,* he reminded himself. He could do this. He had to do it because no one else could.

He reached for the door and gambled it would open since Fischer had been so sure of the safety of his eyrie that he hadn't locked anything else. It swung wide, and Simon had seconds to register William Fischer inside a room with paper-cluttered walls before he started firing his paint gun.

Aim for the chest, he told himself. *Broader target, hurts like a muther.*

He squeezed off four shots. Two hit their target; two more went wide. Then something cold and powerful shoved him, hard, sending him stumbling. He had three balls left in the clip, and he got his footing and fired again. One shot hit Fischer in the shoulder, and another winged his side, while the third missed entirely.

The cold force struck again, throwing Simon against the wall hard enough to make his head spin and knocking the empty gun from his hand. When the power released him, he fell to a crouch.

"Simon Kincaide. You saved me the trouble of coming for you. How…convenient." William Fischer was no Anthony Hopkins. He lacked Ted Bundy's charisma and good looks. His face and build were unremarkably average, but the intensity in his eyes sparked with madness. Fischer stalked toward Simon, ready to claim his spoils.

Simon concentrated, muttered one of the rote spells he'd learned, and hoped for the best. Before Fischer could reach him, an iridescent circle of light surrounded Simon, cutting him off from his would-be attacker.

"Stay back," Simon warned.

"If you wanted me to stay back, you wouldn't have come here," Fischer replied, stopping several feet from Simon. "We both know how this is going to end."

"With you in jail," Simon growled.

Fischer laughed. "Oh, I doubt that. How long can you hold that pretty little parlor trick? I can wait."

Simon didn't know how strong Fischer's power had become, or what he could do with it other than throw someone around. His whole strategy lay in getting close enough to Fischer to stun him, then maybe clobber him with the heavy flashlight and tie him up. Then again, Fischer didn't know what Simon could do, and his smug certainty might give Simon an advantage.

"You've been stealing energy from people with minor gifts," Simon accused.

Fischer did a slow clap. "Give the man a prize."

"Then why try to run me over or shoot me?" The Slitter's obvious change of plan had puzzled Simon.

"I thought you were a fraud at first," Fischer replied. "Then I realized you weren't."

Up close, Simon realized Fischer didn't look so good. He had the pinched expression of someone with a bad headache, or indigestion, or both. Simon wondered how quickly Miss Eppie could put a root on someone, and how fast her curse would work.

The curtain of light was draining Simon fast. Fischer was only a few feet away. "You picked J-ones because no one would notice." Simon wanted to keep Fischer talking, distract him and record him if his next move had any chance to work.

Fischer looked pained, and whether Eppie had sent him a migraine or stomach cramps, Simon realized that if Eppie's curse was working, maybe all he needed was to run down the clock, eluding Fischer's grasp until the root work brought him down.

That might be tricky because Simon was feeling the strain of expending his magic. He'd held the protective curtain longer than he'd ever done in his scant practice, and he wasn't sure he could produce it again without more time to recuperate. Unlike Fischer, Simon had only his own energy to draw from, and it was finite.

"And they didn't—until you started causing problems," Fischer replied, his eyes narrowing. "You and that cop became a real nuisance. But after tonight, after I kill you and take your energy, it won't matter. I'll do what I set out to do—"

Mid-sentence, Simon dropped the protection spell and dove forward, shoving the flashlight against Fischer's chest and setting off the charge. Unlike a stun gun that shot darts to send out an electric zap at a distance, the flashlight had to be in physical contact to work. Fischer gasped as his body jolted and he staggered backward, with Simon in pursuit to get in another shock and bring him down.

Rage twisted Fischer's features, and he grabbed Simon's arm. Simon kept his grip on the flashlight and turned its blindingly bright beam into Fischer's eyes. Fischer ducked his head, and Simon laid his left hand on Fischer's forearm and murmured another rote spell. His hand grew warm, then blazing hot within seconds, and Fischer yelped, letting go and dodging out of reach.

Simon whirled and jabbed the flashlight against Fischer's shoulder, then pressed the button.

Nothing happened. *Cheap-ass $30 stun gun.*

Fischer grabbed for him, and Simon swung the heavy flashlight, clipping Fischer in the temple and opening a gash. Blood trickled down the man's face as he gestured and raw energy tossed Simon against the wall, hard, and kept him pinned.

"I will bleed you slowly for that," Fischer promised. "I could have made it quick and painless, but you need to show respect."

"How long can you throw me around without draining all your stolen power?" Simon taunted. "Won't that ruin your big surprise?" Poking the bear was definitely stupid, given the situation, but he was left with little other than bravado, and he hoped he could marshal just a little of Vic's signature snark.

Immobilized for the moment, Simon got his first good look at the room. It was indeed the lair of a serial killer. Photographs of the victims' bloody bodies were tacked up on the walls, along with newspaper clippings and printouts from websites. A variety of small items were arranged like a shrine, and Simon guessed they were trophies taken from the victims. He couldn't see what the pieces were from where he was pinned, but he imagined they were jewelry or small personal objects, things that would allow the killer to relive the excitement of the murders. Plenty for the cops to use against him.

"Why bother taunting me?"

"Because you were a challenge," Fischer replied. "The others were easy marks. With you, I wanted to enjoy the game."

"What's the plan?" He wondered if Fischer could stop his heart or asphyxiate him with pressure. Enough force could crush his bones. But no. The Slitter needed Simon's blood, and he enjoyed making the kill with his knife, a personal, lethal connection.

Keep him talking. He's not a fucking wizard, just a sociopath with a bunch of stolen energy.

"LDP is holding a big shindig for investors and the business community tomorrow night," Fischer said, his voice scathing, naming the holding company that owned Bolton Construction. "Didn't have money to pay the people who build their fucking buildings, but they can wine and dine the hot shots in style. I'm going to bring the house down on them."

Lowcountry Development Partnership—LDP for short—owned Three Triton Place and half the commercial real estate in Myrtle

Beach. All of the city's leadership would be at an event like that. And with his construction knowledge and his stolen power, Fischer would know which support beams to crack, which load-bearing walls to knock out to collapse a high rise like a house of cards. The death toll would be in the hundreds.

"You planning to die with them, or walk away laughing?" Simon prodded.

"What do you care? You won't be around to see it."

Fischer made another gesture, and the force vanished, dumping Simon on the floor. He motioned again, and slammed Simon across the room, with enough of an impact that his teeth rattled. Two more slams had Simon's head reeling and his body aching from the beating. This time when Fischer let him go, Simon fell to his hands and knees and did not get up.

"I think we've wasted enough time." Fischer kicked the flashlight out of Simon's hand, and his boot connected solidly with Simon's fingers in the process. He grabbed Simon by the hair and dragged him to the center of the room, then used his power to pin Simon spread eagle on the floor.

Simon was pretty sure his hand was broken, and maybe a few other bones after the way Fischer had knocked him into walls. His head throbbed, and Fischer's energy immobilized him. Fischer went to a long table near the window and returned with a silver bowl and a wicked knife.

This is it, Simon thought, and his heart sank.

Fischer walked back to where Simon lay and knelt next to his left arm. "I've used a lot of power on you, but there's more where that came from. And once I top off with your energy, no one will be able to stop me from getting what I want."

"How did you learn the trick?" Simon's body was pinned, but apparently Fischer wanted to hear him scream.

"I've always had a fascination with old books," Fischer replied. "Amazing what you can find when you look. Of course, no one else took the book seriously, but I did. It seemed to speak to me."

Simon wondered if Fischer himself had some native talent, grossly misused. "So you learned how to steal power."

"They weren't using it for anything important," Fischer said with a shrug.

"I'm pretty sure they didn't want to die," Simon shot back.

Fischer gave him a cold smile. "No? How about you? Not much of a life you've got there. Is anyone really going to miss you? Can't imagine the world will notice when you're gone."

Would he be missed? Simon wasn't close to his parents, but they'd notice if he died. Tracey would mourn him. Maybe Jay and some other friends. And Vic…Yes, Vic would care, and blame himself.

"I wanted that witch bitch, but she left town," Fischer fretted, and Simon was sure the killer meant Gabriella. "And the conjure woman won't leave her house, which is warded tight. So that left you."

Fischer talked big, but he looked like hell. Simon wasn't sure how much was the drain of expending so much energy, and how much Miss Eppie's curse was doing its work. Unfortunately, Simon feared the curse wasn't going to move quickly enough to save him.

"Since you're in the occult business, I'll tell you how this is gonna go," Fischer said. "I'll drain blood to fill the bowl. Now, with the others, I made the cuts long and deep so it would be quick. But you've pissed me off, so I'm doing it crosswise, a slow drip."

He leaned closer. "I want you to feel the cold coming for you, and the dark. Feel the life leaving you, your body shutting down. The full death experience. While you're doing that, I'll work the litany. And then, to seal the ritual, I have to drive the blade through your heart while it's still beating. Nothing personal."

He reached over Simon's open palm with the knife, and Simon muttered his flame spell. A tongue of fire flared just under Fischer's wrist, igniting his shirt.

"Damn you!" Fischer shouted, jumping back and beating out the fire with his other hand. His face contorted, and he landed a swift kick to Simon's side, then backhanded him across the face.

Simon didn't have enough in him to try the spells again and pinned as he was they would have little effect. He felt despair well up, and so many regrets, chief among them how he had left things with Vic. *I should have fought harder for him, told him how I felt before it was too late.*

Fischer's knife slashed across Simon's left wrist, and blood welled up immediately, beginning a steady rivulet into the waiting bowl. Simon still could not move except to talk, and right now, he had nothing left to say. He was exhausted in mind and spirit, and as he resigned himself to die, he saw the ghosts of the Slitter's victims gather, ready to welcome him among their number.

The best way to fight evil is with what you have inside you, Miss Eppie said.

Fischer had stepped back with an old grimoire, eyes shut in concentration. Simon saw his last, desperate chance and seized it. He reached out to gather his waning strength and *pulled* with all his will, summoning the angry ghosts and giving them the dregs of his own life energy to help them manifest to take their vengeance.

The temperature in the room plummeted, and the spirits Simon had seen only in his inner sight became visible to the eye. They showed up with their death wounds and bloody clothing, their eyes glinting with rage. Simon supplied the power, and the ghosts became solid. Too late, Fischer opened his eyes and saw himself surrounded by ten furious spirits intent on revenge.

The ghosts swept around Fischer like a maelstrom, shrieking and howling. They clawed at his skin and tore at his hair and clothing, raising bloody welts and leaving long gashes. Fischer dropped the grimoire and tried to fend off the swarm of revenants, flailing and kicking to no avail. He lashed out with his power, but the force that had worked to toss Simon across the room had no effect on ghosts. Fischer, apparently, had no other tricks, and fighting Simon had drained his energy. Between Miss Eppie's curse and the ghosts' vicious attack, Fischer looked like a corpse himself.

Fischer staggered, and Simon felt the power pinning him wane. A few seconds later, the malevolent force was gone, but Simon wasn't sure he could crawl, let alone stand. Fischer went down to his knees next to Simon as the ghosts continued their assault. Outside the door, Simon heard running footsteps.

Everything seemed to happen at once.

The door slammed open, ghosts vanished, and men in riot gear surged into the room. Simon thought he glimpsed Vic and his partner right behind them. Fischer drew a gun and aimed across Simon's body.

Simon forced himself upright, intending to knock Fischer's aim wide. Instead, he plowed into Fischer, and they went down together with the gun between them. Simon heard a shot, felt his body jolt, and then searing pain flooded over him as Fischer threw him off and tried to stand.

A fusillade of bullets flew, a man gave a hoarse cry, and then silence.

"We need a medic!"

The floor shuddered beneath Simon as someone dropped to his knees. "Simon? God, Simon, don't you dare die!" Simon recognized Vic's voice. *He made it, just in time.*

Simon was so very tired. The spells had sapped his energy, and what was left had been used up powering the ghosts to slow Fischer. And the blood...

"Simon! Can you hear me? Hang on. Come on, baby, hang on," Vic begged.

Simon wanted one last look before he fell asleep. He used his remaining strength to open his eyes and saw Vic's panicked features. "I love you," he murmured and stopped fighting the inevitable.

20

VIC

"Vic, you've got to get out of the way." Ross's voice had the tone he used to talk a jumper off the bridge, or reason with a hostage-taker.

Vic fought Ross's grip on his shoulders as his partner pulled him away from Simon, letting the EMTs get in close.

Ross wrestled Vic back to the wall as the room filled with SWAT members, uniforms, and the forensics team. Vic never took his eyes off Simon lying too still and pale in a pool of blood. The EMT chatter they overheard didn't sound good.

"....lost a lot of blood. Get an IV started."

"...keep pressure on that wound. Got a collapsed lung."

"...immobilize him. Expect broken bones."

Vic watched numbly as they loaded Simon onto a gurney. As the EMTs started to wheel him out, Ross released his grip and gave Vic a push. "Go with them. Say it's police protection. I'll handle the Captain," Ross said quietly. Captain Hargrove was busy for the moment coordinating with the other units, but he'd already cast a questioning glance in their direction, and Vic knew his reaction had been anything but controlled and professional.

Vic fell into step behind the EMTs, his presence unquestioned until they got to the ambulance. "I'm riding with you," he said, hopping in.

"Stay out of the way. He's in bad shape."

They had barely pulled out into traffic when alarms squealed. Vic didn't need to be a doctor to recognize the high, flat whine of a heart monitor flatlining.

"Clear!"

Vic watched sickly as they cut away Simon's bloody shirt and placed the paddles. Simon's back arched beneath the electricity trying to jumpstart his heart. Two attempts finally restored a rhythm, but even Vic knew it didn't sound right.

"Blood volume is way too low," one of the medics reported. "Let's hope we don't hit a lot of traffic."

Vic clung to the sound of the monitor all the way to the hospital. It was only a little over six miles, fifteen minutes or less with the siren wailing, but it felt like an eternity, every second measured by the beat of Simon's failing heart.

At the Emergency Room, the ambulance doors flew open, and the EMTs unloaded Simon and whisked him off with the precision and urgency of a SWAT team. Vic followed, numb and dazed.

"You can't go in there," an orderly said, blocking Vic's way.

Vic flashed his badge. "Police escort. Where he goes, I go. He's a witness." Vic's voice sounded flat and cold, even to his own ears.

The orderly stepped aside, and Vic barreled through, keeping his badge out in case anyone else decided to get in his way. At the doors to the operating room, even his badge wasn't enough.

"Sorry, Lieutenant. No one goes past here unless they're holding the scalpel or going under one," a stern nurse with short, graying hair told him.

"How long?" he asked in a rasp he barely recognized.

"The guy they just took back? No idea," she replied. Her expression softened. "There's a family waiting room right over there," she said, pointing to a door. "The doctor always comes there first." She sobered. "You might want to contact the man's family, just in case." The nurse patted his shoulder and headed away.

Vic walked to the waiting room on autopilot. He had no idea

how to contact Simon's family, or if they were still on speaking terms. Tracey. Tracey counted as family. He pulled out the card she had pressed into his hand just before he and Ross left Simon's house, and dialed the number.

"Did you find him?" Tracey answered, not even bothering with a greeting.

"Yeah but...fuck, it's not good," Vic said. "We're at Grand Strand Medical. Can you get here? Hurry."

Vic was alone in the waiting room, for the moment. Elsewhere in the hospital, other people had crises of their own, but none of them nearby. It had been a long time since Vic had been to Mass, except for when his mother begged his attendance at Christmas and Easter. Upbringing aside, he didn't consider himself religious, let alone a praying man. But with his lover fighting for his life, Vic begged whatever powers might be listening to spare Simon.

Vic didn't know how long he'd been sitting with his head in his hands before someone else entered. He looked up, afraid he would see a somber doctor bearing bad news. Tracey was just a few steps inside the doorway, looking absolutely bereft. He stood and put his arms around her, glad she permitted the comfort for his own sake as much as hers. Vic released her, and she stepped back.

"How is he?"

"No idea. They took him right in. No one is saying anything."

They settled into chairs beside each other. Vic recounted what had happened, his voice taking on the monotone that helped distance himself at crime scenes when it cost too much to feel. Now he knew if he let the full force of the horror hit him, he wouldn't be able to hold it together.

Tracey laid a hand on his arm, her earlier animosity set aside, at least for the moment. "He made it to the hospital. That's a good thing. And they're not out yet. That's good, too."

"They said we should let his family know. In case—" Vic couldn't finish the sentence.

"Fuck, no. Not that they'd come," she added with a derisive snort. "This is all too sordid. It wouldn't play well in the papers. Especially since his gift is going to be all over the headlines."

"That bad, huh?" It pained Vic that he and Simon hadn't had enough time together for him to hear more than the bare basics about Simon's family.

Tracey regarded him for a moment, searching for something. "Don't you have somewhere else you're supposed to be? I mean, this is the Slitter. Big case. Important stuff. I thought Homicide detectives would be all over it."

Vic looked away. "Yeah, I should be at the scene. There'll be hell to pay about it tomorrow. Ross will cover for me as best he can, but Cap'll have my ass. That's okay," he said almost to himself. "This is where I need to be."

"Guess you made your choice."

He glanced at her, frowning with an unspoken question. "I told Simon you were going to have to decide what was most important to you if it came down to the wire. I guess you did."

"Yeah, I guess so," Vic replied. He recognized the adrenaline crash after a firefight. But normally he wasn't alone when the aftershock set in. A bust like tonight would go on until dawn, securing the crime scene, escorting the photographers and evidence teams, the forensic crew. Someone would deal with the reporters, who wouldn't take long to sniff out the Slitter's downfall. And after that, paperwork. Vic had only barely glimpsed the walls of Fischer's lair, but from what he saw, he didn't doubt there would be plenty of evidence to send him away for a long time. Vic could only hope that when they tried William Fischer, it was for ten murders, and not eleven.

Vic and Tracey spent the next few hours in companionable silence. They took turns fetching coffee and sodas from the cafeteria. The chairs weren't comfortable, but they were too tired to complain, dozing off when fatigue overwhelmed even fear, waking fitfully when dreams and worry intruded.

His phone buzzed at nine, and he glanced at the ID, figuring Ross might have an update. Instead, he saw Captain Hargrove's number and sighed. "I've got to take this," he murmured in apology to Tracey and got up to pace.

"D'Amato. What the hell was that little display? And now you've called in sick for tomorrow? Talk to me—and it had better be good."

Normally he'd have dragged himself in the day after a major bust even if he was dripping blood and spiking a fever of 104. But until Simon was out of surgery—and hopefully, out of danger—Vic wasn't leaving the hospital.

"I'm not sure what you mean, sir," Vic closed his eyes, well aware of what Hargrove had seen. Vic had broken ranks, run to Simon, begged him not to die, then left a murder scene—on his own case—to accompany Simon to the hospital and never came back. Hargrove was probably going to have his desk emptied out and dump the box of his stuff on the doorstep by morning.

"You knew the victim."

"Yes."

"Let me rephrase that. You were involved with someone who became a victim in the case you were investigating, who had provided material evidence, and you didn't think that crossed a few lines?"

Vic winced. Tracey didn't look up from her game, but Vic felt certain she could hear Hargrove since the captain was nearly shouting. "I'm the one who brought Simon into the case," Vic admitted. "We were at a dead-end, and I figured that psychics have helped other departments, why not us? His information was good. The rest just…happened."

"Jesus, D'Amato! You know better! Especially after last time—"

"This is entirely different. Sir."

"Yeah. Last time you weren't sleeping with a suspect."

Vic took a deep breath and tried to rein in his temper, although between worry and exhaustion, his nerves were raw. "Simon was never a serious suspect, even before the big-deal lawyers showed up."

"Did you encourage him to go play Nancy Drew?"

"Hardy Boys," Vic corrected, and then face-palmed.

"Excuse me?"

Vic cleared his throat. "Um, I said 'Hardy Boys,' Because Nancy Drew was a girl."

The phone was silent long enough Vic figured Hargrove had left the station and was headed to the hospital to smack him upside the head in person. "He cracked the case," Hargrove said finally.

"Excuse me?" Vic was certain he had misheard.

"Your psychic boyfriend cracked the case. He was a step ahead of us on who, why, and where. I read the folder and the notes. Won't say I believe in all the woo-woo stuff, but then again, his system worked."

"He's the real deal," Vic said, unable to keep the bitterness from his voice. If he'd only come to believe that sooner, maybe Simon wouldn't have gone Lone Ranger on them, and maybe he wouldn't be fighting for his life in the O.R.

"How is he?" Hargrove's voice had calmed, returning to the efficient authority Vic had come to expect from the man.

"He's still in surgery," Vic replied, trying to keep his voice steady. "No one will tell us anything."

Hargrove went silent again, and Vic found himself holding his breath. If he got fired, it would be the end of his police career, especially after the clusterfuck in Pittsburgh.

"The SWAT guys who were in front said they saw a gray fog around Fischer that vanished right after they entered the room," Hargrove said. "One of them thought he saw faces in the fog. And I've got to say; someone beat Fischer all to hell. Clawed him up real good, too. Couple of bites, for good measure. Now I've phoned the hospital to check under Kincaide's fingernails and get a dental print, but I don't think we're going to get a match. Got any theories?"

Gray ghosts attacking a serial killer with a wounded psychic bleeding out on the floor? Yeah, Vic had a lot of theories, and he wasn't going to mention any of them. "I doubt I'm qualified to give an opinion on that."

"Huh. Because I'd heard something kinda like that happening to a guy up north a few years ago."

Vic closed his eyes and took a deep breath. "Stranger things have happened." He paused, and took the plunge. "So, um, do I need to come clean out my desk?"

Hargrove's silence stretched even longer this time. "Ross walked me through the timeline," Hargrove finally replied, "and the folder Kincaide put together. I haven't finished counting the protocols you've ignored and 'best practices' you've trampled. Not sure whether or not you broke any rules. Internal Affairs is going to have a field day. I'm gonna have to suspend you until IA is done. But if it's up to me, your punishment is having to put up with me for a good while longer."

Vic realized he had been holding his breath, so certain that Hargrove would be furious. He bit back the impulse to ask the captain to repeat what he'd said. "Thank you," Vic managed, although his throat was dry.

"When Kincaide is on the mend, maybe we can do this the right way, and discuss how it might work to bring him in as a consultant with the proper paperwork."

Tracey gasped, and Vic couldn't help it as a tired grin spread over his features. "That would be great. Thanks, Cap."

"Call me when you know something," Hargrove replied brusquely and ended the call.

Tracey looked up at him expectantly as he pocketed his phone and sat. "Well?"

"I've still got a job. I think. Depends on how much shit IA wants to give me over 'irregularities.'" He should have felt more relieved than he did. But until he knew how Simon's surgery was going, Vic wouldn't have cared even if he'd won the lottery.

"You know, I was all set to dislike you, D'Amato," she said. "But I think you'll do for Simon."

Vic shook his head and looked away. "Pretty sure I lost my chance. That letter…he thought I'd written him off. I was trying to keep him safe. And look how that turned out." No matter how Simon's surgery went, and regardless of where their relationship went from here, Vic knew he'd feel guilty for a long time over leaving Simon on his own.

"That boy's in love with you," Tracey said. It should have seemed funny to hear her talk about Simon, in his mid-thirties, that way, especially when Tracey was several years younger. But Tracey had an old-soul vibe that made it work. "You just have to let him know where he stands with you."

And Vic intended to if fate gave him the chance.

By midnight, Simon was still in surgery, and no one could, or would, provide any information. Tracey had drained her phone battery playing mindless games when their conversation ran dry and now sat close to a wall plug so her cord would reach. Vic began to pace. Over the course of the evening, a few other visitors poked their heads in, then withdrew. Vic wondered if he and Tracey somehow managed to take up all the space by themselves. To Vic, the small room felt airless and constricting, as tight as his chest.

Vic looked up when the door opened, hoping to see a surgeon. Instead, Ross stepped into the room, looking weary and worn. He had two large coffees and a bag of donuts, which Vic and Tracey accepted gratefully.

"Hey," he said. "Anything?"

Vic shook his head. "No one's talking. Even flashing the badge doesn't work."

Ross took a seat beside Vic, with Tracey on the other side. "It's going to take forensics a while to finish up the scene," he said. "But they've got everything I think we'll need to put Fischer away for a long, long time. Assuming he lives long enough to go to trial."

Vic raised his head. "What do you mean?"

"Not counting the bullet wounds to his gun hand and right leg, and the four times he was shot at close range with a paintball gun —" Ross replied with a grin as Vic couldn't help snorting, "—and that he was clawed up like a wrapped roast at a honey badger picnic, the man's dying. Some sort of wasting disease. Maybe autoimmune. They don't think it's contagious, but we have him in quarantine, and the infectious disease folks are giving him the once-over. I'm frankly amazed he was strong enough to overpower Kincaide."

"Guess we'll have to wait until Simon can tell us his side of the story," Vic replied. He filled Ross in on his conversation with Hargrove, and Ross told him what he could with a civilian in the room.

"Sucks you're going to be suspended," Ross commiserated. "That means I have to do all the paperwork myself."

"Beats hell out of the other options," Vic pointed out. "But you know everything I know. And you type better."

"Meaning I was going to be the one filling out the reports, regardless."

"Yep."

Ross yawned, looking like he was about to fall over. "Go home," Vic urged. "I appreciate you coming by, but there's nothing else to tell you. I'll call when I know something."

Ross clapped a hand on his shoulder. "You know where to find me," he said and headed toward the exit. Just then, the door opened, and an exhausted man in blood-spattered scrubs walked in.

"The Kincaide family?"

Vic stood immediately, and pure fear sent a surge of adrenaline that made him wide awake. Tracey was beside him in an instant. "How is he?" Vic asked, and Ross stepped back to close ranks with them in support.

"He's a very stubborn man," the doctor replied, looking even more fatigued than Vic felt. "We almost lost him a couple of times. The gunshot wound wasn't the problem. We fixed his lung, and the rest of the damage—pretty straightforward. He'd lost a lot of blood. That was a big part. And he was exhausted to the point of collapse. I don't know what he'd been doing, but the human body can only push so hard before it breaks."

Magic, Vic thought. *Psychic gifts. That's what he was doing, with every-thing he had.* "So he's going to be all right?" he asked, and Tracey's hand gripped his forearm.

"Yes," the surgeon answered. "He won't be going home tomorrow, or for a while yet, but assuming the next twenty-four hours go as they should, I believe he'll make a full recovery."

Tracey let out a whoop and threw her arms around Vic, and he went with it, lifting her off the floor as Ross grinned. "When can we see him?" Tracey asked, suddenly wide awake.

"He's in Recovery until the anesthesia wears off, and then ICU until we're sure the lung won't collapse again," the doctor answered.

"We're going to keep him under for a while, to give him time to heal. I hope you got whoever did this." The surgeon's eyes flashed with anger. "Because they beat the crap out of him before they shot him. Broken rib, broken hand, and bruises from head to toe. Plus the blood loss."

Those details spiked Vic's protective fury, but he tamped down his feelings and tried to focus on relief. *Simon's alive. He's out of surgery. He's going to make it. Nothing else matters.*

"When can we see him?" Tracey repeated. From the set of her jaw, hearing the extent of Simon's injuries had raised her hackles as well. Vic was glad that she had decided he was acceptable because he didn't want to be on Tracey's bad side. She would be a formidable enemy, but right now, her righteous rage was focused on protecting Simon.

"Give it an hour, and I'll leave word with the ICU desk that you're authorized to visit," the surgeon replied. "Only one at a time and the nurses will be strict on removing you if they think it's necessary. It's well past visiting hours, but a badge can bend a few rules, up to a point," he added, looking to Vic.

"Thanks," Vic replied with a weary grin. "I'd offer to fix your next speeding ticket, but I don't work that beat."

The surgeon gave him an equally tired smile, and after promising that someone would come by to explain more in the morning, shuffled out. Ross followed, with promises to call at a reasonable hour.

The next hour seemed to last forever. Finally, Vic turned to Tracey. "You go first." As much as he wanted to assure himself that Simon was alive and recovering, Tracey had been Simon's friend much longer. And part of Vic still worried that after everything that happened, their reunion might not go as he hoped.

"Okay. But don't go far. I'm pretty sure I'm not the one he wants to see when he wakes up."

When Tracey returned, she looked shaken, and her eyes were red. "God, Vic. The doctor wasn't kidding. He looks like he was in a car wreck. His hand... and they've got a tube down his throat."

"Is he awake?"

She shook her head and sniffed back tears. Vic got the impression that Tracey wasn't usually a crier. "No. But they said it could be any time now. At least, as far as the anesthesia goes. If he's that worn out, he might sleep for a while."

Now that it was his turn, Vic hesitated. Tracey gave him a push. "Go. And don't mince words if you to talk to him. Say what you mean. That's what he needs to hear."

As Vic approached Simon's bed, his heart felt like it would beat out of his chest, and his mouth went dry. He reminded himself that he'd been far more afraid going into the Slitter's bolt hole, but that was a different kind of fear. Then, he was terrified for Simon's safety. Now, Vic was scared that Simon might have decided Vic didn't deserve his trust.

Vic stopped when he pulled back the curtain and stifled a gasp. Tracey hadn't been kidding. Simon's right hand was wrapped and splinted. His left wrist was also bandaged, with stitches closing the wound beneath. The mechanical wheeze of the ventilator kept Simon breathing, giving his damaged lung a chance to heal, but it underscored the severity of his injuries, and how close Vic had come to losing him. A sheet covered Simon to his shoulders, but Vic could see the edge of the dressings over the wound in his chest. *Fuck. A few inches over, and I'd be claiming him at the morgue.*

A hard plastic chair sat to one side, and Vic moved it to the left of the bed, so he could take Simon's hand. "I love you," Vic said quietly. "I should have said it before now, but I was too much of a coward. I was wrong about so much. I believe in your gift. In you. In us. And I want to get the chance to make it up to you, if you'll have me."

His voice caught, and he blinked hard. "Just, get better. You're not going to believe this, but the Captain wants you to consult with the unit, if you're willing. I told Cap about us. Because I made a choice, and I chose you," Vic said, leaning close.

Vic brushed his lips across his lover's temple. An ugly purple bruise spread across Simon's cheekbone. His eyes looked sunken and dark-rimmed, and he still seemed far too pale. A glance at the monitors showed a regular heartbeat—music to Vic's ears—but Simon's skin felt too cool for Vic's liking. Vic couldn't remember his own early recovery after he had been shot, only that Ross had looked like shit from worrying when Vic finally woke up.

"I hope you heard me," Vic said, afraid that a nurse would come at any moment to make him leave. "But if you didn't, I'm going to say it again and again until you do." He gave Simon's hand a squeeze, and kissed him again gently. "And that's a promise."

EPILOGUE

SIMON - THREE MONTHS LATER:

"If you keep feeding me like that, the department will put me on a diet," Vic said with a sigh, indicating a blissful food coma.

"It turned out pretty good, didn't it?" Simon replied as if still surprised their barbecue party had been a success.

He'd spent a month recovering from his injuries. Jay and Tracey had helped him find reliable people to staff the store in his absence, and he had promoted Pete, his part-timer, to assistant store manager. Getting shot made Simon realize he couldn't keep trying to do everything himself, so he intended to hire the extra helpers on a part-time basis. They couldn't do the séances or private readings, of course, but Simon's regular clients had been very willing to reschedule when they realized what happened.

Simon had feared that he would have to cancel all his ghost tours, even though they didn't require psychic ability, but Pete surprised him. As it turned out, Pete was a theater major and occasionally acted in the many stage shows at venues around Myrtle Beach. He stepped into the role with gusto and added his own spin with different costumes and personas. The uptick in bookings made Simon consider just letting Pete run with it, and using that time for better things, like coming home early to Vic.

"Good? Our friends just ate us out of house and home," Vic complained, but his grin put the lie to his words. He and Simon had gone together on the nicest gas grill they could afford and broken it in with a big "thank-you" party for their friends. Tracey and Shayna were there, along with Jay and his girlfriend, Chrissy. Ross brought his wife, Sheila, and Pete introduced them all to his new boyfriend, Mikki.

Vic made pasta with homemade sauce from his nonna's recipe and a big salad. Tracey brought several flavors of cheesecake from the killer bakery that supplied Le Miz's pastries, Ross and Sheila brought a selection of appetizers, and Pete brought a handle of rum and a half keg of beer. Simon cooked up shrimp, chicken, and beef shish kebabs, corn on the cob, and a fluffy rice pilaf, with ice cold watermelon on the side. They all had taken the day off, so the party started with pasta at lunch and lasted through the afternoon into the evening, finishing up around the fire pit Vic had bought as a surprise for Simon.

By ten everyone was happily full, comfortably buzzed, and all too aware that the next day was a workday. Vic and Simon saw them off, promising to do another cookout in the fall, and started cleaning up paper plates and plastic cups so they could head inside.

"That pasta sauce was fantastic," Simon said, something he'd already told Vic but which bore repeating. "My compliments to your nonna."

Vic smirked. "Come home with me to Pittsburgh for Thanksgiving, and you can tell her yourself."

Simon's heart did a little flip like it always did when Vic talked with casual certainty about the future. It was only May, and November seemed a long time away, but Simon loved the fact that looking ahead came so easily for Vic. He brushed a kiss across Vic's neck as he passed to toss more trash into a garbage bag.

"I'd love to. But it's cold up north by then. Won't a Southern boy like me freeze my balls off?"

"Hell no," Vic replied with a wicked grin. "I'll keep them plenty warm for you."

The grill was off, leftovers were in the fridge, and the fire pit embers were covered. Simon hefted the last bulging garbage bag and tossed it into the bin by the curb. Music still played from a speaker, cycling through the playlist Simon had put together.

"All done!" he announced.

"I want to leave the lights up," Vic said, looking at the strands of twinkling white lights he had strung the day before. "It makes the backyard feel special."

They hadn't officially moved in together, but most of Vic's stuff had found a home in the blue bungalow, and Simon was privately convinced all that was left in Vic's apartment was a toothbrush and some dental floss. They had talked about moving forward slowly, building a foundation to make their relationship last, but Vic already stayed over with Simon most nights, and Simon wouldn't have it any other way.

"Anything you want," Simon said. A Springsteen song came on —Simon had made sure the playlist included all of Vic's favorites— and Simon put his hands on Vic's hips, pulling him closer. "Up for a little dancing in the dark?" he asked in his most sinful voice, hooking his fingers through Vic's belt loops.

"Always," Vic replied. His kiss sent Simon's heart racing and hardened his already stiff cock. Their erections rubbed together through their jeans, and Vic's hands slid down to cup Simon's ass.

"What sort of dancing did you have in mind?" Simon teased, as they swayed together under the lights.

"Mmm…maybe start with a little horizontal mambo, or some four-legged foxtrot—"

"Oh, my god. I can't believe you just said—"

Vic kissed his way over to Simon's ear. "How about we go inside and I suck you off and then we fuck each other into the mattress?"

"Sounds perfect to me," Simon replied, losing himself in their kiss underneath the stars. "I love you, Vic D'Amato, and I intend to prove it all night."

OTHER BOOKS BY MORGAN BRICE

Witchbane

AFTERWORD

Myrtle Beach is one of my favorite places. Most of the tourist attractions and landmarks mentioned in the book are real, but all of the businesses and people that are part of the plot are fictitious. The boardwalk (and the Gay Dolphin Gift Cove), however, are real and if you visit the Grand Strand, I totally recommend strolling down to the piers and walking along the beach. The ghosts and wrecks mentioned on Simon's tour are part of local lore.

The inspiration for the Slitter's lair came when my friend and fellow author Jeanne Adams and I were sitting by the fire pit at Coastal Magic Convention in Daytona Beach and looked up at the high rise next door that was closed for renovation. Even though the parking garage was blocked off and the place was definitely not open, a single light blazed, high up in the tower, and we could see that a ceiling fan was turning. Creepy, huh?

Mark Wojcik, Seth Tanner, and Cassidy Kincaide made brief appearances in Badlands. They actually star in series of their own, so you if you want to know more and follow their adventures, there's plenty to read! Seth Tanner is one of the main characters in the Witchbane series (another of my Morgan Brice urban fantasy M/M paranormal romances). Cassidy Kincaide, Teag Logan, Anthony

Benton, and Sorren are featured in my Deadly Curiosities urban fantasy series (under my Gail Z. Martin name). Mark Wojcik is the lead in the Spells, Salt, and Steel series (Gail Z. Martin & Larry N. Martin). Check them out for more monster hunting and supernatural adventure!

Thank you for supporting independent authors!

This book was written and published by an independent author. Independent authors work outside the large, traditional publishing industry, which means we can be more responsive to our fans and readers, bringing you more of the kinds of stories you want to read.

When you support independent authors, you're helping them make a living, providing an income for their families, and helping to guarantee that they can continue writing the books you enjoy reading.

By helping spread the word about the books and authors you enjoy, either in reviews on sites like Amazon and Goodreads or by personal recommendation, you help others discover these books for themselves, and you help make it possible for the writers you enjoy to keep on writing. This is especially important for independent authors, because we don't have a big name publisher promoting our books or the benefit of being shelved in bookstores.

If you've enjoyed this book, or other books by independent authors, the biggest way to show your thanks is by reviewing online and spreading the word. And please, never download 'free' books off pirate sites. Doing so harms the author by robbing him or her of the sale, and makes it harder for authors to stay in business, writing the books you love.

Thank you for reading!

ACKNOWLEDGMENTS

Thank you so much to my editor, Jean Rabe, to my husband and writing partner Larry N. Martin for all his behind-the-scenes hard work, and my wonderful cover artist, Natania Barron. Thanks also to the Shadow Alliance street team for their support and encouragement, and to my fantastic beta readers: Mindy, Trevor, Darrell, Donald, Chris, Cheryl, Laurie, and Vickie plus the ever-growing legion of ARC readers who help spread the word! Many thanks also to the fabulous Jordan L. Hawk, Rhys Ford, Charlie Cochet, and Lucy Lennox for their help, encouragement and inspiration! And of course, to my 'convention gang' of fellow authors for making road trips fun.

ABOUT THE AUTHOR

Morgan Brice is the romance pen name of bestselling author Gail Z. Martin. Morgan writes urban fantasy male/male paranormal romance, with plenty of action, adventure and supernatural thrills to go with the happily ever after. Gail writes epic fantasy and urban fantasy, and together with co-author hubby Larry N. Martin, steampunk and comedic horror, all of which have less romance, more explosions.

On the rare occasions Morgan isn't writing, she's either reading, cooking, or spoiling two very pampered dogs.

Watch for additional new series from Morgan Brice, and more books in the *Witchbane* and *Badlands* universes coming soon!

Where to find me, and how to stay in touch

Facebook Group—The place for news about upcoming books, convention appearances, special fun like contests and giveaways, plus location photos, fantasy casting, and more! The Worlds of Morgan   Brice https://www.facebook.com/groups/143333126341151/

Pinterest (for Morgan and Gail): pinterest.com/Gzmartin

Sign up for my newsletter and never miss a new release! http://eepurl.com/dy_8oL

Twitter: @MorganBriceBook

CPSIA information can be obtained
at www.ICGtesting.com
Printed in the USA
LVHW041449121218
600214LV00002B/411/P